W9-ALN-071

DANCING ON SNOWFLAKES

Dancing on Snowflakes

Malcolm Macdonald

St. Martin's Press
New York

Library of Congress Cataloging-in-Publication Data

Ross-Macdonald, Malcolm.
    Dancing on snowflakes / Malcolm Macdonald.
        p.   cm.
    ISBN 0-312-11256-4
    1. Irish—Travel—Sweden—Stockholm—History—19th century—
Fiction.   2. Man-woman relationships—Sweden—Stockholm—Fiction.
3. British—Ireland—History—19th century—Fiction.   4. Young women—
Sweden—Stockholm—Fiction.   I. Title.
PR6068.O827D36   1994
823'.914—dc20   94-26106
                                                                                CIP

First published in Great Britain by Hodder and Stoughton.

First U.S. Edition: November 1994
10 9 8 7 6 5 4 3 2 1

Laserset by the author using Spellbinder DTP®
in Glyphix™ Palatino fonts
on a Hewlett Packard Laserjet III® printer

to

Axel and Ebba
Count and Countess Hamilton

friends through and through

Contents

DANCING ON SNOWFLAKES

Part One

The View From

Katarina

*K*aty O'Barry was born Katarina Oberg — not in Sweden, which provided her nationality, but in Dublin, where she had lived since her birth in 1876. However, since the Swedish pronunciation of Oberg is closer to "ooh-berry" than "oh-burg," her father gladly accepted the name of "O'Barry" as a gift from the Irish nation. The fact that O'Barry is a nonexistent clan was all to the good, for it meant he could take it with vacant possession. He had been living in it, and living up to it, for more than twenty years by the time Katy, his only child, "came out" — that is, was presented along with several hundred other young ladies to the Lord Lieutenant in Dublin Castle.

The great event had taken place two days ago — an occasion in which tedium and terror were so evenly mingled that Katy had since done her best to forget it entirely; the Lord Lieutenant had kissed the heavily powdered cheeks of more than a hundred females by the time her turn came round and his beard had looked as if he unglued it each night and stored it in a flour sack. But tonight was to make up for it all. Tonight, as a fully fledged young lady, *out* in the world at last and ready to fly the nest, she was to attend her first St Patrick's Ball, which was also, as it happened, held at Dublin Castle. Surely, she felt, it would be the most exciting night of her life.

Indeed, as it proved, it was to be most momentous night of her life, as well.

Part of her excitement lay in the sheer magnificence of St Patrick's Hall itself, which (as any Dubliner will confirm) has no equal throughout the British Empire. Of course, like any other tourist, she had paid her sixpence and gaped at its grandeur. But nothing she had seen on that rather cold, gray afternoon could have prepared her for the sight of it on this great evening of the ball — the highlight of the Dublin Season of 1897. For tonight the windows were all hung about with gay bunting; never had the regalia of the Order of St Patrick — the banners and paintings — been deployed to such sublime effect. On that earlier visit she had felt rather dwarfed by the gold and white corinthian pilasters and the massive cornices and entablatures that soared above them, in tier upon tier; but now, when bathed in the brilliance of ten thousand candles, they seemed warmer and she felt delightfully at home among them.

She wished she might say the same about the throng of guests, for this, the widest, longest, and loftiest of all the state apartments, was already alive with the bustle of ever so many revellers — the greater part of the Upper Three Thousand of Irish society. The men were in court dress or full military undress, and the ladies all in silk and chiffon, in whose folds gleamed every jewel they possessed. The glitter and the sparkle quite took Katy's breath away and, to her shame, as she entered that vast and animated salon arm in arm with her dear friend, Amelia O'Dowd, she forgot all her good resolutions about remaining cool and utterly blasé and metropolitan, and instead gave out a gasp of astonishment that would have shamed a country cousin straight off the bog.

Amelia, as always, covered up wonderfully for the gaffe. "Me, too," she said with a sigh that might almost have been a gasp. "No matter how familiar one is with this place, it still takes one aback to see it in the light of all these candles."

Katy smiled gratefully. It was very brave of Amelia to remind everyone within earshot how familiar she was with the Castle. Of course, what she meant was that the O'Dowds, though Roman Catholics, were very thick with the powers-that-be — "the Castle crowd," in popular parlance. But a mean-spirited listener might equally well have remembered that poor Amelia had attended every ball throughout last year's Season and hadn't managed to catch a sniff of a husband; and this Season she had already been to two state balls and a dozen private supper-dances — with the same dismal lack of result.

"Can you see him at all?" Katy murmured under her breath. "I knew I overdid the belladonna. I'm blind as an owl at noon, now."

"See who?"

"See *who!*" she echoed scornfully. "Who d'you think? I don't want to gawp in case people remark upon it."

Amelia continued to stare at her blankly, pretending she did not understand a word.

"Tskoh!" Katy let go of her friend's arm and looked around, trying to appear as fashionably weary as possible.

Despite the effects of the belladonna — which dilated her pupils to great, dark pools of mystery (and made focusing almost impossible) — she saw him almost at once. The whole world seemed to shimmer and dissolve about her — all except that focal centre where *he* stood, darkly handsome and brooding. Her heart skittered about in her chest like soap in a bathtub. And then a moment later she had to stifle a little scream of terror as their eyes met ... and he smiled ... *and turned and started making his way toward her!*

"Dear God I can't breathe!" she murmured. "Would you look at him there!"

"Oh Kate!" Amelia placed herself between her and the young man — the rather common young man, in her well-bred opinion — who held the poor colleen in such inexplicable thrall. "If anyone else behaved like this, over any other fella but that one, you'd laugh your head off, so you would."

The good thing about it was that Katy was doing all the wrong things to catch and keep Mr Declan Butler; unfortunately, they were all the right things to invite his seduction and later abandonment of her. Katy knew it, too, though she'd never admit it out loud; all she'd say was she didn't care and she couldn't help herself.

She said it again now.

"It's when *he* helps *himself* you'll start to worry," Amelia warned her darkly. "Now be sure to give him no more than the one dance."

"The last waltz," Katy murmured ecstatically. Under her breath she added, "And the last of every other set as well."

"Here's your mother now." Amelia's tone was half warning, half sigh of relief.

"I said to wait," Mrs O'Barry exclaimed crossly. "That stupid cloakroom attendant! If his head wasn't glued on, he'd have fallen out of the last shower of rain."

Mrs O'Barry still muddled her Irish idioms when she was flustered. "Now remember, Pappa expects you to dance with as many gentlemen as possible this evening. We have lots of important *confrères* here."

"Am I in his balance sheets then?" her daughter asked tartly. "What heading I wonder? Stock-in-trade?"

"Fixtures, more likely!" Amelia laughed, to persuade Mrs O'Barry it was just a jolly notion.

"Written-down assets more likely still," Mrs O'Barry muttered — then, catching sight of the approaching Declan, she broke into a wide but frosty smile and exclaimed, "Ah, Mister Butler!"

"Mrs O'Barry, ma'am!" He swept up her hand and kissed it with a fervour too stylized to be anything but mocking. "I never saw you looking so young and alluring, if you'll pardon me for saying so. If you'll take over your daughter's programme, I'll fill every space you have." His eyes dwelled mischievously in hers, leaving no doubt as to what *space* he referred to nor what sort of *filling* he had in mind.

Mrs O'Barry was gripped by two powerful but contrary emotions. Declan Butler was undoubtedly one of the most handsome men she had ever met; more than that, he radiated a sort of magnetic pull that set every danger alarm ringing within her. The very air about him seemed charged with a strangely life-enhancing power; it was as if an invisible limelight followed him around, picked him out, and gave him a golden aura — the sort of aura one feels rather than sees. The contrary emotion was much easier to show for it was the protective instinct of a mother with a maiden daughter to steer through the minefield of courtship into the safe haven of a virgin marriage.

"One dance and one dance only," she said peremptorily — hoping that the flush she felt on her neck and ears was not a visible blush.

"Mamma!" Katy said solicitously. "Do loosen your mantilla. You look quite hot, suddenly."

"The *room* is hot, that's all!" the woman said crossly, and turned toward Amelia so as to break off the exchange.

It was all the opportunity Katy needed. "Here?" she asked Declan, holding up her programme and pointing with trembling fingers to the last of the Irish set.

"Mm-hmm." His tone was uncertain but his nod (unnoticed by the mother) was emphatic enough.

"Here?" The little silver pencil darted on and came to rest in the space for the last of the quadrilles.

"Mm-hmm."

And so it continued inexorably toward the pinnacle of the final waltz. Five dances were earmarked, though no name was scribbled in the corresponding place in her programme. Katy funked the final suggestion. The point of the silver pencil hovered near the final space on her card but no word could she utter.

"Sure why not!" he said lightly, slipping an arm about her waist and giving an amiable squeeze.

Mrs O'Barry bridled at the sight of this intimacy. It alarmed her, too, not so much the gesture itself as the intense feeling it aroused in her — a feeling more of jealousy than of anger. She drew a deep breath and held it, as if determined to crowd out the sudden flush of her emotion.

Declan turned and grinned at her, a lopsided sort of grin that had the effect of closing one of his eyes more than the other; it looked suspiciously like a wink. Mrs O'Barry opened her fan and applied it with vigour. "One dance only?" she asked.

With an air of triumph Katy held up her programme for inspection.

"Hah!" Her mother's feelings were divided between pleasure that Katy had for once, seemingly, obeyed her and annoyance that the single permitted dance was the coveted last waltz. "Why torment yourself?" she asked when Declan had gone to apportion out his favours among the other debutantes. "Your father will never consent to your marrying him."

"Why not?"

It was not, of course, the first time they had pursued this topic. Katy only asked so as to provoke her mother's usual answer — "Because!" It would then allow her to launch into a spirited rendering of her own views.

"Because he's worthless," her mother chose to say this time.

It quite took the wind out of Katy's sails. Before they had time to fill again, the other added: "And he'll never marry you without your father's blessing."

"He might." But Katy's tone carried little conviction; she looked to Amelia for support.

Her friend was adding a young officer's name to her own programme; the subaltern begged Katy to grant him a dance as well. During the time it took to add his name her belligerence evaporated.

Her mother rubbed in the salt: "Your father has too much power in Dublin for you or the likes of that young man to flaunt him."

"Flout him, you mean." Katy's correction was glum and automatic. She knew her mother spoke the truth. And if you had power in Dublin, you could make them uneasy in West Cork and Donegal, too, so there'd be no escaping his wrath — not on this island.

"And what sort of man is he, anyway?" Mrs O'Barry took advantage of her daughter's unaccustomed lack of argument. "A horse coper! A glorified horse coper!"

"He buys Irish remounts for the best regiments in the British army." Katy spoke sweetly to Amelia, as if excusing her poor, eccentric mother's inability to comprehend the difference.

"A horse coper," Amelia said as sweetly back.

"Thank you, dear." Katy's tone was cool as she drew her mantilla primly about her. "Well-well-well! I have secured two dances, anyway. One in an hour's time and one three hours after that. What a giddy evening it's going to be! Will my feeble constitution stand up to such a fantastic whirl?"

Ten minutes later, however, young officers and gentlemen were looking in bewilderment at her programme and wondering why she was claiming no more room. They were too well bred, however, to let it show in their expressions, so Mrs O'Barry was none the wiser — and she, too, had had a drop too much of the belladonna and could see no more than a blur when Katy dared show her how brilliantly she had been engaged. "How one has grown since one last saw one!" Katy said in Swedish, which always had a softening effect on her mother's mood.

"Oh, let's bury the axe this one night at least," she replied, hugging her daughter warmly.

"Hatchet!" Katy flung over her shoulder as the band struck up and a dragoon whisked her off for the first of the dances.

Throughout the British Empire a state ball opens with a quadrille in which only the sovereign, or her viceroy, and half a dozen of the grandest nabobs take part; the rest of the assembly, from belted earls down to plain misters, stand with their ladies behind silken ropes to watch and applaud. The only exception throughout all the length and breadth of those mighty dominions is the St Pat's at Dublin Castle, which Queen Victoria herself declared to be the most magnificent *and* the most sparklingly good-humoured of them all.

True, it was still opened by the viceroy and a few grandees, but instead of the stately quadrille they pranced about to the lightsome strains of Irish jigs and reels. Then, as the applause died down, the silken ropes were removed and the floor opened for the remainder of the Irish set — and the gavottes and waltzes, the turkey-trots and one-steps, the mazurkas, the schottisches, and the Sir Roger de Coverleys enjoyed by the common herd, from plain misters up to belted earls and beyond.

That evening Katy never scaled the giddy heights where belted earls and their heirs have their stamping ground, but she could claim two viscounts and a baronet before it was time to pause for refreshment. By then she had enjoyed three of her promised half-dozen dances with Declan. During the first she had been relieved to see her mother deep in earnest conversation with Mrs Considine, the only sort of conversation that was possible with that particular lady; she was even more delighted when, before the second even began, she saw her slip out to the ladies' room. During the third, however, her luck ran out. They finished the dance mere feet away from where Mrs O'Barry was standing in frosty silence, her back to one of the great pilasters.

"That was not the last waltz," she said sternly. "Katy! Find your next partner and ask him to take you for refreshments. Young man! You and I have a bone to chew."

"Pick!" Katy said as she went in search of her next partner.

He was a rather dashing young Guards officer; the sight of him made her quite forget her mother's parting instructions — and in any case, she wanted to keep an eye on her and Declan.

However, after two fruitless scans of the ballroom, once on each circuit, it became quite clear that they had left the hall entirely. Puzzled, pleased, slightly apprehensive, Katy then applied herself heart and soul to the rituals of the dance. She and her partner talked of the brilliance and success of the Season, the clemency of the weather, the sprightliness of the band, and (a touch of daring, here) the excellence of the musical comedy then showing at the hall in Tivoli. Katy smiled and her eyes sparkled and she threw back her head and laughed prettily and no one would ever have guessed that her heart was now full of misgivings.

She kept up her insouciant joviality through several more dances with other, interchangeable young men, by which time it was the proper hour for the buffet supper; her squire for that feast was one John Fitzpatrick. She knew him well, for they both belonged to the St Stephen's Green Drama Society. The O'Barrys actually lived round the corner in Harcourt Street, but they counted as St Stephen's Green for the purposes of the Dram Soc, which was not exactly awash with pretty young ladies. John talked to her of the brilliance and success of the Season, the clemency of the weather, the sprightliness of the band, and (even more daring, here) the *possibility* of going to see the musical comedy then showing at the hall in Tivoli. Katy continued to smile and her eyes persisted in sparkling, though by now her alarm at her mother's absence was considerable.

They had just reached the sorbet when a nearby conversation intruded on theirs. They were standing in the shadow of a square pillar and the voices — of two young men — came from just around the corner. Katy had been vaguely aware that the rascals were discussing "the fillies" at the ball that night. She had even pricked up her ears a couple of times when they appeared to be discussing someone she knew; but every other word was drowned in the general hubbub so she had soon given up. However, she heard one of them say, "Who was the pretty, dark-haired one who had three dances with Declan Butler early on?" ... and the other replied, "The one with the amazing eyes?" ... and the first said, "Yes." Then, indeed, her every nerve strained to catch their every word above the clamour. For, of course, there was only one pretty, dark-haired girl with amazing eyes in the whole of Dublin and she did not need to hear the second fellow say, "Miss Katy O'Barry," to know it.

In fact, she did not hear the second fellow say her name at all because she was desperately signalling to young Fitzpatrick *not* to intervene — which he was plainly ready to do.

"I'm surprised you don't know her," said the second fellow. "Her father's that Swede with a finger in every pie. More Irish than the Irish, as they say."

"Larry O'Barry? I never knew he had a daughter — certainly not a little corker like that. But God, I know *himself!*"

"Why d'you say it in that tone?"

"He had dealings with my father."

"Profitable, I hope?"

"Sure, aren't they all when that fellow's in it! Poor girl, though — to be stuck on a gobshite like Declan Butler!"

Katy clenched her fists; her nostrils flared; the blood drained from her cheeks. She was just about to step out from behind the pillar when John Fitzpatrick intervened and stopped her. With one oblique nod of his head and one chagrinned pursing of his lips he managed to imply it was too late now to reveal their eavesdropping; she'd made this bed and must lie in it.

Thus she missed the next exchange between the two young blackguards. By the time she picked up the thread they were discussing her amazing eyes. "Oriental," the first fellow said knowingly.

"Depends what you mean by oriental. Old Eli says her mother's from Lapland. It could come from there."

His colleague sounded dubious. "Sure I don't know what sort of eyes the girls would have in Lapland, and I doubt if Eli does, either."

Old Eli was head of the anatomy school, well known in Dublin.

"*Lap*land is it?" the other asked with a sudden, bright chuckle. "Well, I have it on the authority of Professor Gray, Twelfth Edition, that in *Lap*land the girls have only one eye, and they keep it tight shut most of the time. But when it sees a real man, doesn't it wink and weep as well as any other!"

John Fitzpatrick grabbed her firmly by the wrist and pulled her away from the pillar.

"They have no idea what they're talking about," Katy told him angrily. "The Lapps have two eyes like any other Christian soul. Anyway, my eyes are Magyar, not oriental. My great-grandmother was from Hungary."

"They're beautiful eyes, anyway, Katy, wherever they come from — as I believe I told you before."

She smiled at him. "I believe you did, John."

All the young people in the Dram Soc had the privilege of using each other's Christian names.

"Who *were* those two spalpeens?" she asked.

"Medical students!" he sneered. "For my part I rank them somewhere below ratcatchers."

"How d'you know they're medical students?" she asked. "Are you acquainted with them?"

"I'm familiar with the type," he replied darkly. "And the particular sense of humour."

"They were quite complimentary," she pointed out in their defence. "The bits I understood, anyway."

Once she made that qualification he agreed wholeheartedly. "Particularly about your father," he added. "So it's not always true that eavesdroppers hear no good of themselves."

"No. I must tell Mamma about that."

She thanked him and they parted. Only then did she begin to think about that remark of the two students — where they pitied her for being so stuck on Declan. Was that the general opinion of her? She did not know those two young men, and they obviously knew her only by sight. Yet they could see her heart on her sleeve. Lord, was it as obvious as all that? She felt her mouth go dry and her stomach hollow at the thought. Why was everyone so down on poor Declan, anyway? It was pure snobbery. Just because he was related to the Butlers, the great lords of Kilkenny with half of west Leinster in their pockets, though he hadn't a penny to his own name except what he earned by his wit and his dealing.

The thought of the poor dear man and the fight he had against a hostile world filled her with familiar melting sensations toward him. It was so unfair. One day she'd inherit all her parents' wealth. God send it was many years off — that dread hour. Yet, in the very nature of things, it would come to pass. Then she and her darling boy would be enabled to thumb their noses at all the world ... But could they wait that long?

The darling boy himself sidled up to her at that moment. "Thank God I found you," he said in a tone that managed to be both casual and solemn at the same moment. He put up his hands to fend off a hug she could never have brought herself to give him, dearly as she would have loved to.

John Fitzpatrick saw the adoration flood her whole expression — and despaired. How, having just overheard that brutally candid opinion of her infatuation for the Butler lad, could she not step just a little more warily where even a fool would fear to tread?

"Where's Mamma?" she asked, in a tone that implied: "When the cat's away ..."

"Ah!" he dipped his head ruefully. "Something has disagreed with her, I fear. I've found her a quiet corner in one of the anterooms and I'm to ask Mrs Considine to chaperon you and Amelia for the time being." He smiled engagingly at both her and Fitzpatrick, who smiled coolly back.

"I must go to her." Katy was full of concern now, and not a little ashamed of her earlier attitude.

"Fear not!" Declan restrained her with a grand gesture. "All she requires is a little rest and she'll be right as rain."

"But she may be ill."

"Doctor Walshe says not."

"Is he here?" she asked in surprise. She had never thought of Doctor Walshe as being "in Society."

"Don't worry," Declan assured her. "All shall be well and all manner of things shall be well. I'll stand guard over her and keep the world at bay. She'll be on her pins again before the last waltz. No one will filch that from us."

His tone made her aware that, whatever about the last waltz, her mother had neatly filched Declan's two remaining dances with her. Now she began to doubt that her mother was ill at all. A likely tale!

As Katy let him lead her to Mrs Considine, a further and even more disturbing thought crossed her mind. Her mother's motives she could understand ... but why should Declan sacrifice the pleasures of the ball to stand guard in a remote and cheerless anteroom? Any castle flunkey could do that.

At first it baffled her but the more she thought about it, the more obvious the answer became — and a smile spread to her face and her spirit relaxed. At first the thought was so delicious that she hardly dared put it into words — not even in secret to herself. But when she told Amelia what Declan was doing, and the girl immediately voiced the same bewilderment, she could no longer hold her joy back.

"Don't you see!" she babbled. "It's to get Mamma on his side — to make her intercede for him with Pappa."

Amelia frowned. "He's never shown the slightest interest in winning her around before."

"Exactly!" Katy crowed. "So doesn't that prove it? He's taking a serious interest at last! I truly believe he is."

There was a pause. Her friend looked at her with great, troubled eyes and said pityingly: "I know you do."

"Oh, Amelia, it's all coming to a head."

Amelia hugged her tight as she said, "I'm rather afraid you're right, my dear."

Mrs O'Barry was silent as the three of them drove home from the Castle that night. Katy and Amelia relived their more exalted moments with gushes of scorn — to show that they hadn't been in the least overawed by the grandeur of the setting nor the pomp of the occasion. Every now and then they forgot themselves and enthused giddily over a particularly dashing cavalry officer or an especially striking young heir but they always recollected themselves in time; then they drew back from the brink of girlish bathos and dispatched the young hopeful with a wicked barb. And so it continued all the way back to Dawson Street, where Amelia was safely restored to her family.

There they took a small glass of port, and no one was tactless enough to ask if the dear girl was in any way nearer to having an engagement ring slipped upon her finger. Her brittle gaiety and the rather desperate glint in her eyes answered that question before it was asked. Then with sad resignation the O'Dowds retired to their beds for what was left of the night.

And with a similar resignation — though in her case more anxious than sad — Katy followed her mother back to their coach to travel the remaining half mile to Harcourt Street. The woman's continuing silence made her uneasy.

For Katy there was not one adult world but many, all of them remote and full of mystery. Her father's was perhaps remotest of all — a masculine world of nods and winks, of grave countenances and sudden eruptions of laughter, of buttonholings and elbow squeezings, backslaps and handshakes, and of oblique allusions to unknown proverbs ("As the actress said ..." or "All my eye and you-know-what ..." and so forth). Her attempts to penetrate this world of secrets were met with stonewall advice not to bother her pretty little head with such matters.

Her mother's world, though less remote — in the sense that Katy inhabited its outer fringes most of the time — was, curiously, even more secretive. It was full of Significant Looks, Meaningful Ejaculations, and Knowing Movements of the Eyebrows. A single drawn-out sigh of, "Well ...!" could imply a myriad of comments from "... some people can get away with murder," all the way along the scale to "... *we* could have predicted that tragedy from the very outset, couldn't we!" Her mother and the other matrons in that magic circle shared a secret that must never be spoken — or perhaps it *need* never be spoken, since it seemed to be in the forefront of their minds almost all the waking day.

To Katy it was rather like a hastily done-up birthday present — the wrapping was so thin she could feel bits of it and discover its overall shape, though the precise nature of the thing itself remained tantalizingly obscure. It was a vast secret, too, since it impinged upon her life in almost every aspect.

"Put on your gloves *before* you leave the house."

"Change out of that dress. You've been wearing it for hours."

"We don't recognize that person, my dear."

"Practise your scales; if you have no feeling for music, at least you can develop precision." Precision was an especially Swedish obsession — and anyway, she *did* have an ear for music, she just lacked fingers for the pianoforte.

"Unpick that embroidery and do it again. You want to have something you can show with pride to your own children one day, don't you?"

"If you can't account to me for a little pocket-money each week, how d'you expect to account to your husband for the housekeeping money one day?"

"Wait until you grow up and have babies of your own — you'll laugh at such silly notions then!"

It was all to do with answering to husbands and having babies of her own one day — that much at least was clear. The whole of her life

— every little grace note she played upon the piano, every tiny stitch she dabbed into that ever-more-hateful embroidered rose — was shaped, aimed, and dedicated to that one end. Nothing else mattered. Nothing else even existed.

Its practical effect was that her mother burbled with Sound Advice from cock-crow to owl-hoot. Like a cattle drover with but a single heifer to deliver into the ring, she plied her stick in a thousand gentle, unhurtful prods every step of life's way. And that was why her silence on this paritcular night was so unnerving.

Even worse, it was not the silence of the impending storm. Katy knew what that sounded like. It was full of explosive little sighs, as when pent-up breath is let out in mounting exasperation. It implied that her mother was busy choosing which verbal whips and lashes to employ when the storm finally broke. But this silence was ruminative, remote, almost wistful. It was as if, for once, her mother was lost in thoughts of her own rather than in cares for her dear and only daughter's welfare.

In a flash of insight Katy realized that such, indeed, was the case: Her mother was well and truly wrapped up in herself for once. She had a sudden feeling of loneliness. It was not just the feeling of being alone in a room, with the whole household buzzing about her, though not actually present; this was true isolation — an intimation of the life that lay beyond her present horizon, but only just beyond it. Life beyond Mamma and Pappa.

She stared out of the carriage window, into the dark holes between the shrubbery of St Stephen's Green, and thought, *I'm really out there already, in that blackness. This is only a memory of me sitting here.*

Panic seized her. "Let me hold on, let me stay!" a voice cried out inside her head. She wanted to disown it, to welcome the prospect of freedom in that blackness, but her panic would not let her.

At last her mother gave out a sigh too intrusive to ignore. Katy turned to her and found her staring back — not, as she had expected, all angry and critical but with eyes that were wan and pitying.

"Mmm?" Katy asked, perturbed by this unaccustomed mood.

"What are we going to do with you?" her mother said.

It was not really a question. Her tone rose at the end but it carried no suggestion that a reply was expected — or even possible.

"Whip me all soundly and send me to bed," Katy suggested.
"Those days are long gone."

Even this remark was obscure. Those days had never been — that
is, her parents had never whipped her, never raised a finger to her.
Nor had they needed to; the withdrawal of their affection had been
far more terrifying than a stinging bottom. So her mother could only
mean that the nursery-rhyme days of the Old Woman who Lived in a
Shoe were long gone.

Katy gave an awkward laugh. "Actually," she said, "the Old
Woman in the shoe had the opposite problem to you — she had so
many children she didn't know what to do."

"The result is the same, though," the other replied dourly. "We
have only one — and we *still* don't know!"

Then she gave out a sudden laugh and, reaching across the carriage,
grasped her daughter's hand and gave it a strangely congratulatory
pat. "Katy, my darling — you have just hit on the answer!"

"What?"

But her mother had rediscovered her normal flow and could not
be reined in to answer obvious questions like that. "As always, I may
say. There is more wisdom in that pretty little head of yours than
anybody could believe. And we never realize it until a little bit spills
out by accident — like just now."

"Why? What did I say?"

"Everything! The entire answer. We have so few children, Pappa
and I, we don't know what to do. There-fore ...?" She dragged out
the word as teachers do when they wish to encourage a pupil to
complete a thought.

"Therefore what?" Katy was now more bewildered than ever.

"You shall see!" Mrs O'Barry clapped her hands and soaped then
gleefully. "You shall see, you lucky child!"

*T*he day could not help turning into one long string of significant moments. Katy knew she was going to remember it like a catalogue of paintings for one of the Royal Hibernian Academy exhibitions: *The Last Day in the Old Home ... Childhood's End ... Farewell to Dear Dirty Dublin ...* and so on. She felt she was moving with a certain solemn grace from one sombre tableau to the next. Yet the single picture she would have treasured above all others, *The Lover's Parting,* had not been there. From her bedroom window she had gazed up and down Harcourt Street for some sign of Declan, coming to wave his last adieu, and she had merely amazed herself at the number of people who resembled him when wishful thinking wielded the paintbrush.

At her final leavetaking with her home, her eyes brimmed with tears as she hugged her maid, and cook, and Mrs Dobson the housekeeper, and all the other maids, and Favour the dog, and Kissi the cat — and, of course, Granny. Then, surveying the world through that salty veil, she had been quite sure Declan was that chequered, tweedy shape in a rakish bowler hat who swam and shimmered on the other side of the street. But he hadn't waved back, and her mother had said she thought it was going a bit far for her daughter to take her *congé* of every passing piano tuner.

She had next seen him hurrying beside St Stephen's Green, too late to say farewell but just in time to wave back as they passed — except that when he turned to do so she saw it was her father's chief clerk, doubtless on his way to the house. After that, though she spotted Declan at least another half-dozen times on their drive to the docks, she sat on her hands and waited for him to wave first. Which he never did.

So now she stood on the deck of the *Suecia,* leaning against the rail, frantically searching among the passing throng of bummarees, stevedores, porters, lightermen, and idlers for her last possible sighting of the darlingest, handsomest, winningest face in all the world. He *knew* she was being banished to her uncle and aunt in Stockholm. He knew it was all because of him — or because of him-and-her; her mother and father were determined to break it up between them, to "cure her infatuation," as they put it. He knew she would love him for ever and ever, to the grave and beyond. He knew she'd cut her own heart out rather than yield it to another. He knew all this because she had written it to him in blood (symbolically, of course) and sealed it with her tears — and Amelia had faithfully smuggled it to him.

So of course he would come and wave farewell — and find some means to reassure her that his own feelings were in every way the very mirror of hers.

"At least the gale has blown itself out," her mother said.

"Yes!" Katy was bright, almost too effusive; she was determined not to give them the satisfaction of seeing how they had broken her heart. "And the Irish Sea is always quick to settle after a storm."

Declan had told her that once. "Like the Irish people," he had added. Where *was* he?

"You'll get your sea legs in no time."

"I expect so, Mamma. Isn't it exciting!"

There he was!

No — it was another one of her father's clerks. How could she be so stupid? Declan looked *nothing* like an office clerk.

"Now you will be especially attentive to your aunt and uncle, won't you, dear. Remember, Swedish ways are much more formal than anything you've encountered here in Ireland ..."

Katy had no difficulty in believing it. She remembered the almost unrelieved tedium of the visit her Onkel Kurt and Tante Anna had paid them the previous summer. Only the presence of Bengt, her cousin, had made it tolerable; but even he was apt to be stiff-mannered at times. If people were as formal as that *within* the family, she shuddered to think how stiffly they might behave outside the home circle. "Mamma," she replied gently, "you recall Pappa's last words? If you haven't moulded me properly by now, it's far too late to start."

Her mother laughed dutifully; her husband had to be supported in anything he said, of course — though he did not always say the most helpful things. "And you will try to ..." She bit her tongue off.

"What?" Katy knew very well what her mother was desperately trying to avoid saying.

"... live within your ..." Mrs O'Barry tried an alternative ending but could not conclude it. Katy might be accused of many things but being spendthrift was not one of them. She had her father's gifts in that direction at least. He could leave home with a pound in his pocket and come back with two — even though he'd only slipped out to post a letter. Opportunities stood in rows for both of them, somehow. "I mean, don't put your uncle to unnecessary expense."

Poor Onkel Kurt was the opposite. He could go out with ten crowns stitched tight in his pocket and come back with five — and the stitching intact! And yet he was the meanest man alive. He wouldn't give you the steam off his own chamber pot, as the more delicate version of the Irish saying put it. He wasn't going to enjoy having his niece foisted on him out of the blue like this. Still, he would enjoy even less being reminded of his many debts to his rich and successful younger brother in Dublin!

"What you mean, Mamma," Katy said with all the dignity she could muster, "is: I will try and forget Mister Declan Butler, won't I!"

"Yes, that, too." Her mother spoke as if she would never have dreamed of raising the matter on her own.

"If that is your purpose in this 'educational' journey to my ancestral home — and we both know it is — then you should also know how utterly futile it will prove. You shan't see me cry. I shall cry but you shan't see it. I shall not beg nor plead nor cajole. May my tongue wither at its root before I rant and rail at your heartless treatment of me. I bear it all with fortitude. And I bear it all the more lightly because, in my innermost heart, I guard this unswerving conviction that my love for Declan and his for me will, at last, triumph over all adversity. You may postpone my happiness but you can never destroy it."

Of all the declarations she had tried out in her mind, while tossing sleeplessly in her bed last night, this had sounded the finest. It sounded even finer now, in their present circumstances, with the vessel about to carry her off to a remote and unknown land.

Her mother's response was rewarding. Her eyes brimmed with tears and she shook her head at the ineffable sadness of things. Then she marred it by adding, "I remember just such feelings as those. I had forgotten them until this minute, but I remember them now as if it were yesterday." She smiled encouragingly. "How sharp it bites, eh! And how swift it fades!"

"And you married Pappa in the end, see!" Katy added.

The faraway sadness intensified in her gaze. "It was not your father who inspired those feelings in me," she said.

Katy swallowed hard; she could not remember her mother coming within seven days' march of such a confession before. "Who, then?" she asked, barely above a whisper.

Her mother looked her up and down; her fond smile turned speculative. "I suppose there's no harm in telling you now," she replied. "It was all a long time ago — and I was as giddy and adorable as you. And, as I say, I had quite forgotten it until ..."

"Who?" Katy asked urgently, unable to contain her impatience any longer.

"A certain young nobleman — a student friend of my brother's — your Uncle Dagmar — at Uppsala."

"But his name?" Katy watched her mother teetering on the brink of closing the conversation. In a last reckless throw she said, "No! How dare I ask a thing like that? Forgive me. It doesn't matter."

Her daughter's brusque dismissal of something that had once mattered very much indeed to Mrs O'Barry finally tipped the balance. "What does it matter *now*?" she asked off-handedly. "I don't even know if the young count is still alive. He'd be almost fifty, anyway, God save the mark! His name was Hamilton. Count Hugh Hamilton."

"An English count? Is there such a thing?"

"No. They're Swedish. Irish originally — they went over and fought as mercenaries for Gustaf Vasa. He gave them the title."

"A count!" Katy was impressed. "That's like an earl in the English peerage, isn't it?"

Her mother nodded, reluctant to admit to any inferiority. But honesty compelled her to add, "Except for one thing — in the European aristocracy *every* son and daughter inherits the title, not just the eldest boy. So there are *hundreds* of counts called Hamilton in Sweden ... and all the others, the Wachtmeisters, the Wrangels, and so forth. So!" She was quite happy now to disparage her own juvenile affaire. "It's of little enough consequence — though I'd have gone to the end of the world with him once."

Katy saw him then — Declan. Definitely. No mistaking that walk — except that he was walking away from the quayside now. He must have been standing there for the past ... who could say how long? Looking up, seeking to attract her attention — while she had gone burbling on about how unconquerable their love was, and how indomitable her spirit ... until he must have assumed she was ignoring him deliberately and so turned on his heel and walked sadly away. Yes — just look at him! Dejection was in his every step.

She bit her lip until it smarted. If ever there was a moment when she came close to breaking her vow that her mother should never see her weep for her lost love, that was it. But she drew a deep breath, then another one on top of it, and so managed to crowd out the sobs that would otherwise have racked her body and brought her spirits low. While her mother babbled on about gay old times in the Stockholm of her youth, Katy followed Declan's departure until he was but a tiny speck, almost at the far end of Sir John Rogerson's Quay. It did cross her mind to wonder why he was making for Irishtown, the very poorest and least reputable quarter of the city, but then she remembered that the South Wall and the Pigeon House lay beyond it — a perfect place of solitude for the lovelorn lad or lass to nurture such a hurt as they now shared.

And the perfect place, too, from which to give one last wave to any departing vessel — and to that dearest vessel of all upon its decks! Her heart leaped up at the thought and the dangerous brush with grief was past.

"All ashore that's going ashore!" Mrs-Captain Carlsson came bustling along the deck, as happy to see her husband's ship preparing to cast off as Katy was sad. "That's what they say on all the big liners," she added.

"Must I go at once?" Mrs O'Barry asked anxiously.

"Oh, I daresay you have a minute or two yet," the captain's wife replied as she put her head to an open porthole in the housing behind them. "Agneta!" she called within, speaking now in Swedish. "Is Nils asleep?"

"Yes, Mamma," replied a girlish voice.

she always felt her spirit rise, as if it recognized an equal; and something within her would move her to court it almost, to befriend it and make it tame. She was sure she could walk among lions and pass unscathed; in Sweden, the wolves would instil no fear.

Naturally, her reasoning mind shrank from all those stupid impulses to bravado. She stepped back from the cliffs, sought an even firmer foothold beside the waterfall, and — now, at *Suecia's* stern — gripped the rail ever more tightly. Her reason told her she was simply provoking herself into being extra-cautious.

All the same, it was thrilling to stare down into the turbulent waters immediately aft of the rudder and imagine losing herself in it — and surviving.

"It's a fascination that never dies," Mrs-Captain Carlsson murmured at her side. "The hours of my life I've wasted, just staring into that … churning and bubbling."

"The power those engines must have!" Katy said.

"I'll take you down and show you as soon as we've settled down at sea." She looked back at the boiling wake. "It's different from this. This is chaos. Down there everything is so exact. You can hold your hand just *this* far from a flying piston and yet know you're utterly safe. It can't move a fraction of an inch from its allotted course. That's exciting, too."

In the corner of her eye Katy spied the Pigeon House, now passing astern to starboard. "Oh!" she cried guiltily and moved a pathetic three paces closer to it, shielding her eyes and staring hard at the long stone jetty.

Mrs-Captain Carlsson disappeared and returned a moment later with a pair of binoculars. She held on to them when Katy reached out a hand for them. "Are you sure you want to?" she asked.

For some reason Katy understood the question without any need for elaboration; there was a curious rapport between her and this rather unusual woman. She hesitated … almost declined the offer … and then, squaring her shoulders, said a decisive, "Yes, please!"

The woman settled the carrying strap around her neck and said, "Good for you." And then, with a, "Come, Agneta!" she left Katy to her search. Only later did Katy realize what a kindness that was; the woman had already known it would be fruitless.

When she first began to seek out Declan, the Pigeon House was a mere quarter of a mile away. And, since the binoculars had eightfold magnification, she was well able to make out the faces of everybody who stood at the foot of its wall, waving at the brave merchantmen as they passed in and out of the port.

Everybody! There were only three of them — two little girls and an old graybeard, their grandfather, perhaps. They waved and she waved back. And for the next five minutes, while the South Wall dwindled to a black line upon the silvery bay, even when magnified eightfold, she hunted in vain for any shape that could be conjured into something resembling her darling man. Once, when a pair of unnoticed lovers stood up suddenly at the very point of the wall, her heart leaped. She did not want the man to be Declan, of course, yet she was so desperate for one last glimpse of him by now that she would have accepted it nonetheless. But the young swain's hair was as fair as Agneta's and so even that teasing hope was killed.

When her arms ached beyond endurance she lowered the glasses at last and admitted to herself that Declan had not come to see her off at all — not to Harcourt Street, not Stephen's Green, not the quayside, not the South Wall. He was probably knocking back a pint in Grogan's this very minute — thinking of her, of course, but being too manly, too hail-fellow-well-met to show it.

Dejectedly she turned from the rail. "You take them as you find them and be glad for what you get." Her mother had said that once in an especially gloomy fit. She stared about her and, finding she was quite alone, wondered if she dared to cry. Then a movement in the gloom beyond an open door alerted her that she was not quite alone. Tentatively she held forth the binoculars.

"Finished?" came Mrs-Captain Carlsson's voice from somewhere down the passageway.

A moment later she stood at the door, an uncertain look in her eye. Katy took the plunge. "Of course he wasn't," she said simply.

"Oh my dear! I'm so sorry." She took back the glasses.

Katy swallowed hard and forced a smile. "They told you all about it, then," she said.

A laconic smile was her answer. "More than I've any right to know. I'll forget it if you like. I didn't really believe it, anyway."

It dawned on Katy that none of the formal rules of social behaviour were going to work between her and this enigmatic woman. And almost immediately after that, the reason occurred to her, too — that telltale little afterthought about "living by her own rules." Mrs-Captain Carlsson might joke about her motives for sailing with her husband (though it was a fairly common practice, especially where the captain was also master and owner of his vessel), but her true purpose was to live as far as possible outside the fetters of conventional society. Indeed, by now she probably no longer remembered them in all their cloying detail; she retained just enough to assume a sort of veneer when they put into port — like an ambassador's wife at an oriental court: She went through the motions and tried her best not to snigger.

All at once Katy warmed to the woman, more than she would ever have thought possible — certainly more than she had ever done with anyone else upon so slender an acquaintance.

"Never mind!" the woman said when she saw Katy too preoccupied to reply. She slipped an arm about her shoulder and turned her to face Dublin once again. "There it goes," she added, giving Katy a gentle impulsion back toward the stern rail. After a long silence she continued with, "And what *else* are you leaving behind?"

"Everything!" Katy said with an ironic stab at heroism.

The other pretended to take her seriously. "Is that a bad thing?" she asked.

Katy felt a sudden prickling of gooseflesh at the back of her neck. "Perhaps not."

There was another long, easy silence before Mrs-Captain Carlsson spoke again. She said, "Pure feelings are so hard to sustain."

Katy stared at her in mild consternation. "Mrs-Captain Carlsson ..." she began.

"Oh, please!" she interrupted. "Anything but that. Since we are to share the same bed for the next week or so, perhaps we might lay aside titles now and call each other Frida and Katya?"

Until she said *Katya*, Katy had not been aware of speaking Swedish all this while. "Frida?" she echoed uncertainly. She was still taken aback by that reference to sharing the same bed. Would the Captain sleep between them? Or would there be a bolster or what?

"Yes. It's Freda really. I'm Scottish by birth, but I spell it Frida nowadays to avoid endless explanations." The Swedish pronunciation was sufficiently distinct to make the spelling clear.

"I could hear you were Scottish by the way you spoke when we first came aboard. Why did we suddenly switch to Swedish?" *And why,* she wondered, *do I bother with trivia at a moment like this?*

But Mrs-Captain Carlsson — or Frida, as she already thought of her — did not seem to find it at all odd. "The moment the Blue Peter comes down in Stockholm, we switch to English. So it's the opposite in Dublin ... or London, or wherever we sail from."

"What did you say about pure feelings?" Katy — or Katya, as she was already beginning to think of herself — asked.

"The wonderful thing about going to the theatre," Frida replied at once, "is that the feelings there *are* so pure. This character is pure evil, that one pure goodness, or purely comic ... purely idiotic ... purely boring. Everyone is purely what they are. You can't have a romantic hero who scratches his backside and picks his nose — the way people do in real life. Even quite admirable people. In real life you simply can't say, 'Oh she's a saint and he's a devil.' I pity God on Judgement Day, don't you? Because if he can *really* look into all our hearts, he's going to find enough pitch in the hearts of the saints to defile them — and enough gold in the hearts of the devils to buy their redemption. In fact, if he really does the job properly, I shouldn't be at all surprised if every blessed soul in the whole of Creation didn't end up weighing *exactly* neutral in his scales." She laughed. "Poor old God! Still, it's his own fault. He shouldn't have made us so interesting, should he!"

Katya bit her lip and laughed uneasily at such blasphemous humour. Yet even as she did so, she wondered if it was really so blasphemous after all. A deity might actually be rather glad to hear himself talked about in such affectionate terms; it would surely make a change from the interminable sycophancy that poured skyward day after day. "I suppose I'd better busy myself unpacking," she said.

Frida nodded. "I've had your trunk moved into my cabin — or *our* cabin, we should call it now. The Captain will sleep in his watch cabin by the bridge." She laughed to see the relief in Katya' face. "Yes, I saw you worry about that."

"He won't mind?"

Frida gave a knowing grin. "He won't go short."

"Because I don't mind sleeping alone. I've always slept alone. I'm well used to it."

"I promised your mother, I'm afraid. Or, rather, *she's* afraid."

"Oh, but she's so silly!"

"I agree. I'll break my promise with a clear conscience if you like. Move yourself back here if you want?" She laid her hand to the passenger-cabin door and raised an eyebrow at Katya.

The younger woman became aware that this was not a simple choice — it was one of those go-on-or-turn-back decisions one faces at unexpected moments in life. Without even thinking, then, she inclined her head along the passageway and said, "What's our cabin like, then ... ah ... Frida?"

When Katya threw back the lid of her trunk she thought for one awful moment she had brought the wrong one, for there on top of everything, covering all the other contents, was her grandmother's dress. She recognized it at once; it was the dress Granny always wore for special occcasions — dark gray, severely cut, softened only by a few rather skimpy flounces below the knee.

"You're a lady of fashion!" Frida commented.

It forced Katya to see the dress with new eyes. She had always thought of it as a piece of folk costume — not the sort of embroidered crinolines girls put on for dancing and other grim-faced high-jinks, but an everyday, peasanty kind of dress, serviceable enough for church or milking. But now she could see that in its severe lines and almost wilful disdain for any kind of bustle it was, indeed, very like the "rational" dresses that earnest young ladies had started wearing ten years ago and which had now trickled down into the world of high fashion. Clever old Granny!

"There's some kind of note there." Frida's finger twitched at the corner of a scrap of paper sticking out at the waist. "A tenner, I trust."

Any such hopes were dashed when Katya withdrew the pin that held it and pulled out a scrap of notepaper on which was scrawled a single line in Granny's firm, old-fashioned writing. "In desperation," it read, "remember — you can always lift the hem of your skirt!"

Katya turned pale. She read it several times, vainly searching for some *other* meaning between the lines — except that there were no lines for any sort of meaning to slip between. The old woman's advice was quite unequivocal.

"Disgraceful!" Frida exclaimed — though with little heat, Katya noticed. "Some servant girl's idea of a joke, no doubt."

"I'm afraid not," she admitted reluctantly. "That is my grandmother's hand — and that is her dress, too."

Frida cleared her throat. "Froeken Oberg comes from an interesting family. Is your grandmother ... how may I put it tactfully? Senile?"

"Not at all. She's bright as a button." She lifted the dress and shook it to hang. Laughing, she added, "A girl would have a hard time lifting *this* hem. There must be half a ton of lead sewn into it. Just feel the weight!"

She passed it to Frida, who mimed a comic collapse of her arms. "Yes, well, you'd have to be desperate to try. Perhaps that's her point?" She crossed the cabin to the wardrobe and hung it up. "Old people take so much for granted. They forget how little we know."

"I shan't unpack completely ..." Katya began.

"Yes you shall!" Frida said peremptorily. "This is home, not a glorified waiting room between ports. Are you any good at algebra? You could help Agneta with it, if you wouldn't mind. I'm stronger on the classics."

It was a measure of the rapport between them that, long before that first day aboard drew to a close, Katya no longer felt the slightest jolt when Frida made such abrupt changes of subject; it was exactly the way her own mind worked when left to its own devices.

"Butterfly," her father called it, but he was the same. He could switch in the twinkling of an eye from Bolinders business (he was the Irish agent for the giant Swedish steelmaker), to his own affairs, to Irish politics, to that night's dinner menu. Naturally, he never called that "butterfly"; he said it was "all part of the tangled warp and woof of his life."

Thoughts of her father and his employers in far-off Stockholm prompted her to realize that she did not know quite where the Carlssons fitted into the scheme of things. So, as soon as she had promised to pass on to young Agneta what little algebra she possessed, her next question, almost in the same breath, was: "Does Bolinders own this ship?"

"Only under charter," was the reply. Frida went on to explain that she was, in fact, the vessel's owner. Her father, also a sea captain, had left her a smaller freighter called *Caledonia*. "I engaged Carlsson as captain and we traded so successfully we were soon able to buy a larger vessel — this one, in fact, which we renamed *Suecia*." She smiled mischievously. "It wasn't the only thing we were rather successful at, I may say. I married him when we found *that* one" — she nodded toward Agneta, who appeared to take no notice of the conversation — "was on the way."

"How ... ah ..." Katya swallowed heavily. "Romantic," was all she could think to say.

Frida laughed. "There are more ways into matrimony than there are ways out of it — I can tell you that for nothing."

Katya did not quite follow her drift.

"I mean, people get married and *then* discover they can't have children. But it's too late. The door's shut and bolted by then. I wasn't going to let that happen to me."

Katya fanned her face and, rolling her eyes toward the little girl, said, "I'm sorry. I'm not used to such discussions."

"I thought not." Frida tilted her head sympathetically, as if Katya had just admitted to being deprived in childhood.

They said no more on the subject though they chatted the whole morning away on every other topic under the sun — enough to have made Katya allow that her mind *could*, at times, be rather like a butterfly, *if* her father had been there to accuse her of it.

But he wasn't — neither was her mother. And that was increasingly becoming the central fact of Katya's life. She was familiar with articles in the ladies' journals — and discussions around the family table — in which people spoke sentimentally of daughters who grew up and flew from the nest. Increasingly over the past few years she had lived in the certainty that it must one day happen to her. And over the past six months, what with all the arrangements for her coming-out, she had lived in a whirl of daydreaming about just such an occurrence. Yet always at the back of her mind had been the notion that she would fly from one nest directly into another — one of her own making with Declan to support her, she had hoped.

But this well-intentioned banishment to Stockholm put a new colour on the whole business. Onkel Kurt's and Tante Anna's house could by no stretch of fantasy be transformed into another nest; if anything it was, in Frida's phrase, "a glorified waiting room between ports." In effect, then, she was fleeing the nest, *tout court*. There was no waiting nest to receive her; the world itself was her next home.

Somehow, though Frida never spelled it out in so many words, her attitude spoke directly to Katya's spirit and made her aware, within hours of boarding the *Suecia*, of this profound change in her circumstances. It was, she felt, another aspect of that strange mental sympathy that undoubtedly existed between them.

It did not, however, lead to an abrupt change in her thoughts and behaviour; its effect was more subtle. She had always lived in the knowledge that her mother and father were, so to speak, "in the next room." Even when she had gone to stay with friends on the other side of Ireland, her parents had travelled with her in spirit and had settled themselves in the "next room" in her mind. Now, however, she felt that room was empty. She could no longer carry life's little problems and conundrums in there and have them all neatly analyzed and sorted out for her. She was on her own.

She suddenly understood what being on one's own really meant.

It was like standing at the top of the cliffs near Doolin. It was like courting danger beside the Glenmacnass Falls. It was like the chaos of turbulent white water at *Suecia's* stern, challenging her to take the plunge. Disorder beckoned her with a smile but she did not cower back in fear.

She knew beyond all doubt that she could walk unscathed through a whole forest of wolves.

*C*aptain Carlsson came aft to his family quarters for luncheon. He was a jovial fellow with a lively curiosity and a quick smile (and a quick temper, too, Katya imagined, though he gave no evidence of it on that occasion). Within five minutes he had extracted most of her story. At its conclusion he looked her up and down and said he'd no doubt she'd overcome every obstacle in her way. She knew it was the sort of comforting nonsense anyone might babble, yet somehow on his lips — and especially after that swift but penetrating inspection — it carried conviction. She felt wonderfully heartened to hear him say it.

That was the moment when Frida chose to tell him the sleeping arrangements she had determined upon. She said nothing about any promise to Katya's parents; she simply presented it as a decision of her own. It obviously startled him but, whatever his true feelings in the matter, he masked them swiftly and said, "So be it."

There was a masterful gleam in his eye, however, when, a few minutes later, at the conclusion of the meal, he grabbed his wife firmly by the wrist and, turning to Katya, asked if she would mind taking Agneta for her daily walk on deck. His tone made it clear it was more of a command than a question. Frida's expression was ambiguous, part-resigned, part-delighted. "Just give us half an hour," she murmured to Katya as she picked up an apple and let her husband haul her from the stateroom into the cabin. Just before the door closed she took a great bite of the fruit; something about the gesture sent a shiver up and down Katya's spine.

Agneta was already in her oilskins and boots. She led Katya to what she called the "fog locker" to select a set for herself. They needed it, too, for the *Suecia* had strayed into one of those unaccountably rough regions that crop up regularly in the Irish Sea — as if the waves had bounced off four nearby coasts at once and then decided to meet here to complain about it. "This is Mamma's and Pappa's playtime," the child explained nonchalantly.

"I see," Katya replied.

"They get into bed and play together," she added.

Katya was glad of the opportunity to vanish momentarily inside an oilskin that was much too large for her. When they found one that was just her size she changed the subject firmly. "It's like a little country all on its own, isn't it — this ship. Or a town, anyway. It's got everything you could need for a whole town."

"Even a looney bin," Agneta said proudly.

"Oh, really?" Katya assumed she was making some jocular reference to her family quarters so she did not press the matter.

Agneta took her all over the ship, everywhere except the engine room, which she said she was forbidden to go near. "Mamma will show you that," she promised. "The men down there have to drink two gallons of beer a day, it's so hot before the furnace."

"Goodness!"

The tour took longer than half an hour but there was still no sign of the Captain and Frida. Katya decided to stay away from the stateroom a little longer. "When you spoke about a looney bin ... that was a joke, I suppose," she said.

"Oh no. Sailors often go mad," Agneta explained.

"Well, I expect they do. Especially if they drink two gallons of beer a day!" Katya replied. "Is there anyone in it now? Where is it, anyway? Deep in the bowels of the ship, I should think."

"No, it's next door to our stateroom. Come, I'll show you." She held out her hand and dragged Katya back toward the stern. Her smile promised a cabinet of wonders.

On their way they passed the stateroom-cabin porthole. Frida's smiling face was almost pressed to the glass. She held one tortoiseshell comb between her teeth and was pinning another above her left ear. Her shoulders were bare but for two thin straps of some pink, silky material. She winked when she saw Katya gazing at her and held up five fingers, meaning "five more minutes."

Katya grinned and nodded; she felt the strangest sense of complicity.

"Here!" Agneta led her round to the port side of the afterdeck housing, where a steel door led directly onto the deck. She opened this door and stepped back politely to allow Katya to enter before her. She did so with some trepidation for the "looney bin" was windowless and it was black as pitch inside.

The moment she was over the threshold, however, the little imp gave a delighted scream and slammed the door behind her. "You're mad! You're mad!" she shouted. "Stay in there and cool off."

Katya laughed and leaned her head against the door. She was not at all surprised to find it heavily padded on her side. "I warn you — I shall be mad, little girl," she said amiably, "if you don't open that door again this minute."

She fumbled for some sort of handle among the heavy padding but, of course, there was none.

And then her blood froze, for she realized she was not, in fact, alone in that darkness. That absolute darkness. Someone else had already been locked in there. She could hear him breathing — a curiously shallow, wheezy respiration — over in the farther corner. What was he? A drunken sailor? A drunken maniac? Her innards turned hollow.

He was a maniac, certainly. She could hear him snivelling in the far corner. He was lying on the floor, making odd little noises, halfway between whimpering and chattering.

She banged on the door again, furious that its padding absorbed almost all the force of it, making her frenzy seem no more than petulance. "Agneta! Please! Please! Open the door this minute! You've no idea!"

She had to pause and fight for breath.

From the far side of the door came no sound whatever. Not even laughter, now. In her terror the most absurd possibilities seized her imagination. A freak wave had swept the child off the deck ... some sea monster had reached up a clammy tentacle and carried her away ... "Agneta!" she screamed, more frightened now than angry.

The strange gibbering over in the corner grew in intensity.

It struck her then that the maniac might be more frightened than frightening. Perhaps she should try speaking to him soothingly? Anything was better than this.

"Sir?" she called hesitantly.

The chattering died at once.

Encouraged, she went on. "I mean you no harm, sir. I've been shut in here by a little girl who seems to think it's the greatest joke since the camel."

She paused and listened intently. The silence persisted; at least she had made *some* impression.

"I shall try to make her understand," she concluded. A moment later she resumed her hammering.

At once he resumed his gibbering.

"Lord, sir," she begged, "if you've breath in your lungs, you'll raise your voice with me and make that little imp open the door again ..." Her words choked off in a faint, strangulated cry, for while she had been speaking to him, the maniac had crawled toward her and got his hand under her skirts. He was now plucking obscenely at their hem, making little whimpering, drooling noises all the time.

"Oh, please ..." she said vaguely.

It galvanized him into some kind of action, for all at once he clutched her fiercely around the ankle. Then his grip swiftly transferred to the calf of her right leg. When she felt him next touch her knee, she kicked out with her other foot but, to her great surprise, she utterly failed to make contact with him. Indeed, she made no contact with anything, and she almost toppled herself with the recoil. And yet his clutch remained as fierce as ever!

How could she possibly have missed him? Which way was he lying? What sort of contorted, misfit shape did he own?

When she regained her balance she tried again, even harder this time — hard enough, in fact, to make her lose her balance when, yet again, she failed to find the rest of his body.

She fell half on some kind of mattress, half on the deeply carpeted floor. And then, of course, the madman was onto her like ten poor cousins — running his hands right up her body, taking the most dire liberties until at last his finger rested at the neck of her bodice.

"Would you stop that!" she shouted in a fury born of terror. And she gripped his finger to pull it away.

It was hairy! Not just slightly hairy — not merely fuzzy like her father's. (Lord, what would she not give to feel that man's fuzzy arms about her now!) But this was *really* hairy — almost furry.

In fact, it *was* furry!

And it wasn't a finger, either, it was a ... She pushed it away, not daring to think *what* it might be. It was something jointed — like an insect's leg. Only vast! A praying mantis? A giant praying mantis with fur? She did not even dare think the word *spider*, for it was ten times bigger than even the biggest, hairiest spider in the stuffed-animals museum in Merrion Square. And surely no spider would gibber away like that? It sounded more like a cricket. In fact, it sounded more like …

A baby?

A little baby lunatic, matted all over with fur?

With deep repugnance, and yet with a certain provisional tenderness growing in her heart, too, she reached down and discovered that the poor, chattering little creature's outlines were indisputably human. It was, indeed, some kind of tiny, shrivelled baby.

Moments later, though, after a more thorough investigation, she herself began to gibber — the oddest mixture of sobbing and laughter that ever escaped her lips.

"A monkey!" she cried. "A darling little monkey — and half dead with the fright and the cold, poor thing!"

She hugged it to her and called out robustly — all terror gone: "Agneta! If you don't open that door at once I'll boil your head and serve it up with the other cabbages!" She continued soothing the monkey, too: "Go on with you — I know what you want now! Why didn't you say so before? Come away inside here where it's warm. Oh, you poor thing. There's not a pick of flesh on those bones — and yourself shivering like jelly at a ball!"

And that was how Agneta found her when at last she opened the door — sitting on the floor, curled around a little gray monkey, cocooning it in the warmth inside the neck of her oilskin. Now it was the little girl's turn to scream. Not only that, she ran off to the stateroom, as well.

By the time Katya followed her, she was tight in her mother's arms and her father was striding angrily down the passage to discover what could have scared his daughter so badly.

When he saw it, and persuaded himself it was not an illusion, he grew so furious it was all Katya could do to stop him grabbing little Simeon (as she had already decided to call the monkey) and hurling him overboard. For two pennies, she thought, he'd have thrown her over as well. It took the intervention of his wife, and several repeated explanations, before he calmed down and accepted that the blame was really to be shared between his daughter and the unknown idiot of a seaman who had hidden the creature there.

Katya was determined that, no matter what terrors the poor little mite had suffered until then, it should suffer no more. She persuaded him it would be a fitting punishment to confiscate the monkey and release it into her care. However, lacking his experience of monkeys aboard ship, she thought it a little harsh that he insisted on chaining the fellow to a perch — and not in the stateroom, either, but in the empty cabin next door. However, despite all her pleadings, it was the best he'd agree to, and so she reluctantly accepted the decree.

She spent the rest of the afternoon in there with little Simeon, making him a rough-and-ready jacket and pantaloons — with the promise of a decently knitted outfit before the voyage ended.

That night she had the luxury of a hot salt-water bath — "to wash the smell of fear away," she said, for otherwise she had done little to exert herself at all that day. The bath was one of Frida's civilizing additions to the ship, added at the last refit; she had used it immediately after her "playtime" that afternoon.

"What a day!" Katya sighed as she sank gratefully into bed beside Frida. "It seems an eternity since I waved farewell to my mother on the quay this morning."

"And hunted in vain for another — who should also have been there to wave *his* farewell."

"Declan," she murmured.

"Is that his name?"

"Declan Butler."

"And what does he do? Shall I put out the light?"

Katya chuckled. "I don't need light to talk by."

"Oh, I do," Frida replied, though she turned down the lamp nonetheless, until it was the smallest glow. "We never fully extinguish it at sea. Seconds can be vital. You were going to tell me what Mister Declan Butler does?"

"My parents sneer that he's a horse coper. He buys remounts for the British army." She gave a sudden laugh — as of discovery.

"What now?" Frida asked.

"I've just remembered something he told me at the ball last Wednesday. I'll *bet* my parents don't know. Hee hee — otherwise they'd rather have sent me to Timbuktoo than Sweden. They *can't* have known!"

"What? What?" Frida asked impatiently.

"Only this: He's just been asked by a Swedish regiment to supply remounts to them — Irish hunters with a touch of Connemara, they said. Hah!" She clapped her hands beneath the covers and wriggled with delight. "He could be on the very next boat behind me! Sure that's why he didn't come this morning — why say goodbye when we'll meet again next week!"

"Katya — careful! You'll throw a fit!" Frida laid a restraining hand on her arm. "Are you sure it wasn't just talk? You know these young men who kiss the Blarney Stone before breakfast every day."

"No, no — it was serious. He even told me the regiments. Oh, don't you see, Frida! It's Fate! Karma. Kismet. It's our destiny. I don't mind my exile at all now. I shall sing all the way to Stockholm. What *was* that regiment? Tell me the names of some Swedish cavalry regiments — I'll recognize it when I hear it."

Frida laughed. "I haven't the first notion, my dear. That's the sort of thing you miss when you don't grow up in the country. I've only learned the nursery rhymes since Agneta and Nisse came along. Actually, I seem to remember that they're just numbers — K-One, K-Two, and so on. K stands for *kavalri*, of course."

Katya shook her head. "It wasn't as elementary as that. 'They're like the British Life Guards,' he told me. *Liv Gard* ... is there anything like that?"

She felt Frida shrug beside her. "Anyway," the woman said, "how would it help to know the name of whatever regiment it was? Will you camp on their doorstep? Bribe the adjutant to tip you off? Hire some loafer to keep an eye on the regimental gates?"

Each ironic suggestion was a nail in the coffin of her new happiness. She thought furiously. "I could write," she said. "I could write to Mister Declan Butler of Dublin, supplier of remounts to ... whatever regiment it is ... and mark the envelope to await his arrival." In the silence that followed she added, "And I could give him my directions as *Poste Restante*, Central Post Office, or whatever they call it."

"My goodness, Katya!" Frida's tone was genuinely admiring. "For an innocent abroad, you have a wonderfully agile brain. Whatever qualms I may have had for you are quickly evaporating."

"Qualms!" Now that Katya had her problems solved, she permitted herself the luxury of a slight glumness again. "Little's the harm will come to me, safe in the bosom of my uncle's family."

"Mmm," was all the reply to that.

*T*he remaining days of the voyage followed much the same pattern as the first. Katya knitted like a demon to keep poor, shivering Simeon warm — and sat by him and chatted to him and fed him and cleaned him and calmed his fears ... and generally turned him into the happiest little monkey north of Tangier. Agneta did the intensive side of her studies in the morning, which left her free to read and draw and paint in the afternoon. She did a little needlework, too, despite her mother's opinion that the world was awash with women who could sew, and all for a pittance. "She'd do better to study navigation," was her judgement, to which she appended the promise: "And she will when she's older."

And at the conclusion of every luncheon, Frida and her husband had half an hour or so of "playtime" while Katya and Agneta went for their constitutional walk about the decks. The baby Nils, or Nisse, as they called him, slept through it all. Captain Carlsson laid claim to these "playtimes" with an oddly assertive truculence, as if he suspected his wife might on each occasion say no, or make him fight harder for it. But she never did. Outwardly she responded with a tolerant sort of world-weariness; but underneath that veneer, Katya could tell, she was excited, too — excited as well as slightly surprised.

Each day Katya watched the interplay of these fleeting emotions with interest — until the day came when Frida caught her at it. She responded with an exaggerrated mimicry of the young woman's open jaw and then she laughed before she shut the cabin door.

That night, when she turned the lamp down to its all-night glow, she referred back to the incident. "I hope we don't embarrass you, my dear, Carlsson and I, with our little playtimes?"

"Of course not," Katya answered effusively. Her heart skipped a beat and then made up for it in doubles.

"He *wants* to embarrass you, of course. It's only because you're here that he's making such a parade of it."

"Honestly. Truly!" Katya pretended to stifle a yawn.

"I saw you watching us today — with that tolerant, superior smile of yours ..."

"Superior!" she interrupted. "Good heavens, but that's the very last thing ..."

"I just wondered what you were really thinking."

Katya realized there was no turning away from it. Frida had come to bed determined to force the conversation this way, no matter what. Curiously, though, she found herself quite willing to follow.

"I'll tell you what I was thinking. I was thinking, *She's happy to go with him and yet she wants to tease him by pretending otherwise. And he knows she won't refuse but he pretends to believe she will.* And I couldn't really understand why people pretend to feel things they both know aren't true."

"Whooo!" Frida let out her breath as if she'd been hit. "I asked for it, I suppose."

"D'you know why you both pretend like that?" Katya insisted.

"I do. But whether I could explain it is quite another matter."

After a silence, Katya said, "I know what you ... I mean what men and women ... I know the secret of playtime."

"That's a start, anyway," Frida conceded. "Though it has very little to do with why Carlsson and I play our absurd games. Tell me — how d'you know this secret? Did your mother tell you?"

"No!" Katya was shocked at the idea. "Amelia told me. And when I talked with my maid, she told me more. Amelia didn't know you had to move as well."

Frida breathed in deeply and then let it out in one long sigh. "It's a whole mountain ahead of you, girl. I don't know where to begin — or even whether I should. Still, as to Carlsson and me, you have to appreciate he's in an awkward position here. A ship's captain is God afloat, you know. He almost has power of life and death over the crew. Think of the powers husbands try to assert over their wives, then multiply them tenfold — and you're somewhere close to the majesty of a captain. But *this* captain's wife happens to be the absolute legal owner of the vessel. And, to make matters worse, I refuse to share it with him! That's possible in Scots law, you know — which is what applies here. Carlsson accepts it by now," she added grimly. "He doesn't understand it — he'll never understand it — but he accepts it. So, while I own the key to his livelihood — he is my lord and master. We never know *exactly* where we are with each other."

"All at sea?" Katya suggested.

Frida laughed and hugged her arm. "Well said! Well and truly said! All at sea — indeed! Now are you beginning to glimpse what's behind it all? Why we play these games? Why we almost have to play these games?"

"Yes." Katya did see, too; she could not have put it in so many words, and yet she understood it quite clearly.

"So your friend Amelia may have told you about putting it in, and your maid may have added something about moving it in and out — but beyond that ..."

"I beg your pardon? Moving it how?"

"In and out — why?"

"Oh! My maid didn't say anything about 'in and out.' Perhaps she didn't know, either."

Frida laughed uproariously. "Keep going! We'll get to the edge of the world yet! Anyway, as I was saying, those simple mechanical facts don't even begin to scratch the surface of what really goes on."

"Tell me, then," Katya urged. "What really does go on?"

"*War*, darling! The sweetest, savagest, gentlest, most merciless battle that ever man and woman waged. An old old fellow once said to me that the only important things in life all happen between a pair of sheets. I thought he was just trying to shock me — which, of course, he was. Yet the longer I live, the more I come to see that he spoke the simple truth." She turned to Katya and raised her head on one elbow, peering earnestly into her dimly illuminated face. "However, *your* simple truth — as explained to you by your friend and then by your maid — is the *least* important part of it. If you remember that, you'll be spared a lot of disappointment." After a pause she added, "And I shall have served some small purpose on this earth, as well."

"I feel as if I've known you for ever and ever," Katya said. "I hope we can meet every time you dock in Stockholm."

"So do I, my dear. Truly." She plucked Katya's hand above the sheets and kissed the backs of her fingers lightly. "But it does rather depend, you know."

"On what?" Katya stretched out luxuriously. She knew that as soon as she was alone again — a prisoner, really, in her onkel's house — she'd start to mourn her separation from Declan, until, of course, he turned up in Stockholm, too; but for the moment her life was so rich and rewarding she could easily put all that sorrow to one side.

"On whether or not you actually do go and stay with your Onkel Kurt," Frida said lightly.

Until that moment it simply had not occurred to Katya that she had any choice in the matter. This time her heart skipped two beats and then thrashed like mad. "What else could I do?" she asked in a faint, fluttery voice.

"That's not for me to say. How old are you?"

"I'll be twenty-one soon enough. But still ..."

"What languages do you speak?"

Katya gave a baffled laugh. "You know very well — I speak both English and Swedish."

"And French?"

She gave a modest shrug. "Tolerably, I suppose."

"German?"

"I can get by. I speak it better than my father. I always do — I mean, I always *did* the interpreting when German businessmen came to see us in Dublin."

There was a thoughtful pause before Frida asked, "Why would German business men come to see Bolinders' agent in *Dublin*? Or is it true what they say about him?"

Katya grinned. "What do they say about him?"

"They say Bolinders would dearly love to part company with him but they dare not, because he could ruin them throughout the entire British Empire market."

Katya's smile became a laugh. "I'm sure that's true. He says the first thing you should do on entering any room is to lock all the exits — and keep the keys handy where no one else can touch them."

"What an admirable man he sounds! Anyway — here you are, on the verge of coming of age, speaking native Swedish and English, and passably fluent in French and German — and yet you, the only daughter of such an enterprising man, can still lie there asking what you might *do? In the year eighteen hundred and ninety-seven?"*

Her heart was still going pittapat. "Is there anything special about the year?" she asked.

"You mean nobody's told you? You haven't heard of the great Universal Exhibition to be held in Stockholm all this summer ... the great celebration of Swedish industry and enterprise ... people coming from all over the world? And you haven't even heard of it?"

Lamely Katya replied, "I've been utterly preoccupied with my coming-out ball at Dublin Castle, I'm afraid."

Frida laughed richly, saying, "Well! Now that we've got the one major event of the year out of the way, perhaps we can turn our attention to this rather lesser affair?"

*T*he *Suecia* made her final approach to Stockholm on the morning of the last Monday in March. Katya was entranced with the city long before it came in sight. As they steamed up the estuary, threading their way among the hundreds of islands of the Archipelago, she thought that any city which could boast such a breathtaking approach must surely be fair beyond measure. The landscapes of Ireland looked old and raddled by comparison, scarred by man in all his guises — farmer, warrior, pillager, villager. But here, she felt, was a land still new, pristine and stainless — looking very much as it must have done on the day it left its Creator's hands.

It helped, to be sure, that a thick blanket of dazzling white snow covered each rocky outcrop, upon whose samite field the trees were crisply etched; the farmhouses and barns looked like toys, unwrapped that very morning. Even the smoke from their chimneys had an artificial look for it rose against the cloudless azure of the sky in a purely vertical line of pale, warm grey that simply tapered away to nothing, high above. Never in her life had she seen the elements so still. She felt she could almost reach out and touch the little houses ... tap them gently on the roof, perhaps, and watch the tiny ant-folk come scurrying out of doors!

Frida came to lean on the rail at her side. "Well, my girl! If you can't start a new life on a day like this ... eh?" A sigh of contentment rounded off the thought.

"I don't know, Frida," Katya replied, unwilling to give a hostage to fortune now that the moment of decision was so close. "I feel I want ... I mean ... oh, I don't know what I want."

"A sign?" Frida asked ironically.

"Yes!" Katya looked at her in surprise. "I know you're being sarcastic, but I *do*. A sign is just what I want. I want something to happen that will tip the balance for me."

"For instance?"

She sighed. "I don't know — except that I *will* know it the minute I see it. I'll recognize it." She made a contented little noise, as if she had reached some critical decision, and rubbed her hands excitedly.

Frida's gaze was full of pity. "That's not the way of the world, my dear. Life doesn't step up and beg you to join the dance. You've almost got to shout at the top of your voice, and even then ..."

Katya patted her arm comfortingly. "It'll happen," she said.

"And if it doesn't ...?"

She touched the breast-pocket of her coat. "I have my father's letter to his brother to fall back on. Don't you think I've been very noble not to steam it open and read it?"

Frida did not tell her that she had saved her the trouble; in fact, the contents of that letter had largely decided her to put the rather outrageous idea into Katya's mind of embarking on her own independent life in this city of her forefathers. Her strong affection for the young woman had helped, too, together with a conviction that she had the character and spirit to succeed at it — a conviction that had grown stronger with each passing day.

"The thing is," Katya said in a more reflective tone, "it would be so easy just to go on being me — just go on being Larry O'Barry's daughter — or Lars Oberg's daughter, in Stockholm, I suppose. Oh dear!" She laughed. "That's the question, really. Do I go on being

Katy O'Barry or do I become Katya Oberg? I've got to decide today.
It's now or never. I *know* Katy O'Barry so well, you see. She has such
an easy life — this is what I was trying to say just now. She's never
had to do anything. Ever. Apart from obey certain rules and con-
ventions, of course. But that's easy because everyone else is doing it,
too." She chuckled as she stroked Frida's arm with one finger and
added, "Almost everyone." Then, serious again: "What I mean is
Katy O'Barry has never been forced into anything by mere circumstances. She's never wanted for anything. She could go right through
life, simply conforming with her father's expectations, and then her
husband's — like drifting endlessly down a lazy summer river. It's so
easy to be a woman, isn't it — that sort of woman, anyway. But as for
Katya Oberg ...!" She shivered theatrically.

"Forget her, then!" Frida spoke as if that were the simplest matter
in the world.

Katya threw her arms about her and gave her a brief hug. "The
moment I hear you say that, my whole spirit rises up and shouts *No!*
But you know that, don't you. That's why you say it."

"Perhaps that's the sign you say you're looking for? You could
simply be looking in the wrong place — not in the world out there
but inside yourself."

Katya shook her head stubbornly. "It'll happen — and I'll know it
when I see it." She smiled reassuringly at her friend — but was
surprised to see her face still troubled. "Oh dear, what's the matter
now?" she added.

"Me," Frida replied glumly. "It's hard to explain. It's a thought
that just flitted through my mind a moment ago — when you were
describing Katy O'Barry and her easy, easy life. I've been thinking a
lot about my own life lately, ever since you came aboard, in fact ..."
She broke off and stared over Katya's shoulder, toward the bows.
"No, don't turn round," she said. "We're just coming in sight of
Stockholm — but I'll tell you when to look. It's not nearly so
magnificent if you see it bit by bit. Now what was I saying? Oh yes —
well, to cut it short, what I was working my way toward saying was
this — it's a warning, really: Beware of women whose own lives have
left them dissatisfied. They'll try and relive them through you. I've
racked my conscience these last few days to be certain that I'm not

guilty of that crime myself. Of course, *everyone* wants more than they've got — otherwise we'd still be living in caves. But I think I can honestly put my hand on my heart and say that my life is more or less what I want it to be. To desire very much more would be greedy. In other words, I don't *think* I'm a disappointed woman trying to live my life all over again through you. But *you* must be the best judge of that, not me — and not just in my case, either." She smiled wanly. "I'm sure that if Katya Oberg does decide to strike out on her own, she'll meet many unfulfilled women who have tried to relive their lives through their own sons and daughters — and who have failed there, too. Beware of them - they're just waiting for someone like you to come along."

Katya drew her arms tight to her sides and shrank her neck into her shoulders; a thrill, oddly compounded of happiness and fear, moved inside her — because implicit in Frida's warning was the assurance that she'd defeat these ogresses who might try to usurp her life. "Can I look round now?" she asked.

Frida shook her head. "Soon."

"It applies to men, too, I'm sure," she went on.

"With men it's much simpler." Frida chortled. "In the game of commerce you must always assume that the other players want to take as much money from you as they can and give you as little as possible in return. You'll meet the odd exception, of course — the player who is genuinely interested in building something lasting rather than running off with a fast profit. When that happens you'll enjoy a pleasant surprise. But it's a rare sort of treat. Where the majority are concerned, it's best to be ever suspicious, ever ready with a sharp elbow. And it's the same with that other game, the men-and-women game — you understand what I mean? You know what men want — *all* men?"

Katya nodded and smiled gratefully. "Playtime."

"And I mean all men," Frida insisted. "From the age of ten to a hundred and ten."

"Can I look now?"

She sighed. "Yes, you can look now."

When Katya turned she let out a gasp of wonder. If the little farms and summer cottages in the Archipelago had seemed like beautiful toys, the city now spread before her in a dazzling, sunstruck panorama was a veritable fairyland.

"It really is the most beautiful city in the entire world," Frida added superfluously.

Stockholm is a city built upon islands, though from the present position of the *Suecia* that fact was barely apparent. Only the central island of Gamla Stan, the ancient and original settlement was discernible, and even that with difficulty. Its southern extremity merged with the built-up hillsides of Soeder, the southern half of the city, parts of which were almost as old as Gamla Stan itself; and the northern end, too, was half swallowed up in the newer buildings of Norrmalm and the equally populous island of Kungsholm beyond. The immediate impression, therefore, was of a single unbroken sweep of grand buildings, their classical façades of pale yellow or rose stucco shimmering in a myriad of shivering reflections in a vast expanse of bright water.

The beauty of it brought tears to Katya's eyes; she tried to speak but there were no words adequate to the tumult of feelings that stirred within her.

Then Frida grasped her by the shoulders from behind and hugged her tight. "Yours for the taking, Katya," she murmured.

Katya stiffened, for a certain wistfulness had crept into the older woman's tone. Those earlier words of warning were still a faint rumble in her mind's ear, and once again all her decisions were thrown into turmoil.

*T*hey berthed just before noon at the Stadsgaard quay on Soeder. Katya, who had not ceased to quarter the city with her eyes ever since it had come into view, strolled round to the starboard side of the vessel, where she could gaze out over the expanse of the Salt Sea and continue to drink it all in. Agneta came and stood at her side, slipping her hand into Katya's. "Where's your home?" she asked.

Katya gave a single dry laugh. "I wish I knew, little face. Just think!" She stooped until her head was level with the girl's and made a traverse of the entire panorama with her gloved finger. "Somewhere out there is a building I shall soon be calling home. A week from now, if you ask me that question again, I'll be able to point it out at once. And its roof will be like no other roof out there, and its windows will be different, too. So why can't I see it now, eh? Why doesn't something of that specialness already cling to the place?" She laughed and added ironically, "Why haven't I got crystal balls in place of these old eyes!"

"I think you've got lovely eyes," Agneta said. "Mamma says they're the most beautiful eyes she's ever seen."

"I'd like them better if they could see just a little way into the future," Katya told her. "Three hours is all I ask." She stared back at the sunlit city. "It's funny, you know. I've never been here in my life, and yet I've seen so many photographs and met so many people who come from here — and read so many stories set here, too — that I already know my way about! Honestly, now, you could set me down almost anywhere out there and I couldn't get lost. You could put me ashore in Liverpool and I'd lose my way round the first corner. But not here, even though this is the first time I've set eyes on the place. Don't you think that's eerie? It's *almost* like being able to see into the future, isn't it."

"I think you're going to live …" Agneta's slim little finger hovered over Gamla Stan before she jabbed it at a building near the southern end. "… *there!*"

Katya grinned. "You don't like uncertainty, either," she remarked. "Actually, my dear, that is the Royal Mint — so I'd never be short of money! You must come and pay me a visit any time you want to go out on a spending spree."

They laughed. Then Agneta, determined to make some sort of stab at prophecy, said, "I didn't mean right on the waterfront, but somewhere in behind there. D'you know Gamla Stan?"

"Only from pictures. It's full of dear little poky streets and mysterious alleys, where seamen's bars and murky deeds go cheek by jowl, isn't that so?"

"It's where I'd like to live," the girl replied simply.

"I'll bear that in mind, then," Katya promised. "I'll find rooms there if I possibly can. And then, when you next berth in Stockholm, you can come and visit me. I'll come back tomorrow and tell you."

"We shan't be here tomorrow."

"What? D'you mean you unload your cargo and load the new one again, all in one afternoon?"

"No!" Agneta went on to explain that the locks at Slussen, at the southern tip of Gamla Stan, were too small to allow big cargo vessels like *Suecia* to pass into the freshwater Lake Maelar, which bathed the western shore of the old city. They had to unload here and then make a long, roundabout canal journey to gain access to the lake — specifically, to the island of Kungsholm, where the Bolinders factory and head office were to be found. It took eighteen hours or more, depending on how dense the canal traffic was.

Katya's spirit sank at this news. At the back of her mind had been the comforting thought that, if the worst came to the worst, she'd always be able to come back to the Stadsgaard quay and find a bunk on the *Suecia* for the night; but now she'd be on her own for the next forty-eight hours or so — a high-wire act with the expected safety net removed!

"You're sad?" Agneta asked.

"No, no." She tossed her curls bravely. "It's just that I had hoped to leave my trunk on board until I'd found somewhere to stay. But I can just as easily leave it in one of the offices on the quay. I'm sure they won't mind."

She had hoped to leave Simeon-monkey on the same understanding, but that, she now realized, was going to be impossible. Captain Carlsson had threatened to sell him to the first buyer he met along the quays.

She took a final luncheon with the Carlssons — remarking that if the ship didn't start to sway and lurch soon, she'd begin to feel quite seasick — and then there followed a not-at-all-final farewell at the top of the gangway. It might have been quite a tearful affair, but their protestations of friendship and their promises to meet again on Kungsholm in a couple of days softened the blow of parting and enabled her to walk down to the quay with little more than a mist of sadness in her eyes.

"Well, Simeon," she said as she turned to wave again from the foot of the gangway, "here we go."

My native soil! she thought, trying to stir up some patriotic emotion within her. But it looked disappointingly like the cobbled quays alongside the Liffey. Her eye, alert for differences that would spell foreignness and excitement, was equally disappointed. A steel crane is a steel crane the world over. Seagulls are seagulls. Horses and carts are ... but no — there *was* a difference. These horses wore no blinkers! She had never in her life seen draft horses without blinkers.

"Good heavens, Simeon," she exclaimed sarcastically, "we really are in a foreign country now and no mistake!"

She turned and waved again from a hundred paces or so along the quay — and again when she reached the head of it at Slussen. Dear Frida and Agneta were still watching her, instantly ready to wave back. What was she thinking? Katya wondered. Was she reliving her own youth as she watched her young friend set out on her new life? Was she wishing her own might have been different?

At Slussen she faced her first real choice of the day — in effect, the first choice for or against an independent life. Onkel Kurt's house stood in Goetgatan, on Soeder, which was to her left. True, it was also an area of small hôtels and pensionats, so a left turn did not necessarily commit her to following her parents' intentions and lodging with her relatives; a right turn, on the other hand, would take her over the bridge into Gamla Stan, to the area behind the mint, which Agneta had pointed out. Each step would be an immediate flouting of her parents' plans. To turn right would be like making her choice here and now.

"Yet how can I?" she asked Simeon, who gibbered back and tried to snuggle even more deeply under her thick fur collar.

She realized she would have to get indoors somewhere or other, and pretty soon. Despite his own fur and his knitted jacket and pantaloons, he couldn't take too much of this dry, bitter cold.

Left or right, then?

She looked straight ahead and then up, and up ... and up, for looming over her was the tall slender tower of Katarina Hissen, the passenger lift whose upper platform was on a level with the top of the Soeder heights — and was, indeed, connected to that part of the city by a long steel viaduct. Those who did not want to struggle up the steeply sloping streets could pay their twenty-five oere, go up in the lift, and enjoy a horizontal stroll of a couple of hundred metres to arrive on the heights of Soeder.

Katarina!

It was an omen of welcome, surely, that the first part of Stockholm through which she would pass, after leaving the quayside, should bear her own name! It seemed to her then that she had to take the lift. It also had the virtue of postponing that more fundamental choice for a little while longer.

From the platform at the top she could see the whole of the city spread out before her — including all those parts that had so far been hidden behind the fairytale outline of Gamla Stan. The uncanny feeling that she already knew it all — this city she had never visited before today — was stronger than ever, now, for this was the view that her mind's eye, assisted by maps, had long ago conceived. There in the centre was the whole of Gamla Stan, from bustling Slussen at her feet to the serene majesty of the palace away to the north. To her right the Salt Sea lapped the island's eastern shores, free of ice and alive with small craft; the *Suecia* was almost lost among half a dozen or more vessels of a like size along the Stadsgaard quay, which stretched away to her extreme right. On the other quarter, west of Gamla Stan, was the ice-mottled water of Lake Maelar, where the toing and froing of an equal number of small craft was more disciplined, being confined to the broad lanes the icebreakers had opened up. Notwithstanding today's cold, the winter was drawing to an end and the ice had already started to break of its own accord on earlier, warmer days.

On this western side of Gamla Stan, balancing the Royal Palace to the east, so to speak, she could see the characteristic outline of the parliament building. Somewhere near by, she recalled, was the House of the Nobility. She enjoyed a brief daydream in which she went up to it, knocked at the door, and asked to speak to a Count Hugh Hamilton — whereupon a charming old aristocrat came to greet her ... took her inside, stood her a dinner of ambrosia and nectar, and then drove her off to his castle in ... where had he lived? In the country somewhere. And there, of course, he had a room filled with mementoes of the fair young Sarah Sandstroem (who later married some commoner called Oberg). Sarah was the one true and only love of his life. He had never married, of course. And of course he would use his enormous influence to get her work as a guide at the Exhibition — nothing could be simpler! It wouldn't actually open for another two months, mind — but she was welcome to treat his castle as her own home until then ...

This final touch of realism brought her back to the ground — or at least to the panoramic platform — with a jolt. Indeed, the Exhibition would not open for another couple of months! Why had she not thought of that before?

And what was she to do in the meantime?

She seized eagerly upon this new problem and dramatized it in a different way. She always seemed to grasp things more clearly if she set them in dramatic form; her father's way was quite different. He would divide a sheet of paper into two columns and write down all the pros on one side and all the cons on the other; but that sort of cold-blooded reasoning had never worked for her. So — imagine something awful had happened to her parents and she had been sent back to Stockholm to live with her Onkel Kurt and Tante Anna. And then imagine something awful had happened to them, too, while she was on the voyage. So here she was, arrived in Stockholm with a trunkful of clothes and a few sovereigns in her purse — all alone. What would she do?

Granny's scandalous advice popped into her mind — assisted, no doubt, by the fact that she was wearing the very dress to which that note had been pinned. Certainly not that!

But what if there was nothing else?

That was absurd. There had to be something else.

What if Count Hugh Hamilton fell in love with her on the spot — or with whatever remnant of her mother he might detect? What if he offered to "protect" her? She had a vague notion of what that meant, and it wasn't a million miles from Granny's disreputable advice. Her mother had said she'd have followed that man to the ends of the world at one time. Surely living under the protection of such a paragon couldn't be wholly bad?

Simeon's frozen chattering broke into her reverie.

"You're right, little man," she sighed. "This is just foolishness — I'm just thinking scribble. What I need is someone who knows what's going on in Stockholm at the moment ..."

Bengt!

Of course!

She could kick herself for not thinking of him at once, for Bengt was Onkel Kurt's eldest son — her cousin, in fact — about five years older than her. He had accompanied his parents to Dublin last summer and they had got on very well together. In fact they had become much too friendly to fall in love, which had been a great disappointment to her mother, she knew, since the main reason for inviting him had been to wean her away from Declan. But it proved she didn't love him, not romantically, anyway — the fact that she'd hardly given him a thought since then, not even during these last ten days, since she'd known for certain that she was coming to Stockholm.

But never mind about that. Bengt was the answer to all her problems. She could go along Goetgatan to a shop or café somewhere near their house and sit and wait for him to make a showing. Then she could call him over, explain her plans to him, and enlist his help — first to find her some good lodgings and then to get some work to tide her over until the Exhibition opened.

"Simeon, you are *so* clever!" she said, loud enough to startle a couple to her right.

Until then the woman had had not been aware of the monkey that the elegantly dressed young lady was keeping half-hidden behind her fur collar. She gave an almighty start and backed away.

"He doesn't bite," she told the woman in English, as if being foreign would also somehow excuse her eccentric behaviour.

A few moments later she plunged into the shadows where the long viaduct drew close to the tall buildings that capped the heights of Soeder.

Bengt! Her spirit sang.

Bengt was the key to everything.

yléns Conditori was the handiest little café from Katya's point of view, for it stood on Goetgatan, precisely opposite Onkel Kurt Oberg's house; and, what with the sun in the sky behind it and the dim lighting within, the windows would appear impenetrably dark to anyone in full sunlight on the farther side of the street. Katya took up her vigil there shortly after two o'clock.

At first Herr Nylén had been disinclined to let her in. Not that he objected to her so much, but he thought Simeon-monkey was out of place in the sort of genteel establishment he imagined he and his wife were running. His wife, however, took one look at the cut of her clothes, decided she was an eccentric aristocrat who must have her own good reasons for slumming in these parts, and was intrigued enough to admit her.

By four o'clock Katy had drunk more small cups of coffee than she would have thought possible; she was obliged to overcome her embarrassment for the second time and to ask Herr Nylén if she might use the family's water closet yet again. On this occasion he obliged her to wait a moment, explaining that he thought it might be occupied. Actually, he believed no such thing, but he wanted a word with his good wife first.

"Speak to her a little when she comes through here, my dear," he urged. "Draw her out if you can."

Fru Nylén tugged her black, art-silk shawl more tightly around her thin shoulders and snapped, "Why? What is she to do with us? Who is she, anyway?" In fact, she was dying to find some reason for questioning this strange young lady with a monkey in her bosom, but she did not want to give her husband the credit for suggesting it.

He continued to cajole her. "There is some *mystery* there, my dove," he murmured, laying emphasis on the one word that could always be guaranteed to penetrate his wife's indifference. His tone promised scandal.

"Mystery?" she echoed scornfully, but already she was sitting up straighter — almost as if he stood over her, holding strings.

"If my suspicions concerning her are true ... well, who knows? She might be of great service to us. That is why I'd like you to draw her out a little. You are so good at that sort of thing."

"What suspicions?" Now she was all eagerness. "Tell me."

"I'd prefer to tell you *after* you've spoken to her. If you draw the same conclusion without any prompting from me ..." He smiled. "D'you see? I'll tell you one *fact*, though. Both times when she has asked to use our toilet — which she calls a 'water closet,' by the way — she has begged me to keep watch on the Oberg household opposite." Fru Nylén's eyes opened wide at that, but her husband raised his finger. "*And*," he concluded, "she asked me to note especially whether young Master Bengt Oberg goes in or out!"

"But he's away on his military service," Fru Nylén objected.

Her husband smiled. "Our mysterious young visitor obviously doesn't know that, though. And I have taken great care not to tell her — so far. As I say, there is a mystery surrounding that one, and it may be of profit to us to discover it. I say no more."

Nor did he need to. By now a pack of wild wolves would not have been able to stop Fru Nylén from trying to pierce the enigma of the young lady, monkey and all. She rose to her full, angular height, pulled her black, art-silk shawl around her once again, and said, "Show her to our 'water closet,' my dear." She spoke the words in a parody of an aristocratic accent. "Is that really what she called it?"

"Her very words, my dear. 'Water closet,' she said."

"How very interesting. Well, I shall be ready for her when she returns to her place."

And so it was that when Katya came back to the conditori, to resume what now appeared to be an increasingly forlorn vigil, she found the other seat at her table taken by a lady dressed all in black — Sunday black, or respectable-commercial black, not widow's weeds. She was a thin woman, all hunched together, as if she feared she would never get warm this side of summer. Her skin gleamed in the fading afternoon light that stole in through the net-curtained window, but it was the shine you get on old parchment, not the sheen of a fresh-polished pippin.

Katya took up her napkin and cup, intending to move to the only other vacant table in the window bay, but the woman turned to her with a smile, a surprisingly pleasant smile, and said, "My husband has asked me to have a word with you, my dear." She waved a hand toward Katya's chair. "I am Fru Nylén ...?"

The little questioning note she injected at the end of the statement had its desired effect. "Katya ..." she began. "That is Katarina, of course. Katarina ... Carlsson." She could tell by the smile on the other's face that she wasn't believed for a moment. And small wonder, for Carlsson is to Sweden what Sullivan is to Ireland or Smith to the English — a name for unmarried couples in hôtel registers.

Fru Nylén came at once to the point. "Are you in some kind of trouble, Froeken Carlsson?" she asked, putting on her most compassionate smile.

"No, Fru Nylén," Katya replied, still flustered. "Not at all."

The woman sighed and stared across the street toward the Oberg house. When her gaze returned to Katya it was brimming over with a new tenderness. "You are perfectly at liberty, of course, to keep your own counsel and to spurn all offers of help, but ..." A sad, seen-it-all-before sort of smile twitched at the corners of her mouth and completed the sentence.

Katya swallowed heavily and said, "You see, Fru Nylén, I don't believe I need any help."

"Because you are waiting for someone who'll bring it to you?"

Katya nodded.

The woman stared again at the Oberg house. "Over there? Would it be young Master Bengt Oberg, by any chance?"

"D'you know him, madame?"

Fru Nylén laughed. "Since he was so high. I also know he won't be coming home today."

Katya stared at her in dismay.

"Nor tomorrow." The woman hammered as many nails as she could into the coffin of Katya's hopes. "Nor all this week, nor next week, either. In fact, young lady, I doubt he'll be back until spring is well advanced."

"Why?" Katya felt the blood drain from her face. Was he ill? Had some dreadful accident ...

"He's doing his military service, my dear! Somewhere far up in Norrland." She shivered at the thought of all that ice and snow.

Katya felt crushed. What was she to do now?

Well, of course, she was in no immediate difficulty. She had enough money to stay in a modest pensionat for days — even weeks. But that wasn't the point. Some time soon a letter from Dublin would pop through the letterbox opposite. It would be written on the assumption that Tante Anna and Onkel Kurt had read the first and were enjoying the company of their darling niece. And then the fat would be in the fire. Before that happened she must have found both lodgings and work that paid a good living wage. And, to be sure, she must be free to meet Declan when he came; how easy it seemed to forget that *that* was her true purpose in all this!

She was unsure of the legalities of her situation but she'd surely be safely over twenty-one — in June — before the law could take its slow and solemn course. However, without Bengt to help her, she was quite alone and friendless in this city.

A great dark cloud of defeat now gathered over her life; her plans seemed doomed before she even began. A terrible urge seized her to end it all now — to swallow her pride, go to that house across the road, ring her aunt and uncle's bell — and bring her great adventure to an inglorious end.

"Was he the only one who might have helped?" Fru Nylén asked, giving another brief glance toward the house.

"No." Katya sighed heavily. "But he was the one I wanted most to ask. I mean he was the only one I wanted to know about my being ... no, I mean it could have been just between him and me." She smiled wanly. "But the rest of the family *will* help me. I know that." She drew a deep breath and framed herself to the decision.

By now, of course, Fru Nylén understood everything. "Wait," she said with great firmness. "Do nothing rash. There may be another way. I'll have a word with my husband. You know where the toi— the water closet is, I think — should you require it again."

She rose before Katya could say another word and went back into their private quarters. A moment later her husband joined her.

"That girl is expecting Bengt Oberg's baby," Fru Nylén said primly. "She as good as told me so. And she is most certainly no servant girl. We may be sure of that. She says her name is Carlsson, but that was a lie. Katarina Carlsson. The Katarina part is obviously from Katarina Hissen. And Carlsson ... well!"

"How can you be certain she's no servant, my treasure? Any lady's maid could put on one of her mistress's frocks and remember to call the toilet a water closet."

The woman stared pityingly at her husband. "If she were a servant girl, my precious, she would have at least some small skill in lying. This girl has none. But never mind all that. *Whatever* she may be, she's certainly down on her luck. Down and *out*, I'm sure. Perhaps she's a governess. Or was. She and Master Bengt must have met socially, somehow. She seems to know the Obergs quite well. And she's quite confident they'll help her." She smiled a knowing smile. "Unless, of course, we can think of someone else?" Her tongue lingered playfully on her lower lip. "Someone to ... fill the breach?"

Nylén studied the ceiling. "I was thinking of Count Magnus Hamilton, my dear," he said casually. "I recall one or two hints he let drop last time he was here — all to do with filling breaches."

"How curious!" Fru Nylén grinned. "I was thinking somewhat along the same lines myself. If she has already touched pitch and been defiled ..."

"Quite!" He rubbed his hands happily.

She rose to her feet. "I'll send the boy at once. Let's just hope our noble lieutenant is not orderly officer at the palace today."

While this conversation progressed, Katya had resumed her seat by the window — and her now pointless vigil for a cousin who was a thousand kilometres away.

And then it happened. If it had happened five minutes later, the street would have been too dark for her to recognize Onkel Kurt.

He came striding up Goetgatan from Katarina Hissen, swinging his cane with a reckless disregard for the safety of others. Everything Katya disliked about the man was suddenly contained in those loose gestures with his cane, and in the way he puffed at his cigar, and even in the way he tapped the ash into the gutter. A self-made man, full of self-made satisfactions.

A beggar woman stirred from the shop doorway where she had been sheltering from the cold and approached him. She was a somewhat starved-looking woman in her mid-twenties with nothing but an old cotton shawl to wrap her and the baby she cradled in her arms. Onkel Kurt listened to her gravely then groped in his pocket. The poor young woman must have thought he was going for his purse; but instead he fished out his door keys. Then, with the merest shake of his head, he dismissed her and went up to his front door. The key chain was so short he had to stand on one leg and cock his hip. *There* was the man for you — he would even grudge the outlay of a few oere on a proper length of chain!

She turned to Simeon-monkey and stared him full in his big soft eyes. "There you are, little man," she told him. "That's the sign I've been waiting for. Didn't I say it would come? And wasn't I sure I'd know it when I saw it? Come on! We're going to find some lodgings for the night."

She rose and started gathering her things.

And that was the moment when Fru Nylén touched her on the shoulder and said, "Pray come and sit in my parlour, Froeken Carlsson. I think my clever husband and I may have found the perfect answer to all your little difficulties."

*L*ieutenant Count Magnus Hamilton was not the appointed orderly officer at the palace that night. In fact, he rather wished he had been, for he had no idea what to do with himself. A curious restlessness had settled upon his life lately and he couldn't seem to shake it off.

On the face of it he had no cause to feel down. He was tall, handsome, and rich; he held a commission in that most élite of regiments, *Lifgardet till haest* — the Lifeguards of Horse; he had friends in every circle — literary, dramatic, artistic; he was persona grata with every hostess in Stockholm, and, being unencumbered by a wife, persona *very* grata with every hopeful matron, too; and at the moment he was free of a mistress, as well.

Indeed, when it came to the business of freedom, he probably had a greater share of it than any other young man-about-town. Except

Max Lejonkrona, perhaps. So not only did he have no cause to feel down, he had no *right* to the feeling, either. All he knew was that something was missing somewhere. His life was all promise and no delivery. Hence this restlessness. He merely went through the outward motions of being an officer, being a swell, being an eligible bachelor ... while an annoying little voice went on drip-drip-dripping away inside him, saying there ought to be more to life than this.

It was all because of his bloody father, of course.

At last, for want of anything better, he decided to go into the city, to the music hall — Svea Salen, perhaps.

When he was dressed for the occasion — best blues, spurs, sword, cape, and all — he surveyed the result in his looking glass. The general effect was not bad, he decided. The dark blue of the uniform was perfect. But the gray of his cape could be a little lighter for his taste. The best thing about it was its lining of crimson silk — which was not army regulation but his own, personal addition to the uniform. Magnus stroked it affectionately and sighed, for the colonel had ordered him to take it out again. His precise words had been: "Take that bloody awful red stuff out of your cape, Hamilton!" — which, in theory, anyway, would allow him to replace it with any other red "stuff," as long a it was *not* bloody awful.

He considered the matter with fastidious care. Actually, maroon wouldn't look too bad. Also, the whole thing would look snappier if it were, say, five or six inches shorter. (His branch of the family, being extensively involved in forests and the timber trade with England, thought only in feet and inches.) He folded the hem under and supported it temporarily by jutting one thigh forward. Oh, yes! It should certainly be *six* inches shorter. And also it should be lined with maroon silk.

He sighed and stood up straight again, letting the cape fall back to the dreadful regulation length. Army regulations! Was he really intended for the army? Sometimes he thought a life on the stage would be far more attractive.

It would kill his bloody father for a start.

And he could wear any uniform he liked. And he could have the capes cut to whatever length he liked. And he could get them lined in any colour he chose.

He tilted his head to strike a better pose; he moved the lamp to give a better shadow. He moved another to give the better shadow an interesting sort of glow. Perhaps he should be a photographer? He had the feel for good lighting. *That* would kill his father off, too. What *right* had any man to get married again at eighty! Especially to a dashed pretty young bride of eighteen.

No, the stage was the thing. Why spend forty boring years working yourself up to the rank of general when you could step into the part one week and abandon it the next, before you grew tired of it? It must be an exceedingly tiresome rank. Certainly none of the generals he met in real life seemed to enjoy it. Perhaps they'd be happier if they, too, married pretty young fillies of eighteen. It had obviously worked wonders in the case of his revered ...

No! He closed his eyes and drew a deep breath, disciplining himself once again *not* to think of that distressing event. When he opened them at last he moved a little nearer his looking glass. Were his moustaches too long? He'd tried everything, from the softest Russian tallow to the hardest carnauba wax, and every mixture in between. But even the best of them lasted only half an evening, after which the tip would inexorably curl, and then, of course, the whole of Stockholm would start to smirk and pass comment.

Also, it made it damned difficult to kiss a girl properly. He ought to get a new mistress — and put that unfortunate experience with Sara Andersson behind him. Eight hundred and ten crowns for one single dress! He still winced when he thought of it. And for what! What had she given him in return?

Next time he'd get a proper mistress, not a girl who'd just use him as a springboard to something better. No, something *even* better. He should look for a professional mistress, a girl paid not to notice things like unruly moustaches.

Suddenly he realized he'd gone off the whole idea of an evening at Svea Salen. Jugglers, conjurors, jokers — people who lived from hand to mouth with no pattern to their lives at all! He shivered. They were too close to him in spirit for his comfort. That's why one needed the army. It gave pattern and purpose to an unruly life. Look what had happened to poor old Max once he became plain Herr Lejonkrona again, after that unfortunate business with Colonel Stenmark's wife!

Stenmark — there was another dry old toad who should never have married a pretty little moppet just out of school.

Perhaps he'd go and dine at the Opera Cellars? Oh, no ... those *awful* murals by Kronberg.

Kronprinsen, then? No, he'd dined there already this week.

Or should he simply stay in the mess and dine in for once? No, he'd only end up playing billiards, at which he always lost money, or cards, where he'd lose even more, the stakes being higher.

He thought again of poor old Max and decided to go and cheer him up. They could dine somewhere quick, like the Metropole, then go back to Max's place in Gamla Stan, put on their slumming clothes, and walk across Slussen to that cheap seamen's *bordell*, where men could buy a ninety-five-oere coupon and have a girl for five minutes. They could do the same as last time — buy a couple of dozen tickets and give the girl the surprise of her life for two whole hours!

His loins stirred pleasurably at the prospect. It was no permanent answer, of course, but it would postpone the necessity of doing anything drastic for a week or two. He ordered up his coach and set off for Max's apartment in Jaerntorget in Gamla Stan.

But Max Lejonkrona was not at home. Magnus, who had his own key to the apartment, let himself in to see whether his friend had left a note or some other clue to his whereabouts. In fact, he had left Franz, his valet — and a Franz with orders not to answer knocks at the door — which showed that something pretty serious was afoot. All the man would say was that the Count might understand that his master had "found it necessary to repair to his country estate on Ekeroe for a while."

"In March?" Magnus's voice was larded with disbelief.

"Indeed, Count!" The man's tone implied that *that* fact alone revealed what dire straits his master must be in — though, of course, as a good servant, he would say nothing specific.

"And he's left you here?" The skepticism was even firmer.

"I am to remain in my own lodgings, sir. Indeed, I was on the point of leaving for them when the Count arrived."

"And he left no special message for me?" Magnus asked. "Not even a note?"

"Not even a note, sir."

Magnus's vanity was so wounded that he gave his moustaches an extra-special tug as soon as he regained the street. Vexed, he wondered what he'd do with his evening now; his loins were still stirring at the promptings of his earlier plan. He decided to turn about and go up to Svea Salen after all; one could always find a pretty little *chanteuse* and take her on to a *suppé* at a *chambre privée*. All the nice things in life were French, it seemed. He was just giving his coachman the order when the boy from the conditori spotted him.

"If the Count pleases," he said, "Herr Nylén begs him most respectfully to come at his earliest convenience to the conditori, where he will find a situation much to his liking."

This mysterious summons was both timely and intriguing. So much so, that Magnus invited the boy to share the ride back to Soeder — and not out in the wet with the coachman, either, but inside, where he could be further quizzed.

But all the boy knew was that an elegant young female with a pet monkey had been sitting in the conditori since dawn, practically, sipping endless cups of coffee, and staring out of the window. At last Herr Nylén and his wife had questioned her about her strange behaviour — after which they had sent the boy to ask the Count if he would be good enough to call.

Now, leaping to all the obvious conclusions, the Count discovered he could hardly wait for the carriage to arrive. When at last it did so, he hopped down with unseemly haste; then, to force himself to behave with more dignity, he half-removed his gloves and pulled them back on with slow deliberation, finger by finger.

The Nyléns were bowled over by his magnificent appearance. Last time he had been here, he and Max had been in their "slumming clothes," which were, in fact, the sort of thing a senior government official or banker might wear, but which an aristocrat would not normally be seen dead in. Now, to the clink of sword and spurs, he strode into the empty conditori, grasped a chair, reversed it, and sat himself down, leaning nonchalantly against its backrail. "Tell me the story, then," he said.

Fru Nylén told him.

"And is she of good class, d'you think?" he asked when she had finished her tale.

"The Count will be the best judge of that," she replied. "But I'll stake my life she's no ordinary working girl."

"I don't think she's Swedish, either," Nylén put in surprisingly. The other two stared at him in amazement.

"She speaks almost too well," Nylén explained. "Too carefully, if the Count knows what I mean? Like a foreigner."

"Has she a foreign accent, then?" Magnus asked.

The man shrugged uncomfortably, being reluctant to go that far. "It's *like* a Stockholmer ... and yet there's something ... *other*. I can't place it. The Count can decide for himself, of course. I merely offer it to him as an observation."

"Have you told her anything about me?" Magnus asked.

"Not a word, your lordship."

"So what does she imagine is about to happen to her?"

"We are at the Count's disposal," Nylén replied.

"We can tell her whatever the Count thinks best — or nothing at all, of course."

They waited expectantly. The Count tugged at his moustaches, pleased to find them still ramrod-straight. "Perhaps it's better you tell her nothing," he said at last. "Desire her to join me out here."

They hastened to obey. At the doorway Fru Nylén turned and asked hesitantly, "The Count would perhaps be kind enough to inquire about tickets for the next levée?"

"If anything comes of this," he assured them, "I shall ask my ..." He grinned. "Yes, I shall ask my mother — my stepmother, that is — to present your daughter herself. You needn't worry about tickets."

Fru Nylén almost swooned at the prospect. A moment later she swept back into the deserted conditori, trailing Katya like a prize in her wake. "Now Froeken Carlsson, my dear ..." she began.

Magnus winced when he realized the woman was about to introduce them the wrong way round. But then, since the Nyléns were not on a social footing with him, they could hardly do the right thing and present him to the girl, either. To resolve the dilemma he stepped forward and said, "Permit me to introduce myself, mademoiselle. Count Magnus Hamilton, Lieutenant ..." He hesitated.

Katya thought it was because he had just spotted Simeon; in fact, he had just caught sight of her amazing, jade-green eyes.

"... er, of the Lifeguards of Horse," he concluded. He clicked his heels, raised her hand to within inches of his lips — and looked into her eyes once more. What astounding things they were! He had never seen the like of them. They made her look almost Chinese. And such a hauntingly pale green! They stirred such novel feelings within him — uncomfortable and potent — and not at all the ones he had been hoping for on his way here with the messenger boy.

"Leave us, please," he told the Nyléns.

"What regiment, my lord?" Katya asked with barely suppressed excitement. She, too, was in something of a turmoil. She had never seen a man quite so magnificent as this noble young cavalry officer. In his dark-blue uniform and charcoal-gray cape with its lining of deep-crimson silk — not to mention his gleaming sword and spurs — why, he was practically *made* to turn any silly young girl's head. Naturally, she despised herself for such empty-headed feelings. And yet ... and yet!

"The Lifeguards of Horse, Mademoiselle ... did that woman say your name was Carlsson?"

Katya nodded abstractedly, then said, "No, my lord ..."

"Please!" he protested. *"Count* will do for the moment."

His eyes promised warmer intimacies, which made her feel hollow.

It was merely hunger, of course. She should have eaten earlier. She lowered her voice. "My name is actually Oberg but I didn't want those awful people to know it." She tilted her head almost imperceptibly toward the back of the café. "The house opposite belongs to my uncle and aunt — I mean, they live there. I don't wish them to ... Oh dear, it's all much too complicated to explain."

"And certainly not in these surroundings." He glanced about them with distaste. "May I be so bold as to invite Froeken Carlsson to dine with ...?"

She interrupted him, reaching across to touch his sleeve; the metal braid felt chill. "I know why they sent for you, Count," she said.

She'd be a fool not to understand it, she thought. You only had to look at the situation through their eyes — a penniless, friendless girl in need of a protector ... a young aristocrat who could do them some favour at court — get their pastries the royal seal of approval, perhaps. She was annoyed to find that something in her was more flattered than angry at this disgraceful assumption — though she took care to hide both annoyance and pleasure from him.

To his relief he now found himself able to look her steadily in the eyes. "I don't know what they have told you, Froeken?"

"I don't suppose they needed to tell me anything, Count."

She wondered why she did not simply stand up and say she was sorry he'd been brought out on this wild goose chase ... she had been hoping to meet her cousin but without the knowledge of her aunt and uncle ... now impossible ... military service ... etcetera, etcetera ... going to look for a modest but respectable pensionat in town ... could he help?

What could be simpler or more natural than that?

So why didn't she do it?

She was forced to admit there was something exciting about the thought that this dashing young officer had come post-haste to this depressing little café for the express purpose of making an improper proposal to her. It gave her an odd sense of power, which she was unwilling to relinquish just yet.

Besides, she suddenly remembered, he had said those magic words *Lifeguards of Horse!* If she cultivated his friendship, just a little, he'd surely let her know — or even let slip — when Declan was coming next to Stockholm!

Yes, of course, *that* was why she didn't want him simply to bow out of her life this minute.

Magnus, meanwhile, was thinking that Nylén was right about her Swedish. It *was* oddly perfect, lacking some idiomatic looseness. Her actual words, however — that she didn't need to be told anything about his reasons for coming to see her here — threw him into a fresh quandary. Was she simply leaping over what could be a rather embarrassing conversation for both of them? That would reveal her as a woman of very *nice* breeding. A lady, in fact. Or was she also arriving at its worldly conclusion — saying, in effect, "Cut the talk. Let's get down to brass tacks!"?

Nothing in his previous experience of women — and certainly not of ladies — had prepared him for such subtleties. In every way, it seemed, this female had him out of his depth. All solid ground turned to quicksand beneath his feet.

He decided to risk nothing — to put the ball back in her court: "Do *you* need to tell *me* anything, Froeken?"

She closed her eyes and drew a deep breath. "All I can say, sir, is that I am far from home — *very* far from home. That I am tired. And hungry. And that a ... a certain person, who lives in the house opposite and who I was quite sure would help me, is up in Norrland somewhere, playing at soldiers." She opened her eyes wide and put a hand to the shocked O of her mouth. "I'm sorry! I mean, doing his military service."

He smiled, not so much at her sarcasm against the military as at her charming remorse for it.

She for her part rather wished he hadn't smiled at all. As long as he had maintained that solemn, slightly frightened air, she could stay calm. But that smile — and its sudden promise of his friendship, his warmth, his tenderness ... his concern for her — it was too much when set beside all the presentiments of loneliness and rejection she had experienced that day, to say nothing of the dashed hopes and the humiliation of handing over her father's letter to his brother.

"Permit me to assure you of this, Froeken," he said. "Any ... er, commitments ... or, that is to say, *arrangements* that our friends" — again he nodded his head toward the private door — "may have promised you on my behalf, you may ignore. I hardly know what to tell you next." He smiled helplessly, making her feel more helpless yet. "I know what I should *like* to tell you."

"Yes?" She encouraged him with her eyes — little realizing what else it did to him and his resolve.

"Yet I know what you would think, nonetheless — even if your delicacy prevented you from saying it." He raised his hands in a gesture of hopelessness. "We are trapped in our present situation, I feel. You are (let me guess) in difficulties — temporary, I'm sure. You are young and — if I may say so — beautiful. It is quite obvious why *I* have been sent for! This is Act One of a drama few playwrights can resist. We, the actors, could speak our lines in our sleep by now. And anything I might say — anything at all — would seem a mere elegant variation on the same tired old theme! A pretty trope to lead us inevitably to Act Two! And yet, I repeat" — he smiled again — "I know what I should *like* to say to you."

Simeon, who had been staring from one to the other, as if he were actually following their conversation, suddenly reached out a hand toward the man in the glittering clothes. Magnus chuckled and offered him his finger, which he clasped avidly.

"He likes you, too," Katya said. "His name is Simeon."

"Shall I tell Simeon, then?" Magnus asked. Her use of the word "too" filled him with an absurd joy. Then, without waiting for her reply, he went on: "Our playwright isn't going to like this one bit, Simeon. For the fact is, we may never get to Act Two! You see, old fellow, I came to this place tonight expecting to find a pretty servant girl down on her luck — and I expected to make her an offer that, truth to tell, would shame an animal, let alone a human being — let alone a member of the House of the Nobility."

Simeon chattered in reply. "Don't interrupt!" Katya scolded.

The Count continued: "It was an offer of help — but it came with certain conditions. What I'd like to do now, Simeon — you see — is to make that same offer of help but without the conditions. But my trouble is — I can hardly expect *her* to believe it. This may come as a shock to you, but sensible people just don't go about the world making altruistic offers like that. You probably see a lot of altruism where you come from — the Noble Savage and all that rot — but you'll find it's very rare among us civilized humans. The parable of the Good Samaritan is only intended for reading aloud in church. The priest who reads it passes twenty beggars on his way to the service — just as his congregation walks blindly past them on their way home. If we all lived in Samaria, of course, we should behave quite differently! But we don't. We live here, and Samaria is comfortingly far away. So *what* am I to tell her? What do *you* advise?"

Katya tried to think of something clever to say, or even something sweet. But she was torn between two quite contrary desires. Part of her was already laughing at his strange but endearing humour. But the rest of her was close to tears — not so much of sorrow — in fact, not at all of sorrow — but of relief and happiness and ... oh, something that had no name at all. And the only way she could think of to escape these ambiguous desires was to reach out and take one of his other fingers and give it a warm pinch.

"Did you mention dinner?" she asked.

She remembered her trunk down at the warehouse on Stadsgaarden quay. The porters grunted and groaned as they heaved
it out to the waiting carriage, hoping thereby to increase their
tip. Then one of them spoiled it by muttering to his companion:
"It didn't take *her* long!" It was all Magnus could do to stop
himself from striking the blackguard.

"That's what the world will think," she sighed as they set off once
more, heading, this time, for the Metropole in the northern part of
the city.

"Let it!" he replied grandly — then, realizing his words sounded
rather cavalier, he added, "For my own part, I mean, I don't care a fig.
But I would do nothing to tarnish your reputation, Froeken Oberg."

They crossed the bridge at Slussen and entered Gamla Stan; she
leaned toward the window and gazed out with interest. "What
reputation?" she asked jovially. She intended going on to explain
that, apart from her relations, no one in Stockholm knew the first
thing about her — but then she realized it wasn't quite true. There
were people at Bolinders, of course, and several cronies of her
father's who had visited him in Dublin. So then, what with all the
qualifications, it became too difficult to explain.

"I see," he said. "May I ask — is Froeken Oberg, in fact, Swedish?
Please do not feel obliged to answer. I desire to know nothing
beyond what you wish to tell me."

She had not realized until then that she was, indeed, under no
obligation to tell him anything about herself. Her upbringing had
taught her that a lady in difficulties should seek the protection of the
nearest gentleman and tell him everything, whereupon the universal
code of honour would oblige him to assist her to the utmost of his
powers. It was so hard to remember that she was not, in fact, a lady in
difficulties but an independent person about to start making her own
way in life. What she might decide to tell him — and what she might
withhold — was determined by quite different rules. She need tell
him no more than it suited her to reveal. After all, was he going to tell
her everything about his own life!

"There's little to unfold, in all conscience, Count," she replied. "You are very clever with your question. I am Swedish, in fact — of Swedish parents ... and grandparents for a long way back. Except one of my great-grandmothers, who was Magyar ..."

"Ah!" he interrupted. "Your eyes!"

"Yes. Is this the middle of Gamla Stan?"

He glanced out. "Just about. And that answers another question. You are a stranger in Stockholm at least."

"Yes and no. This is my first day in the city but I've heard so much and read so much — and seen so many pictures — I don't think I could get lost here. Are there any good pensionats around this quarter? If we could find one now we could leave off my trunk and I could change into a more suitable evening gown. I feel quite drab beside you."

It was all good sense, of course, but he did not want such a break in their developing friendship; it had already acquired a certain momentum and he didn't wish to lose it. "We can take a chambre privée," he suggested.

Her jaw dropped, though she felt more amused than shocked. "What will the world say to that!"

"They're already saying it. Tell me, do you write letters on lined or unlined notepaper?"

They both laughed — and that was somehow taken as a tacit agreement between them that they considered themselves above such things. They needed no guidelines to run straight and true.

"So," he went on, "your family is Swedish all the way back to Noah. That's more than we Hamiltons can boast, I may say."

"Oh, I know about the Hamiltons," she told him. "You came over here from Ireland to fight for Gustaf Vasa. By the way, is Count Hugh Hamilton still alive?"

"Hardly!" Magnus chortled. "He came over from Ireland more than three centuries ago."

"No. I mean a more recent Hugh."

"Oh, well, there are dozens of them. We come by the dozen now, you know. There's the Royal Palace, by the way — my place of work, you could say. D'you know a Count Hugh Hamilton, then?"

"My mother did once, long ago. He'd be in his fifties now."

Magnus shrugged. "There's one of that age in Lund but I've never met him." He returned to his guided tour. "That's the House of the Nobility — the finest cellars in Stockholm. And this is the new parliament building going up. Each wave of lords and masters seems to get bitten by an urge to build hereabouts. Nowhere else will do. Where will the trades unions go, I wonder?"

"They'll have to flatten the palace," she suggested.

"Yes," he said heavily. "They will have to flatten it first, too. However — we digress yet again. You are Swedish ... but?"

"Did I say *but*?"

"I think you were about to. That's Dramaten, by the way — our main theatre — the Opera's just behind. Tolerable food but undrinkable wines. Tell me the rest of your story when we're comfortably settled at the Metropole."

"*In*tolerable food but drinkable wines?"

"Tolerable both," he replied — and then occupied the rest of their short journey by pointing out the principal buildings and squares as they drove past. "This is the area of the 'goulasch barons'," he said scornfully of some especially grand apartment houses, which looked as if they'd been transported entire from one of the more swell quarters of Paris.

The head waiter at the restaurant raised his eyebrows at the sight of Simeon, but when the Count asked for a *chambre privée* he shrugged and let them pass.

"You have power in this city," Katya said to him as they ascended the stairs.

"My rank carries power," he replied scornfully. "So, too — if I may be vulgar — does my purse. Take them away and what am I?"

She laughed. "Have you ever tried?"

"How could I?"

"Put on a common man's clothes and go slumming."

He cleared his throat awkwardly and said it sounded like fun ... perhaps he'd try it some time.

The *chambre privée* was the most luxurious room she'd ever been in. The walls were lined with red plush and encrusted with gilded plaster swags and opulent mouldings. A crystal chandelier, glowing with soft electrical lamps, hung low over the table, suggesting an enchanted forest. The carpet was so deeply piled it almost swallowed her feet. And the crimson velvet armchair into which her waiter now assisted her received her with a seductive embrace, as if it had been moulded for her alone. An extravagant canteen of crested silver cutlery gleamed on dazzling white napiery, set off by a phalanx of sparkling crystal glasses — the first of which was filled with a pale dry sherry the moment she was seated. Somewhere in the room there must be a large pot-pourri of rose petals.

When she thanked the waiter the man shook his head, barely perceptibly, and she understood he did not exist; she was to ignore his attentions.

He, of course, imagined he was helping an Unfortunate go up in the world.

The Count was so used to not noticing such fellows that he noticed none of this. "Now!" He rubbed his hands in a display of anticipation. "We had reached that interesting little word: *but!*" He toasted her rather formally. "*Skaal!*"

"*Sláinte!*" She watched closely to see if the Irish toast had any meaning for him.

It obviously did — and not a happy meaning, either. "It's Irish," she told him.

"And don't I know it!" he replied heavily.

"Why d'you say it in that tone?" She grinned. "Please do not feel obliged to answer. I desire to know nothing beyond what you wish to tell me."

"A hit," he confessed like a sporting swordsman. "A palpable hit. It so happens that my aged father has lately married again — a young Irish girl named Theodora Hennessy?"

That little hint of a question made her reply, "There are lots of Hennessys in Ireland — it's like Carlsson or Svensson here."

"Ah!" He grinned. "I thought at first that you knew of my father's remarriage and were mocking me for it. How interesting! You seem very well informed about Ireland, Miss Oberg." This time he said "Miss" rather than "Froeken." Then his eyebrows shot up and he said, "Oh, I begin to understand!"

She smiled, knowing very well what connections he was now making. "All right, then — you tell me."

His eyes promised he would, indeed, tell her as they paused to inspect the menu. "May I choose for you?" he asked.

She was about to agree when something made her say, "No, thank you." Then, turning to the waiter with the pencil and pad, she went on: "I'll have the *consommé royale* — made only with the white of the egg, please — followed by the *saumon irlandaise en croûte* with *petit pois*. Then stuffed quail with spinach purée and plain boiled potatoes. You serve the spinach with butter and a little ground nutmeg?"

"We can of course, mam'selle." The waiter turned to the Count, who was smiling at his young companion. Without taking his eyes off her he said, "I'll have the same."

"Why are you grinning like that?" she asked when both waiters had gone.

"*Sláinte!*"

She made all the right responses except for actually sipping her glass. "Not till I have some lining to absorb it, thank you," she said.

He drank a solo toast and said, "I'm smiling, Miss Oberg, because I'm just beginning to realize what a resourceful and quick-witted young lady you are. Conversations with you do not plod from A to B to C ... They leap from A to M to Z."

"If you're lucky!"

"Well I seem to be lucky tonight. You've told me almost everything about yourself, using fewer words than I would need to mount a platoon."

She accepted the compliment with a dip of her head, but all she replied was, "I wonder."

"Just now, for instance," he said, "you showed me you speak flawless French as well as Swedish. Then, halfway through your order, you reverted to Swedish — showing me you *understand* the French, too — which is not always the same as being able to read it off a menu! But that's only a little sample of what I mean. Before that you told me that your father is Herr Lars Oberg, principal agent for Bolinders in Ireland — and that is why you speak perfect Swedish, although your speech also carries this strange hint that you are not from Sweden. You grew up in Dublin, of course."

She stared at him, amazed. "How can you possibly know all that? Just because I say *sláinte?*"

"Ah, but you didn't just say it, did you! You also looked to see if it meant anything to me — that's why I thought you were mocking me about my new stepmother."

"Mocking? Why would it be mocking?"

"Don't change the subject. You keep going off at a tangent. I was explaining how I'm *almost* as nimble-witted as you. Tell me — how many Swedes are there living in Dublin?"

Katya shrugged. "Half a dozen?"

"Oh, really?" He was surprised. "Well I only know of one — so do most people in this city. Your father's quite a well-known character here, you realize?"

She shook her head. "I didn't until now. He's well known in Dublin, of course."

"Well, he is here, too — and Stockholm's quite a bit smaller than Dublin, I think?"

This development, she realized, put rather a different complexion on matters. If she wanted to put herself beyond her uncle's reach — at least until she came of age in June — she could hardly go about under her own name.

"I wonder why he never brought you back to Stockholm — he comes here often enough himself."

She shrugged. "He never did — though it was always sort of half-promised *next* summer — that sort of thing."

"Is your mother still alive?"

"Yes. He's never brought her back, either. Granny says it's because he has another wife here! But she says things like that. I think he's just got his own friends here, his own cronies, his own club, and he doesn't want us taking him away from it."

"Do they know you're here?" he asked. "Is it just your uncle who's in the dark?"

She felt trustful of him now, enough to tell him everything — or almost everything. Some instinct made her withhold any mention of Declan Butler. She said her parents had simply decided she ought to come to Stockholm for a while to gain some first-hand acquaintance with her native land and to renew her ties with the family.

"And you've said yes to the first and no to the second," he commented when she had done.

"In a way, yes. D'you think that's awful? If Onkel Kurt and Tante Anna would agree to let me work as an interpreter-guide when the Exhibition starts ... I think I'd live quite happily with them. Well ... I'd agree to live with them, anyway."

The waiters returned with their consommé. As they withdrew she glanced about the room as if she had not seen it before.

"What now?" he asked.

"I was trying to imagine myself in Dublin, dining alone with a young gentleman like this. My life has completely changed over the past two weeks."

"*Could* you dine like this in Dublin?" His tone was enough to tell her it was pretty unthinkable here, too.

"I could, but it would be social death. Even if we announced our engagement the very next day, it would take years for people to forget." She drew a deep breath and went on: "Yet where's the harm? We're not going to end up on that chaise longue over there, are we!" It was not a question.

He risked replying, "If you say so."

"Be serious!" she chided. "I know that's why it's there. I know what these rooms are for. Oh dear!" She pressed her fingers to her temples and clenched her eyes tight shut. "I can see what I mean so clearly. I mean everybody *expects* intimate dinners like this to end in even greater intimacy there. They wouldn't *believe* it's *not* the inevitable finale. Yet it isn't, is it! Surely you feel that, too?"

He smiled sardonically. "It becomes less and less likely with every word you utter, Miss Oberg. Talk is the enemy of amorous dalliance."

She reached across the table and touched his hand excitedly. "You *do* understand. I like you, Count. You're the first man I've ever been able to talk with — just talk, you know."

"You've tried — and failed — with lots of others?"

"No! I've never been allowed to. That's my point. People like my parents are all so afraid it'll lead to ..." She jerked her head toward the chaise longue. "If only they knew! Isn't this much nicer?"

He nodded; his brows were arched in mild surprise. "Oddly enough — yes! I find I enjoy simply talking to you, too."

After a few delicious mouthfuls the reverberations behind his last reply penetrated the soporific shell of her happiness. She bit her lip and said, "You're not just guessing, either, are you! I'll bet you've dined alone here with hundreds of young females!"

"A few," he admitted modestly.

"And it always ended not a million miles from over there?" Again she tilted her head toward the alcove.

"Or somewhere like it." Now his agreement was rueful.

"Don't pretend!" she teased. "You don't regret it at all. I'll bet you've boasted about it in the mess."

"We never discuss ladies in the mess," he protested. "Ladies, politics, and religion."

"And money?"

"One never discusses money anywhere."

"What a dull place it must be, your mess."

"Why d'you think I came into town tonight?"

Their eyes met. There were so many possible turns for this conversation to take next that they were temporarily embarrassed by their own riches. She was wondering what would be so terrible about ending up on the chaise longue, anyway; and he was trying to pin down what was so utterly fascinating about this strange young woman that *that* was the least thing he wanted of her. For both of them it was uncharted territory and for the moment they each hesitated at the last frontier.

"You can't go about under your own name — I suppose you realize that," he said at length.

"I do." She sighed and returned to the practical here-and-now.

"Carlsson's a bit obvious. You don't *look* like a Carlsson to me. What was your Magyar great-grandmother's name?"

"Something full of esses and jays and letters with funny hats. I'd be bound to spell it wrong if I tried that." The glint on his spoon caught her eye. "Silver!" she exclaimed. "Katarina Silver! That has quite a distinguished ring — without treading on the heels of the nobility, of course!"

"You could say you were a direct descendant of Long John Silver, the famous pirate."

"Yes!" She clapped her hands delightedly.

"You like the idea of having pirate blood in your veins, don't you," he accused jokingly.

"You've got mercenary blood in yours," she fired back.

A slow grin split his face. "What a well-matched pair we are, then," he murmured. "Shall we invent a past life for you? I suppose we ought to know first what sort of employment you'll be seeking." He dabbed his lips and gave his almost empty plate a token push. "I, myself, could offer you a very nice position. Several very nice positions, in fact."

She almost said, "All right!" But she knew he wouldn't take her seriously — otherwise, of course, he wouldn't have said a word. He'd merely assume she was calling his bluff. Also she couldn't be absolutely sure he'd be wrong. Instead she drew her watch from its pocket, consulted it, and said, "Oh dear! Ask me again next week. I'm just so busy at the moment."

"I enjoy talking with you, too, Miss … what may I call you, now? Oberg would be a dangerous habit, and I can't call you Silver — except in public, of course."

She poured out some claret in fresh glasses and then, rather solemnly, held one up toward him. He understood at once — this was the Swedish custom of "laying aside titles," when friends stop calling each other by the semi-formal *ni*, equivalent to the French *vous*, and take up the intimate form, *du*. The moment usually takes months or years to arrive, if it ever arrives at all. But there are exceptions. All teachers are *du* to one another from the moment they meet. So are army officers of similar rank, or civil servants of equal grade. It is a recognition that they are colleagues, not friends. So Katya's decision to permit it now was not an unequivocal sign of intimacy. However, it was done. He was now *du*-Magnus, she, *du*-Katya. Whether that made them colleagues or intimates was now a matter between themselves.

"Froeken Katarina Silver," he said. "Your father, Lars Silver, is now an invalid, which is why you must seek employment. How do we explain your command of English? Stick as close to the truth as possible — the primary rule for all good liars. He was employed for many years in Dublin. At what? D'you know anyone there who'd support a little fib for you? If your employers here wrote seeking a reference or something?"

While she racked her brains to pick the best of the dozens of friends in that category he went on, "Actually, come to think of it, I know an Irishman who'd be delighted to join in this conspiracy. I've never met him but he writes a most amusing letter ..."

"In Swedish?" Katya asked.

"No, no. English. Don't get excited. I'm sure you don't know him — unless you move in very horsey circles. Do you?"

Her heart was beating so fast now she hardly dared reply. "I was once hoping to," she said.

"Anyway, your father was ... I don't know — bookkeeper? At the biggest horse-auctioneer ..."

"Couldn't he be general manager?"

Magnus shook his head. "Don't give yourself airs. People fight shy of employing social equals. It embarrasses them. No. Bookkeeper will do nicely. Sometimes he was out of work, too. You've known moments of poverty before — but the point is you stayed respectable. You see — you're walking along a knife edge."

"We have known poverty, actually," Katya confessed. "Sometimes my father's commercial schemes have gone badly wrong and we all had to pull in our belts."

He frowned. "How deep was this poverty?"

"It was pretty awful," she told him. "We had to cut our sheets and turn them sides-to-middle when they began to wear."

"That's hardly poverty!" Magnus said scornfully.

"Well, we never did such a thing before — or since."

"We do it all the time," he replied.

"Oh." She felt deflated. "Tell me this, then — d'you melt down old candle ends and dip new wicks in them?"

"Of course, always. Talking of sheets, we turn ours tops-and-bottoms-to-middle, as well." He laughed. "We call them sheets for the New Aristocracy — because they've only got four quarterings!"

"Quarterings?"

"You know — the divisions in your coat of arms. You get them by making advantageous marriages. In Vienna you're not considered a true aristocrat until you've got *sixteen* quarterings. It's all nonsense, of course."

"Ah!" She felt deflated. "How many quarterings have the Hamiltons? Hundreds, I suppose."

"None," he said. "We're a Scottish clan, you see. It's a different system. The British nobility think it's rather vulgar to have too many quarterings. Still — enough of that. We haven't finished your story. Why have you *suddenly* come to Stockholm looking for work — and why to Stockholm, anyway? Well, of course, it's your home, so to speak. Even so, there must be some threat in Dublin that drove you back here. Ha! I have it! Last month your mother started making ominous noises about a fine gentleman who would be interested in marrying you. A fine gentleman of *eighty*, if you please!"

Magnus interrupted his stream of invention and gave a bitter laugh. "In my opinion such crapulous old toads should be dragged through the city at the tail of a dung cart!" he roared. "They should have the flesh flogged off their bones every step of the way. And what's left should be thrown to the fishes at the end of it!" After a brief, stunned silence, he added in a much more reasonable tone, "If you want my opinion."

Katya let out the breath she had been holding. "I'll certainly *remember* it, Magnus," she said.

"Yes … well" — he cleared his throat awkwardly — "I know what it's like — from the other side of the … you know. My stepmother. So I know what it's like and believe me, Katya, I sympathize with you."

"Magnus!" She leaned across and patted his hand encouragingly. "It isn't really happening to me, remember? It's a story — *your* invention, in fact."

He shook his head as if to clear it and blinked several times. "Oh yes," he murmured.

"You should go on the stage. You're wasted in the army."

He looked at her suspiciously. "Why d'you say that?"

"I don't know. Because you can get so wrapped up in a part. Anyway, I think your story's jolly good. Who's the man in Dublin who'll bear it out if asked? If I'm interviewed, I shall have to direct their inquiries somewhere."

She toyed with her spoon; no one looking at her would think his answer would have any special significance for her whatever.

"He buys remounts for us," Magnus replied. "Or he's about to start. We've invited him to supply the first batch."

"When?"

"Last month."

"No, I mean when is he going to bring them here? He could accidentally let slip something that would give me the lie."

Magnus shrugged. "I don't know. It's up to him, really. As soon as he can. They're not actually wanted for the regiment. They're for a polo team some of us are getting up. He buys remounts for the British army, though. So he knows his onions."

Katya saw it would be futile to pretend to ignorance any longer. When Declan came to Stockholm, she could hardly conceal the fact that they knew each other already. "Then you must be talking about Declan Butler," she said triumphantly.

He stared at her in surprise — but must then have remembered his own earlier words. "It seems to be a very small town, indeed," he said. "You know him?"

"Know him? I danced with him at the Saint Pat's Ball, not two weeks since. And," she added when she saw a certain hardness enter his expression, "a few dozen others. Including some very dashing cavalry officers, I may say. Shall I run down the list? I'm sure you'll know half of them, too."

"No." He laughed. "One is enough for now."

She had managed that rather well, she thought.

And so the meal progressed, with conversation on every topic under the sun; and when it drew to a close, neither of them made even the most joking reference to the chaise longue in the alcove. She was a little disappointed about that; she would have liked one more chance to say no — because some noes are quite, quite final and some aren't.

Magnus drank rather too much wine, she thought, but he seemed able to carry it well enough — until, that is, they were sitting in his carriage on their way back into Gamla Stan, where he said there were plenty of small, respectable pensionats to choose among.

He intended, in his tipsily good-humoured way, to pet Simeon, who was nestling in her bosom with his head poking out of the opening of her overcoat. But, what with the fuddling of the wine and the uneven motion of the carriage over the old cobbles, his wandering hand found not the monkey near her bosom but the bosom near her monkey.

She gave a startled cry.

Simeon bit his finger.

His immediate response, of course, was to snatch his hand away. Unfortunately he was tight against the upholstery and had only six inches of freedom in which to manoeuvre — which brought it into intimate contact with the other bosom — which seemed to confirm that his earlier contact had been no accident.

A moment later his head rang with a loud explosion, his cheek was stinging from the slap she gave him — but, worst of all, his moustache was in ruins. Then he felt the pain in his finger where that wretched ape had bitten him.

By now the carriage was at a halt and Katya was out in the street again, stumbling and finally tripping over her long, slim skirt. She was shouting up at him in English. The evening was in ruins.

Magnus, white with fury and twirling his damaged moustache in a desperate bid to restore it to manhood, shouted, "Drive on!"

Moments later he vanished into the night.

"My trunk!" she called after him as she picked herself up from the cobbles. Something had torn during that frightened leap from his carriage. Her coat or her skirt — something down there, anyway.

She stooped to investigate — which was when she realized she had left her purse behind in his carriage, too.

Now she really was alone and penniless in a foreign city!

*I*mmediately after Katya's fall, Simeon scampered away in fright. But then he decided that the dark, cold, unfamiliar street was even more terrifying and came back to her. On his way he picked up something that glittered, which he handed to her as if it were a peace offering. He could not have chosen better.

"Why, thank you, kind sir!" she said formally as she took it. Then, when she had inspected it more closely, she cried, "Gold! You *clever* little monkey!"

Then a doubt assailed her. Sweden had no gold coinage these days — not in common circulation. It was used only in exalted *niveaux*.

Exalted! A chilling thought then struck her: Perhaps Magnus had tossed it from his carriage window as he departed? Her blood began to seethe all over again at the very thought. The presumption of that man! The condescension!

"Was it himself did it, Simeon? Did you see him do it?" she asked. "Did his high-and-mightiness himself drop this ... this ..." What was it, anyway?

She sidled into the pool of light under the nearest street lamp. As she went, Simeon climbed up her coat and returned to the haven of her bosom.

"A sovereign!" she exclaimed in delight. "An honest-to-God English sovereign! Heavens! That's eighteen Swedish crowns to you and me, little lad! We're rich again." She kissed it and flourished it at the black-and-diamond sky — a little gesture of thanks to the guardian angel who had put the coin in her way.

The chill of the night reached through her clothing and made her shiver. No matter what opinion she might now hold of the Count, his carriage had felt delightfully warm. And no thanks to any *artificial* heater. He was a warm man. His company was warm. She felt the first small twinge of regret for her hasty temper. What was a little drunken fumbling, anyway? Couldn't she cope with that? Hadn't she fought off worse back home in Dublin?

It was just the surprise of it — and the fact that he'd been such a perfect gentleman up until then.

All men ...

She remembered Frida's warning and sighed.

She began also to regret her certainty that he could not possibly have thrown the coin at her. If he had, it would show that he cared for her even at the height of his anger. But then she'd surely have heard the clink of it, wouldn't she?

After a careful check that there were no open drains or hungry manholes in view, she bent down and dropped the coin onto the cobbles from the height of her knee. The clink of it was distressingly loud. Disappointed, she bent to retrieve it — but as her fingers closed upon the shining disc, she thought the night had gone all out of joint and that sudden magic stalked abroad. For where she had let one sovereign fall there now gleamed ... *two!*

Hardly daring to touch them she crouched right down on her heels and peered hard at the coins to make sure her eyes weren't crossed or something.

And now there were *three* sovereigns! Magic and mystery were surely at work tonight. The third was half-hidden under her skirt. Fearfully, gingerly, she drew back the hem, to make sure — and indeed it was so. Three sovereigns winked up at her from among the icy cobbles. It was so frightening she did not dare pick them up.

Then, with some annoyance, she saw that in stepping so hastily from the carriage — when the toe of her boot got caught in the hem — she must have torn it. Her lovely, warm, fashionable grandmother's dress! She lifted the hem to see how bad the damage was ... and this time she actually saw the sovereign fall out of it. The hair bristled on the nape of her neck. *Lift the hem!* In absolute desperation a girl can always *lift the hem of her skirt!*

She began to laugh — weakly at first, then rising to an almost maniacal shriek. Two elderly gentlemen who, from some way off, had seen her fall and had hastened as best they could to assist her, now assumed she was drunk and veered away again. And in a sense she was drunk — with happiness, with disbelief, with amazement at her sudden reversal of fortune, and above all with thankfulness for a cantankerous old granny who would rather leave a joke like this ticking away like a time-bomb than explain it, even though her family thought her a scandal for the sort of things she often said. But she quickly sobered down and began to feel along the hem to see how many more sovereigns her grandmother might have sewn into the lining there.

To her further amazement there were quite a few. These were what she and Frida had assumed to be the sort of lead weights one finds sewn into the hems of every lady's dress. But now she could feel the difference. Dress weights were cast in teaspoons and had quite a different shape from the perfect discs of a golden sovereign. Counting the four that had already fallen out, she now had twelve. And that answered the other question that had already started to nag her: Had any coins fallen out *before* little Simeon had brought her the first? Twelve was just the sort of number her grandmother would have chosen — twelve or ten. Nice round numbers. So an even dozen it was. Plus the two that were in her purse, which was still in Magnus's carriage — wherever that was by now.

"Lord save us, Simeon!" she exclaimed as she dropped them into her pocket. "Have you the faintest notion of how rich we are? Tell me what's fourteen times eighteen, because that's what we've got now? It's over two hundred, anyway. Two hundred and fifty-something Swedish crowns!"

She looked all around, hoping against hope that Magnus's coach was still somewhere near. She longed to go running up to it, to apologize and tell him it had all been a silly misunderstanding. But there was no one in sight. Just one or two shadowy figures scurrying to get indoors, bent against the chill of the breeze.

Suddenly she felt vulnerable. She feared every footfall; each grim shadow held a new menace. She had to get indoors quickly — and behind lockable doors, too — until she could call at a bank tomorrow and lodge her windfall wealth. Two hundred and fifty-something crowns! She still went weak behind the knees at the thought of it. She stuffed her fist tightly into the pocket that held the coins and set off into the maze of Gamla Stan. She would apply wherever she saw a sign that said *Hotell* or *Pensionat* or simply *Rum*.

Magnus was meanwhile seeking her. Once the sting of her slap had gone, once he had restored his dented moustache, he began to see what a dreadful mistake he had made. That wretched hot temper of his! Katarina Oberg was a pearl among women — a woman he could actually *talk* to, and enjoy it far more than ... the usual — the exchange of scented banalities followed by the scented grapplings on the chaise longue. He knew he simply had to turn back and find her. Despite the bitter cold, he went out and sat beside his coachman, trusting his own eyesight better than anyone else's.

The ten minutes it took him to track her down were the longest of his entire life. Every beat of his sinking heart reinforced his conviction that he had been an utter fool. He had only parted company with her five minutes ago and already it was as if the sun had been turned off. It was not love, of course. It was ... it was ...

He was still seeking a better word for it when he saw her standing a little way up a narrow street, gazing uncertainly at a sign that read *Pensionat* in the window of a house from which gleamed no light of any kind. Then words no longer mattered; the universe stood on its head and the sun came out again all over town.

"Miss Silver!" he called out in English, almost startling her out of her skin. "Can you ever forgive me?"

She stared up at him in utter bewilderment. "What? I mean ... why ..." How strangely alien her native English sounded on her own tongue now!

He wanted to do something special, something he could build upon tomorrow. A deep apology, even if she accepted it, followed by a hasty goodnight kiss on some pensionat doorstep, was not quite what he had in mind.

"I can find you work tomorrow," he continued speaking in English. "Not ... not the stupidity I joked about earlier. I mean real work. A good position."

"What?" she asked warily.

Encouraged, he leaped down beside her and said, "At the university? On a newspaper? With a very chic art gallery? We can do a tour of Stockholm tomorrow and you may choose."

She was overwhelmed at all this. "I suppose it was an accident," she said.

"A stupid accident."

"Your English is very good."

"I was seconded to the Blues in London last year — the happiest time in my life ... before tonight. That's where I heard about young Butler. Come on, you must be freezing."

"Where?"

Inspiration came to him. "I know the perfect place. You'll be quite alone but completely safe."

As he assisted her back into the carriage he said to his coachman, "Back to Lejonkrona's." To her he added, "He's my closest friend, but he's out of Stockholm at present. I have the key — look."

"Well ..." Happy again, she settled back in the snug upholstery. "If you're sure?"

"Quite sure — I promise. Tell me, do you really speak French, too? Or just menus?"

"*Je vous en prie, m'sieu!*" she sighed. "*Je danse sur la corde raide. Je suis presque dans le bleu.*"

"Tiens!" he exclaimed in admiration. "Very well. Tomorrow, I think, you can take your pick of the vacancies in this city."

They arrived in Jaerntorget, an intimate little square near the southern end of the old city, where half a dozen narrow lanes converged. It was precisely the area little Agneta had pointed out, so then she knew it was Fate. He took her up into Max's apartment — one of six in that particular building — and showed her where to find everything she might need. He also demonstrated the workings of the geyser, so that she could have a nice hot bath.

"I'll call for you around noon," he said as he let himself out. He was walking on air. *"A toute à l'heure!"*

W hat the devil!" The manly roar rang through the apartment. Katya gave a little scream. She had been deeply involved in a small love affair with piping-hot water and creamy soap-suds and she had not heard the key turn in the front-door lock. And, of course, thinking herself alone, she had not bothered to slip the bolt on the bathroom door — any more than she had stopped to think what a little scream might do to guide the feet of a male intruder.

The feet of this male intruder halted, turned, and made straight for the bathroom, whose door stood an inch or so ajar. She huddled down beneath the foam. Only her head was showing by the time that inch had become a yard.

There was a gasp, then a delighted chuckle, then a genial voice saying, "Well, well, well!" The actual words were English — but it signified nothing, for that particular phrase was common currency in Sweden, too.

Katya, all but paralyzed with fright, had enough power of movement to tilt her head slightly toward the door and to angle her eyes upward. She discovered a rather plain-looking young man standing in full evening dress, somewhat disordered and bedraggled. He was gazing down at her but having some difficulty with his focus. His topper was tilted well back on his head and his white silk scarf was in danger of slipping off, being one foot long on his left side and five on his right.

"What d'you mean: 'well, well, well'?" Katya asked. She thought it wiser, somehow, to speak in English.

He raised an interested eyebrow and replied, also in English: "I mean they dined me well. And they wined me well. And … *well*" — he waved a hand toward her — "this is surely the height of hospitality! But they didn't breathe a word about it to *me* — the artful devils!"

Katya felt it was time to pull rank. Reverting to Swedish she said, "Your friend Count Hamilton told me you were out of town — that is, if you *are* Herr Lejonkrona?"

"Ah ha ha! The penny drops!" He laughed and wiped bits of his face rapidly — as if he felt little midges crawling over it. Many of his gestures were a little strange — and strangely endearing, she found. "Is that old devil here, too?" He spoke in Swedish, now — where any mention of the devil is considered extremely coarse. Clearly he did not consider her the kind of woman with whom he needed to watch his tongue, no matter which language it spoke in.

Katya, knowing she ought to be shocked, wondered why she was not. There was something utterly *un*threatening about this rather ugly and slightly drunk young man. "He is not here," she informed him. "That is why he said *I* could stay for the night."

"Damned good of him. What was the quid pro quo?"

"That is a most insulting question. If you weren't so tipsy I should ask you to withdraw it. Are you going to let me get out?"

He laughed hugely. "Well, I shall certainly do nothing to *stop* you! Where's your towel?"

Katya looked around and, with sinking heart, saw she had forgotten to bring it through from the bedroom. In an empty apartment what would it have mattered, anyway?

A huge grin cracked open his face. "No towel, eh?" he mused aloud. "Well, this *is* going to be interesting!" He drew up a chair and sat down, rubbing his hands gleefully.

He was so boyish, so harmless, she could not really be angry with him. She *was* angry, of course, but she felt it would pay him an undeserved compliment to show it.

She sighed, "Oh, very well, then!" — rather wearily. Then she stood up, stepped from the bath, and, with the water and suds falling off her in cascades, strode carelessly past him and out into the passage. And he just sat there, pinned to his chair, gaping at her with eyes like saucers.

So there! she thought. *Nothing to it, really.*

Five minutes later he tapped hesitantly at his own bedroom door and asked with great diffidence, "D'you think I could have my nightshirt, please?"

She opened the door and solemnly handed him a little bundle comprising nightshirt, nightcap, and slippers, already tied up.

Then he, seeing what she was wearing, grinned wickedly and added, "And what about my dressing gown?" He poked his nose hopefully inside the doorway.

She chuckled and put a finger to the tip of it. "I'll see you at breakfast, Herr Lejonkrona — if, by some miracle, you're sober by then." She gave a little push and shut the door gently again. As he backed from that finger of hers he pulled some extraordinarily comical faces.

"Is that a live monkey in there with you?" he called out the moment the door was shut.

"You'll meet him at breakfast, too."

"You're sure you won't get cold now?"

"I'm warm again already!" The bed creaked slightly as she climbed back in. "Look to yourself."

She turned down the lamp and lay awhile in the almost-dark, thinking what an extraordinary end she had just made to this the most extraordinary day of her life. Then she realized she had forgotten to slip the catch on her door. Lejonkrona could come stealing in at any time.

And yet she knew he wouldn't. Something told her he was lying out there on his sofa, feeling equally nonplussed by this strange encounter. Somehow — through the accident of her sleeping in his apartment when she thought he was away, and his surprising her, and taking little liberties because of the assumptions he made — and being a little tipsy — and with her standing up and walking past him like that, as naked as Eve — and with dozens of subtler little signals of the kind that men and women exchange all the time without even knowing it hardly ... somehow, thanks to all these different elements coming together by the purest chance at the climax of this amazing day, the two of them had leaped over what would have taken them months to establish in any other circumstances.

Something of the sort had happened with Magnus, too — only there her feelings were more ... different.

Just before sleep stole over her she decided that she was going to like Stockholm very much.

Very much ...

Very much indeed ...

Perhaps she'd never return to Dublin?

No, of course she would! How stupid! After Declan came and found her.

She thought of Declan then, shed a little tear ... and sleep claimed her at last.

*The following morning Katya awoke — that is, returned to consciousness — by stages. The first thing she was aware of was an alien bed. Then an alien wallpaper and alien noises from the back court outside. Then she heard a cough, an early morning throat-clearing, from another room. A man's cough. The timbre of his voice immediately conjured up his face: the dark, deep-set eyes, imperfectly focused, the plain, lopsided features, the amused smile, the firm, unshaven jaw, the arrogant, self-assured stance — marred only by the occasional lurch.

Lejonkrona!

She did not know his other name.

Fragments of their meeting last night began to return now. She cringed with shame at some of her recall — until she realized she was doing it for no one's benefit but her own. Who else cared what she did, or didn't do? It was a novel thought. After that, she realized she actually felt no shame at all about last night. Not that she felt exactly shameless, either. It was just that neither shame nor shamelessness was ... appropriate.

"Circumstances alter cases," she murmured aloud — her father's favourite dictum, which he used whenever he wished to change his mind, or do the opposite of what he'd always done before, or get out of a contract, or rearrange an obligation. But Katya meant something slightly different by it. She meant that when you found yourself in entirely novel situations (and being stared at in her bath by an amusing young fellow, slightly tipsy, was certainly a novel situation!) you didn't scream like a giddy little schoolgirl.

Another phrase popped into her mind from nowhere: "Do you use lined or unlined notepaper for writing letters?"

That brought back her meeting with Magnus, though it had been hovering at the back of her mind all this while, of course. Now it helped her remember the precise quality of his charm and wisdom and ... just his general niceness.

And the fact that he was going to get her a position today.

No — help her obtain a position for herself.

Then she remembered the money from her grandmother — two hundred and fifty-aught crowns! She'd slip out this morning and buy a smart new outfit, just to surprise Magnus. She didn't need his help to go buying good clothes for herself.

She stretched luxuriously, full length in the bed, and let her mind wander over colours and styles. Dark blue was a good, sober colour, and it went well with her eyes. Not navy, though. Blue with just a hint of green. Not enough to call turquoise. Just to stop it being navy. Navy was what school regulations had laid down ...

School seemed so long ago and far away! What had she learned there? Anything that had helped her pick her way through yesterday's minefields? Not even worth answering, that one.

"Cup of coffee?"

The door swung hesitantly open. She panicked for a moment when she realized she had no nightdress on, and then thought what did it matter, anyway? Some part of her already had very firm ideas about the role Lejonkrona was going to play in her life and it had nothing to do with romance or ... all that sort of thing.

"Lovely!" she replied.

He was wearing pyjamas now, a great advance on the flannel nightshirt she had handed him last night. They were of black silk with dark red piping of a toy-soldier kind at the trouser bottoms, and, she assumed, at the sleeve cuffs, too. And his slippers were silk — scarlet and gold with curled-up oriental toes. And his dressing gown was of heavy gold brocade, like a Venetian gentleman's housecoat of two centuries ago. It was a good effort but he really ought to have shaved as well.

"You're awake then," he said, rather superfluously, as he placed the tray on a small occasional table and carried the combination to her bedside. Now he addressed her by the semi-formal *ni*. He drew up a chair for himself. The white carnation from last night's buttonhole now stood in a narrow glass vase, the centrepiece of the tray, which also held crisp, dry bread, butter, and cloudberry jam.

"I was thinking," she said.

"Is that the same thing? I often feel I do my best thinking when I'm *not* awake. I mean, I wake up with problems resolved that not all my thinking of the previous day had even dented. What were you thinking? D'you like cream or black? I do envy people who can think when they're awake. If you're worrying about your monkey, by the way, he's quite happy in the kitchen. I found him a bag of some rather stale almonds."

"You are an angel!" She used the more intimate form, *du*, and added, "You called me *du* last night. You can't go back on it now, you know." (Of course, he had only called her *du* because he had thought she was some kind of courtesan, but he could hardly offer that as his excuse now!) As she spoke she squinted down over the sheets and saw a shawl draped across the foot of the bed. In the same spirit as she had stepped naked from the bath last night she now sat up and reached for it — amazed at how *un*selfconsciously she could do a thing like that.

He chuckled. "Well, you certainly started as you mean to go on!" This time he used the *du* form.

"You remember, do you?"

"Shall I ever forget!"

She draped the shawl round her, neither making a deliberate display of her charms nor coyly hiding them — exactly as if he were not there, in fact. "With cream, please," she said, returning her attention to the breakfast and his earlier question. She moved the tray onto her lap. "I was wondering what I'd learned at school that was of the slightest value in real life — and I decided nothing. Because school isn't real life, is it — it's not even life of any kind."

"And what did you wish to learn?"

"Who I am — my inner me." Even as she spoke the words she realized it was a sentiment she could not possibly have expressed in English — not because it was hollow but because the English way of thought simply does not lend itself to that kind of introspection. She could have said it with a titter; but in Swedish she could say it quite seriously — and be taken seriously, too.

"And who can teach you that?" he asked.

"No one. The only way we can get to know who we really are is to see how we behave in different situations — lots of different situations. D'you play that game in Sweden where you have to guess what someone's thinking about by asking questions, and the person can only answer a yes or a no? It's like that, don't you think?"

"Can I ask *you* a question?"

"You already did. And I replied 'with cream' if you remember."

"Sorry!" He laughed and poured cream in her coffee. "I must have caught sight of something that distracted me! The question is this: Can you tell me how a person who talks perfect Swedish — almost too perfect, in fact — can ask, 'Do *you* play that game in Sweden ...'?"

She sipped her coffee and stared at him thoughtfully. "If I tell you the truth," she said, "the absolute, utter, plain, whole, unvarnished truth, will you promise me on pain of death you'll never tell a soul?"

She saw that he was about to make a flippant reply when some new thought checked him. He bit his lower lip but said nothing.

"Would you rather I didn't?" she asked.

His lips broke into that strange but endearingly lopsided grin. "In the space of five minutes you offer me the two greatest temptations any woman can offer a man!"

"Oh?" She looked down to see if her breasts were still covered.

"Yes, that's the first one. The second — if you really mean it — if you actually carry out your threat to tell me *everything* — will put the first temptation beyond my reach for ever. I still have some hopes there, you see. So do you wonder that I hesitate? For my part, I wonder that you *don't!*"

She shook her head. "I can't follow that reasoning, I'm afraid." But there she was less than honest; he was saying the same thing as Magnus last night — that the more she developed the genuine friendship that had sprung up between them (as another was springing up now between herself and Lejonkrona), the more difficult it would become for him to seduce her in the traditional manner.

He spelled it out for her: "Do you really want me, a total stranger — well, an almost total stranger — to know the absolute, utter, unvarnished, et cetera truth about you?"

She swallowed hard and said, "Yes."

He dipped his head, almost as if he were conceding defeat. "Thy will, not mine," he said. Then, as if the thought had just struck him, he added. "It's nothing too dreadful, is it? I mean, your life's not in danger or anything like that? I only ask because I'm the most awful coward and I couldn't lift a finger to defend you."

She marvelled at his ability to move from total solemnity to total flippancy between one sentence and the next. "Don't be absurd," she replied.

He made another lightning turn. "Don't think me rude, by the way, that I haven't asked your name or title. It's such fun guessing."

She grinned. "What makes you think I have a title, Lejonkrona? May I call you that?"

"I should be honoured. And of course you have a title. The way you tossed your head and said, 'Don't be absurd!' Only aristocrats talk like that. I was in a cigar shop the other day when Baron von Essen came in and asked to be shown some handkerchiefs. The assistant said it was a cigar shop and they didn't sell such things. And von Essen replied at once, 'Nonsense, of course you do!' That's a true aristocrat for you! I think you're a princess."

"Do you have a title?" she asked.

He shook his head, but whether he was actually denying it or merely dismissing the notion she couldn't be certain. "Titles are almost meaningless in Sweden," he assured her. "*Every* son of a nobleman inherits his father's title at birth — and daughter, too. It's not like in England where only the eldest male gets it and only after his father kicks the bucket. How many Counts Hamilton do you suppose there are in Sweden?"

"Dozens, I know."

"Hundreds. Their crest should be a pair of rabbits. A hundred years from now everyone in Sweden will be called Count Hamilton. And they'll all be poor as churchmice." He laughed, as if at some private joke, and then turned apologetically to her. "You were saying, Princess? Or were about to say?"

And so she told him her story, exactly as she had promised, omitting nothing, varnishing nothing — right up until the moment he had discovered her in his bath last night.

When she had finished he rose, went over to the chaise longue, where she had cast aside her grandmother's dress, and inspected its hem. "Amazing!" he said.

"Feel in the inside pocket," she told him.

He brought it to her and she tipped out the contents on the breakfast tray. "It changes everything," she said.

He stared at the golden hoard. "It usually does."

"I mean — the reason everyone was scandalized at Granny for saying that, about a girl lifting the hem of her skirt, was they have no idea of what an *independent* spinster of rising twenty-one would look like. Or what she'd do. A spinster of fifty, yes! Obviously she inherited the money from an uncle or someone. And she would run charities and do lots of gardening. But a slip of a thing like me? Never. Granny's joke was too near the bone — too uncomfortable. D'you think Count Hamilton's right? Is every high-class establishment in Stockholm crying out for English-and French-speaking Swedes?"

Lejonkrona shrugged. "How should I know? Probably. I'd certainly look into it — *if* it's what you really want. I suppose it is?" He stared at her with sudden intensity and for some reason it crossed her mind that he'd make a good detective.

"I don't know, Lejonkrona. I've got to find out. As I was saying — I won't know until I try, will I!"

His eyebrows shot up. "D'you apply that rule to everything in your life?"

"I don't know *what* rules to apply, to be honest. At school we wore navy blue and went about in pairs and every minute was accountable. It doesn't seem much help at a time like this."

He licked his lips nervously and tugged at the tip of his nose.

"May I be as completely and utterly frank with you as you were with me, Miss Oberg?"

"Oh, you'd better not call me that!"

"Very well. Princess, then. May I be frank?"

"If you must."

"I think I must. You say you don't know what's right or wrong until you try it. You could have applied that yardstick to the idea of becoming Count Hamilton's mistress — which is obviously what he had in mind for you. Indeed, he probably still *has*, if you want my humble opinion."

"Not to say humble warning!"

"But you turned him down — or aside, anyway. So you *do* have some absolute rules, you see — things you know without having to try them first."

She was spreading jam on a piece of the crisp bread, a delicate operation in her semi-recumbent position. She took a tiny nibble and lay back more comfortably. Then, with a smile, she said, "How d'you know I didn't actually consider it?"

"Ah!" He spread his own jam and took a thoughtful bite. "I obviously don't move in circles where a stinging slap on the face is equivalent to saying, 'Pardon me while I give your suggestion my most earnest and careful consideration'!" He took a bite, licked a little jam off the tip of one finger, and said, "What about your parents? They'll be worried out of their minds when they realize you aren't lodging up in Goetgatan, don't you think? Are you going to write to them?"

"Good heavens! I only decided to break free yesterday. Give me a chance! Anyway, how can I write to them without giving away my directions?" She sighed. "It's going to be even more difficult finding some way to let my Onkel Kurt know."

"Perhaps not, Princess." Once again he pinched the tip of his nose thoughtfully. "I have — how can I put it? — *friends* in the police here. I'm sure one of them could pass on a message from you without tipping them off."

"That's vital," she said.

This answer seemed to fascinate him. "Why?" he asked. "Are you unhappy at home? It didn't sound like it."

"Not unhappy. Of course not." She closed her eyes as if in pain — and, indeed, it was a painful struggle to marshal these particular thoughts. "But not happy, either. Not really. Not *alive* is what I really mean, I suppose. I've known some desperate moments of *un*happiness these past two weeks, believe me! Being sent away from Declan. He was the sun and moon to me — he still is. But in between times I've also felt *alive*. D'you follow? I never realized *life* like this was possible. Oh God, I know I'm talking like an idiot now. You must think me a complete idiot ... but ..." To her own embarrassed surprise her lip trembled and tears stung behind her eyelids. She had no idea where these emotions were welling up from. "I don't want to go back, Lejonkrona!" She burst out sobbing then but went on speaking through her distress. "I love Declan still ... and ache for him ... and ache for him ... and yet I want to go on, not back. And I can't understand it. And — oh God! — I don't know why I burdened you with any of this."

Somehow she had fought her way through her fit of weeping and had emerged at its farther edge, calm once more. Gently he laid a large, freshly laundered handkerchief upon her lap, removing her tray at the same time.

She took it, wiped her cheeks dry, blew her nose, drew a deep breath, and forced a smile. "Besides" — she waved a hand rather grandly around her — "all this is too exciting to give up."

"Really?" He looked around the room, relieved of the necessity to be sombre with her. "Well — you may have it, of course. The rent is thirty crowns a week, but that's because I'm a bachelor. You could probably beat the landlord down to twenty-five. He prefers female tenants, I know for a fact. They don't smash the place up. He's an awfully decent fellow, too."

"What are you talking about?"

"I'll move into the apartment opposite, on the same landing. By good fortune it happens to be vacant at the moment. It's the mirror-image of this — which will make for an interesting homecoming at times!" He mimed a drunkard so comically she had to laugh.

"Lejonkrona!" she chided. "You know jolly well I wasn't talking about your apartment. I meant" — she waved the same grand gesture — "Stockholm ... the world."

"Whew!" He put his hand to his breast and mimed an absurd relief. "I'm so glad. Between you and me, I would have hated moving."

She offered him back his handkerchief but he consigned it to her with an airy wave. Her shawl fell open — and partly off her, in fact. It was quite accidental — still less had she intended it as any sort of test of him. But, since his eyes were staring directly into hers, she went on staring back.

And so did he. Then, without once lowering his gaze — or even blinking — he reached forward, found the edge of the shawl, and pulled it back round her.

He smiled.

She smiled back.

"Just as I told you," he said.

She nodded. "I'm more grateful to you than I can say."

He made a funny movement of his eyebrows and she realized she had at last managed to embarrass him.

"Well!" She rubbed her hands briskly to change the mood. "The apartment opposite sounds a good idea. Could I really beat the landlord down?"

"Leave the blackguard to me." He spoke with comical menace. "However, our first act today must be to find a proper home for your pet monkey."

She bridled at that and stared at him frostily. "I believe he already has one."

"We'll find him a better one." He stared back at her, waiting for further argument.

She delayed a few seconds too long, enabling him to round off the silence with, "You know it has to be, Princess."

She lowered her eyes and fresh tears gathered on her eyelids.

"We'll go over to Skansen, to the ape house. He'll make lots of friends there."

She nodded but could not commit herself to the actual words. "I must buy some clothes," she said. "And, oh — Count Hamilton promised to take me to lunch — and to help me find an apartment." She chuckled. "Well I needn't tell him until we arrive at the sorbet."

Lejonkrona stood up and soaped his hands jovially. "That's the spirit!" he exclaimed.

*N*ow that her granny's dress was torn, Katya was left with a mere eight other outfits to wear. They were all highly suitable for a young, housebound lady of leisure but none of them was quite the thing for a place-seeker in the great metropolis. They "reeked of domesticity and just-out-of-the-nursery," as Lejonkrona remarked. He found a dress that had been left behind in his apartment by an actress called Sara Andersson — in what circumstances, he did not explain. It was a sumptuous — and obviously expensive — creation in silk, with bold dark-blue-and-white diagonal stripes. He was much happier with the result, especially as Katya required his strength to get all the buttons hooked up. She was less certain.

"It fits like a glove," he said encouragingly, while she continued her dubious survey in the looking glass.

"You mean it sticks out in five obvious places!" she responded. "I can't go abroad in *this*, Lejonkrona!" She pulled in one of the obvious places — her stomach — but that only made the other four swell even more provocatively.

He held up her grandmother's old skirt — which helped her to swallow any further objections. Her remaining wardrobe was now indelibly tainted with his "nursery" sneer. She looked back at herself in the glass and could not deny that the nursery was the very last thing anyone was likely to think of when they saw her.

His valet, Franz, arrived just as they were about to set off. Lejonkrona paused only long enough to tell him the order of the day and to inform him that Katya was called Froeken Silver and would be moving into the empty apartment opposite.

"He didn't seem the least bit surprised to find a young female in your chambers," Katya said archly as they descended the stairs.

"The sight of Simeon didn't raise much of an eyebrow, either," Lejonkrona replied. "Valets who show surprise soon find themselves becoming ex-valets."

As they rounded the bend at the half-landing he nudged her and inclined his head toward the door of the apartment immediately beside the door to the street. It was open a crack, but someone closed it sharply as soon as Katya turned her gaze upon it. "That was Fru Torbjoernsson," he said when they had gained the street. "Our semi-concierge, as we call her."

"Why *semi?*"

"She does only half the duties — the spying half. I'm pointing out all the drawbacks so you can beat the landlord down."

"I thought you were going to do that for me."

"I will if you trust me, Princess. It's a novel situation for me — being *trusted* by a woman."

The temperature had risen considerably overnight; now it hovered around freezing. The sky was filled with bright, fleecy clouds as the pair wandered down Norra Dryckesgraend to the quays, where the ferry to and from Skansen berthed.

"Oh, that's better!" she exclaimed as they emerged into the wide expanse of Skeppsbron and gazed across the Salt Sea to the island of Djurgaarden where Skansen, their destination, lay. "That's the Stockholm I remember — or do I mean recognize? It's very strange, you know, to be in a city that is so familiar — even though I've never been here before. It's almost like a dream."

He took her lightly by the elbow and hastened her on. "It's almost like your own life at the moment, don't you think? New territory that is somehow very familiar?"

It was such an illuminating thought that it kept her silent for at least a minute, by which time they were safely aboard the ferry. The pilot had actually waited for them and the vessel cast off as soon as they were aboard. He greeted Lejonkrona by name, she noticed.

Simeon felt the motion of the water, which he had every reason to hate, and clung more tightly to her. "There, there," she soothed him. "You're going to meet lots of new friends, little man." She turned to Lejonkrona. "It is the right thing to do, isn't it?"

His expression said, *Don't involve me.* He gave his buttonhole a few superfluous tweaks and murmured, "It depends on how you're going to earn the rent, Princess. Can you sing? Can you dance?"

She frowned in bewilderment.

"If you could do either, well enough to earn a crust, then a monkey might be a positive asset. I don't believe you've considered all the possibilities, have you. In fact, I was surprised you agreed to my suggestion so easily this morning."

Her frown deepened. "Were you testing me?"

"Of course I was. Everybody's testing everybody else all the time."

"You mean if I'd dug in my heels and refused to let Simeon go, you'd have agreed?"

He laughed. "You're still looking for absolute yesses and noes, aren't you! Look — there are *five ways* out of Jaerntorget alone. If you're going to work at an art gallery or hôtel, Simeon's a liability. But on the stage he could be a great asset. D'you want to change your mind?"

The thought of herself singing or dancing on the stage and somehow incorporating Simeon into the act was too absurd to contemplate. But his earlier statement — that people spent most of their time testing one another — intrigued her. "Were you testing me with other things you said?" she asked.

"For example?"

"About Count Hamilton. When you remarked that everyone in Sweden would one day be called Count Hamilton, you smirked."

"I did not! I resent that statement more than anything you've ever said to me. I am particularly careful never to smirk."

"Very well! You didn't exactly smirk, you gave a sly sort of smile. Did you expect me to ask why?"

"Did you want to ask why?"

"Yes, but then something else happened and I forgot. Tell me now — why was that so funny?"

He smirked and warned her that the explanation was indelicate. But before she could tell him that in *that* case he'd better desist, he continued, "However, it is an indelicacy of a very *rural* kind, which is never quite so bad, I always think. You have to understand that Count Magnus's branch of the Hamilton clan owns vast estates outside Uppsala. The family castle is called Valholm. It's on an inlet of Lake Maelar — I don't know how many thousands of hectares, but it's big. They've been very active in the Swedish Bloodstock Improvement Society — which is where the indelicacy begins to intrude upon the story. Magnus's father, you see, hasn't confined his interest in bloodstock improvement to, ah, *agricultural* stock. He seemed to consider it a positive duty to improve the *human* stock in the vicinity of Valholm, too."

Katya laughed at his delicacy. "He's hardly the first nobleman in history to do that!" she pointed out.

"No," Lejonkrona conceded, "but very few other noblemen have made such a thorough *system* of it. He gives out trophies, you know."

Her jaw dropped.

"Or perhaps, out of deference to his newly wedded state, I ought to say he *gave* out trophies."

"But how? I mean ... who to?"

"To the lucky females, of course. There's a jeweler in Drottninggatan called Hallberg. They make trophies of all kinds — for sportsmen, mainly. But they make trophies for the old Count Hamilton, too. For *his* favourite sport! What can one call it — poly-philo-procreativeness?" His hands sculpted a small bowl around which his thumbs and longest fingers could just meet. "Pure silver."

"And he actually *awarded* these trophies to the ... the females who ... you know?"

Lejonkrona nodded. "In two classes. Class A was for the lucky local wench who bore him a son ..."

"You're making this up."

"I promise you I'm not. A Class A trophy was filled to the brim with silver crowns. A Class B trophy was for the wench who bore him a daughter. Just a plain silver bowl and no extra cash."

"How typical!" Katya said in disgust.

He shrugged and said mildly, "In bloodstock-improvement circles sires are at least twice as valuable as dams. You have to look at it from their point of view. A sire can father thousands; a dam can bear a dozen or two at most." He scratched the back of his neck diffidently and murmured, "It's a point worth remembering yourself, actually. Ah — here we are!"

They stepped ashore at the Allmaennagraend landing. He pointed to their left. "That's where the Exhibition's going to be — not that anyone could believe it at the moment, but they say it'll all be ready in time."

Gangs of workmen were erecting a tall wooden fence beyond whose unfinished parts she could see scaffolding and the framework of a number of buildings. The cacophony of hammering made conversation difficult until they were several hundred paces away, at Hasselbacken. Lejonkrona told her that some wag had named it the "1897 Chorus" because it was even louder than Tchaikovski's 1812 Overture.

"That's the ape house there." He pointed to a building at the foot of Skansen hill. "But we'll have to go up to the main entrance and come all the way back. What a bore."

On their way he said, "You know all about Skansen, I suppose?"

She replied that her cousin Bengt had described it when he visited them in Dublin last summer. "They've moved houses here from all over Sweden, haven't they."

"Houses, farms, villas, bakeries, workshops ... any old building that stood in the way of progress — they reprieved it and brought it here. And bits of nature, too. They've got wolves here, and eagles ... bears. And plants from all over Scandinavia. It's an amazing place."

She chuckled and dug him in the ribs. "D'you know, Lejonkrona, I think I've at last discovered something of which you actually *approve!*"

The ticket clerk recognized him at once. "Good morning, Herr Lejonkrona," he called out as they approached. "You're out early this bright morning."

"For my sins, Herr Loefgren," he replied. "Men must work and women must weep. We're hoping to find a home for this young fellow at the ape house. D'you know how well stocked they are at the moment? I've never actually been inside the place."

"You may be in luck there, sir," the man replied, "for they have only one ape there at the moment and I've heard the kiddies complaining. He's rather a surly creature. It should never have been called the *ape* house, in my opinion. It's really where they put any sort of exotic animal. Or bird. But you can't explain that to a kid of nine who's heard the magic words 'ape house,' can you."

"And what's the curator's name there, d'you know? What sort of man is he?"

Five minutes later they set off for the misnamed ape house, armed with all the information they might possibly require. Lejonkrona's thoroughness in preparing the way surprised her — but then, she realized, he was the sort of man who would go on surprising her, probably, for as long as their friendship might last. "D'you know *everybody* in Stockholm?" she asked as they skirted the back of the Summer Theatre.

"All the important people," he replied. "Head waiters, doormen, ferry pilots, ticket clerks ... semi-concierges — all the people who can tell you what's really going on. Herr Loefgren back there knows ten times more than the head of the parks department, for example."

The arrived at the path that led to the door of the ape house — the back door, as it happened, though they were not aware of that.

"I'll wait here," he said, dusting a bench with his handkerchief. He settled and unfolded the tourist map he'd bought at the gate.

"Aren't you coming in with me?" she asked.

He stared at her briefly and said, "D'you want me to?"

Somehow he managed to make the words imply, "Can't you do anything on your own?"

She smiled gratefully and said, "All right."

She walked down the path, paused, drew a deep breath, and opened the door. At moments like this she envied Roman Catholics their ability to make the sign of the cross. Out in the world one needed talisman-gestures like that.

It was one of the gloomiest buildings she had ever been in. Earlier that morning she had made a semi-jocular comment about locking Simeon in jail for the rest of his life. Now it proved only too accurate, for the building appeared to be filled with bare iron cages. Each had three walls, a floor, and a ceiling made of solid iron sheet; the one remaining wall, facing the gangway, was a door of iron bars. Most were empty — mercifully. A few were tenanted by a motley of bedraggled mammals and birds arranged without order or apparent reason — a mongoose, two gray squirrels, an unkempt-looking porcupine, a large lizard of some kind, a fish eagle that had lost most of its feathers ...

"Dear God, my little love," she exclaimed, hugging Simeon tightly to her. "I can't leave you here. The Lord alone knows what I'll do with you, but I shan't leave you here. Not if I have to sing and dance till I'm giddy."

She rounded a corner, looking for the nearest way out, and almost bumped into Herr Gullberg, the curator. "Hallo, young lady," he said cheerfully. "And what have we here? An Indian macaque, I believe. The organ-grinder's favourite monkey. What's his name? What's your name, little fellow?"

"Simeon," Katya said.

He looked sharply at her and then burst into laughter. "Very good! It's *the* perfect name, of course. And I never saw a simian look healthier, if I may say so. You clearly know how to look after him."

He continued in that vein for some time. It seemed impossible that such a jovial and kindly man could be responsible for the miserable creatures she had seen near the entrance. When she hinted as much — or at least passed some remark about the poor animals near the door — he shrugged and said, "Well, it's only for an hour or two, just while we clean and disinfect their cages. They don't like it, of course — and who can blame them!" His eyes twinkled. "But I always say it gives them a proper appreciation of their permanent cages once they get back to them."

Katya laughed immoderately — to hold back her tears of relief. Then she explained her true purpose in coming there that morning.

Herr Gullberg was only delighted. They had an ape at the moment but he was a brooding old orangutan called Magnus whose only party trick was to spit at visitors.

She suppressed a smile at the name and asked, "Can I see what sort of cage you'll put Simeon in?"

"Bless my soul, I shan't put him in a cage," the man exclaimed. "Come and see."

He led her to the centre of the building. On the way they passed the permanent cages, where some attempt had been made to re-create the animals' natural homes and landscapes; she felt greatly reassured by the time they reached the open space the curator wanted to show her. "There's a dead copper beech outside there," he said, jerking his thumb toward the north. "You may have seen it on your way in?" And he went on to explain how they could bring it inside and re-erect it on this open space, put a protective fence around it, and let Simeon swing around from branch to branch to his heart's content all day — "showing off to all the populace."

"Lord, but he'd love that," she said. "He's the world's show-off."

"And at night I'll take him home with me," he promised. "He's not the only one who's short of a little company."

When the moment for parting came, however, she still hesitated. "Do it swiftly," he advised.

So she bit the bullet at last. "Well, Simeon," she said in English, giving him a final, desperate hug. "You're a long way from a seasick perch in a padded cell on a storm-tossed tramp steamer. You have to admit that. I've not done *too* badly by you, have I now?"

He knew very well what was about to happen. He clung to her like a limpet, chattering with dismay.

"Come on, now," she said, little above a whisper for her voice was already breaking. "Don't make this harder for me than it is already."

He seemed to have grown two extra arms and two more legs, and he was trembling like an aspen.

"I'll come and visit you, I promise — and then you'll fear it's to take you away I am. You'll see."

Herr Gullberg's fingers slipped between them, slowly and skilfully detaching Simeon from her. From nowhere he produced a couple of cashew nuts — which immediately distracted the creature and made it forget to cling to its mistress for dear life. "Go now," he murmured. "Quickly! Don't look back."

Their antics had attracted a small crowd, for which Katya was grateful; alone, she would not have been able to hold back her tears.

"And don't return here for at least a month," he called after her. "Let him settle well and truly. That would be a kindness."

She went out by the front entrance and walked quickly round to where Lejonkrona was still sitting, perusing his map. He pretended to be nonchalant but she could see he was watching her with surreptitious anxiety. "Want a quick walk round the place, while we're here?" he asked. "Shame to waste the entrance fee."

She swallowed hard, determined not to break down in public, and shook her head. "I just want to get away from here as quickly as possible," she said.

"Good!" He rose abruptly and folded the map. "We'll go back to the apartment, collect your grandmother's dowry, and go and buy lots of lovely frocks, eh?"

*C*ount Magnus Hamilton's morning parade was cancelled; His Majesty was indisposed. The temperature had risen overnight and the southerly breeze felt almost warm. The whole city looked washed and bright beneath an azure sky. Shoals of fleecy clouds drifted northward over the rooftops and spires, serving only to emphasize the blue around them. Magnus, being unexpectedly released from his duties at the palace, decided to make all haste to Jaerntorget and surprise Katya by bringing her breakfast in bed. Then he remembered he had given her his key to Lejonkrona's place. Well, he thought, he could still surprise her — and they could take all morning over buying a suitable dress for her interviews.

In his best blues and cape (for he had hinted to his superiors that he might call on military attachés at various embassies) he strolled down Skeppsbron, on the morning side of Gamla Stan, past the foot of the Royal Palace, and on along the Salt Sea shore, heading toward the ferry stages near Slussen. How clean everything looked in the spring sunshine! The water sparkled. The eddying breeze whipped miniature white horses off the crests of the ripples, cold green flames that dithered in confusion between the strand of the old city and that of the next island downstream, the naval base of Skeppsholmen. And from Djurgaarden beyond came the "1897 Chorus." What a proud city this was going to be when they had finished their work! he thought.

And what a wonderful spring and summer lay ahead of him now — with the beautiful and enigmatic Katya to woo and win!

Or merely to court and seduce?

Yes, that was the one cloud in *his* sky at the moment — a little white fleecy thing as yet; one could only hope it would drift away. His entire instinct as an unencumbered young man-about-town was to woo and seduce her, as he had already done with several other young women of petty-bourgeois origins. It was a game he and they understood well. A game they played with care, so that no lasting damage was done — not so far, anyway. And when he tired of playing it, he always saw them well settled. Two had married well on dowries he had provided, one had a place in a high-class modiste, and one, Sara Andersson, was now a successful actress — none of which would have happened if they had not met. So where was the harm in that?

Thoughts of Sara Andersson brought a flush of annoyance to the back of his neck. Eight hundred crowns for one dress! And he'd never seen her wearing it since. Still, one lived and learned.

One learned, for instance that the Sara Anderssons of this world were ten a penny. Perhaps they knew it themselves — which was why they grabbed all they could before they were found out!

One learned, too, that a woman like Katya Oberg — or Katya Silver, as he must try to think of her — was unique. Her infectious gaiety, her shining optimism, her quick wit, her amazing eyes ...

As he began this euphoric catalogue, old bachelor habits reasserted their dominion. He was walking into a trap — the most ancient trap in human history. Deception and fraud were Woman's patrimony. He was digging his own grave, weaving his own shroud, singing all the way to his own doom.

Doom! He laughed the inner voice to silence. How could one listen to such bilge on a day like this — glittering with possibilities? Blow ye trumpets! Bang ye drums! Let pleasure flow with the wine! Like Mowitz, the hero of Carl Michael Bellman's songs, who must have walked this same strand a century and more ago, he wanted to throw his cap over the waves and drink *skaal* to the whole world!

His euphoria lasted no farther than the approach to Jaerntorget. For, as he entered the little square, he saw his friend leave the building in the company of ... it could not be — yet it was: Sara Andersson! And to add insult to injury, she was wearing the eight-hundred-crown dress *he* had bought her!

The perfidy of people!

What was Lejonkrona doing in Stockholm, for a start? He was supposed to be hiding out at Ekeroe. And if he was coming out of his apartment with Sara on his arm, what had happened to Katya?

The couple turned away from him and strolled off in the direction of Stora Nygatan, the main north-south thoroughfare in Gamla Stan. With his blood at the boil Magnus hurried toward the building they had just vacated.

"Was the Count hoping to find Herr Lejonkrona at home?"

He spun round to find Franz, Max's valet, coming across the square behind him, carrying a basket with the morning's marketing on his arm.

"I see him just turning the corner there," Magnus replied.

"Indeed, sir. Did the Count particularly wish to speak with him? I fear he may be away all morning."

"The Count particularly wished to speak to the young lady whom I allowed to stay in the apartment last night," Magnus replied darkly.

"The Princess," the valet murmured, taking out his key to the front door.

"Eh?"

"That is what my master calls her. I believe she is also known as Froeken Silver."

"Yes. Is she still in the apartment?"

The valet nodded gravely as he opened the door and held it for Magnus to enter. "In spirit, as one might say — in the sense that her luggage and some personal effects remain here. But in body she is in Nygatan with my master, as the Count no doubt recognized."

"Don't be absurd," Magnus responded. "That was Sara Andersson. I saw her myself."

Franz cleared his throat delicately. "It was Froeken Andersson's *dress*, sir, but it was Froeken Silver inside it." Under his breath he added, "... if only just!"

"But how can that be? What the devil has been going on here? Has Froeken Andersson called here already this morning?"

They began to mount the stairs. Fru Torbjoernsson's door opened a crack behind them. "Froeken Andersson has not called here, to my knowledge, for over a week, sir."

"It's news to me that she ever called here at all, I may say."

"Quite so, sir," Franz said. "I distinctly remember my master saying the Count was to be spared the news if possible. As to Froeken Silver, she was already in the apartment when I arrived for duty this morning, so I had not the honour to announce her — or, of course, I should have inquired more particularly as to whether 'Princess' was her first name, her patronymic, or a mere soubriquet."

"Yes, yes!" Magnus said tetchily.

"I suspect it is a soubriquet," the man went on unperturbed as he took out his other key. "And do I understand the Count to say it was the Count himself who permitted Froeken Silver to use the apartment last night?"

"Dammit, I thought your master was away. I seem to remember *somebody* telling me he'd gone to the country! Well, isn't this absolutely typical!" He clenched his fists and ground his jaw. "Where are they off to now, d'you know?"

"They said something about purchasing a suitable outfit for the young lady, sir."

Again he stood aside to let Magnus enter but this time the young Count stood his ground. "What's wrong with what she's wearing? It cost over eight hundred crowns, I may tell you."

"Froeken Silver makes it seem a bargain, even at that, if I may say so, sir. Now if the Count will excuse me? I have luncheon to prepare." He stepped inside the apartment.

"Make it for three," Magnus snapped as he turned on his heel. "I'm inviting myself. I'm damned if I'll let Lejonkrona get away with this! *I'm* going to find her a place in this town, not him."

He fumed all the way up to the corner of Stora Nygatan. How did Max do it? The man was as ugly as a toad, had no idea how to dress, treated women like chums — couldn't be gallant to save his life — and they just flocked around him. They were such irrational, unfair, infuriating creatures!

By the time he reached the main road, however, his ebullient good humour had reasserted itself. If Froeken Silver were as treacherous and as crafty as her behaviour during the past twenty-four hours suggested, then Max had met his match and he deserved everything that was coming to him! At a discreet distance then, making no effort to catch up, he followed them through Gamla Stan, along behind the Royal Palace, past the House of the Nobility, past the new parliament building ... oh, shades of yesterday! How prettily she laughed, how animated was her conversation — he watched it all through a red mist of jealous fury.

On into Drottninggatan they strolled, the fashionable shopping street in the northern quarter of Stockholm. There he almost lost sight of them in all the bustle, for here, too, the workmen were busy, scraping off old distemper and limewash, patching the frost cracks of winter, cleaning eaves and gutters, sprucing up the façades, and in general making sure everything would be ready to greet the armies of visitors this summer-to-end-all-summers would bring to "the Venice of the North." For Magnus, however, the pleasures of anticipation had gone out of the day — to be replaced by the darker enchantments of *Schadenfreude* toward Max, and the nemesis that was even now winging its way toward him.

He caught sight of the pair of them again just as they turned out of Drottninggatan and into Brunkebergstorg. There he watched them enter Augusta Lundin's, the most fashionable *modemagasin* in the city. Grimly he crossed the little square and entered the conditori opposite, where he sat at the window, morosely drinking coffee and never letting his eyes stray too far from Lundin's door.

espite its narrow and rather dark frontage, Augusta Lundin's was large, light, and spacious within. The immediate interior, where they sold small items of haberdashery, betrayed traces of the private house into which the shop had been poured; but the rear, where the entire backyard had been built over, revealed just how much a good architect could achieve with space and money. It was as sumptuous as anything Katya had seen in Dublin and was probably, she thought, on a par with the finest establishments in Paris itself. The floors were deeply carpeted, the marble walls draped with the choicest Persian rugs and oriental silks, and the assistants moved about their business in a reverential silence that proclaimed the place to be a very temple of beauty and commerce. Katya was now glad of the elegant dress she had earlier scorned; but already she doubted that her paltry fortune in gold would be enough to buy even the meanest garment in so grand a place.

"Let's try somewhere a little more modest," she whispered to Lejonkrona as they made their way toward the very rear of the *magasin*, where the day dresses were displayed.

"You needn't buy anything," he pointed out calmly. "Most of the women who come here only part with cash on one visit in every four. The assistants are quite used to it."

She turned and stared at him in amazement. "How d'you know these things?"

He grinned. "Because it's not the first time I've been inside *this* establishment, Princess."

As if to underline his words, a tall, elegant lady in a dark green dress turned at the sound of his voice and called out, "Ah, Herr Lejonkrona. How very pleasant to see you here once more."

By the glint in the woman's eye Katya knew she had overheard that fateful title, Princess; she was filled with sudden foreboding. "And I am Froeken Silver," she said firmly, holding out her hand as if they were meeting socially.

It did not deceive the woman one bit. She smiled knowingly and said, "Quite, madame. I do understand." She even shook her hand with a sort of confidential deference. "Froeken Silver it is. And I am Fru Pihl, the lady manager of this *magasin*. I trust Froeken Silver will find something here to her liking and that this will be the first of many occasions when we have the honour of serving her. What might interest her today?" She snapped her fingers and barked, "Froeken Rydqvist!"

A nervous, slender girl with gazelle-like features appeared out of nowhere; she was about Katya's height and build — and, indeed, age too, though it was the height and build that mattered for she was to model anything that might take Katya's fancy.

Fru Pihl had meanwhile been staring rather curiously at the dress Katya was wearing. At last she turned to Lejonkrona and, still keeping her eyes half on Katya, said, "Has Herr Lejonkrona seen Sara Andersson in her latest piece at Dramaten?"

He made noncommittal noises but Katya fumed, realizing that the woman now knew she was wearing borrowed plumage. She considered trying to explain it by saying that the actress was a dear friend of hers but delayed too long to make it sound plausible. Unfortunately, that only served to make her angrier yet, and she resolved to buy nothing at all, not even if they paraded a dozen perfect dresses for her at five oere apiece.

So she found fault with everything — more with Froeken Rydqvist, alas, than the dresses, for they were so beautiful that criticism of them would be like calling Rembrandt a mere dauber. At last, and to Katya's horror, Fru Pihl rounded on the unfortunate assistant and dismissed her on the spot — told her she hadn't the first notion of how to behave with such a distinguished lady as Froeken Silver and added that she needn't hope for a good character, either.

Katya turned imploring eyes upon Lejonkrona, begging him to step in and smooth everything over. He stared at her quite impassively and then turned his attention to his gloved fingers. So, blushing to the tips of her ears, she drew a deep breath and said, "Fru Pihl?"

The woman halted in mid-tirade.

Not quite able to look her in the eye, Katya went on, "I'm afraid the fault is entirely mine. Froeken Rydqvist is blameless. It so happens that I lost a very dear friend this morning. I came here in the selfish hope that choosing a dress would cheer me up. I did not realize how upset I really was. It was unforgivable of me." She turned to the poor assistant, who had tears running down her cheeks by now. "Miss Rydqvist, will you be so kind as to put on the dark blue dress again, the one with a hint of green in the weave? I think I might very well take that, after all."

The pathetic eagerness with which the young woman leaped to obey was worst of all; nothing could have revealed so starkly to Katya how slender were the ties that held poor but virtuous young women and their respectability together. She bought the dress, of course, and she lavished praises on the hapless young assistant. "I'll take it," she said, even before she heard the price of ninety-nine crowns — two-fifths of her capital!

Lejonkrona saw her blench and asked casually, "Does Froeken Silver wish to open an account while we're here?"

He didn't even wait for an answer but simply nodded at Fru Pihl — who replied that that would be entirely in order. Even in the throes of her shock and confusion Katya realized it was far from being the first time that the two of them had engaged in that particular exchange. Something of her earlier anger returned as she realized what sort of assumptions the lady manager was making *now*. Nor did Lejonkrona help when the woman asked for directions for the dress.

"Send it care of me for the moment," he replied. "Froeken Silver will probably be staying with the Grand Duchess, but that has not yet been arranged."

He smiled so blandly at her that she assumed "staying with the Grand Duchess" was some kind of code.

Fru Pihl accompanied them part-way to the door, grovelling and repeating her thanks to Katya over and over again. Over the woman's shoulder she could see Froeken Rydqvist quietly rehanging the dresses she had modelled; there was no humility in her gaze now — only contempt.

The sudden brilliance of the outside world was like a further accusation. Katya turned from it, facing into the dark shop window, and, leaning her brow against the cool of the glass, murmured, "Oh, Lejonkrona, wasn't that dreadful!"

"All's well that ends well," he replied.

"But it might have ended so … differently."

He rapped a knuckle gently on her arm, as if knocking at a door. "Give yourself a little credit, Princess. I think you pulled the marshmallow out of the fire rather nimbly. And with dignity, too, if I may say so."

She smiled gratefully at him. "I'm still shivering," she said. "Did you see the terror in that poor girl's eyes? Dismissal would have been like a death sentence."

"Or what the English call a fate worse than death."

"You may scoff. You're a man. I don't think I'm capable of being a shop assistant, you know. Not even in the most exclusive establishment. I couldn't live on that knife edge all the time. And I could never bring myself to fawn on customers like that."

When he made no response to this she turned and stared at him. "My God — that's why you brought me here, isn't it! To see what being a shop assistant is like at close quarters."

His grin confessed it. "I didn't imagine anything quite so dramatic would result from it. I take it we may cross that particular career off our list? I wonder if you're going to find the others any better? Chivalry is hard to reconcile with a weekly wage packet. Perhaps even the gilded cage of marriage — and all its other hypocrisies — will come to seem enticing before long!"

"Oh God!" She closed her eyes and pressed her brow even harder against the cold pane.

"By the way," he continued brightly, "you didn't happen to notice an old lady rummaging through the capes and mantles, did you? She left about five minutes ago."

If he'd waited much longer before mentioning her, Katya would have forgotten. "Rather down-at-heel?" she said, struggling to pluck back the image from oblivion. "Yes — vaguely. I wondered why they didn't tactfully escort her off the premises. I don't think I'd want to buy any mantle *she* had fingered."

"Really?" he asked as if he found it hard to believe. "Perhaps you'll change your mind when you get to know her."

"Get to know her?" Katya pulled a face.

"I'll take you there after luncheon."

"Who is she?"

He smiled. "The Grand Duchess." His eyes changed focus and he peered intently into the glass shopfront. "Don't turn round," he said. "But if you move to your right, in front of me, you'll see him in reflection — sitting in the bay window of the conditori on the far side of the square."

She did as he bade and then broke into laughter. "The peacock in all his pride! He is rather splendid, isn't he! But I thought he mentioned something about a parade this morning."

"It must have been cancelled." He chuckled as further possibilities dawned on him. "You realize what's happened to the poor old boy, don't you. Parade gets cancelled. Off pops our hero to awaken the Sleeping Beauty with a kiss — thinking she's still alone in the apartment where he left her. But then, at some point in his happy peregrination, he sees the Beauty herself, no longer sleeping, alas." His laughter increased in pitch. "Worse yet — suppose that dress of yours is one that *he* gave to Sara Andersson just after Christmas!" He considered it critically. "It must have set him back over eight hundred, I'd say. That would hurt!"

She looked down at it in horror; she might have guessed three hundred at the very outside — and she would have been appalled even at that. She was actually wearing enough to pay a scullerymaid's wages for *five years!*

Lejonkrona was still chuckling. "Ho ho ho! D'you think he's got a gun? Perhaps he's just waiting to get a clear line of fire!" He soaped his hands. "Dear Magnus! So tease-worthy! What further mischief can we make of this?"

She did not share his merriment. "I think you've done quite enough for one day, Lejonkrona. If I'd known this dress was as exclusive and as recognizable as it clearly is, I'd never even have considered wearing it. And if I'd known that Count Hamilton had bought it ... well! I *do* think you might have told me."

His amusement turned to wounded innocence. "But I didn't know that myself until — I mean, I've only just worked it out. He *must* be the one who paid for it. I'm quite certain Sara would never spend so much on herself."

"But why must it be *him?*"

He put his head on one side and said, "Princess!"

"Oh!" she said wearily. "And I suppose it would be equally naïve to inquire how it came to be lying around in *your* apartment!"

He nodded.

"It's indecent!" she exclaimed. "Eight hundred crowns!"

"I could be wrong. It might have cost a thousand. Once you get into the range of exclusive dresses, there's no rhyme or reason to it."

"A thousand!" She was even more scandalized. "Why, that's ..." She tried to recalculate it in terms of a housemaid's annual wage.

"... more than little Froeken Rydqvist would earn in a whole year of humiliation such as we have just witnessed," he said. "It is indecent — you're quite right. Yet I wonder? Has our Princess been a little hasty in rejecting certain choices?" He grasped her playfully by the shoulders and turned her to face Count Hamilton once more. "There sits, it would seem, a very generous man!"

"Don't!" She wriggled petulantly from his grasp. "He'll see."

"Seeing is not the same as understanding. Shall I carry your embassy across the square to him? I think I could persuade him to renew his interest."

She backed away from him in a kind of panic. "At least he's straightforward," she asserted. "I knew where I was with him. But you! I thought you were going to be a friend. Now I don't know *what* you are."

His smile never wavered. "I'm your best hope, Princess. Just *use* me. Everyone else does — why should you hold back?"

In the silence that followed she saw him lose the struggle to maintain that smile. The defeat lasted only a moment and then he was as genial as ever, but it was a moment that changed her understanding of him entirely. For it had revealed to her a man both lost and vulnerable — confident only of the petty things in life. When it came to the big, important questions, he was as desolate and uncertain as she was.

It ought to have brought her comfort to recognize a kinship there. Finding none, she realized how much she had been depending on him — to speak to the landlord, find a good bank for her little capital, help her get work, and in general to sweep the path before her in her new choice of life.

"Let's go and mend some fences with Count Hamilton," she said.

But before they had gone a dozen paces across the square the Count himself emerged from the conditori. Katya's heart leaped up, for she thought he intended to meet them half way. How splendid he looked as he stood there in the doorway — tall, lordly, strong ... She began to arrange her greetings to him and her explanations concerning Sara Andersson's dress. But all of a sudden he gave a stiff little bow and strode away.

After a brief silence Lejonkrona said, "Our future guest list grows shorter by the minute."

If they had not been in such a public place, she would have said far worse things to him than she did.

He let another short silence elapse and then, *still* genial, said, "Do make some effort to curb your tongue, Princess, or people will think we're man and wife."

*W*hen they seated themselves for luncheon Franz made to remove the setting he had laid for Count Hamilton, but Lejonkrona told him to leave it. "Every good feast should have its spectre," he said.

Katya's new dress was delivered just as they were finishing their meal.

"Won't you try it on?" Lejonkrona asked as they rose. "There's a little lady round the corner in Oesterlaanggatan who could make any necessary alterations. It's bound to need some. She can mend the hem of that other one, too."

Katya opened the box, looked at it, and said, "I hate it."

It wasn't true, of course. She loved the dress and couldn't wait to put it on; she knew it was going to suit her better than any dress she'd ever had — better even than her granny's hand-me-down. But she hated the circumstances in which it had been bought; she hated the reminders it carried of the horrors of an assistant's life in even the finest *modemagasin* in Stockholm; and above all she hated the fact that her own flaws of character had eaten so deep into her capital.

She could acknowledge these reasons secretly; but she was less willing to admit, even to herself, that she actually wanted to go on wearing Froeken Andersson's dress — not merely because it hugged her figure so closely and flattered it to an inordinate degree, nor because she now knew what an outrageous price it had commanded, but mainly because there was just the slenderest chance that her path might cross Count Hamilton's once again, and she could revenge herself for his snub.

"I can't be bothered to change," she said — which was absurd, coming from a young lady who normally changed at least four times a day.

"Very well, if you say so. Let's go and look at your apartment, then." Lejonkrona produced a key and handed it to her.

"How did you get this?" she asked, turning it over in her hands.

"From the landlord, of course." He ushered her across the passageway, and waved an impresario's hand at the front door of the apartment immediately facing his.

"But you haven't been out of my sight since you first mentioned the idea." She unlocked the door but hesitated to open it.

He laughed. "I sent for it, Princess. I wouldn't treat with that scoundrel in person — and I strongly advise you to have no direct dealings with him either. Leave him to me." He pushed open the door and stepped back, wafting her forward with a flourish.

Katya, who now had severe misgivings about living cheek by jowl with Lejonkrona, breezed in, determined not to like the place at all. Unfortunately, it was *exactly* the sort of apartment she had dreamed of, though with little real hope of ever finding it. Her resolve was shattered the moment she looked about her.

It was, as he had said earlier, a mirror-image of his own apartment in plan, so the number of rooms and their arrangement came as no surprise. The kitchen, the bathroom, dining room, everyday room, and two bedrooms were laid out in the same order except that here they lay to the right of the internal hall whereas in his place they were all to the left. But what especially delighted her was the taste the landlord had displayed in the furnishing and decoration.

Lejonkrona's was rather manly and spartan, with limewashed walls and rugged, no-nonsense furniture; he liked sporting prints and pictures of noble animals; his carpets were plain and the surrounding floorboards were only lightly stained and then thickly varnished — an easy place for a non-resident valet and a twice-weekly help to maintain. The contrast with this unoccupied but lavishly furnished apartment could hardly have been greater. The organizers of the Exhibition could lift it bodily and carry it across the water as an example of the very latest and finest in Swedish style — which was to say English style, for the ideas and designs of William Morris were then all the rage. The walls were papered in the most gorgeous floral prints, which made a splendid foil to the white and pastel shades of the painted furniture. The floorboards were stained in a brown so dark it was almost black, which set off the jewel-like opulence of the carpets to perfection. The pictures — all originals — were of the kind that celebrated light and colour rather than people and anecdotes. Yet, despite its richness, the overall effect was restful and warm, because each part of the design was in such harmony with every other part.

Katya wandered from room to room, finding each more enchanting than the one before. And when she came to what would surely be her own bedroom she could not suppress a gasp of delight, for, unlike Lejonkrona's, which was at the rear of the building, this one had a dear little wrought-iron balcony overlooking the square. She could just imagine herself sitting out there of a warm summer's evening, surrounded by begonias and geraniums, reading, sipping sherbet, and occasionally lifting her eyes from the page to watch the bustle of life in the square below.

"Well, I daresay it'll do till you find something better, eh?" Lejonkrona murmured.

She laughed and flung her arms round his neck and hugged him and said, "Damn you! You knew, didn't you! I'd only have to set foot in here and ... pfft!"

"Pfft?"

"All my good resolutions *not* to rely on you ... to find my own place all by myself ... to stand on my own two feet ... pfft!"

"Oh, I see."

Impulsively then she kissed him, first on the cheek, then on the mouth. It was pleasant but it lighted no fires within her. Indeed, for some curious reason, it made her wish she had found some way to kiss Count Hamilton last night, before he had gone too far.

Then she realized to her surprise that her kiss did not stir him much, either. At length he unpeeled her arms and, cuddling her in a manner more friendly than romantic, said, "It wouldn't work, would it, Princess?"

She shook her head. "Why not, I wonder?"

"Because I'm not looking to marry for some while yet — and, all joking apart now, I would not dream of offering you anything other than marriage."

She kissed him again, lightly, and smiled. "It's good to know that, right from the start."

"Yes."

"For both of us. We both know where we stand."

He refrained from pointing out that she had said quite the opposite, not two hours earlier. "True."

"And it gives us great freedom to be together — if we know that door is bolted from the outset."

"Doesn't it just!" He rubbed his hands and went on, "The Grand Duchess can have the bedroom next door."

"Oh!" She pushed him sharply from her then. "What d'you mean — Grand Duchess? Why d'you keep harping on her?"

A fly buzzed on the windowpane. He took out a handkerchief and swatted it with an expert flick. "Respectable young ladies who hope for respectable positions with respectable employers cannot possibly live in apartments, *toutes seules*," he said.

Her spirit sank. It was a point she had not considered but the moment he made it she knew it was true.

"Perhaps Dublin is different?" he asked.

Glumly she shook her head. "But couldn't I find another respectable young female of my own age?" she objected. "I know I hardly gave that old woman a second glance but I didn't much care for what I saw in the first one. Why must it be her?"

"Because it would earn you the undying gratitude of ... well, never mind their names for the moment. A large number of significant and highly placed people would be most grateful — not a thing to be sneezed at. Also because ..." He hesitated. "Oh dear! No matter what I say — whether good or bad — it's going to sound as if I'm simply manipulating you."

"And aren't you?" she challenged.

"Of course I am," he replied solemnly. "But I'd rather it didn't *sound* like it, you see."

She laughed again and pulled a punch on his arm. "Tell me something about her, then." She sat down hard upon the bed and approved its firmness beneath her.

He thought it over and then shook his head. "No, I've decided against it. I don't want to say anything to prejudice you, one way or the other. Please — just let me take you to meet her? Make up your own mind."

"But I already *am* prejudiced. I'm prejudiced against her. To me she looked like those old ladies who snatch abandoned snacks in railway cafés. Tell me something to bring me back to feeling neutral at least."

He massaged his brow furiously. "You're like a terrier once you get your teeth in!" he grumbled. "All I really know about your father is that you are his daughter. But it encourages me to believe everything else people in Stockholm say about him. All right. I'll tell you two things. First, Roseanna, Dowager Grand Duchess Straczjinskaya, *née* Rosie Nelligan, is probably the world's most fascinating woman. And second, I cannot think of any two people who are more in need of what the other can give — at this particular moment in their lives — than you and her." He assumed the manner of his valet and added, "Does Froeken Silver require anything further?"

Now, of course, all the king's men would not stop Katya from wanting to meet "the world's most fascinating woman"; but she sighed wearily and rose, offering him her arm. "Come on, then," she said. "Let's get it over with."

oseanna, Dowager Grand Duchess Straczjinskaya, *née* Rosie Nelligan, lived in the northern quarter of the city, one floor up in a smart apartment house in Biblioteksgatan. The smartness finished at her front door. Squalor was the only word for what she had put in its place.

Lejonkrona's ringing, followed by his even more peremptory knocking, was answered by a middle-aged porter wearing the livery of the Hôtel Sibylla, one of the more select of Stockholm's hôtels. "Herr Lejonkrona," he said. "I'm sorry I was so long answering. I can't find a thing here."

"Is Her Highness all right?"

"She is now, sir. I put her to lie down while I made a cup of tea — the way she likes it." He stepped back and accompanied them into the wreckage of a once-fine drawing room. "She took one of her turns and came wandering into the hôtel. Didn't know where she was. Thought she was in some Russian palace with an army of serfs, I think! Anyway, Herr Klint calmed her down and sent her back with me. He telephoned Jansson's of Kungsgatan to send round a quarter of Russian tea. I thought that was their delivery boy when Herr Lejonkrona rang."

"Good man!" Lejonkrona pressed a couple of crowns into his hand and told him he could go back to the Sibylla now.

He and Katya followed the fellow to the door, where they were just in time to intercept the messenger from Jansson's, who was mistakenly on his way to the floor above.

They took the packet of tea and, returning to the apartment, picked their way down the corridor to the kitchen. "Rosie?" Lejonkrona called out. "It's Max. I'll bring you a nice cup of tea in half a jiff. Then I have a young lady here I'd like to present to you."

"Cheeky boy!" the old woman called out in English and then gave the most awful old-crone's cackle.

Katya's heart fell. Lejonkrona saw her expression but said nothing.

"She must indeed be an extraordinary woman," Katya said as soon as the kitchen door was closed behind them. "The Sibylla's quite a swell place, isn't it?"

"One of the best." He picked up the kettle and nodded to her to crank the pump handle.

"A *well?*" she asked incredulously. "One floor up?"

He shook his head. "Not exactly. It's one of about a thousand things that need changing here."

"And that's just the kitchen!" she remarked sarcastically as she cranked the handle. "What's outside those windows? It must be a century since anyone took a cloth to them."

"For example," he said.

She returned to her earlier point. "And Jansson's of Kungsgatan, too. Even I've heard of them. They're like Smythe's of the Green, aren't they. Or Fortnum and Mason in London. And yet they'll send round a *quarter pound* of tea to ... to a rubbish tip like this! She *must* be quite a personage, that's all I can say."

Lejonkrona kicked several bits of dubious detritus out of his path between the pump and the gas cooker; he took care to use the soles of his boots, so as to keep his spats clean. "This is another thing that'll have to go," he said, tapping the stove. He sought for matches and gave up, lighting it with a vesta from his own pocket, instead.

By now Katya began to grasp his purpose, of course. He was parading before her the unchallengeable evidence of a batty old lady who was no longer capable of living alone; the awful suspicion now occurred to her that Lejonkrona — and, no doubt, those dozens of important people he had mentioned — hoped to persuade *her* to volunteer herself as the poor old thing's companion. That would be why he had put her off the idea of becoming a shop assistant; it would be hôtels next.

"Perhaps I should apply for a position of some kind at the Sibylla?" she said offhandedly.

"I know the manager there," he remarked. "An awfully decent fellow called Svensson. I'll put in a word for you if you want."

She laughed and butted his shoulder with her forehead. "I'm not going to win, am I, Max!"

He walked over to the sink and cleared enough space to wash up some crockery. "I don't know what you're talking about."

"No, of course not! I'm telling you I might just as well give in now and say I'll take the position."

"What position?" He frowned at her and you'd have sworn his bewilderment was genuine.

"Companion to Her Grace." She jerked a thumb toward the door.

He shook his head and laughed almost contemptuously. "It's not vacant, I'm afraid. Besides, you'd go out of your mind inside a week. Anyway, it's *Her Highness* for a grand duchess, not *Her Grace*. And why am I 'Max' all of a sudden?"

"I don't know. It just slipped out — because you called yourself Max to Her Highness, I suppose. I like it. D'you mind? It suits you."

He smiled and shook his head.

When the water boiled he used half of it to start the tea brewing and the rest for washing up some tea glasses; he left the gas roaring and put another kettleful back to boil. Katya meanwhile found a maid's housecoat, which, though it was none too clean, she slipped on before taking over the washing up. "This is quite fun, actually, isn't it. You'd make a good valet, Max, and I'd be an excellent lady's maid. We could hire out as a couple."

"You keep thinking of the most inappropriate careers, Princess," he complained. He found a freshly laundered tea-towel in a drawer.

"Wonder of wonders," he said as he started drying the glasses. "Look, since you've leaped to the wrong conclusion, I'd better point you toward the right one. The fact is, we've been trying for years to get Rosie out of here. Not permanently, you understand ..."

"Who's we?" she interrupted.

"I'll come to that. We just want her away from here long enough to turn out all this rubbish, tidy up, mend everything that's broken, and redecorate it all from top to bottom ..."

"A year's work," Katya guessed dourly.

He smiled. "Two or three months, anyway. She's not actually as slovenly as all this makes her seem, believe it or not. It's taken more than a dozen years to deteriorate to this state."

"Can't she get maids?"

"She can get dozens but she can't keep one of them. 'We,' by the way, is a group of her friends who sort of look after her affairs. To be quite candid" — he lowered his voice and glanced toward the door — "don't ever let on you know any of this — I mean, the whole of Stockholm knows it but she thinks nobody does — but the fact is, she hasn't a bean. She's let more fortunes run through her fingers than she's got fingers to let them run through, but now she's absolutely smashed. So we — a couple of dozen of her friends — club together and keep her afloat. Not, of course, in the manner to which she was accustomed, but even a couple of dozen Rothschilds couldn't do *that!* So, as you need a chaperon ... et cetera, et cetera. D'you see?"

"Of course I can see it!" The kettle boiled and she filled the teapot. "Why didn't you just say? You want to persuade her to move into my spare room?"

He cleared his throat diffidently. "That was my idea when we set out, but now I think you could do the persuading so much better."

"Oh yes!" She poked him in the ribs. "You see — you didn't need to manipulate me at all!"

"How very true!" he replied. "I'm so glad I didn't even try. You'd have seen through it at once."

"Oh, Max!" She slipped off the housecoat and used it to lassoo him. "You're dreadful! You're the worst of all!" She pulled him to her and hugged him. "D'you realize — we haven't even known each other for twenty-four hours yet — and already I feel as close to you as I would to a brother. If I had one. Are you going to be the brother I always wanted?"

He rubbed his cheek lightly against hers. "If that's what you've set your heart on, Princess, how can any power on earth withstand you — let alone little me?"

"*What* is going on in here, may I ask?" It was a voice that had once kept ten thousand serfs quaking in their boots. The Grand Duchess stood in the doorway, looking with disdain at each of them in turn. Guiltily they leapt apart.

One would not call her fat, for her waist was almost as slender as Katya's. But the bosom that overhung it and the derrière toward which it swelled below were both massive and firm. It was the sort of hourglass figure Katya had seen only in the yellowing pages of her granny's *Drawing Room Companion*. In the flesh — the too, too solid flesh — it was truly awe-inspiring. Yet it was as nothing when compared to the magnificence of the mask and coiffeur that loomed above it. Katya could only call it a mask, for heaven alone knew (and perhaps even heaven had long forgotten) what lay beneath all the paint and cream and lacquer. Of the shabby, bowed nonentity she had seen in passing at Augusta Lundin's that morning there was here no trace.

"Rosie?" Max intoned accusingly.

The tableau collapsed. "Jaysus but these stays is *killin'* me!" the Grand Duchess murmured to herself.

"Cheeky boy!" came a cackle from somewhere up the passage, followed by that eldritch laugh.

"Now then!" Max turned to Katya with a grin. "Put hand on heart and tell me you didn't jump to the wrong conclusion the first time you heard Rosie's parrot!"

*M*ax took a sip or two of tea and then recalled another pressing engagement. Pausing only to make sure that Katya had the droshky-fare home, he rose to leave. He bowed low over the Grand Duchess and kissed her on both cheeks; the old woman's response fascinated Katya. She tilted up her face an inch or so, closed her eyes, smiled a seraphic little smile, breathed in, thrust out her bosoms, and allowed a subtle, almost imperceptible writhing motion to run from her toes to her scalp — the very picture of a woman on the verge of romantic surrender. It was so slight, and so brief, that when it was over Katya wondered if she had not simply imagined it; but she felt sure she had not — and equally sure that the Grand Duchess herself had been quite unaware of it. It was just something her muscles did automatically whenever a man approached within kissing distance.

"Oh, men are such tedious creatures," the Grand Duchess sighed the moment Max had gone. "They amuse one but one is always rather pleased when they depart. Now we can get down to important matters." She presented her rear to a startled Katya and added, "Just untie the knot, there's a dear." In English she added, " 'Twill reach the bottom anon."

Katya goggled at the cruel bite of those corset strings and thought it the greatest mercy to obey; her own waist, which did not chafe at all from the corset that confined it, nonetheless luxuriated in sympathetic gratitude.

"Talking of tying and untying knots," the Grand Duchess went on, "are you and the dear boy ...?" She jerked her head toward the departed Max while her eyebrows supplied the question mark.

"Heavens no! We only met for the first time last night."

"You're his mistress, then? Or are you still haggling?" Her bosom began to subside, like a pneumatic tyre with a slow puncture.

Katya laughed and hoped she wasn't blushing. "Nothing like that, I assure Your Highness."

"But I saw him buying you a dress this morning," she accused. Her lower rib-cage was beginning to assume a stouter and more human form; Katya could just imagine the corset string zigzagging like a snake through the little bronze eyelets with every move she made. "A very plain little dress it was, too. I had to restrain myself from barging in and giving him a piece of my mind. The gentleman who bought you the one you're still wearing now had more ..."

"*I* bought that dress," Katya told her. "Out of my own money."

The Grand Duchess frowned; the notion that a lady might buy a dress for herself, "out of her own money," was almost beyond her comprehension. Her wasp-waist vanished under the advancing swell of liberated flesh. "But how dreadful!" she exclaimed. "You poor thing! And to think I have just entertained him under my own roof. I would never have let him over the threshold if I had known. Next time I see him ..."

Katya interrupted again, realizing it was probably her only means of contributing to any conversation with the old lady. "I would not have permitted him to buy it, Your Highness. Debts of friendship are one thing. But actual financial debts ... no."

At last the Grand Duchess understood. "You have set your sights on some *other* gentleman! Oh but you could still have allowed Lejonkrona to *hope,* you know. Men are often just as happy to hope as they are to actually gain their object. Take it from one who knows! Besides" — she frowned again — "that plain blue thing would never attract *any* man. You have a splendid figure — by modern tastes — it wouldn't have served in my day but one must allow for fashion — a superb figure, as I say, and the most dazzling eyes — but don't make the mistake of thinking that the wrapping doesn't matter! Beauty can all too swiftly ..." She started moving a hand toward her own countenance, then thought better of it and wafted the judgement on toward the world beyond her drawing-room windows. Bosom, waist, and hips were now the merest hints of curves in what was essentially one stout, shiny cylinder of daunting flesh.

Katya would have continued defending her own corner, but the thought struck her that the Grand Duchess's desire to enlighten her into the ways of the world might be just the "hook" she needed. "I know so little about such matters," she said with a sigh.

A satisfactory gleam kindled in the older woman's eye. "Tell me something about yourself," she chirped. "Not the whole truth, please, but enough to be going on with. And let's make a fresh pot, eh? I gave my maid the day off last year and she never returned."

"Herr Lejonkrona and I couldn't find any lemon," Katya said inconsequentially as she followed the woman down to the kitchen.

"It's perfectly proper to drink tea without lemon. The old empress never drank it with lemon. She said it was a Jewish habit."

"And also a French one," Katya put in as she cranked the pump handle once again.

"French-Jewish, yes." The Grand Duchess took a matchbox out of the oven and lit the ring for the kettle.

"What's outside those windows, Your Highness?" Katya asked as they waited for it to boil.

For reply the woman crumpled a handful of what had once been a lace curtain and wiped a cleanish smear on the windowpane. "From here one can see directly into the eighteenth century," she said.

Katya peered down into the courtyard and saw a scene of such poverty that even Dublin would have been hard put to match it. There were children in rags, women in tatters, and men lying in a drunken stupor in the mud. One distraut family was trying to beat a horse to stand up, though the poor beast was clearly dying between the shafts.

"The end of the road for him — and the end of the tether for them," the Grand Duchess murmured. "There is always someone worse off, you see." She smiled wanly. "Didn't they choose well when they selected this apartment for me!"

Katya stepped away from the window and picked up the kettle, which was just beginning to boil. "A sight like that," she said quietly in English, "would scald your heart for many a day."

The Grand Duchess spun round and stared at her in amazement. "Merciful hour!" she exclaimed. "You're Irish yourself!"

Katya grinned. "Arrah! I'd as well blindfold the divil in the dark as say no to that." She held out her hand as if presenting herself all over again. "I'm Katy O'Barry, Highness, of Harcourt Street in dear dirty Dublin. I had an unfair advantage, I fear, for Max Lejonkrona told me you were born Rosie Nelligan."

The other, still bewildered, shook her hand feebly. "Is that why you're here? What else did he tell you?" They spoke English now.

"Divil a word," Katya said. "He refused." She carried the teapot back to the drawing room.

The old lady sat down again, closed her eyes, and tilted her head far back. The turkey-like wattles beneath her chin stretched into threads, which pulled her mouth open, like a woman breathing her last. "Wait till I think!" she said at length.

"Your tea will get cold."

"I must think very carefully."

To assist her in the process she rose and fished among the rubbish behind the tiled stove, returning in triumph with a bottle of pale amber fluid that was obviously precious. She poured a good measure into her tea and knocked back a mouthful. "Oh God!" She breathed out with fiery satisfaction. "It goes down like a torchlight procession, so it does." She handed the bottle to Katya. "A bird never flew on one wing, colleen. Put some in your own tea while you're at it."

Katya did as she was bid; she had tasted spirits but twice in her life, and then only in experimental sips. "Is it poteen?" she asked.

Her hostess was horrified. "Indeed it is not! That's Jamieson's. Twelve years old!" This claim to age stirred her memory and she laughed. "Old Jimmy Hennessy," she said. "He must be dead those many years. He always acted as beater for the Castletown estate on the Saint Stephen's Day shoot and Major Bickford-Smith always put a tot of that stuff" — she nodded toward the bottle — "into their hands. 'Now then, Hennessy,' says he one day. 'Drink up, man. That's twelve years old!' And didn't old Jimmy look him square in the eye. 'Lord-a-mercy, Major,' says he. 'Isn't it *awful small* for its age!'" She threw back her head and cackled with laughter. "Dear dead days!" she said in a dying fall, wiping a little tear from her eye.

"Cheeky boy!" came the cry from her bedroom; the parrot's laughter was a perfect echo of its owner's.

And Katya wiped a tear from her eye, too — partly of laughter, and partly of sadness as she realized how much she missed Ireland and Dublin and the people and the crack and the rare oul' times. And Declan, to be sure.

"Tell me all," the Grand Duchess said. "I want to hear all."

*W*hen Katya had finished, the Grand Duchess pulled out an old rag, once a cotton polishing cloth, and dabbed her eyes. Katya thought the sadness might have been occasioned by her tale but apparently not. "Dear old Prince Belskij," the old lady said. "You've heard of him, of course."

Katya made noncommittal noises.

They seemed to satisfy the Duchess, for she continued: "I was with him once in Saint Petersburg, standing on the Nevskij Prospekt — the day they were slinging the first telephone cables over the city's rooftops. Not great forests of wires like we have here in Stockholm, just a few discreet lines, mostly for the secret police, of course. And there was this young post-office fellow shinning up and down the buildings like a dragonfly on wheels. And the Prince said to me, 'Ah, Rosie,' says he, 'if there was only some way of connecting a cable between *people!*' And at first I didn't see what he meant — or, to be honest with you, I thought it was something indelicate, so I didn't inquire too closely. He had a filthy mind, even for a prince. But then I felt his muscles twitching in sympathy with the lad's exertions, and all at once I knew what he meant. He wanted that young fellow's *energy*, d'you see? I don't mean he wanted to *be* the lad himself. Not at all. He wanted to go on as the Prince, with all his years of knowledge and experience — but he also wanted the energy to be able to make something of it — the youth, the vivacity. What good is all the knowledge and experience in the world to a man when he falls asleep in the middle of undressing his mistress!" She tapped her own breastbone — in case Katya still harboured doubts.

"Couldn't he have told the young lad a thing or two?" she suggested. "It would have been a kindness, I think."

The Grand Duchess caught her drift and smiled. "Ah, but would the young lad have listened?" she asked slyly.

"He would if he'd had any sense. And if the Prince was *willing* to share his wisdom."

"He might have been," the old one allowed. "If he'd thought the youngster worthy."

"Yourself, now, Highness," Katya went on, "you must have a tale ten thousand times more interesting than mine?"

She chuckled. "A thousand times longer, I'll grant. But you're off to a flying start, colleen. The important thing in the race of life is not to fall at the first hurdle."

"Lord!" Katya fanned her face in mock alarm. "And didn't I think I was already over it!"

Her hostess gave a sad shake of her head and then gathered her thoughts in silence awhile. "I suppose the year eighteen hundred and sixty-one would seem like before the Flood to a wee shlip of a thing like yourself," she said at length.

"Is that when you were born?" Katya asked without thinking.

The Grand Duchess laughed ruefully. "I was born a goodly while before that, may I say. No. Eighteen and sixty-one was the year when His Royal Highness the Prince of Wales spent a few weeks with the second battalion of the Coldstream at their summer camp in the Curragh. A famous occasion of scandal. Are any little bells beginning to ring in your mind, dear?"

Katya shook her head.

"Not even if I were to tell you bells is spelled b-e-l-l-e-s?"

Still Katya was none the wiser.

"Ah me!" the other sighed heavily. "Such is fame! Does the name Nellie Clifden mean nothing in Dublin these days?"

Katya had vaguely heard of her. "Wasn't she an actress — about that time?"

"She was. And do you not know her most famous rôle? No? Well, she's the one who's credited with breaking the prince's cherry."

Katya frowned in puzzlement.

"Relieving him of his distress," the Duchess explained. "Lord, colleen, she helped him lose his virginity! Or so everyone believes."

Katya swallowed heavily. "And you mean to say it wasn't true?"

"Oh, she slipped between his sheets all right. And he shot her well and truly, somewhere betwixt wind and water. And she boasted of it for ever and a day. But what she'd never admit — and what he was too much of a gentleman to tell her — was that another wee lassie had got there first!" Another tap on the breastbone revealed the anonymous culprit, as before.

"Whew!" Katya fanned herself. "Such things to be talking about!" And this was the person Max had suggested as her chaperon!

"And what of you?" the Grand Duchess asked sharply. "Have you still your cherry unbroken? Normally, you understand, I wouldn't ask. But, in view of the rather bizarre tale you've just told me ..." She left the rest unspoken.

"Of course." Katya felt flustered still — and wished her boast did not sound like a confession of failure. "What was he like?" she asked. "The Prince of Wales?"

The other laughed heartily. "So you *are* interested in the topic, eh — just a little bit?"

"I'm interested in the Prince of Wales. Who wouldn't be! Was he fat in those days, too?"

"God, he was not!" A misty glaze came over her eyes. "He was like a young stag fresh off the hills and ready to please all the gazelles of the plain. Fit as a yard bull! Poor Prince Belskij I told you of — he should send his magic cable back in time and draw off some of young Bertie's sap! No female east of the Oder would be safe then! There was not a pick of fat on his bones in those days, and the flesh on him like swan skin!" She laughed and shook her head in a slightly dazed manner. "What *I* showed him that night! The gods themselves stopped their sport to look on. *I'm* the one that gave him that thirst — the thirst that's never left him. Little Nellie Clifden only showed him how many wells there are in which a grand fellow like him may quench it!" The metaphor seemed to please her — though that did not stop her from changing it in the very next statement: "I was that blazing furnace where his desire was forged!"

Her head was high; her eyes glowed like coals in that dead expanse of cream and paint that was her face. What fires must be banked within! Katya thought. The Grand Duchess herself had clearly been no mean actress in her day.

"You never regretted it?" was all she could think to ask.

The other sighed. "I did. I did. It taught me a bad lesson, you see — a lesson I had to scald my heart to unlearn, and scald it many times. *He* never regretted it, of course." She drew herself up and threw back her shoulders; for a moment her figure almost returned spontaneously to the shape her corsets had imposed. "The pleasure he found with me taught him to cultivate that thirst and slake it whenever and wherever he could. I suppose you know no woman's safe with him? A friend is a friend only as long as he looks the other way when his wife curtsies low and slips into Bertie's bed — you know that."

Her gaze was so piercing that Katya felt she would show herself up as the worst kind of bogtrotter if she admitted she did not. "Sure it was the talk of the Saint Pat's Ball last year," she replied. "Last month, I mean ... Lord, is it only a month ago?"

"Less than three weeks, in fact," the Grand Duchess reminded her. "But *what* weeks they've been for you, eh! Oh, child! If I had *your* opportunities and *my* experience! I swear I'd have all Europe at·my feet before the summer was out. But perhaps you don't want that? Perhaps you'd just rather be ..." She shrugged expressively and waved vaguely in Katya's direction. "Tell me — what *do* you want out of life?" She licked her lips rapidly — with a surprisingly reptilian motion of her tongue — and waited for a reply.

Katya gave an awkward little laugh. "So far all I've wanted is to survive and not be hurt."

"You amaze me! The limit of your desire was merely to survive? Why, that's a desire you share even with those wretched creatures down in the courtyard beyond. So little! So little! And in any case you've achieved it already. You *have* survived! Now just *think* what you could do if you actually had a *real* ambition!"

"What was the bad lesson you mentioned?" Katya asked, hoping to change the subject.

"Oh!" The woman gave a light laugh. "The same as Bertie's — only, since I'm a woman, it's the opposite way round. It taught *me*, too, to seek that same pleasure wherever and whenever I could find it." She wiped her lips and belched gently into her napkin. "Now d'you know what I'm going to tell you," she said solemnly. "It's this: Don't be bothering your head with any oul' books on this particular topic. Never mind the doctors and professors in front of the names nor the cornucopia of alphabets trailing after them — they couldn't find a hole in a ladder, most of those fellows. They'll tell you there's only two kinds of women. There are good, pure angels — that's you and me, to be sure — and there's bad, impure divils — the type you'd find in good novels and bad houses. And between them there's mountains the height of Olympus itself. And d'you know what I say to that? Balls, I say! There's only *women*. And that's the top and the tail of it." She laughed as an unintended joke occurred to her. "Yes — the top and the tail. There's women who use their tops." She tapped her forehead and smiled shrewdly. "And there's women who use their tails." She grinned naughtily. "Like the squirrel, you know? They cover their backs with their tails. And there's women who haven't the first idea about either. They just do what all their friends do. And what the ladies' journals tell them they ought to do — and the priests. They embroider. They guzzle. They swig. And they snore. And they all believe in the Sleeping Beauty. The *Snoring* Beauties, I call them, because — I want to tell you this — there's nothing easier in all the world for a man to come strolling by and wake up such a Snoring Beauty. And when it happens, Lord, such a fluster and fuss! It's the oul' miracle, they'll swear to you — love's oul' sweet song! True Love — and there's the proof of it. 'I slept and he woke me with a kiss — me darlin' man!' Listen till I tell you, Katya — the world is only full of darlin' men. And if you're content to go on being one of the Snoring Beauties, *any* of those darlin' men will waken you with a kiss, and pop you in his gilded cage for you to chirp his praises till you join the choir everlasting."

Dimly Katya perceived that — somewhere in this opaque diatribe — was a damning description of her own life up until that moment: knitting, chatting, chewing, and snoring! How easy it had been for Declan to go strolling by and awaken her with his kisses! How close she had come to letting him pop her in his gilded cage. By being sent away — and by developing this new taste for independence — she ought to have burst out of that old cocoon. But she hadn't. The experience had taught her nothing. She had simply carried the old attitudes into her new circumstances. She was still a victim of the old expectations, still snoring away, waiting for Prince Charming and calling him Declan ...

But now she felt it was all about to change. Indeed, with her whole life laid out there, illuminated in all its barrenness, what else could it do but change?

"What," she asked the Grand Duchess, "d'you think I should do, then, if you please?"

The other closed her eyes and breathed out mightily; her face settled in a seraphic smile. "Before you do anything," she said, "you must acquire a good chaperon. And wait till I tell you one thing, colleen," she added in the very next breath. "You won't be repeating all *my* mistakes. There now! Aren't you the darlin' of the whole western world!"

O ver dinner that night Max listened more or less in silence while Katya gave an excited and somewhat confused account of her afternoon with Rosie, as she was now privileged to call the Grand Duchess.

"I think she knew, from the moment you presented me, why you'd brought me there," she said.

"Nothing escapes her," Max acknowledged. "Did she agree to come and live here for a while?"

Katya nodded. "She said she'd move in on Friday. Next week, not this — the ninth."

"Good. That'll give you time to establish yourself in the territory. You'll have to fight tooth and nail to hold it, though — I'll warn you of that now."

"Oh!"

"Does that surprise you?"

"No." She laughed. "That's not it. I'm still wondering whether she's even remotely suitable for me, as a chaperon, I mean. Her language is ... well! And the things she talks about, too! She asked me straight out whether I was still a ... oh, and whether you and I ..." She swallowed and laughed with embarrassment. "I can't say it, Max. She probably talks quite differently to men."

He shook his head. "I'm afraid not, Princess. She's a tough old boot who's fought her way up from nowhere ..."

Katya interrupted. "I wouldn't say nowhere, exactly. She has a good-class Dublin Protestant accent. She's not from any old slum — that I'd dare swear."

"Interesting!" He raised an eyebrow.

"*She* is. I think she's the most interesting woman I've ever met."

"Good. I'm glad it all worked out so well. Shall we move on to the blackcurrant schnapps?"

She pushed her glass toward him. "And now are you going to tell me all the things you refused to tell me earlier — for fear of prejudice?"

He poured out good measures of the syrupy liquid. "*Skaal,*" he said. "What did you tell Her Highness about Count Hamilton?"

She shrugged. "What is there to tell? I didn't *need* to tell her what he tried to ... you know. I think Rosie was disappointed in me. She thought I ought to have accepted."

"Is that what she said?"

"Not in so many words. But then there are lots of things she doesn't actually need to *say*. Not in words. She does it all with her eyes. She must have been magnificent on the stage. But as a chaperon for a respectable young lady, Max? You must have taken leave of your senses."

"I'll find you a proper one if you wish?"

Katya grinned and shook her head. "I can manage Rosie."

"If I doubted that, I'd never have suggested her."

"She imagines she's going to manage *me!*"

Max soaped his hands. "And she hasn't a hope, of course."

Katya gave an awkward shrug. "It's not as simple as all that. I'm not going to reject everything she says, just because she's trying to manage me. I mean, a lot of it makes very good sense. She certainly made me feel I've wasted most of my life until now — or misdirected it. The trouble lies with her remedies — they're so old-fashioned. They all revolve around men — how to manipulate men, flatter men, cheat them, trick them into ... She told me I should have duped you into buying that dress for me this morning. She said I could have dozens of men, here in Stockholm, bringing me presents by the cartload, paying for everything, and I could keep them all at arm's length. I needn't give them anything — except hope. Just spin them out eternally."

"How dreadful! I trust you told her what you've learned about the dignity of earning your own living and making your own independent way in the world?"

"Oh, you may scoff, Max, but you must admit there *is* a simple sort of dignity in earning your own living — compared with being that sort of deceitful parasite."

He nodded as if he was forced to agree. "We saw it this morning, did we not? The dignity that simply shone out of little Froeken Rydqvist's eyes — in among all her tears!"

She let out a toneless whistle. "Unfair, unfair, Max! It doesn't have to be like that."

"We shall see," he said grimly. "But I'm sorry — we were talking about Magnus Hamilton. I was going to warn you that you have to be very understanding where that fellow's concerned. You know what unreliable, hysterical, emotional creatures we men are even at the best of times. And this is not the best of times for poor Magnus. His father has just remarried, you know."

She laughed and settled much more happily to this new conversational line. "I do know. He told me all about it. Rosie was most interested in that, because, of course, the new countess is Irish, too. She's only eighteen, I gather?"

Max chuckled. "You know his butler's comment? The old count asked the butler what he thought of the new countess and the butler said ..."

But Katya was not listening. "Poor creature!" she murmured.

He pulled a dubious face and shook his head. "Why does one say things like that? For all we know she could be having the time of her life. To jump from nowhere in an Irish bog to the rank of countess, all in one — to say nothing of marrying into one of the richest families in Sweden ..."

"Are they?"

"Ha ha!" He pointed an accusing finger at her. "Even the great standard-bearer of female independence is suddenly interested!"

Katya shook her head impatiently. "Good luck to her then," she said. "I still think girls of seventeen and octogenarian gentlemen make a poor mix."

He nodded sagely. "What would you call a good mix, then?"

"Oh," she replied airily, "the man should be about your age, I believe, and the woman ... well, about mine." She wrinkled her nose at him as if to say, *so there!*

He poured another large schnapps and leaned back in his chair. "The reason I asked what you told the Duchess about Magnus is that the poor chap called on me earlier this afternoon. Perhaps his ears were burning. I'm sure he was hoping to find you in."

The news jolted her out of the torpor into which the burgundy and schnapps had allowed her to slip. "What did he want?"

"Absolution, I think. He went down on one knee and chanted, 'Bless me, Lejonkrona, for I have sinned'."

"Be serious," she said crossly. "Did you tell him where I got the money from — to go shopping this morning?"

He shook his head. *"Skaal.* It slipped my mind."

"Good." She took a draught and said, "Keep it to yourself. I don't want him ever to know."

Her vehemence surprised him, though he hardly showed it; all he did was raise his left eyebrow.

She stared back at him belligerently. "I know very well what conclusion he must have jumped to when he saw you and me go into Augusta Lundin's this morning. I just *hate* the assumption that when a girl is in a spot of bother she's got to do *that* to get some money."

He chuckled. "You don't like it because it touches a raw nerve, eh? It couldn't be that in your heart-of-hearts you very nearly agreed to that same proposition?"

"Not at all!" She tossed her head.

"Anyway, you're quite right," he went on. "I absolutely agree. It's absurd to believe a girl only has *that* to fall back on — when everyone knows there's a much easier alternative."

"What?"

"You know! She just gets Granny to sew a dozen English sovereigns into the hem of her skirt and make risqué jokes about it. Easy! I don't know why more girls don't think of it."

She stared wearily into her schnapps and then tossed it down in one easy gulp.

"That's the way!" he said, refilling her glass instantly. "You have an enviable head for liquor, I'll say that." He refilled his own glass, too. "So tell me — which of the four dozen young men in your life did the Ugly Duchess think you should marry?"

"None." She poked her tongue out at him playfully. "She's been married six times, you know. All of them mistakes, she said."

"All of them buried," he commented, as if that somehow evened the score.

She peered at him cautiously. "Are you going to break silence and tell me about her now?"

"If you insist." He began to count the tally on his fingers, one by one. "First there was an actor-manager chappie. Don't recall the name ..."

"Vincent Maundy," she told him.

"For example." He dipped his head. "The only important thing about him was that he toured Europe — and the theatres he played were always the *crème de la crème*. Stacked from floor to ceiling with the Almanac de Gotha. She left him when they reached Vienna, where she became the mistress of the Grand Duke Otto."

"The present Prince of Wales introduced her to him," Katya put in. "She was the Prince's first mistress, before even Nellie Clifden."

"Ah ha? I didn't know *he* made the introduction. Anyway, when the actor-manager, Maundy, died, she became properly available once more — and promptly married a duke, an ordinary duke. Did you know, by the way, that a Swedish count ranks equal with a European duke? That was decided at the Congress of Somewhere-or-other. Ask Magnus Hamilton one day. Anyway, the duke who was husband number two died with a certain smile on his face, as the saying goes — actually during their honeymoon. I've forgotten his name for the moment."

"The Duke of Hohë-Tatra — something like that."

"If you say so. Of course, news of his death — especially of the manner of his dying — spread like a plague among the noble but geriatric bachelors and widowers of Vienna. And Potsdam. And Paris. Most of them had wanted to die for years and couldn't wait to try the Rosie Way to Paradise. That accounted for husbands three and four."

Katya drew breath to supply their names but he held up a finger. "Three was a count of the Holy Roman Empire, a Spanish grandee called de Roja. And four, I think, was only a baron, but with vast estates in Pomerania. A Baron von Winterhalter — a cousin of the painter. Did she show you her two paintings by him? Two lovely little landscapes — nothing like his great bombastic portraits. She'll bring them here with her, I'm sure."

He continued with his tale. "The baron was made of sterner stuff than the others, though. In fact, he dawdled along the Rosie Way for five blissful years before the dreaded cardiac plethora carried him the way of all flesh — or, at least, the way of all flesh that gets tangled with Rosie's."

"I must say, this is a very different version of the story she told me," Katya said.

"The money just ran through her fingers like water," he went on unperturbed. "The Kaiser couldn't stand her. You know what a frugal lot the Hohenzollerns are! I've seen them doing their own Christmas shopping on foot in Potsdam — and carrying their own parcels home under their arms. The Kaiserin sorts the palace laundry each week, I'm told!" He shook his head as if even his long familiarity with these scandals had not dimmed their power to shock him. "So you can easily imagine how they felt on being held up at a crossroads by dear Rosie with her carriage, her spare carriage, her servants' carriage, her running dogs, and her running footmen, all in the Winterhalter livery! They took longer to pass than an entire regiment of foot guards."

"She hated the Hohenzollerns, too." Katya felt she ought to say something in her new friend's defence.

Max chuckled. "And with cause. The Kaiser used to invite the Winterhalters to every state ball and then keep them outside the golden cord. Rosie was a superb dancer, too. Graceful as a swan. But all she could ever do was watch."

"Oh, it's all so petty!" Katya brought her fist down angrily on the arm of her chair.

"Don't tell *her* that," Max warned. "She thinks the earth revolves around such matters. Anyway, it did her some good in the end, because after old Winterhalter died the Empress of Russia ..."

"Yes!" Katya chuckled. "The *Empress!* I made the mistake of calling her the Tsarina!"

Max's eyes opened wide in mock-horror. "That's the biggest *faux pas* you can make — in the circles where Rosie moves. Emperor and Empress, if you please! Anyway, the Russian Empress could always be counted on to adore anyone the Kaiserin hated, so she took the inconsolable widow under her rather ample wing — married her off to Count Molotkin."

"They owned over a hundred thousand serfs!" Katya threw in. "She told me she was sewn into her dresses every day — sometimes six times a day. Some of their estates she never even saw. They had a palazzo on the Grand Canal in Venice and she never even visited it. And a château in the Midi. She never saw that, either. How can one go from a life of such unimaginable wealth to ... the way she has to live now?"

He smiled sadly. "I'm sure it puzzles her, too, Princess. I'm sure she spends half her time wondering where she went wrong." He stared keenly at her. "She must sit there in that filthy apartment in Biblioteksgatan thinking, ah, if only I could live my time again!" He arched his eyebrows to see if she took the warning.

She grinned back at him. "You can't bear it, can you!" she taunted.

"What?"

"The notion that one old woman who knows the world and all its sly ways might be passing on her knowledge and wisdom to me! You hoped *you'd* be the one to corner that market. Men are all the same."

"She should know! She's sampled enough of 'em!"

Katya shook her head. "That's not something Rosie told me. It's my own opinion." She drained the last two drops of her schnapps and said, "Perhaps one more?"

"After all," he said, taking up the bottle again, "a centipede never walked on only twenty legs. That's an old Irish saying."

"*Skaal!*" She was tipsy enough by now to do it meticulously — keeping her eyes fixed on his as she sipped and then returning it to the third button of her shirt (or what would have been the third button of her shirt if she were a man) before favouring Max with the second little bow of her head. Then she leaned back in her chair and asked him what else she imagined the Duchess might have advised.

He chose not to answer the question in quite the form she put it. "The trouble with Rosie's ideas," he replied, "is that the world has moved on. In our lifetime, Princess, the possession of land will turn into a millstone round the necks of the landowners. The possession of a noble title could soon be enough in itself to warrant a certificate of execution."

"The world has moved *on?*" she echoed sarcastically. "Did you somehow miss the French Revolution, Max?"

"*Plus ça change* ..." he reminded her. "Well now! With Rosie moving in at the end of next week, I take it we shan't be looking for positions as a hôtel bedmaker or lady waiter or anything simple and dignified in that line, meanwhile?"

"Hardly," she agreed.

"And what rent have you and Rosie arrived at?"

Katya was shocked. "I shouldn't dream of charging her rent."

Max winced. "Oh, Princess! You have all the decent notions and none of the right instincts. Whereas Rosie has all the right instincts and hasn't had a decent notion in her life." He grinned into his glass. "What a pair you're going to make!"

Part Two

near Sibyllegatan

Home Thoughts
From Abroad

2:*a v.*
Jaerntorget 17
Staden-mellan-broarna
Stockholm
Thursday, 8 April

My dearest darlingest Declan,

I know it is probably futile to write this to you for even now you are surely on the high seas with every nag you could muster for the Swedish Life Guards, as anxious to see me again as I am to see you. O how my eyes ache for that moment, and my heart, too. Day and night I fret that you are not here, that I cannot see your dear face nor hear your darling voice nor feel your arms about me and taste your lips on mine.

O but I could fill these pages with nothing but my own woes and the emptiness of my life without you! But that will not do. There are practical matters that will not wait.

First, when you come to Stockholm (if this letter should reach you before you depart) you are on no account to seek me at my Onkel Kurt's house, for, as you will see by the above directions, I am not to be found there! Second: neither he nor my Tante Anna have any idea where I am — or even that I am come to Stockholm at all, for I have my father's letter to them unopened and about me still.

How this has come to pass would consume so much paper in the telling that it would sink the ship that brought it, so must wait until you are here and can see for yourself that all is well. On the other hand, the bare story would, I think, fill you with so many alarms that I should waste even more ink calming them. Suffice it to say that my wilful nature would not submit to simple banishment from you. I would not humbly deliver myself to my gaolers here — not when I knew that you would be arriving almost hourly with your remounts for the Lifeguards of Horse.

My parents know nothing of your commission, of course, or they would liefer have sent me to Siberia than here. (Actually, that is rather funny, because there is a part of Stockholm nicknamed "Siberia" — being all of <u>two miles</u> distant from the centre! Now you know how small a city it is.) You must hasten, though, if you have not already left, for Pappa will surely get to hear of it, and then the telegraph wires will hum, and all his Stockholm cronies will be pulling every string and turning this city upside down to shake me out of hiding. (I should add that, simultaneous with this letter, I intend to let him know what I am doing — but not exactly where!)

Therefore (and I assure you, <u>for that reason only</u>) I have cultivated the acquaintance of two helpful gentlemen, which you are not to take amiss since I do it only for you. One is Count Magnus Hamilton — a nobleman I am sure you know, since he is largely instrumental in placing the order with you. He got your name in London, when he was seconded to the Blues. He will alert me to your arrival. The second is my landlord, an ugly but amusing gentleman who has many friends in the police and is a sort of quidnunc who knows everything that happens in this city even before the people it's happening to are aware of it. What a confuffle of a sentence but you know what I mean!

As to what I am living upon, you should know that I am engaged as companion to Roseanna, Dowager Grand Duchess Straczjinskaya, an ancient lady of impeccable pedigree and virtue, who seems to have taken an immoderate liking to me for some reason best known to herself. I sleep in the next room to her and am attentive to her every whim, which is mostly to have her pillows plumped up and to be read to. (When I say "my" landlord, I mean, of course, <u>ours</u>.)

A new page! I could fill it with loving endearments, my darling, darling man, and still not say one millionth part of all I long to tell you. If I let my heart rule my head, I should be scribbling until you came knocking at my uncle's door in Goetgatan — which would certes bring the world down round our ears! Yet it is such a pleasure to write to you, I fain would stop. You must let these few lines stand for all those unpenned thousands, then. Think of me as I rise each dawn, aching and yearning for you. Think of me at noon, wondering how I can bear this burden of my unsymmetrical love (unrequited I cannot

call it, since all I mean is you are not here). Think of me as I climb
exhausted into bed, there all alone in the dark, weeping an ocean into
my pillow, and all for lack of you. And think of me at every spare
moment in between, sighing only for you and longing for the day
when we are in each other's arms once more.

A million times a million kisses!

All my love my darling man!

Your own, your very own, tender and true!
Thine 'til death!
Thine beyond the grave!

Katy

XX X X X XXX X XXX X XX XX X X XX X X X X XXX X XX X X XXX!

Katya read the letter through and wondered in all conscience how
much of it she dared send. She glanced at the clock across the square
and saw that, if she was also to dash off a letter to her parents, she
had no time to rewrite anything.

Actually — and in all conscience — she could let every word of it
go to Declan. The untruths it contained were informed by the
profounder truth of her love for him. Nothing there was intended to
deceive him, only to set his mind at rest. How would it be if she
described that first evening in Max's apartment, when he, tipsy as a
lord, had watched her taking a bath! And she had stood up without a
stitch on and walked within inches of him to fetch a towel! *She* knew
how innocent it was, and how it had done nothing but help further a
jolly fine friendship between them — but how could she ever convince
Declan of that?

The only thing she would like to change was the occasional false
"literary" note, where her language became unconvincingly high-
flown. But there was no time for that, either.

She signed her name with a flourish (and a lightened conscience) and added the row of kisses. Then she turned to the even more awkward letter she had to write to her parents. (The one to her Onkel Kurt could wait a few more days, she decided, until the Grand Duchess really had moved in and she herself had found a secure position somewhere in the city.)

Stockholm Thursday, 8 April

My dear Pappa and Mamma,

1: I am safe and well.

2: I did not go to Onkel Kurt and Tante Anna.

3: I am living independently in this city and in circumstances of impeccable respectability.

4: I shall leave the rest of this page blank because I know you will need some time to overcome your anger and alarm at the foregoing.

Taking a new sheet she continued:

I hope you're a little calmer now — enough, at least, to permit me to explain. I know you think of me as a child still — foolish and headstrong, a prisoner of every passing enthusiasm, and so forth. Perhaps I am — or was — for when was I allowed the kind of life that would encourage me to develop any deeper traits?

Actually, I'll tell you when: it was from about noon on the Saturday after that fateful ball in Dublin Castle, when you set me down alone upon the high seas. Seven days on a featureless ocean is an eternity to a girl who previously found five minutes of soul-searching too daunting to contemplate. At first, naturally, I could think of nothing but Declan, my loss of Declan, the thought that I might never see him again. If you knew how close I came to throwing myself overboard, you would never have banished me as you did!

But the hottest blaze burns itself out the quickest and so I soon found my mind wandering down unfamiliar byways. I began thinking, for instance, not of what I had lost in Declan but of what he had (or had not) lost in me! Yes! Your flighty, flippertigibbet daughter was actually questioning her own merit for a change! The answer was sobering to say the least. Not (as you might think) that I began to value myself very low — though in my mood at that time it should have been easy enough in all conscience — but that I had no scales whereby to value myself at all!

Who was I really, I wondered?

I thought of that gay young creature at her first St Pat's Ball — supposedly ready to come out into the world — and I wondered what distinguished her from the hundred other gay young girls who were also coming out that night. She had attended the same academies as they, read the same approved books and journals, played the same piano pieces, painted the same views, embroidered the same charming texts and flowers, assisted at the same concerts, laughed at the same pantomimes, strolled the same ... need I go on? I was Amelia O'Dowd was Janet Cosgrave was Maude Frewen was Jemima Bryce-Smith ... ad infinitum. Except that I knew I was not!

I imagined myself in some kind of court or seat of inquisition with people asking me to prove I was me — someone quite different from all those others. "Give me a chance!" was all I could say. And so — to cut the tale short — that is what I have seized. My chance to discover if I am worth anything more than the crowd.

And now to particulars. I am living in Stockholm, as you desired of me. I am engaged as companion to an elderly noblewoman, late of the court of the Kaiser and of the Russian Emperor. The other minutiae of my daily life would meet with your unreserved approval.

If you are content to know this and will not insist upon my cloistering myself at once with Tante Anna and Onkel Kurt, please write to tell me of it. You may direct poste restante to Centralen on Gamla Stan. I shall then write again, with my true directions and closer particulars.

That I love you both still and miss your dear faces and voices goes without saying, I trust. You may think me unruly but I feel no trace of rebellion in what I have done. It is to me the merest continuation of the education you have always sought to give me — though it has been artificially hastened, I concede, by your artificial banishment of me in such haste.

Yr ever-affec. dr.

Katarina.

PS Please to tell my Granny that her advice took a great weight off me!

It was a measure of how far she had come that she had no idea how her parents would recieve this mixture of olive branch and gauntlet. It was an even better measure that she did not much care, either.

atya knocked lightly at Max's front door and went in at once, calling out, "Only me!" She found him already dressed for a promenade. "Any letters?" she asked. "I'm just on my way to the post office."

He tried to read the addresses on the pair of envelopes she was holding but she turned them at too oblique an angle — without making it obvious she was foiling his efforts. "Oh, Franz can take those for you," he said nonchalantly, holding out his hand. "No trouble at all."

She tapped his fingers with the letters in gentle reproof, moving them too rapidly for him to read anything but the name DUBLIN, written in large capitals on the uppermost envelope. "I'm going out anyway," she said. "I'm on my way to my interview at the Hôtel Sibylla, as a matter of fact."

"I thought you were going to leave that until next week — after Rosie moves in."

"They seemed eager to bring it forward for some reason. Then I thought I'd go and see Frida Carlsson."

"Again?"

"They sail again tomorrow morning. And, what with Rosie moving in after lunch, I shan't be able to see them again until they get back here next month."

He shrugged. "That's entirely up to you, of course." Then he returned to the topic of the letters. "There's nowhere to post those between here and the ferry. Franz would love a little stroll up the road." He put out his hand but snatched it back when she threatened to smack it again.

"I'm going to walk. And think — or try to. And plan my nefarious campaign for the interview as I go."

He consulted his watch. "How fortunate," he said. "I'm going in that direction myself."

But when they gained the street he turned toward Skeppsbron and the ferries. She reminded him he had said there was no post box down there.

"I said between us and the ferries," he replied. "There's a perfectly good post box at the other end, near Kungstraedgaarden." He gave a catlike grin.

On their way down to the landing stage he made several further attempts to squint-read the envelopes, which she artlessly dandled before him, always at an impossible angle. Sometimes she shook them like a baton to emphasize some point she was making. He was still no wiser when they boarded the ferry, where she tucked them both into her handbag.

Max then seemed to lose interest in them. "D'you know who you're going to meet at the Sibylla?" he asked.

"You mentioned him — Herr Svensson, your friend."

"Acquaintance. He's possibly Rosie's friend. What d'you know about him?"

She gave a slightly baffled laugh. "Everything you told me — which isn't much, I know. But the important thing is that he has already as good as agreed to employ me, surely?"

"He might only have said that, Princess, just to please Rosie and me. He could find any number of reasons to say no when it comes to it. What are you going to say to convince him he *must* take you on?"

She shrugged awkwardly. "I was just going to let him ask the questions. Oh dear — I haven't really thought it out very thoroughly, have I!" She brightened. "But look, if he's a gentleman, which I'm sure he is ..."

"Ha!" Max exclaimed, as if she'd committed some elementary howler. "In the world where men and women seek employment, old girl, there's no such species as *gentleman*. Don't even think of him in that light. Don't imagine he'll show you the slightest favour or deference as a lady, nor accord you a single one of the privileges of that rank. D'you know the best way to approach this interview?"

"What?"

"Remember Froeken Rydqvist at Augusta Lundin's? Try and put yourself in her shoes. Imagine her with a working knowledge of English and French. Imagine how *she'd* approach this interview."

Katya pulled a face. "Oh, Max, I don't want to go now."

He sighed with relief. "Good! I thought it was going to be much harder to talk you out of it. We'll send Herr Svensson a polite note and then we'll just sit in Kungstraedgaarden and enjoy this lovely spring day, eh? And don't you worry your pretty little head about where the next meal's coming from. Rosie's friends will give you a generous honorarium for putting up with her." He smiled seraphically across the little billows of the Salt Sea. "And just think, Princess! You'll be able to tell your grandchildren that you once *almost* worked as a menial in an hôtel."

After a brief, unhappy silence, Katya said, "I wouldn't dream of taking a penny for putting up Rosie."

"Ah." Max rubbed nothing in particular off the top of his silver cane. "I see."

"And it wouldn't be *menial* work. Not necessarily."

He gave a dubious tilt of his head. "That would be up to you, Princess. What sort of work are you going to suggest to Herr Svensson that you might do?"

Katya had given no thought to the matter at all. She had blithely assumed that Max, Rosie, and Svensson had, between them, thought up something to keep her busy for so many hours a day; she had imagined that this interview was merely to inform her of the result. "Something to do with my languages," she suggested.

"For example." He nodded encouragingly.

"I can teach the hôtel servants English and French."

"Tiens! By jove!" His eyes were full of mocking admiration.

"The basic things," she insisted. "And not all the servants, either. Just those who associate with the guests."

"You've brought your teaching diploma along with you, I suppose." He peered down at her over an imaginary pince-nez and she realized he was pretending to be Herr Svensson.

She laughed with relief. If it was a matter of acting — well, two could play at that! "Oh, you Swedes and your bits of paper!" she exclaimed scornfully. "If you really imagined that some professor with Big-A in medieval English literature from Uppsala could help your waiters cope with Paddy Reilly from Ballybunion when he's asking for 'rashers and eggs,' you'd already be employing him." She broke out of her ebullient character and added in a rather thoughtful voice, "Actually, that's not a bad argument, is it!"

"It's a start," Max said coolly. "Suppose he puts you to the test?"

"And it's not just one hungry Irishman asking for *his* kind of breakfast, either — it's the German asking for his, and the Frenchman asking for his, and the American — *and* the English. And the poor little waiter running in circles like a bluebottle." She rubbed her hands gleefully as the interview at last began to take shape in her mind — and as the prospect of directing it in her own favour beckoned.

"If he puts you to the test?" Max persisted.

But she rattled on. "And it's not just food. Think of some rich family arriving with two dozen pieces of luggage. Every piece might have a different name — trunk, valise, carpet bag, and so on. Think of the poor hall porter when the husband tells him which piece is to go where!"

Max turned an imaginary clockwork key in his ear, winding himself up for one further try: "And what will you do if he puts you to the test?"

She breathed in deeply, threw back her shoulders, and said in English, "Not for nothing, my good man, have I toiled in the vineyards of the Saint Stephen's Green Dramatic Society. Friends! Romans! Countrymen! *That* is the question!"

He raised an admiring eyebrow. "You have played Mark Antony *and* Hamlet?"

She laughed, floating now in the sea of her own confident exuberance. "No. They made me Second Citizen and Mute Acrobat — the producer invented that part, especially for me, he said. But don't worry, Max. If Herr Svensson asks for a demonstration, I'll make his hair stand on end."

They stepped ashore at the Opera stage, under the statue of Charles II, and made a beeline across the square for the postbox at the end of Kungstraedgaarden. When they reached it he held out his hand casually, as if popping the letters in the box were part of a gentleman's duty to a lady.

Laughing, she held them up to him as a teacher holds up reading cards in school. Then, as if she were already a crammer putting a scholar through his grind, she read both legends with elocutionary precision: "Declan Butler, Esquire, care of Dobbs's Stables, Kingsbridge, Dublin, *Irland*. And Mister and Mrs L. O'Barry, Harcourt Street, Dublin, *Irland*. Now are you any the wiser, Max?"

He made a vague movement of his hand and then, taking her by the arm, started walking across the foot of the park in the direction of Sibyllegatan. "Don't you think the best way to bring Declan to you might be to write absolutely nothing? Keep a mysterious silence — and keep him guessing?"

She slumped dramatically. "Oh, Max! Not you, too!"

"What d'you mean?"

"This is beginning to sound like the carriage drive home after every ball I've been to in the past couple of years. I dance with him too much. I throw myself at him. I make him conceited and neglectful. I make myself cheap ..."

"And do you?"

"I don't know. And I don't care, either. I'm just being honest. They say I'm obsessed by him — and I agree. I am. They say I'm infatuated. I don't deny it. Why should I pretend to be what I'm not? I'm *not* hard-to-get — which is what they'd like me to be. Scheming. Wily. You know — *womanly*."

"How awful for you! But tell me: Does all your honesty bring its own reward? Is he your devoted slave, living only for you?"

"Yes. That is — I mean ... well, he *would* be ... except he has a living to earn. He has his reputation as a man to keep up — he wouldn't want all his friends to think he was tied to my apron strings. Surely you understand?"

He nodded. "I think I'm beginning to. Tell me — have you given them your exact directions?" he asked.

"Declan, yes, my parents, no — though I've told them if they accept what I'm doing, I will let them know where I am."

"And you've told them what you're doing?"

She pulled a face. "Sort of."

"Hmm."

She glanced nervously at him, sidelong. "What does 'hmm' mean?"

"It means, Princess, that you should be thinking about your interview. We'll continue the conversation later if you wish. Meanwhile ..." His voice dropped to a murmur. "Permit me to point out that the Sibylla is a very *discreet* hôtel."

She looked at him askance. "Max!"

"Architecturally speaking," he added, nodding toward the building across the street.

"Oh, is this Sibyllegatan?" She looked around in a slight daze. "I didn't even notice when we entered it. Real goulasch-baron country, eh?" she added, remembering Magnus's comment.

The memory of Magnus gave her a sudden, sentimental pang.

Max chuckled and nudged her to cross the street.

The hôtel was as large and as anonymous as all the other grand apartment buildings that lined the street on both sides — at least, down here at this rather fashionable end. She could see smaller, more commercial premises farther up the gentle rise toward the northeast.

In fact, the Sibylla was not quite anonymous, for its name was carved in modest letters no more then three inches high over the entrance. "Here we go!" she said as the porter opened the door.

To her surprise, Max stayed put. "Here *you* go, Princess," he said. "I have one or two things to attend to. Shall we meet at that little terrace-conditori in Kungstraedgaarden in an hour and a half? You can stroll round the shops if you finish here with time to kill."

*K*atya was lucky that the porter was the same fellow she and Max had met at Rosie's apartment the previous week — and that his name came back to her without effort. "Albert!" she cried, rather loudly in her sudden nervousness. "How nice to meet again!"

He was flattered to be recognized — and not merely recognized but remembered by name — by a girl he had admired for her prettiness but who, he felt sure, hadn't looked twice at him. He bowed and swept her in as if she were a rather grand guest — an act of deference that was not lost upon those other hôtel servants who saw it.

Had she been any other place-seeker he would have taken her no farther than the opening of the passage that led to Herr Svensson's office; there he would merely have pointed out the rest of the way. But Katya he escorted to the very door.

"You were most kind to the Grand Duchess last week," she told him as they went. "D'you know she's coming to live with me while her friends refurbish her own apartment?"

He sucked a tooth in sympathy. "Froeken Silver will have little time on her hands, then."

"Time enough to spend a few hours here each day, I trust. I suppose you know why I've come this afternoon? I hope the boss is in a good mood?"

The porter halted and, after a careful glance in both directions, murmured, "Herr Svensson's not the one to watch, if I may be so bold as to advise Froeken?"

"Please do!" She smiled encouragingly. "Who is the one to keep an eye upon, then?"

He held up a finger. "I'm not saying the boss is an easy man, if you follow. But he knows how much the Sibylla depends on the goodwill of Herr Lejonkrona and Her Highness and their circle."

"You mean he'd take me on as a pianist even if I had no arms!"

Albert chuckled. "Not quite, Froeken, though he'd go some way. But then there's Herr Klint!"

"Herr Klint?" she echoed. From the way Albert spoke, the name already sounded laden with doom.

"He's the one who counts every penny. He could weigh you and me to half a gramme. He can hear through walls and see round corners. He never sleeps, they say — he just hangs himself up in his wardrobe, still in his suit ..."

The picture was so comical, and Katya so nervous, she had a fit of the giggles. They dried up, however, the moment she was ushered into the manager's office and was introduced to the terrifying monster — Klint himself.

Actually, he was quite handsome — tall, slim, somewhat craggy, with shiny jet-black hair, beautifully groomed. His complexion was a little sallow — but that, she realized, went with his calling. It was his eyes that unsettled her most — dark and utterly dead; indeed his whole face, for most of the interview, remained completely devoid of any emotion. He showed neither sympathy nor antagonism toward her; he might have been that automaton Max had parodied earlier, with a clockwork key in his ear. It was a relief to address herself to Herr Svensson, who was as unlike Klint as a man could be — short, bald, rotund, and genial.

"Ah, Froeken Silver!" he exclaimed as the impassive Klint assisted her into a chair immediately in front of the desk.

Klint himself took a seat at right angles to her line of vision, so that she could not easily turn and include him in anything she might say — nor, more importantly, was she able to observe his response, if, indeed, that masklike face ever betrayed anything so human.

"Her Highness has spoken of you in the most satisfactory terms," the manager assured her.

Katya, determined not to be too ebullient, dipped her head solemnly and murmured, "She is most kind."

"And vague," Klint said from her right.

"I beg your pardon?" She turned to him. Their eyes dwelled in each other's and, for some strange reason — probably because he, too, was rather handsome — she remembered equally stubborn "eye battles" with Declan. Well, she knew how to win those! And, sure enough — just like Declan — this Klint fellow yielded first. But he made it seem as if he were turning to prompt his superior to explain.

Svensson obliged. "What Herr Klint implies," he said, "is that, for all her kind words, Her Highness doesn't actually say what contribution Froeken Silver might make to our ... ah ..."

"Our income?" Klint suggested.

"Yes. That, too, of course," Svensson said.

Klint continued. "When I pointed out to her that we do not engage new staff, no matter how temporary, on the basis she was suggesting, she simply replied, 'Nonsense! Of course you do!' Which was not a great deal of help to us."

Katya, recalling Max's test of a true aristocrat, was hard put not to smile. However, a rather grim decision was now taking shape in her mind. She realized she'd rather engage in any other employment, even change shoes with Froeken Rydqvist, than work in an establishment where this Klint person might enjoy some kind of authority over her.

Rosie and Max must know plenty of other hôtels.

She relaxed as she decided to jettison the interview. "Far be it from me," she said offhandedly, "to tell you your business, but I would have thought that someone fluent in English, Irish, Scottish, Welsh, American, and French — and Swedish, of course — and with a passable familiarity with German — would be quite useful to have around over the next few months."

Svensson smiled and glanced at his assistant, who said, "English, Irish, Scottish, Welsh, and American are all, in fact, the same language, are they not?"

She noted he put the nations in the order she had used; he clearly had a memory for every detail. It did not endear him any further to her, for she liked to trundle through life with the unimportant details constantly falling off the tailgate of her mind. She looked at him with a hint of pity. "A hôtel where they believe that, Herr Klint, is in for a rude shock this summer."

He was tough, all right. She would have expected a man whose livelihood was challenged so directly to show a touch of nervousness at least. But not Klint. He smiled thinly and came back at once with: "Froeken Silver does not seem to understand that the Sibylla has been catering quite successfully to an international clientèle for almost a quarter of a century."

Now that she knew she was working *not* to be taken on the Sibylla's staff — without, of course, embarrassing Max and Co. — she found that she, too, could patronize with the best. "By the *thousand,* Herr Klint?" she asked.

This time he hesitated; indeed, she saw a little flicker of interest behind those dead-fish eyes. Seeing her chance to rub in a bit of salt she said: "Imagine the scene, if you like. It's breakfast time here and the Exhibition's in full swing. Your poor waiter is trying to serve his tables, which are *packed.* It's not just that fussy French family sitting over there, calling for their *croissants et café au lait* — I'm sure he's used to that. But sitting right next to them is a group of rather loud Germans demanding *Bauernfrühstück.* And beyond them is a Scotsman whining 'Wheer's ma haggis, laddie?' And behind your man there's a jolly American saying at the top of his voice, 'I know you do omelets, son, but can you fix me a *jelly* omelet?' Not to mention Paddy Reilly from Ballybunion, grumbling that all he wants is 'a plate of loose rashers and eggs, be all the holy!'." She paused to catch her breath.

The two men were just staring at her. Didn't they understand — even now?

She pressed the point further: "So there's your poor waiter, who's still trying to work out what German *farmers* eat for breakfast — and wondering how do you *fix* an omelette? And what in the name of God are *rashers?* Lord save us — the man's a nervous wreck and your guests are going hungry."

After a moment's silence, Klint recovered his poise and asked in that infuriatingly bland, neutral voice of his, "And what, pray, *are* rashers, Miss Silver?"

He spoke in English this time — quite good English, too — which surprised her. But the question itself was foolhardy — if he hoped to trip her up. Did he really imagine she'd have put that in if she couldn't explain it? She gave him a weary smile and said, "They're what the English call *bacon,* Herr Klint. But if an Irishman asks for bacon, he wants what the English call *a bacon joint.* The nearest we have in Sweden is a ham — though it's cured differently. And I'm afraid we don't have anything they'd dignify with the name of rashers — or bacon."

He nodded gravely at this intelligence but she could not tell whether she had made any dent in that infuriating superiority of his. "Does Herr Klint still maintain that the Americans, English, Irish, and Scots speak the same tongue?"

He twitched. She knew he'd noticed that she'd changed the order — *and* left out the Welsh; it probably annoyed him that he could not think of a way to point it out without sounding extremely petty.

Herr Svensson cleared his throat and glanced awkwardly at his assistant. Katya, knowing her time was almost up, saw one last chance to rub Klint's nose in it. "You still don't believe me?" she said. "Come on — I'll show you what I mean. It's not just the waiters. Let's see how your porters can cope."

Springing from her seat, she slipped out of the door and back down the passageway, forcing the two managers to trail in her wake.

"Porter!" she called out in English to Albert, "What's your name?" She winked where Svensson and Klint couldn't see it.

God be good to the man, he played along at once. "Albert, ma'am." He replied in English, and tipped her a smart salute.

"Froeken Silver is wasting her time," Klint warned her. "Albert understands English. All our porters do."

The man's adamantine calm was unnerving; she had to remind herself she didn't want the place, anyway, before she could recover her own. It did not entirely work this time for she discovered that, whether or not she wanted to work here, she wished very much to convince them she was right. She drew a deep breath, turned back to the porter, and forged ahead: "Albert," she said, begging his cooperation with her eyes, "imagine I'm a rich English lady just arriving at the hôtel. You understand?"

"Yes, milady." He went over to the desk where he would normally receive a guest and turned to face her.

"Very well," she said, feeling suddenly alone and a little foolish. "Here I come. I'm holding a dog on this lead — imagine." She cleared her throat portentously and threw up her chin. Then, advancing across the foyer she declaimed, in her best St Stephen's Green Dram. Soc. English: "Ah, porter! Please find me someone to take this fellow for his constitutional. My baggage is hard on my heels — if those nincompoops in Customs have finished playing games with it. There'll be seven bags, with labels coloured after the rainbow. The trunks with red, indigo, and violet labels you may put in your lumber room, for I shan't be requiring them for a week. The rest are to go up to my suite and you may unpack the valise with the orange label at once. I fear my maid was — shall we say — a little under the weather last night and I've sent her off with a flea in her ear. Would you kindly find me another? She absolutely *must* speak French — if possible, of course." Then, with a final winsome smile at poor Albert, she added, "And now I turn into an Irishwoman and tell you: " 'Clare to God, I could eat a horse!' Did you follow all that, Albert?"

He simply stood there and gaped.

In Swedish she asked, "Did you follow *any* of it?"

He stared uncomfortably over her shoulder at the two managers and shook his head.

Katya turned round. "Well now, gentlemen, I guarantee that in two weeks from now I could have him able to follow every word."

Svensson was tugging his lower lip and laughing feebly — the way people do when they've watched a conjuring trick from about six inches away and still have no idea how it was done.

Klint's face, as ever, remained blank and unreadable.

Goaded beyond caution, she blurted out, "But perhaps Herr Klint can do it instead? I'm sure *he* followed every word!"

" 'Clare to God, I didn't," he replied — in English and without a trace of a smile.

She saw it was the closest he'd ever get to conceding she might have just the teeniest bit of a point. Well, what did it matter? It was time she got out of here, anyway. They could jolly well stew in their own juice. "I'll leave you to think it over, gentlemen," she said as she turned toward the door.

But now Klint held up a finger. "What is there to think over, Froeken Silver?" he asked. "She has made a most convincing point, I think. Don't you agree, sir?"

The question was directed at Svensson, who sucked his teeth and nodded wholeheartedly.

The assistant manager turned back to her and added, "The matter now requires further discussion." He gestured toward Svensson's office and the two men left her to follow them back there.

"Was that really *English*, Froeken Silver?" Albert asked.

"Every word of it," she assured him. "I wish they'd give me the job of teaching you and all the other Sibylla servants how to cope with things like that. But you're right about that fellow Klint. I'd not work for him for a thousand pounds."

"Oh, don't take my words amiss now." The man seemed quite distressed by her assertion. "I only meant he'll test you till you want to strangle him. But he's not a bad fellow to *work* for. Strict, yes. But fair and straight — you'd never meet fairer. And I'll tell you one thing — you've certainly made your mark on him!"

The news amazed her. "Me!"

"Oh, indeed, Froeken. I was watching his face over your shoulder while you were ..." He cleared his throat, not wishing to say the only word that occurred to him. "I'll swear he almost smiled. I never saw him nearer to smiling in all the years he's been here."

"Froeken Silver?" A thin youth called her from the entrance to the manager's corridor.

"That's Herr Lindgren," Albert muttered. "The boss's secretary."

"I'm coming," she told him.

As she followed Lindgren to Svensson's office she thought back over what Albert had just told her. She was still disinclined to take a position at the Hôtel Sibylla, but her determination was no longer quite so absolute.

Klint began in his dry monotone: "Let's leave aside for the moment the question of whether or not we have a vacancy here for the sort of tutoring Froeken Silver is proposing ..."

The Swedish custom of addressing people in the third person was made for this man, Katya realized.

He continued: "Suppose we were to offer Froeken Silver some such position, by the hour, what would be her fee?"

It was the last question Katya had been expected to be asked. She had assumed that every position in a hôtel — indeed, in every trade and profession — already had a recognized fee attached to it. "Nine crowns ninety-five," she said, picking a number almost at random — on a principle familiar to haberdashers.

Svensson gasped; and even Klint, for once, showed some tremor of emotion. His eyebrows shot up at least a millimetre and his lips sort of *considered* whether or not they might form themselves into an astonished O.

"Well, it depends, of course, on how many hours a day," she added hastily.

"Ah," Svensson said as if she had thrown him a lifeline — or a weapon, perhaps? This kind of discussion was not merely novel to her, it also had an air of something vaguely dishonourable. *Ladies* simply never haggled over money.

Then she remembered Max's wise advice to her on that particular subject.

Svensson was starting to dig little redoubts. "Inevitably it will entail some disruption of our rosters ..."

"Oh, but I wasn't intending to hold school classes," Katya said at once, wondering why she bothered to meet their objections — except that she *wanted* Klint to admit he'd been wrong. And in any case it would be good practice, and it would give her some idea what to ask at the next hôtel.

"What, then?" Klint asked.

"A hall porter may learn English while polishing a brass plate with an otherwise vacant mind, Herr Klint. So can a chambermaid while she's making the beds — instead of singing, or chatting with whoever's doing the dusting. They can both learn together *and* continue with their chores. A little ingenuity is all it will take."

The man appeared to be thinking it over seriously. Svensson turned to him in alarm. "It's unthinkable, Klint," he murmured. Katya barely caught the words. "Even if it's only for four hours each day — which, frankly, is all I think we should offer. That's forty crowns a *day!*"

Katya could not believe her ears — they obviously thought she meant nine-ninety-five an *hour!* She was on the point of interrupting to say that she'd assumed a full ten-hour *day* for that fee, when she heard the assistant reply, "We could stretch to eight, though, sir — don't you think? A four-hour day — one week's trial? Thirty-two a day. It's not so very much to lay out on what could be highly ..." He glanced at Katya and nodded solemnly. "Pardon me, Froeken Silver," he added as he leaned forward and murmured something that only Svensson could hear.

Thinking it over later, Katya felt sure he was pointing out that if the Sibylla didn't take her on, one of the other big hôtels would. Nonetheless, whatever he had murmured in his senior's ear, Svensson smiled reluctantly and put a good face on things. "Very well," he said to her. "We'll give Froeken Silver a week's trial — beginning tomorrow morning at eight? Four hours a day. Eight crowns an hour — I'm sorry, but Froeken Silver must understand we *absolutely* cannot go higher than that!"

Katya was having a little trouble understanding anything at that moment — except that she was sitting there, feeling more unreal than at any time in her life, trying to comprehend the fact that they were going to pay her the equivalent of one pound, six shillings, and eightpence — more than a labourer's wage for a *week* — and for a mere four hours' work. And you could hardly call it work, either — thinking up little scenes like she'd just played with Albert, and acting them here and there all over the hôtel!

Klint stepped into the unexpected silence. "Normally, Froeken Silver will realize, we would not engage anyone without making exhaustive inquiries. But she comes so highly recommended that we may waive all that. She has a work permit, of course?"

Katya's heart dropped a beat. A work permit was something she had not even thought of.

But Svensson, consulting the papers on his desk, said, "Herr Lejonkrona is arranging that."

Klint needed no further assurance. When Herr Lejonkrona promised to arrange something, it was obviously as good as done already. The assistant rose to his feet. "I'll see you out, Froeken Silver," he said.

So — now that she was a member of the staff she was "you" all of a sudden, though still the semi-formal *ni,* of course. She felt disappointed. Addressing him in the third person had been rather satisfying.

The man turned to his senior and said, almost as an afterthought, "Unless you, sir, have anything else to add?"

"No no!" Katya noted that Svensson seemed mildly surprised to be consulted after Klint himself had made up his mind. She began to understand what Albert had meant when he told her that the assistant manager was the real power to watch at the Sibylla.

"May I suggest you come at ten o'clock tomorrow morning?" Klint told her as he led her back to the foyer. "Eight would be a little early. You may work until twelve. Take half an hour for your luncheon, which, of course, you may eat in the senior staff dining room." He heard her draw breath and assumed he knew what question she was about to ask. "Without deduction, of course. Meals you eat on the premises are a perquisite. And so you may finish at half-past-two. But I'm afraid it will be different hours each day if you are to get round all the day-and all the night-staff. However, I'm confident we can devise a mutually acceptable roster." They were crossing the foyer as he concluded: "And may I add that I believe this is going to make a most interesting experiment."

He left her, somewhat dazed still, several paces short of the door, almost as if he were some nocturnal creature, afraid of the full glare of sunlight outside.

"Well!" Albert exclaimed as he escorted her the final yard or so. "Did I hear that or did I just imagine it? *Interesting*, he said! I never heard him use such strong language in all my life!"

M ax was already seated in the terrace-conditori by the time Katya finished her wishful-thinking window shopping — though, since she was now going to earn the price of two new dresses *a week*, the activity leaned more toward thinking than wishfulness. She had no idea how she was going to break the news to him, or even whether she ought to.

"My!" He grinned happily as she approached. "We *are* in a good humour. Do I take it we landed the position at the Sibylla?"

"As if you didn't know! That was a foregone conclusion — thanks to you and Rosie. But what d'you think they've agreed to pay me?"

He made an apex of his fingers and rested his lips against it briefly. "Fifteen crowns?" he guessed.

She realized that he, like herself, was quoting a daily rate; even so, his studied nonchalance and the twinkle in his eye showed her that he believed he was pitching it outrageously high. She saw the chance to play the same game with him as Svensson and Klint had unwittingly played on her. "Be fair," she chided. "It's less than a half-day."

"Oh well," he said. "Eight crowns?"

She pouted. "You cheat, Max! You must have telephoned and asked them."

But he was delighted to hear it was so high. "Are they *really* paying you that much?" he asked.

She nodded. "For four hours a day."

Now he began to doubt her − not her veracity but whether she had understood things properly. "Eight crowns a day for only four hours' work!" he asked incredulously.

"No! Not per day − per hour! Eight crowns an *hour!* It's thirty-two crowns a day."

He laughed and waved away this obvious persiflage. Evidently she had muddled it all up.

It took some time before he would − reluctantly − accept she was telling the truth. She had to describe to him, word by word, glance by glance, how the interview had gone, until it was clear to him how the fortunate misunderstanding had arisen.

What amused her most was the subtle change that then took place in his attitude toward her. He had obviously imagined that Svensson would offer her mere pin money, which she, being a thorough lady and used to that sort of patronizing treatment, would accept gladly. His guesses had been jocularly lavish, to tease her. But the teasing and the banter dried up completely the moment he accepted she was speaking the truth. He began to look at her with a more respectful light in his eye. He spoke to her less as a girl he might tease, more as a woman he could converse with on equal terms. It was not a sudden and dramatic shift from pole to pole − more of a gentle swing away from the one and toward the other. But it was enough for her to notice it at once.

"I don't think we'll tell Rosie anything about this," he said judiciously. "Poor dear, she belongs to another age, to a generation that could never understand."

"She was an actress, wasn't she?"

Max smiled indulgently. "Come, Princess! Even you don't suppose that's how she earned her money, do you? *That's* what she'd never understand — that a professional lady could earn eight crowns an hour in any other way."

Katya dipped her head, acknowledging the probable truth of that. "Even so, she's bound to ask."

"I don't think so. She certainly won't ask Svensson — and I doubt he'd tell her, even if she did. If she asks *you*, just be vague. Say it's enough to manage on ... something like that. She'll be satisfied it's only pin money and she won't press the point."

Katya was still dubious. "She's obviously much more ladylike with you than she is with me. The things she says to me sometimes!"

"For example?"

Katya shook her head. "I'd die of shame."

"Put it in other words, then. Now you're a teacher of English you should be able to do that."

She sniffed dubiously. "She told me there's no difference between the ladies of the town and the ladies of the court. I leave it to you to guess how *she* expressed it."

He shook his head. "She's wrong, anyway. There *is* a difference."

"What?" Katya was looking forward to having some answer with which to trump the old reprobate.

"Oh — easily a couple of thousand crowns."

She kicked him gently under the table.

"Your ears have gone quite pink," he accused.

"I've obviously led a very sheltered life, Max."

"I wonder if they'll still blush so readily after a few weeks in the hôtel business?"

She stared at him in alarm. "The Sibylla is a very select and respectable establishment."

"That's what I mean! However, enough of this persiflage. We had better go back to ... oh! Just look who's coming this way. No, don't! He won't recognize you in that dress." He raised his silver-knobbed cane and waggled it raffishly above his head to someone behind her.

Even before the newcomer spoke she knew it was Count Magnus Hamilton; her heart missed a beat and then started hammering away like the 1897 Chorus.

He, for his part, was furious when he saw that Lejonkrona had tricked him. He clicked his heels, barked "Mam'selle!" at her, and bowed with such brittleness she feared he'd snap in two.

"Join us, old chap," Max said jovially. "Froeken Silver's had a bit of luck. We're celebrating."

Katya glared at Max. Magnus, who had been about to refuse the invitation, saw her annoyance and accepted eagerly, though he did not seat himself at once. "Let me guess," he said, tweaking his moustaches and smiling to himself. "Froeken Silver having gone so far already in the footsteps of the divine Sara Andersson, has decided to go all the way. She will now make a profession of a talent that has so far been mere amateur — upon the stage. The piece of luck came when the theatre management took one look at the ape on her shoulder and — knowing genius when they see it — engaged her on the spot! Am I getting warm?"

Katya tried so hard not to smile, but it was so neatly put — and the criticism was so justified from his point of view — that she yielded the opening salvo to him. "Better a little ape on the shoulder than a large chip," she said sweetly.

Now it was he who tried hard not to smile. "You can hardly blame me," he pointed out.

"For the conclusion — no. For jumping to it so readily — yes."

He bowed his head and said, *"Touché."*

Max leaned toward her and murmured, with stage-confidentiality, "I like to see a bit more resistance from a girl than you're giving him, Princess. This isn't much fun for me, you know."

Magnus rounded on him. "You're the cause of more than half the trouble," he snapped.

"I?" Max was full of wounded innocence.

"Yes. Permitting me to believe ... all sorts of vile insinuations."

Max turned back to Katya with a smile. "Listen carefully now, my dear. He's as close to an apology at this moment as he ever was in his life — believe it or not."

"Pay no attention to him, Count," she said brightly. "Apologies are not called for — or rather, shall we agree that they cancel each other out?"

He bowed. "If Froeken Silver so wishes."

"No! Only if we both so wish. Do sit down, man. You're making me quite dizzy."

At last he grinned. But he refused her invitation, pleading that he was on his way to an engagement he could not break. "Perhaps Froeken Silver will do me the honour of dining with me on the next ladies' mess night?" he asked.

"The honour would be mine, Count," she replied, turning to Max to see if he had one more pearl to cast.

"Let me know when the next storm breaks," he said, pretending to settle back for a snooze. "It will. It will."

Magnus clicked his heels at his friend and bowed stiffly. "Lejonkrona!" he snapped as he left.

"And the same to you!" Max laughed after him. His laughter continued until Magnus had quite gone. "I adore that man," he said, wiping his eyes. "How dull this city would be without him!"

But when he turned to Katya and saw that her eyes were fixed on the place among the trees where they had last seen Magnus, the smile faded. "Oh dear," he murmured. "Oh dear oh dear oh dear."

*I*t was a little over a kilometre from the terrace café in Kungstreadgaarden to the Bolinders wharf on Kungsholm — a stroll from a world of fashion and elegance to the grime and poverty that supported it. The filthy river that separated the island from the northern quarters of the city was like a border between two nations. Nowadays, whenever Katya saw poverty like this, her thoughts inevitably strayed to poor Froeken Rydqvist, who must carry such scenes in her mind's eye all the time, nudging her conscience, whispering, "Don't give trouble!"

Frida Carlsson saw her visitor as she crossed the bridge upstream from the wharf; she was up on deck by the time Katya reached the quayside. "Don't come aboard," she shouted. "There's iron dust everywhere. I'll come down. Did you get the position at that hôtel?"

"Yes," Katya called back.

"Huzza!" Frida flung on a shawl and skipped down the gangway. "Well done!" she cried, throwing her arms round Katya and giving her a hug. "I don't think I could have left Stockholm if you hadn't."

Katya looked at her in surprise. "Why ever not?"

"Because I feel responsible. Shall we stroll down to the lakeshore?"

"What about Agneta?"

"One of the ship's officers has taken her and Nisse to the zoo in Skansen. One of their favourites."

The way led past Bolinders' main shipping office. Katya glanced up into its grimy windows. "I wonder how many times my father has stood up there, looking down at this scene?" she murmured. "And if only he knew — what wouldn't he give to be looking down now!"

"That's one of the things I wanted to ask you," Frida said. "What do I say if I meet him in Dublin — which I'm almost certain to do?"

"I've written and told him — in general, you know."

"Good for you, but that's not really an answer. It doesn't help me."

"Don't you want to hear about my interview at the Sibylla?"

"Of course I do — so let's get the dull bits over and done with. What do I say to your father when we meet?"

Katya stopped suddenly and stared at her. They had reached the end of the quay and now stood in the shadow of the Karolinska Hospital. "I never even thought!" she exclaimed.

"Well, think now."

"No. I mean — you could be in trouble — for the way you've helped me."

"Good heavens!" Frida's jaw dropped. "You didn't tell your parents about all that?"

"No, of course not." She relaxed a little. "No, I suppose there's no way they could ever find out. Except that my father's as cunning as a fox. He'll guess I would never have taken such a huge step entirely off my own bat. He'll suspect we must have talked about it at least, you and I. If you do meet ..."

"There's no *if*. We always see him."

Katya took her friend's arm and started to stroll again; she gave a reassuring squeeze as she said, "I'm shocked at my own thoughtlessness. It never occurred to me that by running off on my own like this I might be getting you in hot water."

"Our charter with Bolinders, you mean?" Frida was dismissive. "It's for four years and would cost them a small fortune to tear up. Besides, I have a nephew on the Baltic Exchange. We pick up all our return cargoes through him as it is. We wouldn't lie idle a single day. So don't you fret about that!"

Katya shook her head. "You're missing the point. The point is I didn't even *think!*"

"All's fair in love and war," Frida said vaguely.

"What has this to do with love?" Katya asked.

The other stared at her in surprise and then burst into laughter. "Why don't you ask what it has to do with *war?*"

"Because it *is* war. Life is now a daily battle ... earning a living — all that. That's war, believe me!"

Frida shook her head. "I can see I'll get no sense out of you until you've told me all your news."

So Katya told her how the interview at the Sibylla had gone. Having already rehearsed it for Max, she made a very polished tale of it now, which left Frida even more stunned than she would have been if she had heard the earlier, stumbling rehearsal.

"You're like one of these new Board of Trade maroons," she said breathlessly. "The first time we set one of those off, we couldn't *believe* how high it shot." Then she pulled a punch on her companion's arm. "Oh, Katya! I'm so glad for you — so glad!"

They had reached Norr Maelarstrand, which skirted the northern shore of Lake Maelar at this, its eastern extremity. Across the road, right on the shore itself, was a little patch of green, a sort of unofficial, unadopted park where people could sit and watch the life of the lake unfold before them, especially on sunny days like this.

They found an empty bench, in full sun and out of the breeze; there they sat and stared out across the water, relishing the view in silence for a long moment. Frida rearranged her hat to ward off the sun; but Katya, obeying an urge deep in her Scandinavian blood, took her hat off altogether and raised her face to luxuriate in its feeble kiss.

It was now well down in the afternoon sky, falling aslant the green, snow-mottled slopes of Laangholmen, over the lake to their right, and the built-up heights of Soeder, immediately to their front.

On their left, Riddarholmen and Gamla Stan basked in the full glare of it — although from where the two women were sitting most of those islands lay hidden behind the vast, anchored hulk of the city swimming schools, which looked like three ornate riverboats from which the paddlewheels had been removed to allow them to be bolted together into one enormous vessel.

"It still is the most beautiful city on earth," Katya said.

"But?"

"It has a dark side to it, too."

She told Frida about the scene she had witnessed from Rosie's window — the view "directly into the eighteenth century," as Rosie had called it. Then she told her about Froeken Rydqvist, too.

"I wonder what became of her?" Frida asked. "Have you ever been back to see?"

Katya shook her head. "I made it quite clear it was my fault. I presume she's still employed there."

"Oh." Frida sniffed but said no more.

"D'you think she might not be?"

"You forced her superior to discharge her — then to take her back. Not a happy situation for any underling. I'd think she's been on borrowed time since then."

"Oh God!" Katya sank her head in her hands.

"I'm sorry. Perhaps I should have held my tongue."

"No, no! You did absolutely right — the right thing. I've had it in mind to go back a couple of times since then but I've been too ashamed to show my face. I'll go tomorrow — on my way to Rosie's. Oh — that's another thing I want to tell you." She brightened, as if her good deed were already done, and then went on to tell Frida all about the final arrangements she'd made to take Rosie into her apartment. "And I *do* remember your warning," she concluded. "Even so, I'm not going to ignore the old crone's advice completely. I shall pick and choose."

Frida reached up and pinched her cheek playfully. "Haven't you grown since I last saw you!" she exclaimed.

Katya smiled at her. "Yes."

"So tell me — what *has* all this to do with love? It's your question, not mine."

"I wrote to Declan, too," she replied lamely. "I posted the letters on my way to the interview."

"Come to think of it — what do I say to *him?*" Frida asked. "D'you want me to try and meet him, too?"

"Yes!" Katya exclaimed. Then, in the same breath, "No!" Then, in a confusion of breath, "I don't know. Perhaps he won't be there. Surely he's already on his way here to Stockholm?"

"With how many horses?"

"Ten? A dozen? They're starting a new polo team so it'll need quite a few."

"Well, unless he also has a relative on the Baltic, he'd need some time to arrange that charter." After a pause she added, "He could go Harwich—Hamburg and continue overland, of course. It would all depend on how eager he is."

Katya, staring moodily into the waters of the lake, said, "Why does everyone take that tone when they talk about Declan?"

"Everybody?"

"Max Lejonkrona, my mother, Amelia, you ... my cousin Bengt last summer ..." She sighed. "I notice you didn't ask what tone!"

There was quite a pause before Frida turned to her and said, "Is that the only part of you that *hasn't* grown — the part where you store feelings like these?"

Katya just went on staring into the water.

"Mmm?" Frida prompted after another long silence.

Katya sighed again. "I'm afraid to let go, Frida. Then *everything* would be gone."

"That would rather depend what you put in its place."

Katya laughed grimly. "That's just what I'm afraid of. The fire is sinking. I thought all those beautiful things I wrote in my letter to him this morning would make it leap up again. But it's still sinking. And somewhere in the dark out there ... beyond the reach of its light ..." She shivered rather than complete the thought.

*A*ugusta Lundin's was smaller than Katya remembered it — though it was still large enough, apparently, to conceal Froeken Rydqvist somewhere. She was not in the millinery, nor the haberdashery, which Katya passed through on her way to the dress department, where she had last seen the woman. Fru Pihl recognized her the moment she saw her — and she recognized, too, that Katya's dress was the one she had bought that first day. She came forward, smiling broadly, and complimented her on how well it looked. She dared to wonder if Froeken Silver were hoping to find another dress to go with it?

"I thought there would be no harm in looking, at least," Katya told her. "Is the young lady who modelled this dress for me available? Froeken ..." She pretended to fish for the name.

Fru Pihl's face hardened. "Froeken Rydqvist?" she asked coldly.

"That's the one! Is she here today by any chance? She did it so well — and I was so wretched to her!"

"I'm afraid she is no longer in our employment, Froeken Silver. Indeed, I supposed Froeken Silver would already know that."

"How so?" Katya frowned. "I have not so much as set foot in this place since that morning."

"And nor has she, Froeken Silver. Not since the following morning, anyway." Fru Pihl stared askance at her, almost as if she suspected her of playing games.

Katya was appalled. "You didn't ... she wasn't dismissed?"

The woman's lips vanished in a thin, compressed line. "No, Froeken Silver — more's the pity! She handed in her notice, bold as brass. Forfeited all her wages." She shut her mouth like a trap and the breath rushed in and out of her nostrils. She was clearly in something of a rage about it.

Katya then remembered her earlier, enigmatic remark. "Tell me, what makes you think I would already know all this?" she asked.

Now the woman was flustered. "I ... I ... I don't know," she concluded lamely. Then, in a tone almost pleading: "I don't mean to be in the least bit disrespectful, but I imagined Froeken Silver was in league with her. I see now I was ..."

"With Froeken Rydqvist?"

The manageress nodded unhappily and repeated: "I see now I was wrong and I apologize."

The more the woman explained herself the more mystifying the whole business became. "Have you an office where we might retire and discuss this properly, Fru Pihl?" she asked.

A frightened look came into the woman's eyes. "There really is nothing to discuss, Froeken Silver. I made a stupid mistake — for which I unreservedly apologize. That is all."

"Well at least tell me why you thought I was in cahoots with her. I promise you — contrary to whatever impression I may have given last time I was in here — I am very slow to take offence."

Fru Pihl bit her lip but remained silent.

"Please tell me," Katya added, "How on earth could I have formed any kind of association with that girl?"

She drew a deep, anxious breath and said, "The circumstances suggested it so strongly. The fact is ... oh dear! The fact is, Froeken Rydqvist herself was in here not twenty minutes ago."

"Asking for her old place?"

Her lips curled in a sneer. "Not a bit! She waltzed in as if she were the queen herself! Ordering my assistants around like scullerymaids — yes, her former colleagues! And nothing on earth would induce me to repeat the things she said to *me*."

"But good heavens! Is she deranged? She seemed so ..."

"I never liked her," Fru Pihl muttered. "I never trusted her — her and that revolutionary brother. Always sneering at the rest of us ..."

Katya interrupted: "But see here, Fru Pihl — I still don't understand why you think *I* should have been in league with her. Just because I happen to come in here shortly after she paid this distressing visit. It suggests that she left here ..."

"She did not leave — she was ejected!"

"Whatever. It suggests that we then met somewhere — in that dam-café across the square, perhaps — and then hatched a plot for me to come in and inquire after her. I find that a little far-fetched, frankly. More than a little."

Fru Pihl looked trapped again. "I said it was stupid of me, Froeken Silver. I have already apologized for it. If Froeken Silver cannot accept ..."

"No, no, no!" Katya laughed to show she was not offended and it was not a matter for apologies. "I just want to know why you made that connection between her and me. Why is she behaving in this extraordinary manner, anyway? Do you understand that?"

"Ha! Because she is *protected* now — that's why."

"Protected?" Katya echoed rather loudly.

The other looked around anxiously and put a finger to her lips.

"I'm sorry!" Katya said, almost whispering now. "Listen — I will buy another dress. I'd be so grateful if you'd come and assist me to choose it. And meanwhile you can explain this mystery-upon-a-mystery to me."

The manageress, loath to turn away a sale, ushered her morosely to the back of the dress department and pulled out the rack containing their latest modes.

Katya had meanwhile been thinking hard — and not too happily — over what had been said so far. "I realize now what you mean by 'protected,' Fru Pihl," she said calmly. Then she smiled, for the words she was about to speak could so easily be taken amiss: "And I think you must be under the misapprehension that I, too, am 'protected' — by Herr Lejonkrona. Am I right?"

The other closed her eyes and said, "Really, Froeken Silver! This is hardly ..."

"No, no. It doesn't shock me. I understand it very well. I imagine that down the years Herr Lejonkrona has brought a number of 'protected' females here to choose their dresses?"

The woman stiffened, to prevent herself revealing anything by an accidental nod or unconscious movement of her eyes.

"You needn't confirm it," Katya said soothingly. "I rather admire your discretion, indeed. The fact is, I'm about to take up a position at the Sibylla — where I suspect I shall need as much discretion as you. So I am not entirely disinterested. I think I could profitably take a leaf out of your book."

Fru Pihl relaxed sufficiently to show a little genuine surprise. "Froeken Silver is going to work at the Sibylla?" she asked. *"Work?"*

Katya nodded. "I am fluent in many dialects of English, and I have more than a smattering of French. Herr Svensson has engaged me to coach his staff — to bring their foreign languages up to the standard they will need during the Exhibition."

The other almost laughed to hear this. "I'm so glad, Froeken Silver," she said — several times.

"You mean glad I'm not like all those others?"

She bit her lip. The smile vanished but the merriment did not leave her eyes. "I'm afraid I can say nothing as to them — I mean as to *that*, Froeken Silver."

"No. I realize that. I shall say no more. Thank you for being as frank with me as you have. I know it can't have been easy."

For the next fifteen minutes they got down to the serious business of choosing a dress. The trouble, as before, was that they were *all* so gorgeous. But in the end, remembering the sober decor of the Sibylla and the need to dress modestly, she chose a dark-blue taffeta creation, severely cut when seen from the front but softened by a column of furbelows each side of the back-centre seam; it had not even a hint of a bustle.

As she was leaving Katya said, "To hark back to what we were discussing earlier — of course there is now one question I'm absolutely *dying* to ask Fru Pihl."

"I realize that," she replied with a twinkle in her eye. "But Froeken Silver will understand it is the one question above all others that I cannot possibly answer!"

Since Katya's interview at the Sibylla had been brought forward, the arrangements for the Grand Duchess had changed. Katya was to take her new lodger to the hôtel, where a day-suite had been arranged for her accommodation until Katya finished in mid-afternoon. Meanwhile Max and friends would move some of her possessions to Jaerntorget — the things she would need over the next two months or so — while the rest would go to a repository in Soeder.

When Katya called at the apartment, on her way between Augusta Lundin's and the Sibylla, she found the door ajar. Max was already there. In fact, having heard her tread upon the stair, he was standing at the drawing-room door pressing one finger to his lips. She tiptoed behind him into the room and found Rosie fast asleep in the smothering clutches of her enormous armchair.

What a face! she thought. It looked as if a dozen women had each lived a very full life inside it. She tried to picture Rosie as a young girl — the beautiful young actress who had been the first to seduce the now elderly prince who would be England's next king. Alas, the present raddled reality was too strong for her imagination to overcome. Yet the raddling was part of it, of course — the countless seductions that had followed that first royal playtime, the marriages, the courtly intrigues, the quarrels ... the money that flowed like wine and the wine that flowed like the Danube, the Oder, the Volga, all in one. The mighty estates, the hunting forests as large as petty kingdoms of old, *châteaux, palazzi, dachas,* villas, and Wagnerian castles ... the vaults full of jewels and gold, the priceless tapestries, the wardrobes that would have furnished a hundred grand operas ... the armies of hangers-on, the maids and minions and serfs beyond number — all had come and gone, and their only memorial was now written here, in the lines — or *between* the lines — of that ancient face, in the blubber of that tired old body, in the few pathetic trinkets that had survived that magnificent voyage, only to wash up like jetsam in the dubious haven of these squalid chambers.

The correlation between all that grandeur and this, its pitiable rump, was impossible to draw. Katya could only marvel that one who had enjoyed so much could now make a tolerable life among so little. Did she ever wonder what it had all been *for?* Had she ever, in those days of her glory, imagined it might all come down to this? A chill tingle ran down Katya's spine as she realized that such, indeed, had probably been the case. Roman generals in their triumphant parades through the Eternal City traditionally had a slave at their elbows, murmuring the timely reminder: "You are but mortal!" Katya herself, about to take the greatest stride of her life so far, was only too aware she could fall flat on her face. The child within her, whose death would begin today, was already fighting hard, urging her to fall back into the old, protected ways, where, if she could not make anything of herself, at least she wouldn't make a fool.

Katya took Max's arm and clutched him tight to her side. "D'you think she ever suspected that all her glory might one day shrink down to this?" she whispered.

He gave a dry, almost soundless laugh. "I think she must often have prayed for it to happen," he whispered back.

"Is she dreaming of her glorious past, d'you suppose?"

"I doubt she sees such an absolute break between then and now, Princess. Not the way we do." In a more normal voice he said, "Have to wake her up, I'm afraid. It's going to be a very busy day for us all."

Rosie woke so instantly to his touch, and was so immediately *au fait* with her surroundings, that Katya wondered whether she had been asleep at all. Had she overheard? On the other hand, did it matter if she had?

Soon, however, the bustle of that day's agenda shouldered all such musings aside. Life's ineluctible mysteries were swept up in, "have you got a spare handkerchief? ... where's the key to that writing case? ... take both shawls to be on the safe side" ... and other matters of briefly absolute importance. Katya felt worn out by the time Rosie was ensconced in her suite at the Sibylla — and her own work had not even begun!

Herr Klint was waiting for her; he did not exactly have his watch in hand but he was tucking it away in his fob pocket at the moment she first set eyes upon him. She was coming down the main staircase from Rosie's suite; he was standing at the entrance to the corridor that led to his office.

"Ah, Froeken Silver," he called out — not a trace of a smile, of course. "May we have a word?"

That *we* sounded like the schoolmarm's usage: "We *are* late this morning, Miss O'Barry!"

He met her halfway across the foyer and touched her elbow to steer her toward the restaurants. "I was wondering what your plan might be for today?" he said.

"If it doesn't sound too odd, Herr Klint," she replied, "I was planning to spend the first two hours learning rather than teaching. I need to learn people's names, first of all. And then I must discover how much English they already know. I'm sure you don't wish me to cover ground already familiar to them — nor to leap so far beyond their present abilities that ..."

"Good," he barked — and turned on his heel and walked away.

Actually, while Katya followed that plan, she became aware that Klint never "walked away." His feet might march his physical body to some other part of the establishment but, as Albert had hinted the previous day, something of his presence remained. Klint was, in fact, ubiquitous in that hôtel. No chambermaid ever made a bed without looking at it and wondering if it would pass muster with him. No waiter could straighten a silver setting without thinking, "Now *he* would approve!" Whatever the menu might say, the chefs made every dish *à la Klint*. Even the tradesmen who called with their deliveries each day would glance up and down the corridors, asking, "Is he around?"

When her four hours were up and she could safely slip into Rosie's suite, all she wanted to do was sink into an armchair and rest for a century. Rosie, however, was ready to go.

"And what have we learned today, little bird?" she trilled.

"Please don't call me *we*," Katya begged. "It makes my flesh crawl. What have I learned today? First, that I've bitten off more than I can chew. Did you know there are *seventy-five* members of staff here who come into personal association with guests!"

"You'll manage that," Rosie told her scornfully.

"I will," Katya agreed. "I don't know how, but I will because I've got to. The other thing I've learned is that I must find some way of putting Herr Klint out of my mind. I don't wish to sound blasphemous, but he's like God within these four walls — or these four hundred and forty-four walls, to be more precise."

"I know exactly what you mean," Rosie said when Katya explained her situation. "Grand Duke Otto was like that. People quaked when he came within a hundred miles. Even the Emperor was known to run a nervous finger round his collar. But not me! *I* had a way of dealing with him!" She gave out her rich laugh.

"What?" Katya asked eagerly.

"Whenever I felt that little squirt of fear in my bowels — because he was a most chilling sort of man, you know ..."

"I know!"

"I used to say to myself, *Well, my little Otto, you don't impress me. I've seen you naked!*"

Katya burst into laughter — which she then tried to stuff back down her throat, spluttering and biting her lip. "*Rosie!*" she exclaimed reproachfully. "What a thing to say!"

"It's true! It worked wonders as well. There's only been one man in my life who was more frightening to me after I opened my thighs to him than before — and he was a wrestler, a serf on our Siberian estate. A vast, gentle bear of a man ..." Her mind hopped off the delicate twig of her voice and flitted away into a silent land where Katya could not follow.

"He was gentle?" she asked. "And yet you feared him?"

The old woman nodded, still lingering fondly among her memories. "*Because* he was so gentle, you see ... the one man who could ..." There was a long pause before she murmured. "That was *real* power!" She looked at Katya as if she, Rosie, had been talking away all this while, explaining everything. "When a man gains power like *that* over a woman — that's when she should fear him, little bird!"

Thus Katya learned a third important thing that day: The best lessons in life can be fully learned even though they may be only half taught.

*T*he Grand Duchess settled so well in her new realm (nowhere that Rosie lived could be called a mere abode) that Katya began to appreciate how threadbare her life in Biblioteksgatan must have been. She became almost young again, certainly in spirit. Her memories became less rambling — though more distressingly graphic, not to say pornographic at times. Katya passed rapidly through the phases of what Rosie quaintly called a woman's "sentimental education" — from horror to shock to curiosity to unblushing interest ... all the way to over-reaction in a nonchalant acceptance of things that would have brought on an attack of the vapours in the old Dublin days.

The turning point came when she realized that, to Rosie, these scandalous mysteries were simply part of life's unending commerce — not commerce in the sense that led to the *bordell*, but that which extended to the buying and selling of great art, grand palaces, rare books, and beautiful clothes. Rosie had inspected the hundreds of men in her life in precisely the same spirit as that in which she had looked at the Raphaels, villas, and sumptuous gowns that had been offered to her for sale from time to time — and she assumed without question that the men had made the same careful choice of her. In that sense, *all* of life was a commerce to her; concepts like "sin" and "virtue" had their uses but their boundaries were moveable — as with giant parasols, one redirected them from moment to moment, placing them where they would protect one best.

In a curious way, these new insights had many parallels with the life that was opening up for her through her work at the Sibylla. There, too, commodities that were elsewhere given from the heart — hospitality, shelter, and warmth, for example — were quite openly put into commerce, each with its own ticketed price in a bill of fare. Everything a private host might do to increase the comfort and enjoyment of his guests the Sibylla did with a smile, a bow, a parade of almost infinite willingness to serve — yet always in the background there was the barely audible *ding!* of the cash register, inexorably totting up each tiny favour.

Between Rosie at home and the Sibylla abroad, Katya's restricted and rather sentimental view of life soon hardened into something more useful and realistic. It was a tribute to her upbringing that she did not become utterly blasé. Those who had furnished that upbringing, however, would have been horrified at her knowledge of the world (no matter that it was still largely theoretical as yet) and her acceptance of its ways.

But what can I do? she asked herself on those increasingly rare occasions when such thoughts crossed her mind.

At the end of her first week at the Sibylla, when she was fairly certain that her new life was going to "take," she wrote to her Onkel Kurt and Tante Anna. She enclosed her father's letter to them — unopened still — and told them that while it would explain how she came to be in the city, it would say nothing about what she was doing there. As to that, she had decided it was time to cease plaguing both her parents and them and to make her own way in life instead. She went on to inform them that she had found a respectable position in Stockholm where she could make full use of her gift for languages; though it was only part-time, it was better paid than many a full-time post. For the rest of the while she was companion to an aristocratic lady of impeccable breeding. She had communicated all this to her parents and was daily awaiting their approval of her independence — on the receipt of which no one would be happier than she to renew her acquaintance with them, her dear aunt and uncle, and all her cousins. They were to remember her especially to Bengt. Meanwhile they must realize how futile it would be for them to come looking for her — and how well placed she was to resist any attempt to deviate her from her present course. She remained their loving and dutiful niece ... et cetera.

"But mainly et cetera!" she exclaimed as she sealed the envelope.

And so, with the nagging problem of her aunt and uncle out of the way (or put back on the long finger, at least), she threw herself into her work at the Sibylla. She continued as she had started — by taking on the rôles of various awkward guests who spoke nothing but English or French. It suited her histrionic talents, and to the waiters, porters, and chambermaids, who were all expecting to drown in an ocean of foreign visitors that summer, it was like the sudden gift of water-wings. Few teachers can ever have been blessed with such willing pupils.

She also helped untangle some genuine problems with genuine foreign guests — an elderly couple some of whose luggage had gone astray, two young parents whose little boy had a colic and who were too distraut to talk sense to the doctor ... that sort of thing. These situations, in turn, fed into her teaching and kept it fresh and realistic. The only flaw in the scheme of her life was, as always, Herr Klint.

She did her best to keep out of the man's way but soon realized what Albert had meant when he said that the man could see round bends. Katya almost wished he would exercise that talent rather than observe her directly. Time and again she would catch him in the corner of her eye, always as far from her as possible while still remaining in view — just observing. If she turned to ask him whether he wanted anything, he would just shake his head and go. The other staff said he was like that with all of them but she felt he was picking especially on her. They said he made everyone feel like that.

"One day I'll just step up and ask him directly if I'm giving satisfaction," she vowed to Max. Only the fact that Max egged her on to carry out this threat held her back.

Otherwise she hadn't a complaint in the world. The work took up little of her time, it paid well, it had no set pattern, and above all it allowed her to mix with people she would otherwise never have met at all — both rich and poor. She made dozens of new friends very quickly. True, none of those friendships was profound — indeed, outside the hôtel they ceased to exist; but inside it they could be quite intense. It was the sort of friendship that springs up among actors thrown together for a particular production, or soldiers sent into the front line for a particular battle; she often felt her work had much in common with both those professions.

To be sure, her life was not entirely smooth. Flies can breed, even in ointment. Her next troubles came with the arrival at the Sibylla of a certain Arthur Dalyrimple, as his passport called him (though he insisted on pronouncing it "Dample"). In dealing with him, however, Katya also found a way of dealing with Klint — the equivalent, for her, of Rosie's, *Ha, little man — I've seen you naked!*

Arthur Dalyrimple, Esquire stated his claim to be one of the Grand Old Men of English Letters loudly and baldly within minutes of his arrival; and, since it is the rule in all good hostelries that guests be indulged gratis in any whim that costs neither time nor money (and be charged handsomely for those that do), he was, as far as the Sibylla was concerned, the world's greatest writer, no matter how unsung or unread. He entered Katya's life on the morning after his grandiose arrival, by which time she had been at the Sibylla for more than three weeks and felt all the confidence of a seasoned professional.

Her hours on that particular day were from eight until noon, so she arrived while the maids were carrying trays of tea, coffee, and shaving water to the guests' bedrooms. She was on her way upstairs to the little closet where she usually hung her hat and coat when Sophie, one of the chambermaids, stopped for a brief chat, having delivered one such tray to Mr Dalyrimple on the floor above. They had hardly exchanged a word, however, when the GOM of English Letters opened his door and bellowed, "Girl! This tea's so cold there's a polar bear swimming round in it!"

"A humorist, too!" Sophie lifted her eyebrows wearily and raced back up to him. Katya finished hanging up her things. A moment later, the maid came back down again, bearing a tray with a fresh pot of tea and some shaving water. Her face was livid. "Look — he hasn't even tried it," she growled. "Just wants to throw his weight about."

Katya felt the pot, and, finding it almost too hot to touch, said grimly, "Give it here."

The maid saw the gleam of battle in her eye and clutched the tray tighter to her. "Pay no attention, Froeken," she said. "It happens all the time in this life. One must learn to accept it, that's all."

"I know what to do with him!" Katya reached again for the tray — and again Sophie clung to it, uttering this time what she must have thought was the ultimate argument: "Herr Klint wouldn't like it if you upset a guest, Froeken Silver."

A huge smile split Katya's face. "No!" she exclaimed. "He wouldn't, would he!" And this time she grabbed the tray so fiercely that Sophie had to let it go for fear of an accident.

A few moments later, carrying the tray and its rejected contents, she knocked at the door of the Great Author's room, drew a deep breath, stretched her lips in an enormous hôtel-style smile, and breezed in. "I heard you upbraid the wretched abigail, sir," she said in her best literary style — and in English, of course. "So I made you a fresh pot, *instanter*, of 'the cup that cheers but not inebriates'! I hope it will prove more to your liking." And she placed the tray deftly on his bedside table.

"Wait!" he barked when she was halfway back to the door. Then, as if it were part of some quasi-religious ceremony, he poured a solemn cupful (milk infirst, Katya noted with scorn) and sipped it. It scalded him, though he hid his discomfort manfully. "Excellent!" he barked again.

She smiled and backed a further pace or two.

"No, wait!" he cried, holding up a solemn finger.

She watched in some trepidation as his hands dived beneath the bedclothes and began fiddling with something distastefully near his midriff. Then his left hand emerged bearing a golden sovereign, which he thrust self-importantly toward her. He wagged his upraised finger at her again. "Now you shall make my tea for me *every* morning, young lady," he said loftily. "What is your name, pray?"

Katya told him — but she pocketed the coin before she let him know she was not there *every* morning at that early hour. "However, I shall instruct the girl to prepare your tea the way we British like it. And," she added, giving him the same commercial smile as before, "you should experience no further disappointment, sir."

She recalled a phrase Magnus had used about his father and spoke it with relish when she rejoined Sophie on the stair: "What a crapulous old toad!" she said, handing over the sovereign. "You're the one who deserves this."

The maid stared at it in what looked incongruously like horror.

"Take it," Katya urged. "He gave me something far more valuable."

Sophie's look turned to one of suspicion.

"A warning on how *not* to behave when *I'm* as rich and 'world-famous' as he is!"

Their subdued laughter was cut short by the sudden appearance (or *apparition,* as it seemed) of Herr Klint at the foot of the stairs. Katya kept her eyes fixed in his as she descended. Her next port of call was the dining room, to see whether any early breakfasters needed her assistance.

"Is anything amiss, Froeken Silver?" he asked as she neared the foot of the stairs.

On any previous morning she would have done her best to gloss over what had just happened. Now, slightly to her own surprise, she heard herself say: "It has all been taken care of, thank you, Herr Klint." And she walked past him without a pause.

The flesh at the back of her neck crawled; she knew his eyes were fixed on her as he tried to overcome his surprise. At every moment she expected him to call her back to give a fuller account of herself. Instead, she heard him turn and walk away.

I've done it! she cried out in the safety of her own mind. *I've broken my chains at last!*

To her dismay, the GOM of English Letters, who must have washed and shaved in record time, entered the breakfast room before she had moved on to the next of that day's appointments. He made a beeline for her and announced that he was so pleased with the Sibylla that he intended to stay for several months while he drafted his new novel. Its entire action was to be set in Stockholm during the period of the Exhibition.

He invited her to sit at his table while he told her all about it. She replied that she had other duties to attend to. Unabashed, he kept her standing there while he told her the entire plot — or, rather, three versions of it — whose contradictions his capacious mind alone was able to reconcile, it seemed. She managed an occasional smile by silently repeating Magnus's wonderful words, and promising herself she would one day utter them aloud to him. Toward the end of his long monologue he began to include her in his plans — the research she could carry out for him, the drafts she might make at his dictation. He asked if she'd had any practice as a typewriter.

She was about to tell him, rather sharply, what she thought of these plans when Klint materialized at her elbow and tactfully extricated her. The unstoppable GOM said he had stayed at the best hôtels in the world but at none had he found a member of staff as courteous, as helpful, and above all as intelligent as Miss Silver. The assistant manager assured him they were well aware of her talents.

For the first time she felt a little warmth toward the man, not for his slightly ambiguous endorsement but for having rescued her. She mumbled her thanks as they left the dining room.

"I thought it was time to intervene, Froeken Silver," he replied.

"You mean you were watching from the very beginning, Herr Klint? You could have rescued me sooner, I think."

"I could have," he agreed mildly. "But then I should never have discovered the length of your fuse."

When she recounted these events to Rosie, the old woman took Klint's side. "A servant with a short fuse is no asset to any master — no matter how well qualified beside."

She was far more interested in Arthur Dalyrimple, Esquire.

"When you took the tea back to him," she said, "d'you think there's a chance he overheard you and the maid?"

"Of course not! He'd have been livid. That man needs a gallon of *amour propre* a day to keep him going."

But Rosie shook her head knowingly and said she wasn't so sure. "Try speaking to him sharply one day," she advised, giving a shrewd little grin.

"I try never to speak to the man at all," she replied. "I spend half my time avoiding him."

"Try it all the same, Princess." She had adopted Max's form of address with a kind of ironic glee. "I think the result might surprise you. Try telling him, for instance" — her eyes closed as she sorted through a mental treasure trove of insults — "yes! Try telling him he's not worthy *to lick your boots!*" She cackled heartily at her words.

"Cheeky boy!" cried her parrot and cackled along with her.

Katya told her she'd do no such thing. "He'd have me out on my ear," she said.

"I doubt it." She dabbed her eyes. "He's far more likely to offer you ..." She broke off and thought better of whatever she had been going to say. "Perhaps it's wisest not to get mixed up in that sort of thing," she concluded with a sigh — and then refused to be drawn any further on the subject.

When Katya repeated this odd conversation to Max, he, too, refused to be drawn — beyond the comment that it sounded "intriguing."

Katya herself was intrigued to learn, a week or so later, that Max had called at the Sibylla and taken Dalyrimple out to dine.

The number of questions she was storing up to ask Max, "when the right moment came," was growing by the day, she thought.

*L*adies' Night at the mess of *Lifgardet till haest* was set for the first Thursday in May. That was only ten days before the grand opening ceremony of the Exhibition, and the Sibylla was already packed with guests who wanted to get the usual tourist visits over and done with before that day dawned — the tours of Skansen, Drottningholm Palace, Saltsjoebaden spa ... the trips up Lake Maelar to Uppsala ... and so forth.

What with all the extra work, and the excitement of being Count Magnus's guest that night, Katya quite forgot that the *Suecia* was due back in Stockholm that same day and that she had arranged to see Frida Carlsson again and hear all the desperately awaited news from Dublin. The afternoon was well advanced before she remembered — in the middle, as it happened, of a particularly tedious encounter with the GOM. He was telling her his latest idea, which was to have the heroine of his novel walk around Stockholm with a pet monkey on her shoulder. He seemed to think that was exquisitely funny. Naturally, it made her remember the *Suecia*.

"What d'you think of my wheeze?" he asked, fixing her with his tiny eyes.

She told him she hardly felt qualified to give an opinion.

"But I would welcome it, Miss Silver — truly. I know you would not stoop to the flattery one would expect from other hôtel servants. You will tell me the honest truth. If it be *severe*, then *scourge* me with it, I beseech you."

"Well, Mister Dalyrimple," she risked saying. "You could make your hero a world-famous writer. But his tragedy is that all his originality deserts him. He is reduced to dining out with the heroine's friends and stealing ideas from them." She smiled thinly. "Or d'you believe one should not write from one's own experience?"

He snapped his writing case shut. "I'm probably keeping you from something more important," he said.

Yet there was something strange about him, she thought. He was only pretending to be angry. Curious now, she decided to goad him, saying, "In the very nature of things, Mister Dalyrimple, that is bound to be the case."

As she left him she heard him say the one word, "Magnificent!"

At the bottom of the main staircase — inevitably — she found Klint waiting for her.

"Are you on your way out, Froeken Silver?" he asked in that neutral tone which passed for affability with him.

Katya explained about meeting the *Suecia* at Stadsgaard — and that she was late already.

He nodded gravely. "Some other time, perhaps," he said. "I hope Mister Dalyrimple is not making a nuisance of himself?"

She shrugged awkwardly. "I think I can manage him tactfully enough, Herr Klint. In fact I find him more of a bother than an out-and-out nuisance."

"I will ask him to leave if he becomes really annoying."

"Oh please!" The thought horrified her. "I must learn to manage such people."

"I believe you are wrong," he said impassively. "No lady should be required to manage a man like that."

It was the first time she had ever heard him refer to a male guest as anything other than a gentleman.

"However," he went on swiftly, "I see this is more mystifying than enlightening to you, so I shall say no more. But please remember — if he makes too much of a nuisance of himself, you may speak your mind to him. Try to do it out of the hearing of other guests, that is all I ask. And remember, too, that I shall not hesitate to ask him to leave. Quite the contrary. It would make me very happy."

He bowed to her, turned on his heel, and made for the street door. It was a day of firsts with him, for she had never seen him leave the hôtel before, though she had heard from the others that he went for a walk at an unpredictable hour every afternoon. He took his hat and cane from the stand beside the entrance and gave her another little bow as he left.

She turned to Albert at the desk and said, "Well!"

"Well, indeed, Froeken Silver," he replied.

"Did *you* understand any of that, Albert?"

He shifted uneasily. "Yes, Froeken, I'm afraid I did."

"Why? What is it? Do you know something about Mister Dalyrimple that I don't?"

He chewed his bottom lip and said at last, "Again — I'm afraid I do, Froeken. But it's something no well-brought-up lady should know, so please not to press me. Maybe one of the girls will tell you."

These gnomic remarks of Albert's and Herr Klint's kept her puzzled all the way down Sibyllegatan and along Nybro Hamn to the Opera landing stage. There she was just in time to catch the ferry to the Saltsjoebaden spa. The boat itself actually went no farther than the Stadsgaard railway station, which is on the line to the spa; but that, of course, was as far as she needed to go, anyway.

Only when she was on the boat did she remember the other rather odd thing Herr Klint had said: "Some other time, perhaps?" It would have registered more strongly with her if she had been aware that he was dressed for a stroll; but the more she thought about it now, the more likely it seemed to her that Klint had intended asking her to accompany him while he took his constitutional!

"Some other time!"

She wondered if she would.

The trip across the Salt Sea lasted no longer than ten minutes. For the first half of it the Royal Palace and other grand buildings in the north-west corner of Gamla Stan obscured her view of Stadsgaard. But even when the far docks came into view, the intervening thickets of masts along Skeppsbron made identification impossible. She was kept on tenterhooks until the very last reach, when the ferry drew level with the southern end of the old city; by then there could be no doubt. Not only was it *Suecia* berthed at Stadsgaard but, from the lack of activity around her cargo hatches, it would appear that she had been tied up long enough to be fully unloaded, too.

Frida must be on tenterhooks by now. And she wasn't going to be too pleased to be told, in effect: "Hallo, goodbye, I'm dining out tonight, so I've no time for you."

And in any case, nothing could be farther from the truth. She was dying to hear whether Frida had met her father — and what they had said. And, of course, she was longing to see her dear friend herself again. Also Declan, she remembered — perhaps Frida had seen him, too.

As the ferry docked she caught sight of Frida, already down on the quayside. Of course, she knew Stockholm well and would have realized that this was the ferry line Katya would take from Norrmalm, where the Sibylla was situated. But poor woman! Had she been meeting them every fifteen minutes since midday?

With mounting guilt Katya waved and yoo-hooed until Frida saw her and began waving back; she even gave a few on-the-spot jumps, like a schoolgirl. Katya found herself wishing she wasn't going out with Magnus tonight — except that she knew the moment she saw him she'd change her mind again and be very happy to be dining with him.

Like a pair of schoolgirls they rushed into each other's embrace and Frida, the bigger and stronger, though not by much, lifted Katya off her feet and whirled her round.

"Oh but I've missed you!" Katya cried, giving her a desperate hug.

"Me too," Frida agreed. "I've been burned up with curiosity to know how it's all worked out. Let me look at you!" She stopped spinning and held her at arm's length. "Well, the answer's in those bright eyes and rosy cheeks! Life is still being good to you, no?"

Katya, not wishing to give a hostage to fortune, said, "Yes and no. It's good but it's complicated. And *one* of the complications" — she took up Frida's hand and clasped it between hers — "happens to fall this very evening, I'm sorry to say."

"Oh?" Frida stiffened.

"I should already be at home, washing the grime of honest toil from my pores and preparing to dine with Count Hamilton at the officers' mess tonight."

"Is that all!" Frida laughed and turned her toward Slussen. "I'm very happy for you. Come, I'll help you dress."

"And tell me all the news as we go!" Katya glanced back at the *Suecia*. "Is Agneta not with you?"

"We called at Greenock and left her and Nisse with my parents. They don't come with us on every voyage."

"Well then!" Katya linked arms, making a pretend-prisoner of her. "Did you see my father when you were in Dublin?"

"I saw Declan," Frida replied artlessly. She leaned forward to see how Katya took the news.

"I was saving him till last," Katya replied.

"Oh really? Are you quite sure you want to?"

Katya licked her lips nervously. "You mean it isn't good news?"

"Not very. He said this Swedish commission is so speculative — I mean, they aren't firm orders yet — and he daren't let it interfere with his regular business with the British army — and in any case, they can hardly require *polo* ponies until the beginning of summer ..." Her voice trailed off, suggesting a further long litany of good commercial reasons for *not* coming to Stockholm just yet.

"That's all true, of course," Katya said.

"Of course," Frida echoed. "Such a *sensible* young man, I thought.

Not an ounce of romance in him."

"All right, Frida," she said heavily. "You've made your point."

"Mmm," the other replied, giving her voice a pensive rise and fall. "I was so afraid it would leave you utterly desolate and heartbroken."

"No you weren't!" Katya gave her a sharp little dig with her elbow. "Tell me about my father, then."

"I'll leave Amelia till last, shall I?"

Katya's whole countenance brightened. "You saw her, too?"

"Did I! She sought me out at every possible occasion. She wanted to hear everything about you. Again and again."

"I'll bet she was horrified."

"On the contrary. She's absolutely thrilled. You've become some kind of heroine among the young ladies of Dublin ..."

"Oh, my God!"

"Why? I thought you'd be pleased."

"What do they know about me? How *much* do they know? Lord, if they know anything at all, it'll surely get to my father."

They had reached Slussen by now and Katya was startled that Frida turned right without being told, or being nudged in that direction. Then she remembered that the woman knew very well where she lived. Katya was so used to living a sort of double life by now that she was beginning to lose touch with which of her friends knew what. Actually, a double life would have been child's play compared with the series of overlapping lives that she now led.

"They know all the facts but none of the details," Frida reassured her. "Relax. Actually, I have a letter for you from her — and from your parents — but I've just remembered I left them on the *Suecia!* I didn't expect you on that ferry, either. Shall I go back?"

Katya took her arm again as they reached the broad cobbled square at the southern end of Gamla Stan. "I wouldn't have time to read them now, anyway. That sounds awful, but it's true."

"I'll bring them back while you're out. Carlsson is taking me to dine at the Metropole tonight."

"Ah," Katya told her airily. "Tolerable food and tolerable wines — and (take a tip from me) the best *chambres privées* in Stockholm."

"Minx!" Frida exclaimed. Then, in quite a different tone, she asked, "Are they really?"

Katya chuckled. "See for yourself."

"I think I shall, you know. Ooh! You've made me go all goose-fleshy, you wicked girl!"

"What's in the letters?" Katya asked.

Frida gave a protesting sort of laugh. "I haven't steamed them *open*," she said — or, rather, that is what she meant to say. But what actually came out was: "I haven't steamed *them* open."

It took a moment for this unintentionally honest stress to register with Katya, but then she was onto it at once. "You mean you did steam open my father's letter! The one I was to take to Tante Anna and Onkel Kurt!"

Frida hung her head ruefully, more in chagrin at being caught out than in shame at admitting it. "Someone had to," she said.

"What did it say?"

"In a word? Lock you up! Except that he took about four pages to say it."

Katya's mind was racing. "So for three weeks my uncle has had that letter ..."

"You sent it to him?" Frida was aghast.

"Together with my own letter telling him not to bother looking for me. It seemed the only honest thing to do."

"Oh, Katya!" Frida halted and gripped her arm. Staring at her intently, now into her left eye, now the right, she said, "If only I had known! It never occurred to me you might do that."

"Never mind!" Katya pressed on toward Jaerntorget. "What's done is done. It means that for three weeks he's had a letter telling him to keep me under lock and key ... actually, come to think of it, how *dare* my father write a letter like that! Ooh, I wish he were here now — wouldn't I just give him what-for!"

Frida cleared her throat awkwardly. "You may get the chance quite soon, my dear. Or, when I say soon, I mean some time this summer. We didn't need to pick up a catch cargo in Dublin this time, you know. The *Suecia's* laden to the gunwhales with your father's contribution to the Bolinders stand at the Exhibition."

"Of course!" Katya murmured. "It never struck me, but of course he'll come over here for that. Well" — she rubbed her hands and smiled savagely — "I'll be twenty-one then, so he can just ..." She stopped her mouth dramatically. "No! I must try to be a lady tonight, so I won't say it."

"Take a long walk off a short pier?" Frida suggested.

"That'll do very well instead." They were crossing Jaerntorget by now. "Where were we when I got all hot under the collar? Oh yes — your meeting with my parents. What did they say? How did they take it? They're in good health, I hope? They always are, anyway."

"Your granny was delighted when I told her you'd deciphered her message. She offered to send more but I told her you wouldn't need it. Your parents are in good health — and, I'm sorry to tell you, are absolutely *aghast* at what you've done."

"Frida!" Katya exclaimed bitterly.

"What?" She was all innocence.

"I'm going out to dinner tonight, remember. I've got to be bright and sparkling and relaxed and gay. What a thing to tell me!"

But Frida was not in the least abashed. Her gaze was level and unblinking as she said, "Are you saying you won't be all those things? And that this news will knock you for six?"

It was Katya who lowered her eyes first — masking it by fiddling with the key in the lock. "All the same ..." she grumbled vaguely.

One of the more subtle changes that Katya began to notice in herself at around this time was that she had stopped accepting the world at face value. It became very clear to her during that Ladies' Night dinner at Magnus's mess. She had known many young officers at home in Dublin and it would never have crossed her mind to question why they had chosen their profession. Officers were officers the way lions were lions, or mountains, mountains. It was their nature. It was somehow part of the natural order. The matter of choice was really something of a formality.

If she had ever put it to herself in that elementary fashion, she would have seen its absurdity at once, of course. But she never had. The world and almost everything in it was *given*. She had no power to change even the smallest part of it — therefore it was pointless to ask whether it might be otherwise.

No longer. As she sat there, listening for the most part to the formalized conversations going on around her, mingled with carefully coded gossip about people she did not know, she began to wonder what on earth a man like Magnus was doing here. True, he *looked* every inch a cavalry officer; as a tailor's manikin for military uniform he was unrivalled. But his wit, his gift for expressing himself in that oblique but compelling manner of his — where could such talents find their outlet here? She listened to him talking to the colonel's wife, seated at his other hand, and thought he must be going quietly insane with boredom.

When it was all over and they had settled themselves in his carriage for the return drive to the city, he let out a huge sigh. She did not need to ask him why. "A country like Sweden ought to have two separate armies," she said.

He chuckled. "What now?"

"All through dinner I was trying to work out why this army is so different from the British, which is the only other one I know."

"Oh, that's easy. The British army has never stopped fighting. *Pax Britannica* is a fraud. There has always been a little war going on somewhere. But the Swedish army hasn't fired a shot in earnest for almost a century now."

"Exactly. That's why I say there should be two armies — a standing one for ..." She laughed and began again. "I mean a *sitting* one for pen-and-ink soldiers like those people, so they can spend all their peacetime years waging paper wars with the government — and keeping the guns and ammo ready for when war comes and the real army can take over."

"And who's in the real army?"

"Men like you — charging over the landscape with a sabre between your teeth. That's what you're good at, Magnus. You must want to curl up and die most of the time."

After a silence he said, "I'm sorry. You obviously didn't enjoy this evening very much."

"I wouldn't have missed it for worlds," she assured him. "But I still wonder what makes you stay."

"I'd go all to pieces if I bought myself out," he replied. "Like poor old Lejonkrona."

She laughed in disbelief. "You keep hinting that about Max but it's not true. He's not going to pieces at all."

"Yes but what does he *do* in life?"

For a moment the question had no meaning. Max was rich and unattached. He didn't need to *do* anything. "He enjoys life. He keeps his eyes open and his wits about him. Come to that, Magnus, what do *you* do?"

Magnus bridled at this direct challenge. "Lejonkrona would have gone to pieces if you hadn't come along. You didn't know him as he was before that. He was turning into a drunken young bore. Have you seen him the worse for wear since you moved in?"

Katya left her seat and came to sit at his right side, away from his sword. Resting her head on his shoulder she murmured, "Don't talk like that."

"Have you?" he insisted, though less challengingly.

"No."

After a pause he slipped his arm around her and said, "Talk like what? How was I talking?"

"About me 'moving in' in Jaerntorget — there's nothing going on between Max and me. And it was he who insisted on Rosie moving in — as a sort of chaperon."

"Ha!" he exclaimed. "I'm sure she's a great champion of virtue! I'll bet Lejonkrona is only asking a nominal rent. He could get two-forty crowns a month for your apartment — easily. And double that while the Exhibition's running."

She was silent after that, wondering why she hadn't even suspected it. Of *course* Max was her real landlord! All that persiflage about "beating the blackguard down" and so forth. The sly fox!

"You weren't aware that the dear boy is your landlord?" Magnus asked shrewdly.

"Indeed, I was not. But it's not the only crow I have to pick with that man," she replied.

He heard the threat in her voice and let the subject drop. As the carriage crossed back into Gamla Stan, he said, "D'you feel like a bit of a stroll?"

It was getting on for eleven o'clock, almost two hours after sunset, but they were at that latitude — and that time of year — when night yields to one long twilight. The warm breeze, which had persisted all day, had dropped now, leaving the air balmy and still beneath a gibbous moon.

Katya made a deliberate effort to change their mood. "I could stay up all night. Time has ceased to have any meaning."

"We could go to a dance hall?" His voice trailed off and he grabbed his sword and shook it vehemently. "Not in *this* uniform. Oh damn the cavalry! You're right."

"Never mind," she said soothingly. "Perhaps it would be wiser not to. I'd regret it tomorrow. I'm sure we'll be rushed off our feet at the Sibylla. Let's just walk a bit — I'd rather do that."

"Are you sure? I could go back and change, if that wouldn't be ..."

"I'm positive. Let's walk down the lake shore of the island. I see the Salt Sea side every day."

They alighted in the square in front of the House of the Nobility. "They have a superb cellar in there, too," he told her. "Or have I already mentioned that?"

"Why this obsession with wine?" she asked. "You don't drink all that much, do you?"

"That's why the wine has to be good. Ask Lejonkrona — if you're going to drink a lot, the quality doesn't matter a bit." After a pause he added, "Actually, that's true of everything in life."

They reached the narrow waters of the Knights' Canal and turned south. The lapping of little waves against the stone walls and wooden fenders reminded her of childhood picnics by the lake in Dublin zoo. The last time she had visited Dublin zoo she had been with Declan. He could have written a letter at least. He knew the *Suecia* was coming straight back to Stockholm.

"I know a man in Dublin," she said, "who believes in both kinds of wine — a rough, gulping wine for every day and a fine one for special occasions."

"Are you beginning to miss your home?" he asked.

She hesitated.

"You know what my real question is," he went on. "Especially when you say, 'I know a man in Dublin'."

"The *Suecia* docked at Stadsgaarden today. Frida Carlsson brought me some letters from home."

Her tone was so neutral he had to ask what they contained.

"I haven't opened them yet," she replied. "I didn't want to spoil this evening."

He laughed dryly. "You knew you could safely leave that to me!"

"Magnus!" She shook his arm gently. "I told you — I wouldn't have missed it for worlds."

"But never again?"

She cleared her throat tactfully. "I'm sure you know many other interesting and rewarding places to show me. And I hope you will."

They reached the end of the canal, where the broad waters of Lake Maelar stretched out before them, black and silver-tongued by the light of the rising moon.

"If I left the army," he said abruptly, "would you leave the hôtel?"

"Goodness!" she exclaimed. "Why?"

"We could buy a boat and sail down the Goeta Canal, all the way to Gothenburg."

"And then?"

"Onward! England. Dublin. America. Greece!"

"Or even to navigation school!" Her heart was suddenly racing.

"Would you?" he insisted, ignoring her joke.

"Magnus!" She leaned her head on his shoulder and hugged his arm tight. "It's just a bit early to be asking things like that, my dear."

"Oh, I'm not suggesting we should start tomorrow. But ... well, some time before summer's quite gone."

"Oh dear!" She straightened herself and they resumed their stroll down the lakeshore. "Just let things take their course, eh?"

"We get on splendidly together."

"That's what I mean, my dear. But it's still such a little plant. Don't let's do anything to stifle its growth. Let's see a few leaves and branches on it before we decide whether to give it a permanent place in the garden, eh?"

"If that's the way you want it, Katya — of course. For myself, I'm as sure now as I'll ever be."

You could start by offering to kiss me, she thought.

"I'll keep my eye out for a good boat, anyway," he promised.

They ambled on, talking of everything under the moon and nothing in particular, until they arrived at Jaerntorget; his coach, having gone ahead, was waiting discreetly at the far side of the square. When they reached her front door and he still had made no move to kiss her, she turned her face toward him in the most obvious invitation she dared offer. For a moment she thought he was going to accept, but then he paused and said, with a frown, "There's just one thing."

"I'm a good sailor," she assured him. "No worries on that score."

"It's about Lejonkrona — and the Grand Duchess."

"What about them?"

"They're not a good influence, Katya. I'd be much happier if you saw less of them."

"Good God!"

"And happiest of all, of course, if you saw nothing at all."

She turned him to face the street light, unable to believe he was being serious. But he was. "I thought they were friends of yours," she said.

"What has that to do with it?"

"And aren't you part of this group that helps support Rosie?"

He shrugged. "I still don't see the connection. The fact is, I have many friends with whom I should not wish a ... a ... with whom I'd not like you to associate."

What had he been about to say? she wondered. A ... what?

"All desperate and disreputable characters, eh? Like Max and Rosie! Really, Magnus!"

"You rush to extremes — as always," he said coldly. "A character does not have to be 'desperate and disreputable' for me to wish ..." He heard her draw breath and said, "Listen!"

"No, *you* listen," she fired back at once. "I'm sure you don't *intend* to insult me, but that's just what you are doing."

"I assure you — nothing could be further from my ..."

"So you believe. I'm sure you honestly believe that — otherwise I wouldn't even be wasting my breath on you. But this absurd request of yours is deeply insulting to me. You imply that your own character is so wonderful and so strong that you may safely associate with people like Max and Rosie without being defiled. But *my* character is apparently so questionable to start with — and so weak into the bargain — that *I* am not to be trusted within a million ..."

"Listen!" he roared. "I'm not saying that at all."

"It sounds very much like it to me. What are you saying, then?"

"Will you listen this time?"

"Not if you're going to make me angry all over again."

"All I'm saying is that ... oh dear! Of course I don't think your character is dubious. Nor feeble. You are beyond reproach — and I'd demand satisfaction from anyone who said otherwise. But that's the point, Katya. I don't want to hear people saying otherwise — which they will do if you continue to live cheek by jowl with Lejonkrona and keep the Grand Duchess under your roof. Everyone knows she's an old ... well, never mind. It can do you no good."

"But you haven't answered my point, Magnus — which is that you seemingly *can* associate with them, and, for some curious reason, people won't talk about it."

"Of course they'll talk. People will always talk. But I'm a man."

"There's no doubting *that!*" she said bitterly.

"I don't know why you take that tone. The point is, a man's character can tolerate a certain degree of mud-slinging. A lady's can't. It's as simple as that."

"Have you finished?"

"I don't write the rules, Katya. I'm sorry — but that's the way the world is."

"Are you sure you don't want me to give up working at the Sibylla, too?"

"Well ..." he confessed reluctantly. "I have to admit, it doesn't help matters."

"Aaargh!" She clenched her fists and shook them at the moon.

"What now?" he asked in a wounded tone.

"You're impossible!" She stabbed her key at the lock and was astonished at the fluke that turned her wild shot into a bullseye. "Don't bother to go looking for that boat," she sneered.

"But you don't understand ..."

"No, I don't! I don't understand why it would be perfectly acceptable for me to go sailing down the Goeta Canal, all alone with you. That wouldn't harm my reputation at all! But as for living perfectly respectably here ...!" She gave up the struggle. The slam of the stout wooden door behind her was highly satisfactory.

"I meant we'd get married first!" he complained to its cold, unyielding exterior.

She did not hear him, even though she was less than a foot away, leaning wearily against it, eyes tight closed, willing herself not to burst into tears.

The "semi-concierge" came bustling out into the hall.

"Froeken Silver!" she said acidly. "That officer outside ..."

"He's yours if you want him, Fru Torbjoernsson." Katya dragged her way past the woman and on up the stairs. "You'll get no complaints from me."

The woman suddenly thought better of confronting Katya in that mood and backed away into her apartment.

Katya stood on the landing above, undecided between her own door and Lejonkrona's.

Rosie or Max?

Or neither?

Scurrilous and unscrupulous advice from a woman who had learned her lessons too late to help herself? Or a manly shoulder to cry on — belonging to a man who owed her more than comfort. Like a few timely explanations, for instance?

She had just decided she was not in the mood for either when Max opened his door anyway. "Where's the turkey in all his pride?" he asked brightly.

"Thank you — just a small glass," she replied, walking past him into his apartment. "It's peacock, anyway."

Though far from complete, it was a three-*skaal* explanation and she felt rather proud to reach the end of it without yielding to the temptation to cry. "The damn fool!" she raged. "He doesn't understand the first thing about me."

"Don't say that!" he cried in alarm.

She stared at him. "Why ever not?"

"Because that's an excellent reason for marrying him. I'd never dream of marrying a woman I understood. It could lead to some highly improper situations."

"Oh Max!" She laughed and punched him on the arm — rather

harder than she intended. "I shall never understand you, either — so beware!" But she still could not get over Magnus's stupidity. "Did he honestly think I'd give up living here, give up being friends with you and Rosie — give up my work at the Sibylla? For what?"

Max frowned. "Didn't you ask him?"

She smiled grimly. "Actually, I didn't need to. He'd already offered it." And she went on to tell him of Magnus's absurd fantasy about the Goeta Canal, which she had omitted from her first account.

He shook his head in amazement. "And you still think you understand him — which is what you implied when you complained that he *didn't* understand you?"

"Well, I understand *that* sort of offer very well!"

"*Do* you?"

"Yes." Her tongue slowly licked her lower lip while she wondered how much more to say.

He saw the gesture and his expression became truculent, challenging her to say her worst.

She breathed in deeply and told him, then: "It's precisely the offer any idle young man-about-town might make to a pretty little shop assistant whose tenure had become a little shaky." She grinned fiercely and added, "For example!"

She tossed back her glass and pushed it forward for a refill. He refused to oblige, so she poured out her own.

When she had set the decanter down, he snatched the glass beyond her reach. "No, Katya!" he begged, shielding it from her gaze. "Try anything but this, I beg you! As my father said to me quite recently: 'Liquor is a demon. It is the father of wickedness, the mother of corruption, and the daughter of all depravity.' Mind you, I suspect he had a monstrous hangover at the time."

"How *could* you, Max?"

She saw him wondering whether to fob her off again with more persiflage. Then he said, "It was simple. I made Froeken Rydqvist an offer. She was perfectly free to turn it down."

"Oh yes! She had so many choices!"

"On the contrary. Before I came along she had no choice at all — or only one, which is as good as none. I actually *doubled* the number of choices in her life!"

"I don't imagine she sees it in that light."

"Why not go and ask her? She lives in the house with the blue door in the centre of the terrace on the western side of the square known as Kronoberget —, which is on Kungsholm. Only don't expect to find the downtrodden little mouse who burst into tears at Augusta Lundin's."

"I know she isn't that. She almost had *Fru Pihl* in tears — though they were tears of rage, not fear."

"Oh?" His eyebrows shot up.

She described what had happened, which made him laugh delightedly. "Good for her!" he said. Then his eyes narrowed. "When did Fru Pihl tell you all this?"

"The day I started work at the Sibylla."

"You mean you've known about it all these weeks — and yet you've said nothing?"

"Why does that surprise you? D'you think I should tell you *everything*? You don't tell me *anything*."

"For example," he said, yielding the point to her.

"What d'you do with her, Max?"

He looked at her askance.

"I mean, how often d'you see her, for instance? What does her life consist of now it's so rich in choices?"

"Oh, you imagine it isn't?"

"Tell me."

"I see her often. She is an interesting young lady, as a matter of fact. I take tea with her. We walk in her garden or in the square outside. We sometimes go to picture galleries. Today we went to the Panorama. We frequently go to the theatre. She writes poetry and favours me with bits of it. We play duets on the piano ..."

"So you must see her every day?"

"For example! I didn't wish you to think that 'seeing her' was a euphemism for just one elementary activity — if you follow."

After a longish pause, Katya said, "It seems it's rather like being married, then."

He reached across the table and took her hand between his, patting it comfortingly while he said, "Alas, no, my dear. It's what people fondly imagine that marriage is like *before* they try it."

*B*efore they parted company that night Max warned Katya not to arrange anything for the coming Saturday evening, which was only three days away. She asked him why but he would not say. Katya returned to her own apartment, looked in on Rosie and found her fast asleep, and then, at last, she opened the letters from Dublin.

Frida Carlsson had prepared the ground well, for they added nothing of substance to what she already knew. Her father claimed to be shocked — so much so that he threatened to disown her unless she went at once to stay with her Onkel Kurt. Her mother added a little footnote to say that he didn't really mean it but he was, nonetheless, most vexed at her disobedience. Neither of them referred to her success at making an independent life in Stockholm. It was quite irrelevant in their eyes; for no amount of success could be set in the scales against her disobedience.

The letter from Amelia was the very opposite. Katya's success was the wonder of Dublin. She and her friends could talk of little else. They were all so envious. She was trying to persuade her parents to visit Stockholm that summer, to see that wonder of Sweden — the marvellous Exhibition, which was in all the journals. Katya was to keep her fingers crossed. They might meet yet!

Katya relished her dear friend's praises and resolved — now that the secret was out — to send her a message via Frida, when the *Suecia* returned to Dublin. Her parents' letter didn't lose her a minute's sleep — not that she'd be happy to be estranged from them but she believed it would never come to that.

The following day, Thursday, she hung back at the Sibylla to see whether Klint would renew the invitation she imagined he had been going to make the previous afternoon. But a large party of German tourists arrived unexpectedly early, and then she realized he'd be busy far beyond the length of time she was willing to wait. So it was "some other time" once again.

She set off in the direction of Kungsholm, thinking she might cry in on Frida; not until she arrived at the bridge onto the island did she remember that the *Suecia* would by now be on the long detour through the canal and would probably not dock at the Bolinders wharf until late that evening.

Then she recalled Max's boastful suggestion of the previous evening — inviting her to go and see Froeken Rydqvist for herself. She realized it had been sheer bravado. He never for one moment expected her to take him up — and that fact alone was enough to make up her mind to do it.

She asked the way to Kronoberget and discovered it was a straight walk along Fleminggatan, all the way — about a kilometre. She covered the distance briskly though her pace began to slacken as she drew near the turning into the square. Perhaps it wasn't such a good idea, after all. She remembered a time at school when one of the girls in her form had been accused of "borrowing" another girl's india-rubber. "Search me!" the accused had challenged. "Go on! Turn out all my pockets if you don't believe me!" Everyone else had accepted that as proof of innocence — all except Katya. She had taken up the invitation and found, not the missing india-rubber but a packet of cigarettes. A prefect had been watching from near 4y. The girl had never forgiven Katya. So it was dangerous to take up challenges that were merely rhetorical.

She decided then not to visit the woman after all. However, as she had come so far, it was silly not to look at the place at least, if only to see what "a fate worse than death" was valued at these days.

It took her breath away. The house was magnificent, with tall windows and rich mouldings of cut stone between each floor; a romantic circular turret, like a miniature tower on a French château, marked it off as the central house of the terrace and the grandest one of them all. Katya just stood on the opposite footpath and stared.

All *that* — just for ...

She could not close the equation in her mind.

Just for a bit of playtime!

How *could* it be worth ... all this?

She was still puzzling it over when one of the windows flew open.

Max!

Hoping she could deceive him into thinking he had made a mistake she turned and set off, back the way she had come. She walked away slowly to show him she had no particular aim in mind at all, really.

"Froeken Silver!" It was Froeken Rydqvist's voice.

Katya hesitated.

"Yes!" the woman called out. "Up here! It's me — Froeken Rydqvist. Surely you remember?"

She had no option then but to turn back once more and, this time, cross the road. When she drew close enough to speak without raising her voice she said, "Is ... is *he* there?"

She hadn't actually seen Max at the window; it was conscience that had driven her away so guiltily.

"Not today. I'm *off duty* today." Her smile was almost triumphant. "Will you come in and take some tea? It's nice and warm in the garden, and we can sit in the sun."

Katya was even more astounded when she saw how opulent the interior was. Froeken Rydqvist saw her roving eye and said, "Would you like to see around before we go outside?"

"Oh ..." Katya was dubious.

"Go on! I know you're dying of curiosity. I can remember how *I* felt the first time Max showed me over this place."

Katya swallowed heavily. "You're sure he's not coming here?"

"Not today. Not for a few days, I imagine. He's all wrapped up in arranging the masks and costumes — I thought you'd have known. In fact, I felt sure that was why you'd chosen today to call." She took a few paces up the stairs and looked back. "We can start at the top and work down." Then she laughed. "That was *his* joke, of course."

Katya remembered Max's telling her not to arrange anything for Saturday evening. Masks and costumes — so that was it. He was going to hold a masked ball somewhere. Well, she'd just have to look bewildered when he finally decided to break the secret.

"I'm amazed you're even willing to talk to me," she said at last.

The amazement, however, was all on Froeken Rydqvist's face. "Why on earth?"

"Because of what happened that day at Augusta Lundin's. I behaved appallingly."

The other was still baffled, as her laughter showed. "But all rich women behave like that. Anyway, if you hadn't … none of *this* magnificence would have come my way at all." She gestured proudly at her surroundings.

That, of course, was what Katya had meant — though she could hardly say so now! "So all's well that ends well," she said vaguely.

"I'll say!"

A housemaid came to the foot of the stairs, curtseyed, and said, "Froeken rang?"

"Don't shout, you good-for-nothing creature!" Froeken Rydqvist snapped. "Come up here and speak respectfully!"

The girl trudged wearily upstairs but just before she spoke again her mistress said, "My friend and I will take tea in the garden in twenty minutes."

The maid bowed her head and returned below stairs.

Froeken Rydqvist smiled at Katya. "One has to keep them in their place, you know."

"I suppose so," she replied.

"Actually that one will have to go. She's too pretty by far. I've seen Max with his eye on her more than once. There can only be one mistress here!" She chuckled. "Did I say the right thing, by the way? You *are* my friend, aren't you?"

"Of course!" Katya was taken slightly aback.

"I'm Marianne." She held out her hand.

"I'm Katya." She shook it.

From then on they were *du* to each other.

The house had five floors plus a basement and attic. The fifth floor and the attic — including the pointed turret — were servants' quarters; Marianne did not bother to show her those, merely explaining that she had four servants and a lady's maid. The fourth floor had two bedrooms and a library. The latter had a lived-in feeling and Katya remembered what Max had said about her writing poetry. "You work in here?" she said.

Marianne looked at her sharply. "He's told you quite a lot about me, then."

Katya shook her head. "In fact, no. It wouldn't fill half a dozen lines all put together."

"But he obviously told you I write poetry." She opened a notebook on the desk and turned it for Katya to see. She read:

> *Time, not as our times of old*
> *would swoop upon our wasted hours*
> *and break each leaden minute*
> *with its mighty wings of gold,*
> *hangs — eagle-like —*
> *a vulture!*

"Very modern," she said feebly.

Marianne laughed. "Very Swedish!"

Katya felt challenged to try again. "Grasping its meaning is like trying to paint a shoal of darting fish. You can see them clearly, but only in flashes. And you can't begin to draw them with your brush."

For the first time Marianne put aside her slightly belligerent graciousness and looked at Katya with respect. "That's not bad," she said quietly.

"Have you written a lot?"

"I shall have by this time next year — and then we'll see whether my virtue and maidenhead were worth the sacrifice."

Katya had an intuition that this woman would have made "the sacrifice" sooner or later, no matter what had happened between them at Augusta Lundin's that morning. She said, "I went back, you know — to see Fru Pihl — or really to see if she'd kept her word about withdrawing your dismissal."

"And perhaps to buy a frock or two as well?" the other suggested. "I hear you can well afford it now."

"Aha! He's told you a fair bit about *me* as well, then!"

Marianne grinned. "I could boil it down into about six lines, too. What did La Pihl say?"

Katya laughed. "She thought I was in league with you. Apparently you'd been in only half an hour before me, behaving like Lady Muck! And so when I came in and asked if you were still serving there, she naturally jumped to conclusions."

A rich peal of laughter greeted this. "She thought you were Max's mistress, too."

Katya blushed. "I know."

"Well, we all did, of course. You needn't feel embarrassed. Half the women who shop there are some man's mistress."

"Really?"

"Really. I mean, even if they are legally married, it's a mere formality. They're giving the same ... how shall I put it? The same quid pro quo. Some of the gentlemen are thirty or forty years older than their wives — pretty little things younger than you and me. What else can they have in common? You ask your Grand Duchess all about it — she knows the tariff for the whole of Europe! Come on! I'll show you the room I know you're dying to see!"

She dashed past the next floor entirely, saying it contained only two more bedrooms, a drawing room, and a bathroom.

"And here," she said, throwing open a door, "is where I do my best to persuade darling Max to go on allowing me the use of all the rest of this lovely house."

Katya, who had been expecting something after the style of the *chambre privée* at the Metropole, only larger and even more opulent, was disappointed. No red plush shrouded the walls, no gilded mirrors hung on the walls, no deep-pile carpets swallowed her feet, no incense left its cloying fragrance on the air. It could have been a dressing room in any upper-middle-class home in Sweden.

"What a let-down, eh?" Marianne remarked.

"No," Katya replied without much conviction.

"I thought it was dreadful the first time I saw it. I thought, if I'm going to live in sin, it should at least be in luxurious sin." She threw open the connecting door. "This could be my bedroom at home — or the home we lived in before my father went smash."

"I'm sorry." Katya touched her arm.

"Not half as sorry as I was! God — another month at Augusta Lundin's and I'd have died of screaming boredom." She turned to Katya with an odd sort of appeal in her eyes. "This *is* better, you know. Honestly it is."

She shrugged awkwardly. "I'm sure you're right. You know why Max took me to that shop? It wasn't really to buy a dress at all. It was to prove to me I couldn't possibly look for a place in establishments like that."

"You mean he wanted to make you his mistress *before* you felt humiliated enough to say yes, no matter what!"

"No ..." Katya screwed her face up, almost as if in pain. "I honestly don't know what he wanted — except to prove to me how wrong *I* was, no matter what *I* wanted. I still don't know what he hopes for with me. Not marriage. Nor" — she waved a hand about them — "this. Has he spoken about it to you?"

Marianne shook her head. "I asked him if you were also his mistress and he said 'Good God, no!' — as if he found the thought" — she shrugged awkwardly — "distasteful. Sorry, I didn't mean it to sound like that. I meant as if he would despise *himself* if he tried anything like that with you. I can't fathom him, actually."

"Nor me." Katya went over to the window, mainly to try to peep into the room beyond the bedroom. "Just when you think he's your dearest friend, he says something, or does something, that pushes you right away. D'you feel you can get near him ever?"

Marianne grinned sourly. "Only there." She jerked a thumb toward the bed. "And in there." She crossed the room and opened wide the door through which Katya had been peeping. Here at last were some of the elements she had felt cheated of — the chaise longue, the polar-bear rug, the dozens of silken cushions ...

"Mirror, mirror on the wall ..." she murmured, looking at all three of them.

"And the ceiling!" Marianne pointed it out. "Max calls it *theme and variations*," she added. "Theme in that room, variations in this."

"What do *you* call it?" Katya asked.

"As I said — quid pro quo!" Marianne drew a breath and asked, "Would you go to bed with him if he suggested it?"

"Did he tell you to ask me that if we ever met?"

"God, no!" She drew a finger across her throat. "He'd kill me if he knew, I think. Don't ever tell him. Don't tell him any of this conversation, will you!"

"Of course I shan't, in that case."

"So — would you?"

Katya licked her lips nervously and said, "Yes." She knew she ought to feel surprised, shocked ... something. But she didn't.

"Because you love him?"

She shook her head. "Because I don't, I think."

"That's wise." Marianne nodded glumly. "That really is wise."

"Aren't you afraid of having a baby?"

"Oh no, he's very careful like that. It's quite possible not to have babies, you know."

Katya drifted back into the bedroom — and on into the dressing room once more. "I didn't know," she said. "I know almost nothing about all that. How did you find out? Was Max the first?"

"Of course he was!" she said indignantly. "What d'you take me for?" She closed her eyes and added, "Sorry! It's a giveaway, that, isn't it — being so touchy! No — Max was the first."

"And he's taught you everything?"

"Taught isn't quite the word. He somehow lets you understand things without actually teaching you."

Katya laughed. "I know exactly what you mean. He's like that in everything. Art, music ... everything."

Marianne took her arm as they went back onto the landing. "Who are you in love with, then, Katya? Am I allowed to ask?"

Katya hesitated before saying, "I'm sort of in-between at the moment. There's a beau in Ireland — I *think.* And maybe there's one here, too — except that every time we meet we quarrel like two terriers and don't speak again for weeks."

Marianne laughed, not unsympathetically. "That sounds the more promising of the two, if you ask me."

They went downstairs and out into the garden — a small, rather formal area full of paving, stone tubs, columns, and niches. It felt hemmed in and airless. To one side was a square-cut marble pool. A nude alabaster Venus bent sylphlike over it, staring at her reflection through sightless eyes.

"What about you?" Katya asked when the too-pretty maid had safely withdrawn.

Marianne became flustered. At first she tried to pretend she had lost the thread and didn't know what Katya was referring to. Then she said, "Me? Oh God, no!" rather too earnestly.

Katya understood why she lied; she had everything to lose if she, Katya, carried the tale back to Max. One good confession did not — in this case — deserve another.

Marianne, aware that she had not deceived Katya, tried to repair the damage. "There *was* someone," she confessed. "A married man. I'm trying to forget him."

"I'm sorry. I didn't wish to pry. I only thought ... you know."

"I know. Actually, he's a very *good* man. Has Max told you about my brother?"

For one awful moment Katya thought she was about to confess to an incestuous passion; then she remembered something Fru Pihl had said. "The revolutionary?"

"So he has told you."

"No, that was Fru Pihl — just a casual aside. She said she couldn't bear the sight of you — you and your revolutionary brother. Something like that."

"Actually, he's only my half-brother. Oh, it's too complicated to explain. Anyway, this man I'm talking about is a friend of Leif's. That's my half-brother. Leif von Kieler. Have I lost you?" She passed Katya a cup of tea, adding, "Help yourself to lemon or milk. And the ginger snaps."

"I think I follow. You have a half-brother called Leif von Kieler, a revolutionary — whatever that is ..."

"A socialist."

"Oh, I see. And he has a friend — this married man — who is the man you're trying to forget."

"Perfect!"

They sipped their tea and sat awhile in slightly embarrassed silence. Their intimacies had run ahead of the friendship and they were both seeking a way back to more neutral ground. Being unable to find one Katya risked asking the one question she still wanted answered. "Does it hurt?" she asked.

"What? Trying to forget him?" Marianne sighed. "Less and less as time goes by — which is a double sadness, really."

"I know." After a brief silence Katya confessed: "Actually, that isn't what I meant."

Marianne frowned — and then the penny dropped. "Oh! You mean" — she gestured up toward the bedroom window — "does *that* hurt?"

"Yes."

There was a peculiar knock at the front door — two quick, two spaced, and two quick.

Marianne pulled a weary face. "Talk of the devil!" she muttered.

Katya was agog. "Your married friend?"

"No! Leif von Kieler. He's got a nerve, coming here. I'd have quite a job explaining him to Max."

"Why?"

"You'll see!"

A moment later Katya did, indeed, see — when the maid ushered out quite the handsomest young man she'd seen in a long time.

*H*andsome or not, Katya soon found Marianne's half-brother quite the most tiresome fellow she had ever met. Thus he earned himself two superlatives in her estimation, and all in the space of half an hour. He sneered at the dainty teacups — though he gulped down the tea; he said the silver biscuit salver cost enough to keep a poor family for a year — and then gobbled up all the ginger snaps upon it. He said Max Lejonkrona, and everyone like him, should be stood up against a wall and shot.

Marianne laughed at all this and finally turned to Katya and asked if she had ever met such an idealistic young man.

Katya made the mistake of saying that Dublin was full of them — which started him off on a lecture about Irish politics. To her surprise he proved quite well informed, though his views were the opposite of hers. One thing he had not grasped, however, was that the middle classes, whom he thought were lackeys of the English, were actually the most ardent Home Rulers of all. They wanted the power in their own hands, not London's.

Before she became interested enough to set him straight, she rose and said it was time to go.

At once he said, "Me, too!" and followed her out. "I'd like to show you something very interesting," he explained as soon as she had taken leave of his half-sister.

"I really am rather busy," she objected.

"It's all right. It's on your way home. It won't take long. It's a part of Stockholm you really ought to see."

The breeze had dropped while she had been talking with Marianne; now the sun shone down directly into Fleminggatan, turning it into a bakeoven.

He linked arms with her and said, "D'you mind?"

She shook him off and snapped, "Yes!"

He appeared not to worry in the least. "You're very beautiful," he said. "You have the most amazing eyes I've ever seen."

Her exasperation mounted — not least because she was beginning to suspect that the only way to get rid of him was to humour him, at least in the little things. "I'm sure it's extremely kind of you to say so, Herr von Kieler …"

"Leif, please!"

"Absolutely not!"

"You call my sister *du*-Marianne."

"That's our affair. I'm not going to call you *du*-Leif. I was going to say that you shouldn't make personal remarks like that — even complimentary ones — on so short an acquaintance."

"Who says."

"*I* say." She laughed, though unwillingly.

"You see! You're softening already. You'll give way in the end."

She sighed and looked around for some means of escape. "I don't know what makes you say that."

"Because I mean no harm to anyone — and because love and frankness and socialism always win over the mean-spirited and the grasping in the end."

"I am *not* mean-spirited — nor grasping, I hope. I just think people should observe a proper reticence when they've only just met."

"But we have done so much more than just meet. I love you! I fell in love with you the moment I saw you. Why should I be reticent? I have so much to give."

She stopped and stared at him. "Have you by any chance been drinking?" she asked.

He shook his head and smiled; he really was *embarrassingly* handsome when he smiled. If he was drunk, it was the strangest drunkenness she had ever seen. "Can't you find it in your heart to show me a *little* compassion, Froeken Silver?" he asked.

She started walking again, briskly despite the heat, leaving him to catch up. "I think I'm showing you a great deal of forbearance, Herr von Kieler. Most other girls I know would have handed you in charge long before now."

"Oh no they wouldn't."

"Oh yes they would."

"Wouldn't!" He waited for her to say *would*; when all she did was quicken her pace still further he added, "I shouldn't have behaved like this to them — so they'd have had no cause! See?"

"See what? The only thing I see is that you seem to have some special mission to persecute me!"

He chuckled. "How can it possibly be persecuting you to tell you you're beautiful, to say you have lovely eyes, to confess I love you? The truth *cannot* ever be persecution."

"What is this ... this *thing* you wish to show me?"

"It's just round the next corner."

"Thank God for that!" She slowed down to a saunter before she got out of breath.

"Just round the next corner" proved to be another wide, sunny street, called Scheele Gatan.

"Well?" she asked, searching in vain for anything special about it.

"Just down there." His tone promised horrors. He was no longer smiling now; his pointing finger was trembling.

"If this is some trick ..." she said vaguely.

As she followed him down Scheele Gatan he said — quite seriously now, "This always distresses me more than I can say. But you have to see it to believe it. You have to know it's *there!*" He turned to her, his eyes full of sorrow, and said, "I'm doing it for your sake."

"I must be mad," she murmured to herself.

He halted suddenly. They were about a hundred paces from the top of Scheele Gatan, opposite an alley so narrow she had not noticed it until then. It was what the French call an *impasse* — a ravine between towering cliffs of crumbling stucco, or, in this case, of crumbling patching plaster that had long ago replaced the original stucco; that must have crumbled shortly after the Ark grounded on

Ararat. "Getgraend," proclaimed the fading municipal paint on the cracked stucco at its entrance.

Von Kieler took a few paces into those sunless confines and then turned, waiting for her.

She shrank from him. "I'm not going up there."

He held out his hand and said, "Just come and see. You'll never forget this."

"You've already made sure of that!"

"I want you to meet someone — a friend of mine."

"You mean to say have friends *here?*" She stared past him, up the cheerless alley.

"He's a friend of Marianne's, too."

Katya had a sudden intuition that this was the "married man" she had spoken about — the love affair she was trying to put behind her. Curiosity began to get the better of her but she still made no move.

A young woman came shuffling barefoot out of a doorway and limped past them, eyes averted, into Scheele Gatan; she was dragging one almost useless leg behind her.

"She had the face of a woman of fifty," Katya remarked when she had gone. "But you could still tell she was young, really."

Von Kieler stooped and asked an urchin a question in a variety of Swedish that Katya hardly recognized. The answer was given in the same slapdash tongue. The urchin ran off with his five-oere reward and von Kieler turned again to her. "Just fifteen minutes," he said. "Is that so much to ask?"

Full of foreboding Katya followed him up the alley, making for the door the young urchin had pointed out. The reek of misery — and human midden — began to choke her from the moment she left the broad, airy main street. Looking back, she could see the sun shining aslant the expanse of Scheele Gatan, and already it seemed far, far away. She doubted that same sun ever put more than a toe inside Getgraend; surely even the rain that fell here would be a kind of second-hand water by the time it reached the cobbles, so foul was the air it must pass through.

"Herr von Kieler," she called out. "I'm going to be sick."

"It'll pass," he assured her. He had changed since coming into the alleyway, throwing off his waywardness and becoming more subdued.

And, oddly enough, from that moment on, she began to feel ... not exactly better but at least inured to the worst. When they gained the sanctuary of the friend's house the piggery stench of the alley was softened by the smell of stale cabbage water, half-laundered bedlinen, and those other, less-definable odours that breathe from the cracks of ancient tenements the world over.

If the street had been strangely underpopulated, the same could not be said of the stairways and landings up which von Kieler now led Katya. It reminded her of an occasion, one Christmas Eve back in Dublin, when her father took a lantern up into the roof space in an attempt to unfreeze a water cistern — cursing the English every step of the way for having such stupid things in the house at all. With great daring she, then only fourteen, had followed him up the ladder — and had then almost died of horror at what she saw up there. Bats! Little squeaky, twitching, furry balls of terror, hanging in impossible ways from impossible slopes of roof-timber, all with their pinhole eyes on her, and each deciding in its pinhead brain which part of her flesh it would bite first. To prise her free, her mother and aunt had had to drag a dressing table into the attic passage and tug at her skirts while her father beat her clenched fingers from above.

And now they were all around her — bats of human size — soft, chattering, skeletal shapes of darkness, clinging to an impossible life, all with their pinhole eyes trained upon her ... She prayed for the moment when she would once again breathe the blessed and welcome air of Getgraend, four floors down.

Von Kieler knocked at a door so old, so battered, so peeling that one could no longer be sure whether its last coat of paint had been black or green or brown — or, indeed, any colour at all.

"What are all these people *for?*" she asked him while they waited.

He drew breath to reply but before he could speak the door opened to reveal a great bear of a man, standing at bay. At first he was nothing but a menacing silhouette against the dimly lighted room beyond. He obviously recognized von Kieler, though, and stepped back. His shaggy, bearded face was split by a huge, gap-toothed smile of welcome. "Von Kieler!" he cried, raising his arms as high and as wide as the mean doorway allowed, which was little enough. "My dear fellow!" His stance was that of a schoolboy miming a ghost. He was barefoot and wore only pantaloons and a shirt, open almost to his waist. "How is your sister? Is she still ..."

His eyes strayed to Katya then and, whatever he had been going to say, he thought better of it. Something crude, no doubt, she thought — though his tone and speech were cultured.

Von Kieler had meanwhile advanced into his restricted embrace and was kissing him heartily on each bearded cheek. "Ursus!" he said. "I heard you'd been evicted from the old place but I never thought to find you thus."

The man gave a resigned smile, took another pace back, and wafted an invitation to enter. "It was a risk one had to take," he said. He pretended to notice Katya at that moment — pretended to von Kieler, that is, for he had been running an appreciative eye over her from the moment he had noticed her. Von Kieler turned to her with a smile and said, "This is Ursus. Everyone is *du* here." To the man he said, "Katarina."

She bowed coldly to the man and said, "Froeken Silver. Herr Ursus has a surname?"

He responded with a formal little bow and replied, "Herr Ursus has the misfortune to live in a world where surnames are dangerous currency, Froeken Silver."

There was something so repellent about him that she beheld him with a kind of awe. He was undoubtedly a dangerous ruffian, and clearly on the run from the authorities — though the danger they might see in him was different from the one she now perceived.

Or was it? she wondered. She could imagine this ragged giant addressing a large crowd, holding it spellbound with the power of his oratory and that indefinable magnetism which seems to concentrate in certain people. It was the same power, she realized, that had ensnared Marianne and now held her under his spell. If she was not careful, Katya warned herself, he would do the same to her, too — despite the fact that her very flesh crawled to be in the same room with him.

And what a room!

It was barely large enough to contain them — and it was stifling. A small, narrow window, though opened wide, shed no more than a fitful light over a crudely made deal table, presently covered with papers. Ursus picked up one sheet and handed it without comment to von Kieler. While he read, Katya made a more leisurely survey of the place — aware that the man's eyes were fixed upon her, not on von Kieler. He knew very well that a certain power smouldered in his eyes; she avoided them.

Behind the table a bed did double duty as a chair, there being no room for both items of furniture. A large wooden trunk filled most of the space beneath the table, making it impossible to sit there in comfort. However, as even the most cursory glance confirmed, there was nowhere else for it. The trunk and a crude wardrobe made of planks, standing at the foot of the bed, held all the family's belongings — except for the patched stockings and threadbare shirt that hung over the tiny cast-iron cooking range behind the door. Next to the range was the smallest sink and draining board she had ever seen. Since the stockings were a woman's while the shirt was a child's, Katya inferred that Ursus had a wife and at least one infant. She wondered where they were.

"I'm sorry about the heat, Froeken Silver." Ursus waved a hand vaguely toward the range. "It's our only means of cooking."

"Of course," she replied, feeling oddly inadequate. She was wondering if she could ever be reduced to living like this. She just wanted to turn and run.

"Froeken Silver asked what all these people — my neighbours — are *for*," he went on.

"I'm sorry," she replied. "I didn't mean to be overheard."

He chuckled as if she had said something unintentionally funny. Then, more solemnly, he said, "They are *for* a better future." He pointed to the papers on his desk. The *Social Democrat* newspaper was prominent among them.

"Ah." Her wandering gaze alighted on a cubbyhole, half-hidden beside the wardrobe. Where they kept the coal, perhaps.

"Froeken Silver is not interested in politics?" Ursus only just made it a question.

Von Kieler looked up briefly from his reading and said, "Froeken Silver is interested in the whole of life."

Katya was too annoyed to speak at all.

"Is that so?" Ursus asked.

She shrugged irritably. "I'd be interested to know why Herr von Kieler has brought me here — or what he thinks I can do to help."

Ursus laughed pleasantly and punched von Kieler on the arm. His implication was that she'd wiped the floor with him. She wanted to tell the man that he didn't deceive her for a minute; she knew he was the sort who'd say anything to ingratiate himself with any good-looking woman he happened to meet. She wondered what sort of woman fitted into the stockings hanging over the range.

"That's powerful. But what a tragedy." Von Kieler finished reading whatever it was and returned the paper to the table. "Where's Gunilla?" He stared about him as if the tiny garret might still be concealing her somewhere.

Ursus pulled a face. "Scrubbing floors for the gentry ... to put bread in my mouth."

Von Kieler hung his head. "You know they allow me *nothing* — not even the fare for a bus."

"I wouldn't dream of it," Ursus assured him.

"Marianne gives me a bit." His voice developed a sneering tone as he added, "... now she can afford it."

Ursus did not repeat his earlier question, asking after Marianne. Katya realized he did not wish to mention that connection in her presence. She cringed from all that that implied.

"And little Olof?" von Kieler asked sympathetically. "Where is he buried?" To Katya he added, "Their son."

Ursus closed his eyes and shook his head. There was something slightly shifty about the gesture, she realized. "I'm so sorry," she said gently. "Did he die quite recently?"

"It can't be long." The man said reluctantly and nodded toward the cubbyhole.

"He's not actually dead?" von Kieler asked in a bewildered tone.

It took Katya several seconds to realize what that nod toward the cubbyhole meant. Then she turned to him and asked in a horrified tone, "Is he in *there*?"

Ursus shrugged. His eyes fell to the floor.

She wondered why von Kieler had assumed the child to be already dead and buried. "What is it?" she asked. "A fever? Or what?"

"I don't know. Some kind of wasting disease."

"What does the doctor say it is?"

He stared balefully at her but made no reply; perhaps he had not called in the doctor at all.

Too poor?

Surely not. Surely they'd buy medicine rather than ink, paper, and copies of the *Social Democrat?* In any case, the Stockholm Hospital for Sick Children was only just up the street — they'd never turn away a dying child, no matter how poor the parents.

"Well ... we must fetch a doctor at once," she said.

"*We,* Froeken Silver?" There was an edge of irritation in his voice.

She looked at von Kieler, who had not expected this interruption to his parade of *real* people for her benefit. He seemed quite put out by it.

"Tskoh!" She strode to the cubbyhole and squatted to peer inside — inevitably blocking off most of the light. It was a mere three paces and she realized that if she'd taken only one of them earlier she'd have seen the little boy's tousled head, lying on a rolled-up overcoat for a pillow, just inside the low arch that framed the alcove; if he lived another year, he would outgrow the space entirely.

He was shivering gently but lay otherwise still — unnaturally still, she thought — not tossing and turning as had other cases of fever she had seen. Yet he was certainly hot. She drew off her gloves and touched his brow. It almost burned.

"Your kind-heartedness does you great credit, Froeken Silver ..." Ursus began. But his voice petered out when she turned and stared at him.

She felt the boy's lips. They were hot and dry. All his skin was hot and dry. "He's parched," she said. "Bring me some water."

Ursus shrugged and turned to stare out of the window. It was von Kieler who filled the tumbler and brought it to her.

She had to draw the little lad half out of the alcove and prop him against her lap before she could offer him a sip. Several times he opened his eyes and stared unseeingly about him, rolling them at random. She held the cup to his lips but he made no response.

She dipped a finger in the water and wiped it across his slackly open lips. His face was angelic. Then she repeated the action, this time putting a little on his tongue. She had to repeat it several times more before he responded, extruding his tongue, following her finger for more. She gave him more. He smacked his lips feebly.

"We've been through all that," Ursus told her sadly. "Froeken Silver is merely prolonging his torment."

She ignored him and held the cup to the boy's lips. By instinct he supped greedily at the water — sucking mostly air, for she was afraid of choking him with a flood of water. He coughed and gasped. Katya, feeling the power of his muscles against her lap, realized he was stronger than his present state of collapse made him seem. She put the cup again to his lips, this time allowing him to sup deeper. And he, by some instinct — for he was still unconscious — moderated his gulp to something his enfeebled tongue could cope with.

"I'm sure it's very good of Froeken Silver," his father said crossly.

She continued to ignore him. Soon the boy had taken half the cup.

"He'll bring it all up in a minute," Ursus warned. "He hasn't kept anything down for days."

"How long has it ...?" von Kieler ventured soothingly.

"More than a week. He's not been well for months, though."

"Is it merely lack of money?" Katya asked.

"Is it *merely* lack of money!" Ursus echoed scornfully. "No, Froeken Silver, it is capitalist greed. It is the indifference of the full-bellied world. My son must die so that Max Lejonkrona and his like can keep von Kieler's sister, and women like her, in luxury for a few hours' pleasure each week." He stared out of the window again and repeated in disgust, "Is it merely lack of money!"

He had used Max's name deliberately, she realized — to see whether it meant anything to her. She hoped she had given nothing away. "All I meant," she insisted, "was — is it merely lack of money that has prevented Herr Ursus from calling in the doctor?"

"The doctor came last week," he replied grudgingly. "It was he who told us to abandon hope. He took no fee."

Katya was uncertain of herself now. "Has Herr Ursus tried the hospital?" she asked in a much softer tone.

Ursus saw it as a chance to rub in a little more salt: "It's nothing remarkable, Froeken Silver. Not in tenements like these. The doctors round here see dozens of equally hopeless cases every week — and dozens of deaths to prove they were right."

"But … the hospital?"

He became angry then. "Who in the Devil's name do you think you are!" His use of *du* was contemptuous. "You come waltzing in here like Lady Bountiful …"

She started to speak over him: "What you're saying is that one doctor has told you to allow your son to die, and because he very decently charged no fee, you have very decently decided not to bother him or anyone else!" She turned to von Kieler and snapped, "What's that article about? I'll bet it's a graveside oration for this poor child!"

He could not look her in the face.

"My God!" she shouted at Ursus. "You can't wait for it to happen, can you!"

The boy stirred on her lap and gave a little croak; again he opened his eyes and rolled them around at random.

"Well let's see about *that*!" she exclaimed, gathering his little birdlike body into her arms and staggering a little as she rose, hugging him to her.

"Where are you taking him?" Ursus asked.

"Where d'you think!" She thrust herself past him. "You two carry on." She nodded at the table and its litter of important papers. "Don't let this interfere."

"Katya …" von Kieler murmured unhappily.

"Goodbye, Herr von Kieler," she called from the door. "I'm sorry your clever little lesson has turned out to be directed at you rather than at me!"

"I'll come with you." Ursus reached his coat from its hook.

Common sense restrained her anger long enough for her to point out, quite reasonably, that the people in the hospital might be more inclined to accept the child if she brought him in alone. "I'll say I found him in a doorway," she told them.

As she started down the stair she heard von Kieler say, "She's probably right, old fellow."

And Ursus actually laughed! "A tactician!" he cried. "We could do with a lass like her." She thought she heard him add, "Don't lose touch, whatever you do!"

*H*e was waiting for her when she left her apartment the following Saturday morning, two days after the incident with Ursus in Getgraend. "Oh no, Herr von Kieler!" she groaned. "If you do not leave me alone, I shall find a policemen and hand you in charge."

"Little Olof is out of danger," he said.

"I know. I telephoned the hospital last night from the … from where I work. His *devoted* father will have to devote his funeral oration to some other poor child."

"I've seen through Ursus," the young man replied bitterly. "I'll have nothing more to do with them."

"I suppose it's too much to hope for — that you might also have taken a disliking to me?"

"You were magnificent, Froeken Silver!" He was calling her *ni* at last. "My feelings toward you are … are …"

She walked past him and set off at a brisk pace across the little square. "I shall be magnificently late for work, if I stand here any longer," she called back to him. "Thank you for your compliments but please leave me alone now."

He ran and caught up with her. "You mean to say you *work?*" he asked in amazement.

"Very hard."

"Where?" His tone was suspicious.

"That's no business of yours." They had reached the far side of the square by now.

"I hope you don't imagine that Max Lejonkrona is in love with my sister," he exclaimed suddenly.

"And that is no business of *mine*," she replied. "It's hardly any of yours, either. She's only your half-sister."

He ignored her objections. "He's made her his mistress for one reason only — so that he can continue to spy on me."

They reached the waterside. It suddenly occurred to her that, if she took the ferry, he'd only follow her aboard — and she doubted he'd moderate his absurd style of conversation just because there were other passengers near by. She glanced about for some sign of a droshky but, with the city filling up for the Exhibition, they had grown rarer than hens' teeth. She decided to walk up Skeppsbron, then, even though it would make her late. They'd almost certainly meet a policeman up near the palace, and she could be rid of him after that.

When she turned away from the ferry he said, "Hah! I called your bluff, didn't I! I was right in the first place. You're not going to work at all. Parasites like you and Lejonkrona don't know the meaning of the word."

She gave him a pitying glance as she set out at her usual cracking pace, up the quay toward the palace. "Max must have hurt you very badly once upon a time," she remarked.

Von Kieler paid her no heed. "I suppose you know he is in the secret police?" he said. "Getting cashiered like that was a very good cloak. A gay bachelor dog! No one would ever suspect."

She halted and stamped her foot angrily. "One more word like this and I'll push you over the edge of this quay."

"I already tried that," he said calmly. "It didn't work. Anyway, it's the truth. D'you realize something? You always lose your temper when I tell you a truth you'd rather not hear."

Again she had the suspicion that the only way to deal with him was to humour him in little things. "Secret police!" she sneered. "You haven't a shred of evidence for saying such a thing."

"You'll see one day," he told her with that maddening calm of his — or was it a *mad* calm? she suddenly wondered. "He's been spying on me for some years now. And as for evidence — you just don't know what to look for. To a trained observer like me he gives himself away all the time."

"Let me hear one example," she challenged him.

"All right. Haven't you noticed, for instance, how he makes friends with people everywhere he goes? Letter carriers, janitors, ticket collectors, park attendants ... waiters. Not the usual chums for leeches of his class. And have you noticed how he's forever asking them questions? He's a big, bland, genial sponge — going around Stockholm, soaking up little puddles of information."

She stopped and stared at him balefully. "This is absurd, absurd, *absurd!*" she told him. "Max Lejonkrona is just a naturally gregarious ... No! I am not going to dignify your charges by replying to them. Just go away, will you? You are a pathetic ... absurd ..."

"Likeable?" he suggested with a smile.

She stopped in her tracks, closed her eyes, and shook her head. "You *could* be," she urged. "You could be *very* likeable."

"If?" he asked eagerly. "Oh, Froeken Silver — I'd do anything to make you like me!"

"If you weren't *you*," she told him harshly.

"You don't even know me."

She saw a chance then — at least to keep him under some kind of social restraint until she could point out a policeman and compel him to behave. "Tell me about yourself, then," she said gently; she even linked arms with him and patted his wrist encouragingly.

"The only thing you need know about me," he said, "is that I cannot get you out of my mind. I think about you all the time. You're in great danger, you know — staying in Lejonkrona's place. I can't stop worrying for you."

She sighed with exasperation. From their present position on the quay, Sibyllegatan, though almost a mile away on foot, was just beyond the National Gallery; and the gallery lay just across a narrow strip of water. It was tempting to leap in and swim for it. Or push him in and run.

"You really are asking for that ducking," she warned him.

"I told you — it didn't work."

"What d'you mean?"

"I tried to drown myself yesterday ..."

"That is not a fit subject for joking," she said severely.

"Oh, I'm not joking. It's in all the papers this morning. I saw how disgusted you were with me over what happened in Getgraend, and so I thought drowning would be a way of purifying myself ..."

She clutched tight to him. "Please!" she begged. "Please tell me this is all a joke — in the worst of taste — but a joke."

"I think the reason I thought so strongly of death," he went on, as if she had not interrupted, "is because *you're* so full of life. Most people aren't. In fact most of us are dead. I thought it was capitalism that killed them but I can see now I was wrong. So now I don't know what it is. But there's *some* kind of malevolent power stalking the land and burying the dead inside the brains of the living. We have these rituals where we carry our corpses out to the cemetery and put them in nailed-down boxes into a deep hole and then pile a couple of tons of earth on top of them ..."

"Not to mention the dead weight of insincere graveside eulogies!" she commented. It was no joke but a forlorn attempt to escape from the toils of his madness — for she was now quite sure he was mad.

"Exactly," he said. "We think we leave them safely buried out there in the frozen ground. But somehow they get free again, and we carry them back home with us." He tapped his forehead. "Like scars inside here. We wear their shrouds as if nothing else can protect us from the world."

He stopped in his tracks, closed his eyes, hung his head. "Oh, God, my brain hurts so much sometimes! I thought about all that while I was under the water, waiting to drown. And then I thought of you — and I realized you are not like that. If any of the dead ever made the mistake of hiding away inside *your* mind, Froeken Silver, you'd bring them back to life! That's when I wanted to live again. I wanted you to bring *me* back to life."

"But you only jumped into the water in the first place because of me," she objected. "Or so you claim."

"I know!" He laughed and turned his baby-boy eyes on her. "Isn't it insane?"

By now they were at the foot of the battlemented wall on that eastern side of the palace. There a triangle of stone steps rose to a small, central gate. He let go of her, shuffled over to it, leaned his forehead against the stone, and communed with his own shadow.

Katya, now frightened as well as bewildered, stared about her and then turned her gaze skyward. To her surprise she found herself looking straight into the eyes of Count Magnus Hamilton. She felt sure it was him. He was standing between two of the castellations, silhouetted against the sky, which made his features hard to discern. Then the sun emerged fully from behind a thin veil of cloud and at that she was certain of him. He'd probably been changing the guard.

All her fears vanished and, on impulse, she blew him a kiss. A moment later she realized there had been an element of unconscious calculation in the gesture — she was reassuring him, in case he had seen her arm-in-arm with von Kieler.

The madman himself saw her shadow miming the kiss upon the stone near his feet. He glanced sharply at her and then upward to the battlements; but Magnus had withdrawn as suddenly as he had appeared. "Why did you do that?" he asked.

"*Le bon dieu,*" she replied, waving at the sky and assuming a gaiety she certainly did not feel.

"Ah yes," he said enthusiastically, picking up her lead at once. "Life is good! We should take it by storm! In both hands. We should shake its fruits off the branches. That's another thing I really wanted to tell you. Never do things by halves!"

They set off again in a much happier spirit, making for the bridge to the northern parts of the city. But when the shadow of the northern ramparts to the palace engulfed them, his mood darkened again. "I'll bet I'm right about Lejonkrona," he said aloud, but as if to himself. When he heard her groan he added, "No, listen! I'll bet he asked all about me when you got home on Thursday evening."

"Of course he didn't! Look — see that policeman over there?"

He ignored her question. "Well then, he's biding his time, you see — putting you off your guard."

"Since I'm not particularly *on* my guard, that would be a fairly ..."

"I'll bet he mentioned me *last* night, then. I'm absolutely sure our visit to Ursus was noted."

"As a matter of fact, the only thing he mentioned last night was a grand masked ball at Valholm tonight — to which he is escorting me. In other words — not only do I have to do my normal day's work at the ... my normal day's work, but I also have to snatch a few hours' rest and then change into my mask and costume. So the last thing I want or need is this sort of outpouring of utter gibberish from you."

"Oh well, in that case I'll burden you no further," he said cheerfully. And, hands in pockets, whistling a tune like any errand boy, he turned on his heel and walked back the way they had come.

"If only I'd known it was as easy as that!" she murmured to herself as she watched his receding figure. She did not know then that he, too, was invited to the ball at Valholm.

osie had also been invited to Valholm, not just for the ball but for the whole Friday-to-Monday. She was an old friend of Magnus's father, whose new young countess needed someone who could talk her native tongue. So Rosie had travelled up to the castle by steamer on the Friday morning. It was early Saturday evening, however, before Katya and Max — and several dozen other guests — joined the special coaches for the hour-long train journey to Uppsala. Naturally they were all masked already. Katya was wearing her St Pat's ballgown for the first time since coming to Sweden. Since most of the revellers knew each other, they soon formed pretty good guesses as to who was who. Max had posed no challenge at all; everybody knew him and he knew everybody. But Katya set them an intriguing problem, for nobody could think who on earth she was. She thus became a kind of *tabula rasa* on which each wrote his or her own fantasies large. She was Max's new mistress. She was a foreign princess … a member of the Russian court, some of whom were then on a private visit to the Swedish court … an ex-mistress of Magnus's whom Max was bringing as an embarrassing joke. Someone overheard her make a remark in English and then she became the new Irish Countess's elder sister, coming to surprise her.

It was shortly after nine o'clock as they emerged from the station.

"I must say, Max," she told him. "I had my doubts that a masked ball could possibly succeed in circumstances where practically everybody knows everybody else. But now I realize it's the only kind that *could* succeed."

He looked at her, surprised she could think such an obvious discovery worthy of the slightest comment. "Of course, Princess," he said. "A masked ball among strangers would be just like daily life in fancy dress."

Every droshky in the city was pressed into service that night as well as every carriage in the Hamilton stables; even two large hay wagons had been fitted out with benches, turning them into giant jaunting cars. These lumbering vehicles, though the slowest, proved the most popular, for the evening was warm, bordering on hot, and the chance of an open-air ride was inviting. Katya and Max were lucky to find a place on the second wagon, which set off as soon as they were seated.

Valholm lay in open country about one Swedish mile — or a little over ten kilometres — south of the town, carrying them back in the direction of Stockholm. The sun, half an hour short of setting, was an enormous ball of dull red fire, weak enough to stare at without discomfort. It hung, slightly egg shaped, over the treetops to their right, colouring everything it touched and lending even the pale city-dwellers the outward hues of a rude, bumpkin health. And more than the mere outward hues, perhaps, for the whole party, which had rather languished in the heat of the train carriages, now burst into effervescent life. Jocular insults were exchanged, embarrassing memories revived — all under the pretence that none of the speakers realized that the subjects of the jokes and reminiscences were among the company. And many a half-promise was given, too, with eyes that sparkled in the lambent fire of that summer's evening. Their laughter rose like thistledown and floated away on the breezeless air of the evening.

Despite their lumbering pace they were soon out into the country, for Uppsala was a village of a city. The landscape had changed little since the days of the Vikings — an intimate mixture of grazing and woodland, interspersed with numerous rocky outcrops that neither farmer nor forest could colonize successfully. The road, unfenced for the most part, meandered this way and that, as if it had been forced to make do with whatever land the plough and the axe had grudged it; every now and then — and with surprising frequency, Katya thought, considering how unpopulated the countryside seemed — it spawned a dusty lane that snaked across the terrain, leading, no doubt, to some hinterland farm. A mere handful of these dwellings were built close to the road — plain, stolid structures of wood, all stained a uniform reddish brown with a waste product from the copper smelters in Falun, the accidental colourists to the Swedish nation. Katya tried counting and never saw more than five dwellings in view at any one time.

"Not tired already, I hope?" Max asked when he noticed she had been silent for more than a minute.

"No, I was just thinking how different this is from Ireland. It's the same sort of farming — pasture, cattle, a bit of corn, barley, and so on — but you couldn't have a more different landscape. There's nothing here an Irishman would recognize as a village. Houses all tightly huddled together."

"Oh, here they feel stifled half to death if there are neighbours within a kilometre!"

She chuckled. "D'you think one could turn Swedes into Irishmen just by moving all their houses closer together?"

"It would be an interesting experiment," he commented. "It would certainly fill a wet Sunday afternoon."

"Why d'you keep looking round like that, Max?"

"Habit."

"Rubbish! You have eyes like the Sphinx, normally. Tonight you're like a travelling rat, as we say in Ireland."

He leaned toward her and murmured, "I just want to see which dresses go with which ladies while it's still light enough to be sure which ladies go with which dresses. If you see what I mean?"

"I'm trying not to, I think. Why bother? Don't the women here keep going into the cloakroom and exchanging dresses to confuse you? That's what we do in Ireland."

For a moment he believed her; then he pretended to shoot himself in the head.

"Anyway," she said, "if you're squiring me, you shouldn't be taking *any* notice of the other ladies, at all."

"Dear Katya!" He raised a finger and brushed her cheek. "I'll be lucky to snatch one dance with you — and well you know it. You'll prance the night away with every last man between the ages of sixteen and a hundred. And, despite the crippling handicap of a mask, you'll leave a string of broken hearts in your wake."

She laughed. "Oh yes — and on the stroke of midnight I'll go dashing down the front steps, leaving only a glass slipper behind!"

He conceded the point with a wave of both hands. "For example."

They were interrupted by a burble of pleasure from the front of the wagon. Valholm was in sight at last.

"Actually," Max said when he realized how close they were, "you'll have to rewrite the scene with the glass slipper. As you see, there are no front steps."

But Katya hardly heard him. She had turned right round and was kneeling on the bench, with the last of the setting sun now behind her. Had they arrived a few seconds later, her image of Valholm — an image she knew she'd carry for the rest of her days — would have been entirely different.

She thought she had never seen anything quite so lovely. The sun, already half-consumed by the western skyline, touched every stone with gilt and set a pearly fire in each pane of glass, making the whole sing out against the darkling purple of the eastern sky. The castle itself — the original stone tower — had been augmented and civilized down the centuries by wings and annexes of a more graceful order, classical buildings with pedimented windows and porticoed doors. Like a perfect model, this precious cluster nestled on the shores of a long, narrow bay, part of Lake Maelar, whose waters also lapped the freshwater shore of Gamla Stan and, indeed, stretched a further ten Swedish miles to the west. Between it and the approaching wagon was about a furlong of well-cropped deerpark; this grass, in turn, was bordered at the road's edge by a stout wall of stone, high enough to keep back a herd of complaisant deer, low enough for the passengers on the wagon to see over it.

Thus the view divided into a series of more or less horizontal bands of vivid colour — the pale ochre of the stone wall, the verdant green of the spring turf, the every-green-in-the-paintbox of the trees by the water's edge, the hot, dark ultramarine of the inlet, and the thunderous prussian blue of the approaching night — all with the golden, nacreous jewel of Valholm as their focal point.

And then, to complete what even the most epicurean taste would have to concede was already a sensual feast, the strains of music came drifting over the park, spanking country gavottes whose energetic pace filled the latest arrivals with impatience for their journey to be done.

By a perfect stroke of accidental timing, the sun vanished — abdicated, one could say — as they turned in at the gate and plunged into the gloomy maw of the tree-lined avenue. In that sudden tumble into darkness, the night claimed them and they became its creatures until dawn.

"Damn!" Max muttered under his breath.

"What?" she asked, and then changed it to, "Actually, do I know you, kind sir?"

"The lady in the blue floral dress — I've already forgotten who she is. Is she Ann-Sophie von Falkenberg or Ingrid Berzelius? I'm sure they were side by side."

She laughed. "You'd make a rotten policeman, Max."

He turned and looked at her sharply and then hung his head and sucked a penitential finger.

"When are you going to put on *your* mask?" she asked.

He punched her playfully.

The trees gave out into open deerpark about two hundred yards short of the castle. Once there had been a moat at that point, when the castle had been a fortress; now it was a haha, where periwinkle and ferns vied for supremacy. From there to the castle door their way was lighted with flares of burning pitch whose fat, lazy flames were like beckoning witches' fingers.

A tall, dashing corsair with a gashed kerchief as his mask, greeted them at the door, naming himself as Barbare and welcoming them by whatever absurd name they chose to give themselves. In case anyone should be so foolish as to suppose from his waxed moustaches that he was Count Magnus Hamilton, he explained he was, in fact, a distant cousin of the family — chosen to welcome them precisely because no one would recognize him.

"Madame de Pompadour," Katya said as he kissed her hand — or, rather, "Madame de Peaume-pa-deauer," in the heavy Scanian accent she now assumed, knowing that her "Dublin-Stockholmska" would give her away at once. She was sure he did not recognize her.

She was surprised there was no control of the arrivals at all — no invitation tickets to collect, no servants making discreet inquiries by the haha. But then she realized she was comparing metropolitan Dublin with rural Sweden; she doubted they'd have any controls in Ballyjamesduff, either.

The moment that hurdle was over, Max grabbed her by the wrist and cavorted with her through the great hall. It was a vast, gloomy, echoing barn, the barbaric heart of the Hamilton dynasty in Sweden, displaying more implements of sudden death than she had ever seen gathered under one roof. She felt glad there was a proper ballroom beyond; the only dances suitable for this ancient mead hall would be sword dances, flings, and hoolies. They swept onward, into the ballroom, where they joined in at once, in the middle of a lively jig. After two energetic circuits they became aware that the ballroom windows, which were really glass doors of the kind known as "french windows," were open onto the terrace and that people were dancing out there as well. Max led her that way to join them, for the ballroom was somewhat airless.

They had not realized there was a small band playing out there, too — the same tune but not quite in the same tempo. Their failure to synchronize was not for want of trying, but the harder they tried, the more they "hunted around" the rhythm set by the interior band, sometimes giving the timing to the dancers, sometimes taking it from them. As it happened, both bands were in exact if accidental agreement as Max and Katya danced across the threshold between the two. So there was a curious moment when the sound seemed to be coming from both sides at once — or, rather, from no side at all; it seemed, instead, to be springing from somewhere in the middle of her head. It was a curious sensation, like the early stage of intoxication but without the fuzziness and nausea. Several times before the jig came to an end she induced Max to lead her back and forth through one or other of the french windows to enjoy the sensation once more.

When the music ended they cooled off with refreshing draughts of a wine cup, which Martin, the old Count's valet, assured them had hardly a drop of danger in it. The old Count himself made his appearance before the next set of dances began; his new Countess was on his arm. They were masked, of course, but Katya would have known him at once, simply by his bearing. Give or take half a century, he was Magnus to a T — tall, slim, graceful ... the very image of self-assurance. A peacock in his pride, indeed. The new young Countess, by contrast, looked as if she were barely out of the nursery; her mask did nothing for her confidence and she clung to her husband and peered about her in smiling bewilderment, like a child being allowed to stay up late.

"Poor thing!" Katya murmured. "How can Magnus be so harsh about her? She looks as if one gust of a breeze would carry her off!"

"Poor thing, my foot!" Max retorted. "Don't you worry on her account. She wears the old boy round her little finger."

Katya stared again at the couple and was bewildered, not knowing whether to trust her own eyes or Max's confident assertion.

Max chuckled and said, "You know what the old count's valet told him? The day after the wedding he said, 'Well, Martin, what d'you think of my new countess, eh?' and old Martin just sniffed and said, 'The Count is dining on what should have been his breakfast!'"

Then the music began again and she was whisked onto the floor by the first of many young gentlemen, all determined to discover who she was — without, of course, breaking the law of the occasion and asking her directly. But, as she replied only in French and claimed to know nothing very much of Swedish or any other tongue, they got no more forward than when they started.

One or two tried pumping Max. "She's not French at all, is she!" they insisted. "The way she rolls her rs — it's too too horribly provincial if she's French. She's only pretending not to speak Swedish. She's from Scania, isn't she!"

"For example," Max said.

Of course, Katya did not mind in the least, for it guaranteed her a steady flow of invitations to dance or promenade and she was never short of a partner all evening. Shortly before midnight, when the masks were to come off anyway, she faced her greatest test when Magnus, still hopelessly "disguised" as Barbare the Corsair, asked her onto the floor. It was a rather stately waltz of the old-fashioned kind, which allowed plenty of time and breath for conversation.

After a few conventional pleasantries in French she relapsed into her own parody of the Scanian dialect, saying, "The Hamiltons are so lucky to have a place like this, don't you think, Barbare? I understand they stole it from the original owners — but then I suppose you, as a pirate yourself, would approve of that?"

There was a moment of tension, a fumbled step or two, and then he smiled knowingly; she felt sure he had penetrated her disguise. But he went on pretending he hadn't. "Not a bit of it, Madame de Pompadour," he retorted scornfully. "When it comes to piracy these

Hamiltons are mere babes in arms. The way they stole Valholm dishonours the noble profession of thief, I assure you. They took it with the king's *blessing!* Did you ever hear of anything so tame! But when a true pirate steals something, he waits for no man's permission — nor woman's either."

"Oh, and what, pray, have you stolen lately?" she teased.

"Plenty of these," he said, pressing his lips suddenly to hers.

She forgot everything then and yielded to the moment, kissing him back with fervour. He had timed it perfectly, beginning his kiss when they were a few paces short of a niche between the last of the windows onto the terrace and the balustrade that protected its edge; he swept her into the recess and pressed her tight against the still-warm stone, and all without once breaking the delightful contact between them. She shivered. Her lips tingled. There were stars in her veins. Her innards turned hollow as she put her arms around him and pulled him tight against her.

Then she felt the tension grow within him once again. Subtly, his hands began to move up and down her back, as the blindfold person's hands stray in a game of blind-man's-buff, trying to identify the victim he's caught. She realized he had not, in fact, recognized her earlier.

"Who are you?" he gasped as they broke for breath. "Please! I have to know." He lifted trembling fingers to her mask.

But she held it tight where it was. "No! There are some laws that even pirates must obey. Besides, it's only five minutes to midnight."

"And then I'll know anyway! So why can't I know now? What's five minutes?"

She snuggled into his arms. "Time that is surely given us for some purpose," she murmured, dabbing several warm little kisses on his lips. But then, in sadder tones, she warned him: "Actually, I'm sorry to have to tell you that you won't even know at midnight. That's when this dress turns back into rags, don't you know, and I flee from your castle leaving only a glass slipper behind."

"*My* castle! You know who I am, then?" he asked in dismay.

In fact, Katya had guessed wrongly that they had five minutes to go, for at that very moment two footmen went through the ballroom and out onto the terrace, beating brass trays with soup ladles. A moment later they fell silent and then the midnight chimes of the stables clock rang out. Champagne corks popped and everybody surged back into the ballroom to take up a glass. Magnus and Katya came somewhat reluctantly out of hiding to join them.

When everyone had a glass, the bands, now combined in the one room, played "Sweet Maidens Say Not No!" — the Second Epistle of Carl Michael Bellman's Rabelaisian hero Fredman (described as "a watchmaker without a watch, a workshop, or a business"). When they reached the final lines — to the effect that the putting down of liquor and the laying down of girls is the central dogma of "Saint" Fredman's religion — there was a universal *skaal!* and a frenzied tearing-off of masks all round.

"You!" was the universal cry, simulating an amazement hardly any of them felt.

Magnus turned to Katya and raised a hand to her mask, but she gripped his wrist and held him off a moment longer. "You may be very sorry if you do," she said — still in her heavy dialect.

"I do know you, then?" he asked.

"Sometimes I wonder. If you had ever kissed me before tonight, none of these doubts would be possible. Shall I run away and leave just a glass slipper behind?"

She darted from him and tripped back outside, laughing gaily. Dozens of eyes followed her. Bewilderment changed to intrigue when they saw, storming in her wake, Count Magnus Hamilton, mask in hand, revealed at last — or, rather, not so much revealed as *relieved* of his absurdly inadequate disguise.

He slipped his mask back on again when he spied her standing at the balustrade, staring out into the dark. Then, as he drew near, he made a parade of taking it off, saying, "You already know me, anyway. Now for you!" He reached to unmask her once again.

It was too good a joke to resist. She plucked her own mask off and stared at him in horror. "You!" she exclaimed. "Oh my God!" She crammed all her fingers between her teeth and backed away, appalled.

His jaw clamped tight and he held his breath. She saw that he genuinely had not recognized her but was now determined to pretend he had. Perhaps his earlier smile of apparent recognition had been a kind of insurance against a moment like this — for she was not the only female at Valholm that night with the power to embarrass him, one way or another. "Don't imagine you can deceive me," he said coldly. "You knew it was me. Why else did you talk about running away from *my* castle?"

"My dear man!" She stared at him as if she thought he was unhinged. "I thought you were your *father*, of course!"

The horror in his expression was worth it. But that, she decided, was enough. She burst out laughing and said, "Oh, Magnus, my dear! Every time we meet, we quarrel! Why do we always quarrel?" She raised her arms and slipped them round his neck. "Didn't you like it when we kissed?"

Still disgruntled, he nonetheless succumbed to a temptation that would have stripped the budding halo off St Anthony himself and lost himself once more in her embrace. "Did you really think I was my father?" he murmured. "I knew it was you all along. You came with Lejonkrona — who else could you have been?"

She rested her head on his chest and gave a happy sigh. "So when you kissed me like that just now — with such wonderful passion — you knew it was awkward, quarrelsome old me! Oh, Magnus, does that mean we're now going to take it nice and slowly? And not rush at any fences?"

He made several noncommittal noises and said it was time for supper. He offered her his arm.

"You're very like your father in some ways," she said fondly as she took it and walked with him back to the ballroom.

"Oh?" he asked warily. "Name one."

"Well, you can now have for *supper* what you might very well have enjoyed for *breakfast* — if you hadn't been so stubborn."

She clutched his arm tight to prevent his running away.

Eventually he gave way to his laughter.

*T*he moment she saw the young Countess close to and without her mask, Katya was certain they had met somewhere before. They spoke in English from the start, of course, for the girl had acquired only a little Swedish in the few months since her marriage. Her first words to Katya were to compliment her on her command of the difficult "foreign" tongue.

She was like a delicate china rose, Katya thought; you wanted to swaddle her up and put her away somewhere safe. "Well, now," she replied, "to tell the truth, I'm Dublin born and reared. And — if I may presume, Countess — I fancy we've met there at some time. You are a Hennessy by birth, I gather? Is it your father is the wine importer — with premises down on Ussher's Quay? And you live out along Ailesbury Road?"

The Countess was delighted. "The very same!"

"Then I know where we've met before. In fact, we've never met — if that's not too Irish. But we had adjacent boxes at the subscription concert last ... September was it?"

"Oh stop!" The other fanned her face. "It was October, and I don't ever wish to remember it again. I dropped my programme and it fell on the Dean of St Patrick's lap. Don't you remember?"

Katya chuckled. "Well, I do, but I wasn't going to bring it up now. Anyway, what of it? Sure that could happen to anyone."

The Countess pulled a naughty-girl face. "But you see I'd drawn a heart pierced by a Cupid's arrow on it. I was going to write the Count's name there and mine but I dropped it before that part. And the *look* the Dean kept giving me after that! Well, I swear I got married just in time. A modest, pious Catholic girl like me — throwing myself at a grand Protestant fellow like him — and in public — what must he have thought!"

They laughed, but Katya realized how neatly the Hennessy girl had disposed of the question that lies uppermost when any two Irish people meet. The Hennessys were a well-known RC family in Dublin;

there was no need even to mention the fact as the Countess had done. But that had not been her purpose; she had answered the *other* unspoken question: "Did you have to change your faith in order to marry the Count?"

"But in that case you *are* Swedish, Miss ... did you say Silver?" The surname puzzled her.

"Wait till I tell you." Katya put a conspiratorial finger to her lips. "I'd not wish it to go all round Stockholm, but if you'll keep it to yourself, here's the way of it."

She recounted her story briefly to Dora — as the Countess asked Katya to call her — stressing all the reasons for not using her proper name until next month, when she would safely come of age.

"And so far," Dora asked, "it's all going well?"

Katya smiled and held up her hands, showing her fingers gripping both thumbs.

"You mean it's a bit of a fight?" Dora guessed.

"No! You know — hold thumbs? Wish me luck? Touch wood. That sort of thing."

The penny dropped and Dora laughed. "Actually, in Dublin we say 'keep your fingers crossed,' in case you've forgotten." She broke off and her eyes, staring over Katya's shoulder, lit up. "Oh, Magnus!" she exclaimed. "Do come and sit by me. Your friend's just been telling me all her adventures — and it turns out we sat in adjacent boxes at a concert in Dublin last autumn. Isn't it amazing!"

From Magnus's demeanour Katya was sure he had just been hoping to flit unnoticed past the doorway; she had never seen him so ill at ease. He did as she bade and, though the little sofa allowed only an inch or so of space between them, he made the most of it. When she leaned back, he sat forward, and vice versa. And every time her hand brushed against him, or even a stray frill of her dress, he jumped as if it gave him electric shocks.

They talked of this and that for a while — chiefly of the guests and which of them had come in the cleverest disguises; and then the conversation turned to those who had sent their regrets instead. Dora surprised Katya by her gift for remembering so many people, most of whom could have been nothing more than names on a list to her. Her ears pricked up, however, when Dora remarked, "There was also a young man called von Kieler. He sent a very strange note of regret. Your friend Lejonkrona brought it." The young Countess became aware that her words were significant to Katya and, though she spoke throughout to her stepson, her eyes darted toward Katya several times, eager to miss nothing of her response to this news.

Katya realized that this "porcelain doll" had a formidable side to her character, just as Max had said. A lot of people were going to underestimate her, and to their cost.

Magnus shifted uncomfortably. "I believe they have family trouble of some kind," he said, darting several glances at Katya as he spoke.

"Would that be a *Leif* von Kieler?" she asked.

He nodded. "D'you know him?"

"Why do you ask? You saw me with him yesterday — below the palace wall."

He lowered his gaze.

"Actually," she went on, "I wouldn't claim to *know* him. I doubt anyone really knows him ..."

"Lejonkrona does. They've been friends since childhood."

Katya frowned. "And yet he didn't recognize Leif's ..."

"What?"

She shook her head — remembering that Marianne's remark that it was all too complicated to explain. "Max didn't say a word to me," was all she said.

"He probably didn't want to spoil the occasion for you."

Katya took the bull by the horns then. "Is Leif von Kieler in trouble with the police?" she asked directly.

He shrugged. "I honestly don't know." He still found it difficult to look her in the eye.

Dora's head went right-left-right-left throughout this exchange.

Katya pressed him. "But you've heard something, I can tell."

He yielded to her persistence at last. "I *heard* he was arrested but I don't necessarily believe everything I hear."

Katya thought of the handsome but strange young man who had pestered the life out of her over the last three days and she felt a sudden, and surprising, sympathy for him — and anger, too, at the stupid people who could imagine he was a threat to anyone but himself. On the other hand ... he had been exceedingly vexatious.

Perhaps a brief visit to the cells might be just the sort of shock the young fellow needed.

"Dear me!" Dora realized she had extracted the last nugget from the present lode. "Poor young man! Still, the von Kielers are a very good family from all I hear. I've no doubt it can all be smoothed out amicably when the brouhaha dies down." She smiled at them. "And now, Magnus!" She leaned back and, catching him by the arm, pulled him back beside her. "Your nerves are all on edge, man. Relax a moment and tell me what sort of evening you've had and who you've danced with — and who's the Cinderella of the ball for you?" She winked at Katya.

The change in Magnus was extraordinary. He trembled; his voice shook; he hunted for words that would normally trip off his tongue; he kept wiping the palms of his hands along the sides of his thighs. The more Dora teased him — and Katya could see she understood very well she *was* teasing him — the worse he became.

At last Katya came to his rescue. She stretched out her hand and said, "Come on, Magnus! We're wasting two very fine bands down there. Let's go and hunt for that glass slipper."

He took the offer gratefully but the moment they were out in the corridor that led to the top of the grand staircase, he lowered his eyes again and mumbled, "Actually, Katya, there are ... er, one or two things I have to do behind the scenes. Would you think me terribly ungallant if I were to postpone our glass-slipper hunt for ... an hour or so?"

By way of reply she drew him into a doorway and raised her lips for a kiss. But he kissed her with such passion, and his heartbeat was so violent against her own bosom, that she grew frightened and pushed him away again. Their eyes dwelled a moment, each in full audit of the other — and then she understood what effect Dora had had on him.

He turned and drifted away from her, a picture of shame and dejection. She wanted to run after him, tell him she understood, say it was all right. But she knew that would only horrify him all the more. He was not ready to believe that she *could* understand such feelings. He would then have nothing left to live up to.

"What that fellow needs is a long cruise up the Goeta Canal!"

She turned to discover that Rosie had suddenly appeared at her side. Katya chuckled though she did not feel at all happy. "With or without benefit of clergy?" she asked.

They spoke in English now, as they often did at home.

"Without delay, anyway," Rosie replied.

"Did you see what happened?"

"Where?"

Katya sighed and took the old woman's arm. "Let's go and see whether they've put out more of that lovely sorbet," she said. As they moved off she added, "And let me put my question in another way: How *much* did you see?"

"Of what was taking place on that sofa? Enough to make me say what I said."

They started down the grand staircase. "You've spent most of the day with Dora, I suppose," Katya mused. "Two fellow-countrywomen on the same day! She must think it only amazing."

"Nothing will amaze that one!" Rosie commented. "Unless she wants it to. Some commoners are just bred-in-the-bone to it."

"To what?"

"To marry into the aristocracy, of course."

They reached the halfway landing and paused a moment. "Meaning I am not, I suppose?" Katya said glumly.

Rosie chuckled. "I was referring more to myself, if you want to know. But yes, you're in the same boat, colleen."

"You have boats on the brain tonight, Rosie. Boats in the belfry!"

They started down the last flight. "I doubt he'll repeat the offer now." Katya sighed.

"Did you have words again, or what?"

Katya pulled a face. "We're always having words. I wouldn't mind that. But did you see the look in his eye just now? He's ashamed. What can I do? I want so much to help him." She smiled at several people who passed them, going up; she hoped they were not too proficient in English.

Rosie patted her arm soothingly. "Patience," she said. "That's the only balm. 'Twill serve you well in the end. Men *need* to feel unworthy of us. They have to put us on a pedestal. To them we're the shining example of the western world or we're nothing. Worse than nothing.

If you want my advice — never let him know you understand a thing like that."

Katya nodded glumly. "I know."

They reached the ballroom door. Rosie paused at the threshold and said in a much sprightlier tone, "Meanwhile there's no call to mope. Life is long." She waved her hand at the couples on the dance floor. "Six to four the field — bar one!"

*A*fter several lively dances Katya felt in need of a rest. Also, her conscience was beginning to tug a little; she felt she ought to seek out Max and discover what had really happened to Leif von Kieler. She asked around and was told that Herr Lejonkrona was reliving his student days with a crowd of admiring acolytes in one of the upstairs rooms.

They were all singing when Katya entered — mainly young men and women, sitting around in a circle, some on the floor, some in chairs. It was a student song commemorating one of the worst nights in the history of Uppsala University — the night the whole town ran out of liquor. Max was sitting, pasha-like, on a cushion between two occupied chairs. When he saw her he raised an eyebrow, gave her his lopsided smile, and nudged one of the chairs farther away, making room for her beside him. He managed it all without disrupting the rhythm of the song.

She la-la-lahed the tune as best she could. When the song ended, a woman to Max's right pointed across the circle at him and told him he ought to sing a solo for refusing to join in.

"And what about this young lady?" Max asked, clamping Katya's arm briefly in his fist.

She protested that she'd done her best though she hadn't even known the song.

"Goodness me, how feeble!" He stared about in mock astonishment. "Does the court consider *that* an adequate excuse for not singing?" he asked scornfully.

There was a jovial chorus of noes and boos and calls for her to pay her forfeit and stop whining. She laughed and told them they just wanted their revenge on her for *not* being a Russian princess. However, she was not at all reluctant to sing in public. Even the stiffest and most formal dinner-party in Dublin would always break out in a rash of songs and party-pieces at some stage.

Her favourite Dublin song was the rumbustious "Captain Phibbs's Kitchen," which tells the tale of a cocky young grocer's apprentice who, setting out to seduce a kitchen maid, has the tables turned on him when she forces him at last to the altar. However, since the previous song had also been rather sprightly, she chose instead a slow, tender song, "The Bantry Girls' Lament" — *Oh, who will plough the fields now, and who will sow the corn?* She plunged straight in before her nervousness could overcome her, and she put in all the trills and grace notes of the traditional Irish ballad.

By the end of the second line — *And who will tend the sheep now, and keep them nicely shorn?* — she realized she was singing it with a skill she would never have dared reveal at home in Ireland. There, of course, you could find singers by the dozen who'd put her well down in the halfpenny place when it came to this style of song; she would have died sooner than croak a single note in their august company. But here, free of competition and free, too, of a critical, knowing audience, the talent she did not even know she possessed came welling up from nowhere and took her by surprise. Indeed, it took *her*, most of all, by surprise.

Singing that would bring an Irish gathering to its feet simply poured from her, though she had never attempted any such thing before. When it is properly done, the voice does not so much produce the melody as flutter around it, as a butterfly dances through a sylvan glade, from sunbeam to sunbeam, in and out of the light and shade, never quite settling, and astounding all with the virtuosity of its flight. And here she was — producing those same virtuoso flights for the very first time, but as if she had done them for ever! She had goose-pimples down her spine and she could feel the hair bristle at the nape of her neck, just to hear it.

Her listeners were not to know all this, of course, but even the dullest among them could not help but realize they were hearing something quite out of the ordinary. The silence that fell was absolute as they strained to catch every little nuance of her rendition. The tension was electrifying — the most thrilling public emotion Katya had ever felt.

When she finished — *since Johnny died for Ireland's pride in the foreign land of Spain* — with about eight grace notes for the word *foreign* while the last three words shared a single monotone between them — there was a silence you could have built a church on. The men swallowed hard; several of the women had tears on their cheeks. And there was no applause; it was as if that would be somehow vulgar, or even profane. But it had been a short song, only three verses, and they clearly wanted more though none dared suggest it. They looked to Max, but he seemed to have fallen into a trance. Eventually Katya herself said, "Will I sing you another? Just a short one?"

There were murmurs of relief and a great sigh of contentment went up.

She would dearly have loved to startle them with "Captain Phibbs's Kitchen" then, but the contrast would have been too great. On the other hand, she didn't want another lament; it would give them the impression that the Irish were altogether too Scandinavian in their merrymaking. So she settled for the lyrical strains of "The Sweet Maid of Bunclody and the Lad She Loves so Dear" — *Oh, were I at the moss-house where all pleasures do dwell ...* The words were so ancient and timeworn as to be almost meaningless; but the melody was clear and sweet, and she laid it so simply on the air that you'd swear you'd heard it before somewhere.

This time the final words — *and all I would ask is one kiss from you, sweet* — brought no tears. But smiles there were in plenty, profound smiles, thoughtful smiles, which lingered on like chords from an untouched piano when some sympathetic instrument plays near by. And this time someone dared to say it: "More!"

And everyone chimed in: "Yes ... do! Please!"

"Oh, really!" Katya protested, blushing with pleasure. "I came to listen to you people, not to hog the stage myself. There are so many Swedish songs I don't know."

"Just *one* more," they persisted.

So she gave it them at last:

> Come single belle and beau
> To me now pay attention
> And love I'll plainly show
> Is the divil's own invention!

... all two hundred and fifty verses (or what seemed like it) of "Captain Phibbs's Kitchen." When it was over they laughed genuinely enough but there were no requests for encores. They sang several more songs — student songs, drinking songs, coy hymns to Venus and Bacchus — before someone pointed out that they could sing any old time but meanwhile, the dance floor still beckoned. Most of them rose then and returned to the ballroom; Katya would gladly have overruled her conscience and joined them if Max had not tugged at her sleeve.

"Why have you been hiding this amazing talent all these weeks?" he asked.

"You mean singing?" she replied.

"For example."

"I don't know." She shrugged awkwardly. "I didn't know I could, I suppose. I mean, Ireland's full of people who can sing like that, only much better. I wouldn't have dared ..." The excuses petered out.

"And you *enjoyed* it, too," he went on, as if he had merely been waiting for her to run out of steam.

She nodded, slightly confused by his train of thought, or seeming lack of it.

"Well, well!" he said briskly, rubbing his hands and rising to his feet. "Let's go and dance."

He reached out a hand to assist her.

She rose of her own accord and kept her arm to herself. "Let's talk first," she said. "About Leif von Kieler."

He bridled. "D'you know him?"

She shrugged. "Slightly. Is it true he's been arrested?"

"How did you meet him?"

"Does it matter? He introduced himself to me in the street — with a plausible enough tale ..."

"When?" He became almost agitated — for Max. "You never mentioned it."

"It was only the day before yesterday. After we parted I never gave him a second thought."

"Did he pester you?" Max sat on one of the vacant chairs and pulled her down onto the other.

"Slightly. There's no harm in him. He kept saying he'd fallen in love with me — love at first sight." Apart from discovering what had happened to von Kieler she also wanted to find out whether Max knew of the young man's relationship to Marianne Rydqvist; but she could as yet see no way to approach the subject.

To her surprise he seemed crestfallen at her last statement. She explained: "He told me he'd tried to drown himself because of me — but then he added that the very thought of me was enough to make him abandon the attempt. All sorts of rubbish like that."

Max frowned. "And all within a few hours of meeting you?" he asked dubiously.

Reluctantly she confessed that von Kieler had waylaid her outside the apartment that morning — "Or yesterday morning, it is by now," she said. "What is the mystery about him, Max? Magnus tells me you've known him since childhood."

"Did von Kieler mention me at all?"

She made a hopeless gesture, implying it was all way over her head. "He called you a social parasite. He said you were in the secret police — because you talk to janitors and park-keepers and so on. He's not right in the head, is he."

Max nodded, biting his lip thoughtfully. "He's fallen in with a socialist crowd who give him crazy ideas."

"A man called Ursus," she said. "I met him."

Max almost fell out of his chair. "You? Met Ursus?"

"It was only for about five minutes."

He leaned forward and said earnestly, "Tell me — everything. Precisely how *did* you meet von Kieler? Was Ursus with him?"

He was so eager she began to wonder if the tale about the secret police didn't have the ring of truth after all. She avoided a full confession, however, merely explaining that she had gone to see Frida Carlsson that afternoon, only to realize that the *Suecia* wouldn't be docking until evening. She had met von Kieler on the bridge to Kungsholm, talked awhile, and then he had told her there was something he'd like her to see. "I believe he had an engagement with Ursus and didn't wish to bid farewell to me," she explained — and went on to tell him what had happened in Ursus's garret.

It brought the first tiny smile to his lips since this conversation had begun. "Poor Leif," he sighed. "He stretches his hands toward the fires of life — and they flare up and burn him."

"You do know him, then?" she asked.

He nodded.

"Since childhood?"

"For example."

"And has he really been arrested today?"

He drew a deep breath and let it out again. "*Arrested* is not quite the right word."

"What *is* the right word, then?"

"Detained?" he offered. "Assisted to a place of safety?"

"Whose safety — his or the public's?"

"Both, I imagine. I wasn't there, myself, but apparently he shinned up a street lamp at Stureplan this lunchtime and started giving out a lecture on the necessity of demolishing the whole of Stockholm and rebuilding it again properly. Most people thought it was a student prank but unfortunately he was being quite serious. The more they laughed the angrier he grew."

She sat, head bowed, eyes closed, shaking her head.

"Need I go on?" he asked.

She nodded. "Please."

"He said he'd drawn up plans for the complete rebuilding of the city and it was so brilliant it wouldn't cost a single crown. But the city council had stolen it from him and he was appealing to the populace to form a column and march on the City Hall to recover it."

The tears were rolling down her cheeks by now; she was glad all the others had gone downstairs before them. Max rose to his feet, lifted her up, folded her in his arms, and stroked her back as if she were a kitten. "Katya, Katya, Katya! My dear! You should have said! I had no idea he meant anything to you."

She shook her head and blew her nose in the handkerchief he

offered. "It's not that," she assured him. "It's just that I think he was asking me to help him — and I simply didn't recognize it."

"How could you have — if you think about it? I've known him all my life, and I, too, met him this morning — or yesterday morning, rather. And even I didn't recognize it. You mustn't blame yourself."

She breathed in deeply and recovered something of her composure. "You're very good, Max. But I have to feel a *little* guilty, otherwise I'll get hard-bitten." She gave him back his handkerchief. He tried to make her keep it but she refused, saying, "I can't go on taking them. I still have the one you gave me that first morning, remember?"

"No," he lied. "What did you cry about then?"

She frowned. "I can't remember."

"There you are, then."

"Actually," she said, "going back to poor von Kieler, not everything he said was rubbish. In fact, he said a lot of sensible things, too. Quite profound things — about death and the impossibility of accepting it. Poetic things. Anyway, until you meet a madman like that you have no idea how convincing they can be." Casually she added, "What are his parents like? D'you know them? Is there any sign of instability among them, too?"

"Not a trace of it. That's the mystery. His father's a very senior civil servant. Solid as a rock."

"Did he marry twice?"

Max raised his eyebrows in surprise.

"Just something that von Kieler hinted at," she remarked. "He mentioned a half-sister. Part of his delusion, I suppose."

He shook his head. "It must be. I've never heard of one."

He was telling the truth — insofar as he knew it; she felt quite convinced of that. So, to end the conversation on a lighter note, she said, "And you *aren't* in the secret police, are you?" — putting just enough doubt in her tone to make him smile.

"Unfortunately, Princess," he said, biting one of his knuckles penitently, "there *is* just a grain of truth at the heart of that accusation. When he came to live in Stockholm his parents asked me to keep an eye on him. He always was a bit of a wild character, but no one ever suspected — you know — *this!*" He took a pace toward the door and stretched a hand toward her. "D'you feel ready for more fun?"

She sniffed heavily and said, "To my shame — yes!" Then, as they went out into the passage and started down the staircase, she added, "He's not ... not in a straitjacket or anything like that, is he? Not a padded cell?"

He patted her arm. "I should think he's fast asleep in a nice warm bed, with his veins full of laudanum. If they can keep him asleep for a couple of weeks — it might be all he needs."

"I must go and see him."

He sucked at a tooth. "I doubt they'll want him to have any visitors for quite a while, Princess. Let him settle down."

She laughed as an odd congruence of thoughts occurred to her. "That's what Herr Gullberg said to me about Simeon, remember? Actually, now I think of it, I probably *could* go and see him again quite soon."

They reached the ballroom to discover a commotion of some kind near the french windows. Couples were running toward them, pressing their noses to the glass, opening the catches and staring out onto the now darkened terrace in amazement. The word "snow!" was repeated, again and again, in an excited babble.

The dance came to a halt, though the band played gallantly on.

Snow in May! It was unheard of — and yet there it was — fat, gentle flakes like puffed-up helpings of sorbet were falling through the still, warm air out of an apparently cloudless sky. The three-quarter moon silvered each one before it touched the flagstones and vanished.

"Dancing on snowflakes!" someone exclaimed.

Amid general laughter the phrase was taken up and repeated to the newcomers who came rushing into the ballroom to witness this freak of the weather: "Dancing on snowflakes ... dancing on snowflakes!"

Katya was a mere fraction of a second ahead of several others when she cried, "Come on! We'll surely never have the chance again!" And she hauled Max out onto the terrace and twirled away into the moonlight. They drew the lazy, unhurried flakes into pirouettes behind them. But they melted to nothing the moment they settled.

*T*he Sunday following the masked ball was the first Katya had had free since starting at the Sibylla; she ignored the church bells and snoozed between the sheets until gone noon. Rosie was still at Valholm, of course. Then, fearing she wouldn't sleep that night if she lingered further, she rose and took a long, luxurious bath, refilling it several times before the horrid sight of her wrinkled skin drove her out of it.

She nibbled some fruit and tried to read an improving tract by Ellen Key but could not get poor Leif von Kieler's face out of her mind — his bright-eyed earnestness, his unshakable conviction — his exquisite lips.

At last she crossed the landing and knocked gently at Max's door.

It was Franz's day off so Max answered in person, fully dressed but for his cravat and jacket. "How did you know it was me?" she asked when she saw he had not even bothered to throw a dressing gown over his dishabille. "By my knock?"

He shook his head. "By the way Fru Torbjoernsson no longer responds when it's you. *She's* the one who recognizes your knock — and I suppose she knows it's hardly worth any effort to spy on me when *you're* my visitor."

She laughed. "Oh, Max — you're just what the doctor ordered. Shall we go out for a stroll?"

He looked at his watch.

"No Froeken Rydqvist today?" she asked archly. "Won't she be pining for you in that little medieval tower on top of her house?"

She could see that the question intrigued him, for he knew very well he had not described the tower to her. But all he did was sigh lugubriously and say, "She, too, has the day off."

That as good as settled the matter for her; if he knew of Marianne's relationship to von Kieler he would surely have gone to her — unless, she suddenly thought, he had done all that yesterday afternoon, before they left for Uppsala.

"I'll get my coat," he said.

"And cravat."

"For example."

Katya left a note for Rosie on the kitchen table — in case she changed her mind and returned early — gave the parrot a stick of celery, and joined Max on the stairs; they reached the square without benefit of semi-concierge — which brought the comment from Max that everyone seemed to have the day off.

"Where shall we go?" he asked. "There's a little pavement café up near the bourse. It's not very far, though, if you want to walk for walking's sake."

"Let's go up Oesterlaanggatan and then cut across," she suggested. "That'll make it longer."

"By as much as three minutes."

"At least we can say we tried." After a few paces she took his arm and said, "D'you know anywhere where we can telephone the Hospital for Sick Children on Kungsholm?"

"The café's probably on the telephone," he told her.

They walked in easeful silence a while and then she said, "I keep thinking of Leif von Kieler."

"I know," he replied. "Me, too. I passed a drunkard once, writhing in the gutter. Of course, I didn't stop and help. Later somebody told me it had been a man I knew slightly — and he hadn't been drunk at all. He was having a seizure."

"And he died?"

"Oh yes. That's how I feel about poor von Kieler now. Where did I walk on past him? Where could I have stopped and helped?"

"But you said last night that no one could have guessed."

"True."

"Anyway, it's probably all for the best. He's being looked after properly now. We might have made matters worse."

"What we're both trying to avoid," he said, "is the fact that we all share a general responsibility for everyone — including the *unknown* drunkard. By the time people start climbing up street lamps and haranguing the populace, it's too late."

She thought of her uncle, walking past the beggar woman that day. "We're even responsible toward people we hate," she said. "Whether we like it or not. There's a shining thought for the sabbath!"

He looked at her sharply. "I can't imagine you hating anyone, Katya — except, perhaps Herr Klint?"

"Oh no!" His words shocked her. "I don't hate him. Not any more — not since the interview, really. There's nothing *to* hate. I feel desperately sorry for him, mind. He's so ... empty of feeling. I don't suppose he's ever had a genuine feeling in his life. He just lives for the hôtel and making everything more ... effectual! His favourite word. But there is someone at the Sibylla who does possibly need help — a guest. I think you know who I mean?"

He cleared his throat. "I thought we might get back to him one of these days — the Grand Old Man of English Letters?"

"Yes. D'you think it's possible he's just as unhinged, in his own way, as poor Leif?"

"For example?" Max asked warily.

"You *know* I'm not just imagining it," she said in an accusing tone. "I can tell by your voice. You already *know* there's something very odd about that one." She went on to describe Arthur Dalyrimple's extraordinary response to her rude attack on him the previous Wednesday, and the way he'd wriggled and gone red in the face when he suggested she should act the schoolmarm and *punish* and *scourge* him for each shortcoming. "And yesterday," she added — having quite forgotten it until then — "he thrust half a dozen sheets of paper into my hand. All covered in tiny writing. And d'you know what they said?"

He closed his eyes and shook his head. "Actually, I don't think I want to, Katya."

"Oh, it was nothing offensive or indelicate. He simply wrote, *I must not be such a naughty boy* — five hundred times!"

"Oh dear," he said when her tale had finished.

"Is that all?" she asked when he volunteered no more.

"No." He sighed. "What I should have said was, 'oh dear, oh dear, oh dear'!"

"I'm sorry I interrupted, in that case."

"D'you have them still — these pages of lines?"

"I tore them up and threw them away. Was that wrong?"

"It would have been better to show them to Klint."

"Klint!" The suggestion bewildered her.

"He'd have had a quiet word with Dalyrimple and you'd have had no further trouble. As it is — without the evidence — I think Dalyrimple could start making trouble for you. Serious trouble, too."

"Why? Klint said he'd be glad to throw him out — if that was what I wanted."

Max's whole demeanour changed. "Oh well, in that case, you'll be all right. Forget what I said."

She sighed. "I'm missing something in all this, aren't I! There's something I don't understand about Dalyrimple. Rosie understood it at once, when she told me to make him lick my boots. And you understood it, too, the moment I told you what Rosie had said. And now you're implying Klint would have understood it immediately if I had showed him Dalyrimple's five hundred lines. But what is it? I can't for the life of me see what it could be. All I have is this intuition — since last night — that he's every bit as mad as Leif von Kieler. Except that it's a madness everyone knows about and winks at. Everyone except me."

There followed a long silence on his part.

She said, "You're not going to tell me, either, are you!"

"Oh dear, Katya!"

"You said that bit."

"Oh! *Dear* Katya, then — it's not the sort of topic one discusses with innocent females of your tender age."

"I thought as much!" she cried triumphantly.

"Phew!" He took off his hat and fanned his brow. "Thank heavens that's behind us, then!"

"Behind us?" she echoed scornfully. "I'll have you know I'm going back into the lion's den tomorrow. It most certainly is *not* behind us! And if you don't tell me ... I ..."

"What?" he challenged.

"I'll make you write it out five hundred times!"

He laughed. He sighed. He said, "If you're going to go around issuing threats like *that*, you'd better know what it would mean to a certain kind of gentleman."

At that moment his eye alighted on a discarded newspaper, lying in a shop doorway. He picked it up and saw — with satisfaction, apparently — that it was *Aftonbladet*, one of the more popular sheets.

He turned to the classified advertisements and soon found what he was looking for. "There!" he said, folding the page and thrusting it into her field of view. "Why should *I* write the explanation out five hundred times when the good 'governesses' of Stockholm have done it for me!"

His thumb rested on a small, boxed advertisement: *Strict schoolmistress will discipline unruly children for distraut parents. Own birches, etc. Box 1729.*

The one below it read: *Iron discipline for naughty boys! Box 556.*

There were others, all in a similar vein.

"Well?" she asked after reading several of them in search of some cryptic message.

"Have you ever noticed advertisements like those before?" he asked casually.

"Lots of them. They have them in some of the Dublin papers, too."

"And you've never wondered?"

She hesitated. "Well, I wouldn't say never. I've often wondered where all these hundreds of unruly children are — and why their parents can't do a simple thing like sting their bottoms."

"What if I told you they're not children at all?" He watched closely to see the moment when understanding dawned.

Not yet, anyway. He added, "The fact is, Princess — the secret you referred to just now — is that these 'naughty schoolboys' are all men like Arthur Dalyrimple." He dropped the paper in a rubbish bin.

"There are *no* other men like Arthur Dalyrimple!" she asserted. "He is unique, thank heaven!"

"I'm afraid there are," Max continued sadly. "Hundreds of them in Stockholm alone. Don't ask me to explain it, but it's a fact. Show Dalyrimple that advertisement — assuming he hasn't seen it already, which I'm sure he has — and he'd carry his answer in person to Box ... whatever it was."

"One seven two ..."

He put a finger to her lips. "Forget you ever saw it."

The implications of his words were beginning to strike her. "You mean he'd go to that strict schoolmistress and ask her to birch *him?*"

He nodded. "Not just ask her, little face. He'd *pay* her to do the job! Quite a lot."

"Great God above!" She laughed uproariously. "But I'd do it for nothing! I'd *love* to birch the skin off the back of that ... that ...!"

"Aaargh!" He gave a strangled cry and raised his fist to the narrow slot of sky that loomed over them. "Don't say it! Not even in jest. And never, *never* offer the faintest hint of it when he's around. *Please*, Katya. I'm being quite serious now. Just don't!"

His urgency got through to her at last. "I still can hardly believe it," she said soberly, but the impulse to laugh had gone.

They turned into the street that led toward the bourse. "But in that case," she said, "don't you think it's as mad as anything Leif von Kieler said — or did?"

"If you want to know more," he said wearily, "ask Rosie. It's not something I've enjoyed telling you. But you made it a duty."

"Oh!" She took his arm. "The sacrifices you men are willing to make in the line of duty! How can Ellen Key say we are your equals! You outshine us in ..."

"I'll turn round and go home," he threatened. Then, in a more encouraging tone, "Tell me about Magnus. Was he as fine a Prince Charming as he was a Barbare?"

She told him what had happened at the ball between her and Magnus. And, since frankness was now in the very air, she also described the extraordinary scene between Magnus and his step-mother — and Magnus's subsequent ashamed behaviour. "Rosie says patience is the only remedy," she concluded.

They arrived at the square in front of the bourse and were lucky to take the last two vacant seats on the café terrace. "Can we talk in English?" she asked. "There are things I want to say."

He glanced around, ostensibly for a waiter but actually sizing up their nearest neighbours. "All right," he replied. "Is it about our tall military friend?"

"Yes."

The waiter came and left them two menus.

"They haven't put the prices," she complained.

He tapped his own menu and smiled. "What about him?"

She chose two *smoergaasar* and then, her eye falling down the menu, said, "Ooh! Would the lobster salad be too-too outrageous? I could eat a horse."

"What a language!" Max muttered under his breath.

The waiter brought them Ramloesa spa water and noted down their orders.

"Our friend," Katya said. "I felt very dispirited when he left me last night. I know what Rosie said — and I know you probably agree with her — but I felt I'd been a coward. I still feel it." She smiled. "We've never spoken English before. Am I going too fast?"

He shook his head and encouraged her to continue with a lift of his brows.

"You see, I felt I ought to have been honest with him. I ought to have told him I know what it's like to have those feelings."

"He wouldn't have been pleased."

She pointed a finger at him and exclaimed, "There! *He* wouldn't have been pleased. He'd rather I didn't have such feelings — but I *do* have them, Max! What about me?"

He held up hands to pacify her.

"Sorry." She grinned. "But it's what Ellen Key says. We're to be like beautiful wax fruit under a glass dome. Worms will never gnaw at us. We're to be protected. It's what you were doing on the way here — protecting me from ..."

He pursed his lips and whistled a warning.

"... from things that — it now turns out — are common knowledge. I don't want to be like that. And I don't want *him* if he wants me to be like that."

"So he's off your list."

"Oh, you and your lists! He's not struck off any list. That's my difficulty. I melt at the thought of him. My blood races when he's near. But I still don't want him if that's what he wants of me. How can I make him see that?"

Part Three

Through
and
Through

*M*ax was no real help — chiefly because he had no sympathy with her aims. Yet his advice to get the ear of Klint ahead of Dalyrimple, in case the GOM turned sour and started pouring in the poison, was certainly worth taking. She plucked up her courage several times the following day, but never quite enough; it always failed her at the last. Even when the assistant manager himself took her aside to let her know that the Hospital for Sick Children had telephoned to say little Olof was being sent home — which would have been an ideal chance — she flunked it. His passionless way of passing on this wonderful news was so chilling.

Her hours that day were from four to eight in the evening, so it was easy to promise herself she'd have a word with him at the end of that time. Fortunately, Dalyrimple was dining out that night. But when eight o'clock came around she learned to her surprise that Klint had gone out for a walk. He was taking his constitutional late that day.

"You only just missed him," Albert told her. "If you're quick, you could catch him up. He always goes down to Skansen."

She hastened into her hat and coat — a light summer cape — and dashed out into Sibyllegatan, where she was just in time to see him turning into Strandvaegen at the bottom of the street. He was easy enough to spot in a crowd for he even walked like an automaton. By the time she reached that same place, he was crossing the bridge to Djuurgaarden. As she crossed it herself, she realized it was almost the last day on which anyone — or any member of the public — would be able to do so; the new stone bridge, built a hundred metres or so to the east, especially to commemorate the Exhibition, was to be opened the day after tomorrow. She hung slightly back from him all the way to Skansen, thinking it would be easier to arrange an "accidental" meeting once they were both inside.

She was by now well known to all the staff of the great open-air museum for she was always bringing guests there and showing them the glories of the place. Herr Loefgren, who issued the tickets at the entrance gate, liked to stop for a chat if the pressure of his work allowed. Unfortunately for her, this was one of those occasions. He kept her an inordinate length of time, telling her how popular Simeon was with the children — and their parents — and relating several anecdotes that would have delighted her on any other day. This time, however, it caused her to lose sight of Herr Klint.

"Come to see the little fellow yourself, have you, Froeken Persson?" he asked at last.

She frowned. "I hadn't really thought ..."

"I only ask because I never saw you come alone before."

She realized then that it would explain her presence there. And why shouldn't she go and see her little pet, anyway? She was just as likely to bump into Herr Klint there as anywhere else, she supposed.

She hastened along the path at the foot of the hill, behind the summer theatre, to the ape house. The dead and barkless copper beech had, she noticed, been removed at last — she only hoped it was in fulfilment of Herr Gullberg's promise. For weeks it had stood there, silently accusing him of promising more than he could achieve.

And indeed, the first thing she saw on entering the evening gloom of the building — by the front door, this time — was the bleached skeleton of the old tree. Eagerly her eyes sought among its branches for the first sight of Simeon.

But even when she stood directly beneath it, there was still no trace of him. True, some of the branches were rather large and he could easily be taking a nap out of sight on any one of them. Still ...

"Is Froeken looking for the ape?" asked a little boy near by.

"Yes." She turned hopefully to him.

"He's sulking up there on that thick branch near the top."

She smiled her thanks. "Would you like to see him?" she asked. "Shall I call him down?"

He gazed at her scornfully and said, "Huh!"

She looked up toward the branch he had pointed out. Her heart was racing suddenly. "Simeon?" she called in English. "Come to Katya now! Come on, me little darlin' man!"

If he had done what any human would do — glanced out, stared, put his head on one side, grinned, and then come to her — she would have been better prepared. But he did none of those things. Before she was halfway through calling him for the second time, he flew at her like a shot off a shovel. Like a warm-grey dart of furry energy he flung himself down from branch to branch, heedless of life and limb, and, in one last, mighty leap, hurled himself at her head, almost bearing her back to the ground with the momentum of his impact.

She laughed and struggled to get him off her — at least far enough to let her breathe. "There, there, now!" she cooed when she had some wind to spare. "Sure 'tis only me. 'Tis only your old Katya. Were you after thinking I'd never come back? Well here I am."

The boy gawked at her, half fearful she was a witch — with powers to summon dumb creatures — in her strange tongue, and all.

Except that *dumb* was the last word anyone would use of little Simeon at that moment. Still clinging to her head with what seemed like a dozen arms and legs — and almost as many tails — he gibbered and chattered and shrilled and screamed. And all the while his little body shivered with the ecstasy of this most unexpected reunion.

"God love you!" she kept saying, still laughing at the frenzy of his joy. "Did you think I'd never come again? What sort of heartless wretch do you take me for!"

Every word out of her seemed only to double his delight.

"Well look now, this can't go on," she said nervously.

By now a small crowd had started to gather, fascinated that the little creature, who had lain so morose and still only ten minutes ago, should be capable of such effervescent joy.

"You'll give yourself a heart attack, so you will," she warned him. "Would you ever just calm down!"

She tried to pull him off her, just to look him in the face, but the terror it aroused in him made her desist. "I just want to look at you," she told him. "To see are you brushing your teeth and combing your hair the way I taught you."

At last, after much more cajolery in this vein, he consented to let her unpeel his arms at least and look him in the face. His huge, dark, loving eyes — mournful even at the height of his mischief — stared up at her with a mute appeal that transcended all need for language. *Do not leave me here again*, it said. *I don't care where you go — only take me with you. Please!*

"Oh, Simeon!" she said, fighting back her tears, "I can't, love. I just can't! I'm sorry. I should never have come."

Herr Gullberg appeared at that moment, attracted by the unaccustomed buzz of the crowd. The moment he saw her he burst into a broad smile. "Froeken Silver!" he exclaimed as he came to her. "How glad I am to see you! I was about to send for you, but I suppose some instinct got there first. You've been feeling the call all day, I expect?"

He nodded so encouragingly, what else could she do but confirm his guess?

"I knew it!" he chortled and, tickling Simeon under the chin, said, "Didn't I tell you so!" He looked back at her and added, "But he wouldn't believe me. I said you'd come."

"He hasn't been sick or anything?" she asked.

"Bless you, no. Pining, that's all. For the first week or so he was happy as a sandboy. Then he went down a bit. Then last week we moved this tree in here for him ..."

"It's the perfect playground," she said.

"It quite restored his humour — until yesterday. Then he started moping again. So I was going to send for you."

She laughed nervously. "I don't think he's going to let go too easily, now I've come at last."

The keeper nodded ruefully. "What he really needs is a mate. I've been scouring Stockholm for one and I think ..." He put up his hand to hide his lips from Simeon — who wasn't even looking at him, anyway — and mimed the words: *I've succeeded!* Then, speaking again, he added, "We don't want to raise his hopes, eh?"

She pulled a face. "I rather think that's just what I have done — by coming here at all. He's sure he's coming away with me now." She licked her lips. "You don't suppose ..."

He shook his head. "He's still your property, of course, Froeken Silver. But unless you can give him all the attention he gets here — you or *someone* ..." He left the rest unsaid.

Her sigh conceded it was impossible.

"And as for getting him off you ..." The man's hands shot out — yet the movement was not in the least bit hasty — and deftly unpeeled Simeon from her.

The monkey did not struggle.

"Don't linger," Gullberg said quietly. "Come back tomorrow or the next day. He'll get used to it."

Simeon just cowered in his arms, his wide, soulful eyes imploring her not to let this happen. She backed away from him and, at last, turned and fled.

The spectators clapped. She could not believe it.

Outside, the evening being so warm and the breeze so balmy, the crowds had grown more plentiful. Even here she could not yield to her sorrow. Already this second parting from her little friend was a deeper hurt than the first, and a sharper hurt, too; but she put it from her mind and tried to remember if there was a way out through the Summer Theatre, or would she have to stumble through the crowds, all the way back to the entrance, and there run the gauntlet of Herr Loefgren's sympathy?

The question made her realize how little she wanted either the quick way or the roundabout way to the ferry; what she really wanted was to be alone for a time. She had completely forgotten Herr Klint by then.

The wilder parts of Skansen were on the far side of the hillcrest from where she now stood; it was where some of the wolves and wolverines were kept under almost free conditions in large enclosures. True, visitors could not enter those enclosures but, by that same token, she could not be seen from them by anything other than the animals themselves.

She turned again, along the path that led up the hill to the wolves' enclosure.

She walked slowly, as if calmness of body would somehow translate into calm of spirit. To keep her mind off her misery she imagined she was leading a party of guests, saying, "This type of farmhouse was very common in central Sweden a hundred years ago ..." and "Over there is Gunilla Bjelke's summer house ..." The Swedish for summer house, translated literally as Lust House, always raised a snigger when they found it on the Skansen plan. And so she continued on her way, deliberately numbing herself to her anguish, past the summer restaurant — now doing a good trade — past the North American bear pits ... until she found herself at last on the thickly wooded slope where the wolves were confined.

One of them was right beside the path, just four feet away from her, separated by a double stockade of iron railings. For a moment their eyes dwelled in each other's. His were gray and cold — and somehow wise, seeming to look right into her. He sniffed the air, being downwind of her, and then followed her in some excitement as she continued along the path.

"Sure I know what tasty little creature *you* can smell," she murmured — which brought her face to face with her own present grief, and in solitude at last.

She turned off the path then, away from the wolf, and stumbled a short distance in among the trees, until she felt safe enough from prying eyes. There she laid her forehead against the cool bark of a silver birch and gave her misery rein.

"Oh, Simeon," she whispered, "what have I done to you at all?"

Large, hot tears overflowed the cisterns of her eyelids and coursed unashamed down her cheeks.

"How will I live without you?"

The tears doubled.

She remembered again his bright, ever-curious eyes, his delicate fingers, his soft, furry arms, the affection of him, the loyalty, the sense of humour ... his mischief, his remorse ... his infantile need to be cuddled and loved.

And, oh God, how she loved him!

"My baby!" she whispered.

Then, realizing she was doing herself no good by yielding to such maudlin grief, she drew a deep breath and peeped out from behind the tree. Was the wolf still there?

He was.

But now he was not alone. There was a man there, squatting on his haunches, staring at the wolf through the two sets of iron railings. She had never before seen Herr Klint do anything so undignified as squat, so it was several moments before she recognized him.

*F*or a long while Herr Klint did nothing but stare at the wolf; and the wolf did nothing but stare back at him. Then he took off his jacket, shifted his stance a little, and glanced rather nervously over his shoulder. He satisfied himself that no one was approaching along the path in either direction but he failed to notice Katya, some thirty paces directly to his rear. She was now behind the silver birch again — and wishing it were a mighty oak. She drew in her shoulders and bent her body to get as much of herself into its meagre concealment as possible, but she still felt dreadfully exposed.

What would he think if he found her there? He'd never believe she had arrived at this particular place before him. What was he doing here, anyway? Was it his habit to come to this lonely corner of Skansen and commune with the wolves? The creature's behaviour suggested he was no stranger. Had it been waiting for him? She hardly dared breathe.

He, meanwhile, being now sure he was alone, reached an arm through the railings on his side and stretched his hand toward the wolf. It whimpered like a dog — as a dog whimpers with pleasure to see its master — and its tail shook the bushes behind it. It tried to poke its muzzle through the railings to reach Klint's outstretched fingers but the most painful effort on the part of them both, man and beast, left them inches apart still. Eventually it reached out a paw and they touched briefly.

After several further contacts, finger-to-paw, Klint stood up and stretched himself. The wolf stared at Katya.

Something about the fixity of that gaze must have alerted Klint, for, in the middle of putting his jacket back on again, he turned round and stared directly at her, too. His eyes met hers so instantaneously she could almost believe some kind of telepathy existed between him and the wolf.

"Froeken Silver? Is that you?" His tone carried an odd blend of outrage and shame.

"I'm afraid so, Herr Klint," she replied — but her voice was cracked and salty with weeping.

He was intrigued enough to suspend his anger. He took a few steps toward her. "I'm sorry. Are you ... in some kind of trouble?"

"No!" She tried to laugh, to reassure him. Then she stepped out from behind the tree and walked toward him. "It's all right. I'm all right. I was just ... I'm not in any kind of trouble."

Her voice trailed off when, on drawing closer to him, she realized there were tears on his cheeks as well. All during that time when he had — apparently — been playing with the wolf, he must in reality have been weeping.

The tears on her cheeks were much less of a surprise to him for the crack in her voice had already prepared him to see them. He fished out his breast-pocket handkerchief and, leaving his own cheeks wet, handed it to her.

She dabbed her face and passed it back to him with a mumbled, "Thank you."

That was probably the moment when they could have exchanged explanations but he hesitated, waiting for her, while she, ill at ease with him still, said nothing; then he assumed she was exercising her prerogative *not* to explain — after which, he felt, any explanation of his own grief would seem like a rebuke for her silence. So all he did was wipe his own cheeks dry and smile thinly.

The wolf had meanwhile vanished.

"Twenty past nine," he said as he tucked the damp handkerchief away in one of his pockets. "We could still get a cup of hot chocolate and a Vienna at Idunshallen?" He nodded in the direction of the restaurant at the farther end of the ridge. "Did you eat before you left the Sibylla?"

She shook her head. "I had little appetite then, I'm afraid."

"Ah!" He clapped his hands and soaped them jovially, as if seeking to blot out the memory of their unexplained tears. It was something she had never seen him do before; in fact, he was an altogether different man out here. "Do I detect a note of regret, Froeken Silver? Has your appetite returned?"

"I'd love a Vienna, Herr Klint." She smiled reassuringly and together they set off toward Idunshallen.

At the corner of the wolf enclosure he paused; beyond the double railing nothing stirred.

"Is he there?" Katya asked.

"He?" Klint asked.

"All right — *it*." How typically pedantic! "Is *it* still there?"

"It's there, all right," Klint replied quietly.

"Have you given it a name?" she asked.

"White Fang." He smiled apologetically. "How very original!"

After that she hardly needed to say a word. He marvelled at the fine weather and hoped it would last all summer. He pointed out places in the Salt Sea where a number of ships had sunk over the years. When they emerged from the trees they paused awhile to admire the effect of the setting sun on the Exhibition buildings. He pointed out the steamboat *Soedra Sverige*, which, he said, had sunk in over fifty metres of water down in the Archipelago; its salvage had been a triumph of modern Swedish engineering, using breathing apparatus and underwater electrical lighting. And there she lay now, quietly at anchor once again, a floating advertisement of Swedish skills to the visiting hordes.

She felt she ought to offer some wonder of her own, so that poor Klint wasn't left to do all the conversational work. "It snowed at Uppsala on Saturday night," she said. "I danced on snowflakes on the terrace at Valholm."

He looked to see if she were pulling his leg.

"It's true," she assured him.

He made a vague gesture with his hand, implying that he wouldn't argue. The gesture continued, becoming less vague — in fact, it pointed quite unambiguously to the landscape before them, to Skansen itself, in the immediate foreground, and to the Exhibition beyond. "It's an odd combination, don't you think?" he said.

"When I bring our guests here," she replied, "I always like to point out this rampart, which once kept the world at bay, and yet now brings the world to Stockholm instead."

"That's good! I like that." He actually made a noise that could be mistaken for a chuckle.

She wondered why he never showed this side of his nature down at the Sibylla. "Isn't that what you meant?" she asked

"Almost," he replied. "I had a slightly different irony in mind. Here in Skansen we've assembled the best of Old Sweden — just in the nick of time — before it's lost and gone for ever. And what is going to destroy it?" He lifted his hand and pointed at the Exhibition beyond. "Universal Art and Industry!"

He returned to the theme after they had taken their seats on the restaurant terrace and the waiter-girl had brought them their chocolate and Viennas. "It's a grand word, isn't it, Froeken Silver — *universal!* A word to stir the blood. Universal brotherhood, universal peace, universal happiness — until you realize it means literally everywhere. Every little valley. Every forest glade. Where will people go to weep in solitude then, eh?"

"Ah!" She stared down into her chocolate.

"That was clumsy of me," he said apologetically.

"Not a bit!" She smiled at him, a brisk almost playful smile. "I've been wondering how to explain it to you. I had a pet monkey, you see. Called Simeon. But when the Grand Duchess came to stay with me — and her parrot — poor little Simeon had to go to the ape house." She nodded toward it, almost immediately below them at the foot of the hill. "I went to visit him tonight, for the first time since then, and ... well ..." Her voice fluttered a little but she managed to smile. "We both became a bit emotional."

"I'm sorry." He stared awkwardly at his hands.

"Well, I'm glad I met *you*, Herr Klint, so soon after. I feel much better about it now."

"All the same, Froeken Silver, I'm sorry I asked, because ..." He scratched his forehead diffidently and gave her a trapped sort of grin. "I suppose I owe you some kind of explanation, too — and yet I honestly cannot explain what came over me back there. It is not my habit, I assure you."

"The wolf — I mean White Fang — seemed an old friend."

"Oh, it is indeed. But I have never ... you know ... broken down like that before. And, as I say, I don't know why it happened now. But looking into those eyes — you didn't see its eyes ..."

"I did. I was there about ten minutes before you. It was waiting."

"Ah, yes, it does. I don't know why. I've never fed it. All I ever do is ..." He breathed deeply and gave a shrug. "Just talk to it."

"Before you came along, I was as close to it as I am to you now, so I know what you mean about those eyes. It's a gaze you never see in a dog's eyes — deep ... cold ... forlorn."

"Ah!" He settled back in his chair, truly at ease for the first time in her company — the first time ever — and he let out a vast sigh of satisfaction. "You understand it, then. Forlorn!" With a shy grin he repeated the word in English. "Forlorn! The very word is like a bell to toll me back from thee to my sole self!"

His tone was so conversational that she did not recognize it as a quotation until the last three words — which he now repeated, staying with English: "My sole self. I don't suppose you know the meaning of the words, Miss ... Oberg — may I call you?"

"You know!" she exclaimed.

He nodded. "I'm afraid I do."

"How long have you known?"

He shrugged as if it hardly mattered. "From the first week you joined us."

"But how? Did the Grand Duchess ...?"

"No, no, no! Never! It's quite simple. I made inquiries. Your friend Lejonkrona has ... connections, shall we say. And so do I — the same ones, as it happens."

"So you know all about my being sent to live with my uncle in Soeder and ... and everything?"

He nodded reluctantly.

"That's where I acquired my pet monkey, actually. On the *Suecia* — the ship that brought me here from Dublin."

"I guessed as much when you mentioned him just now. The thing is, you see, Herr Lejonkrona had to give his friend in the ministry your true name in order to get a work permit in ... I can't call it your *false* name because you have done so much to dignify it. Your *other* name, let's say."

"And so you know ... everything! Who my father is — everything!" She laughed. "Even English. Your English is far better than you've ever allowed me to believe, Herr Klint."

"Please!" he replied. "As we are colleagues, Miss Oberg — and senior colleagues at that — it would be quite in order for you to call me Peter when we are not actually ... why do you stare like that?"

She was staring because, by Swedish custom, it was most decidedly *not* in order for her to call him by his Christian name. Not that she minded, but she wondered what his real purpose might be. "Was I staring?" she asked, shaking her head as if to clear it. "I'm sorry. I just realized that — in all this time — it's never struck me that you ... I mean I never knew that your name was Peter."

He laughed ruefully, knowing full well that the words she had almost blurted out were: "It never struck me that you had a Christian name at all!" He said, "Well, it is. English is so much easier where you don't have to think of *du* and *ni*. May I call you Katarina? Or d'you prefer Katya?"

"Oh, Katya, please," she replied. "Sorry! I'm unused to these rituals. Also, I'm still trying to work out why you said I wouldn't understand the meaning of those words — my sole self. Why should you think that?"

"What I meant was, tonight's the first time I've ever seen *you* alone, Katya."

His use of her name brought an odd thrill of pleasure to her. "But I arrive alone every day — and leave alone, too."

He smiled and tapped his forehead. "Not up here. You bring the whole world with you into our little hôtel. I see it in your smile, your ... eyes. You're always on your way to meet someone or coming from a meeting with someone. But tonight you were really *alone*. Sole — it means alone, doesn't it? Am I wrong about you, perhaps? Are you ever truly alone?"

She stared past him, down into the darkening archipelago, and said, "Almost all the time, Peter."

He seemed amazed that she used his name — even though he himself had requested it.

She, mistaking the cause of his surprise, went on: "I didn't realize it until lately, but it's always been there — the loneliness *you're* talking about. The desolate sort of loneliness you can feel in the middle of a crowded room."

"Or in a large hôtel with hundreds of guests."

"Yes. That loneliness. I've never told anyone this before. When I lived at home, it was very easy to ignore. I mean, it was so easy that I never once noticed it."

Their eyes locked briefly; his were as unreadable as ever but that no longer repelled her. She stared away from him in the other direction, toward Maelaren and into the last of the setting sun. "No," she murmured. "I'm wrong. We *aren't* alone before we leave home because really we aren't a complete person there, are we. We're just ... something the rest of the family expects us to be." She shifted her gaze again, toward Soeder. "I remember the first morning I was in Stockholm, standing on Katarina Hissen with the whole city spread out before me. It was a very strange sensation because, you know, in our family, I've grown up with talk of Stockholm, and pictures of Stockholm, and news from Stockholm ... it's always been like a sort of second home. But there I was — *in* Stockholm at last — and it was so different from anything I'd ever thought. Everything was in the right place — Gamla Stan, Slussen, the palace, Norrmalm, Kungsholm — it was all there, *precisely* where I knew it would be. And yet" — she shivered — "alien! I suddenly realized I didn't know a single, solitary soul. All right — I knew a few cousins. Or I knew where they lived. But they didn't count. Because I no longer wished to let them know I was there, you see. But as for the rest, all those hundreds of thousands of people — I didn't know one of them. *And they didn't know me!* That's the point I'm labouring to get to: They didn't know *me!* They didn't know how I'm expected to behave. Can you understand what a difference that makes? I can't walk down any street in Dublin without meeting someone who knows me. And then there are all sort of expectations set up about the way I'll behave. And if I behave a bit differently, word'll get about. 'Met that Katy O'Barry in Grafton Street this morning.' That's what I'm called there, by the way. 'Thought she was a bit odd!' But here in Stockholm, I suddenly realized — I could be *anyone!*"

She saw a flash of amusement in his eye and said, "It wasn't in the least bit funny, Peter. There I was, completely unknown in an alien city, and I suddenly realized I could be *me* at last. And that was a *dreadful* thing to discover, you know."

The word astonished him. "But why?"

"Don't you see? Because the next question is, 'What *is* me? What is this ... this *thing* in here" — she tapped her breastbone — "that's free at long last to express itself? And I'll tell you what it is: *Nothing!* A great big blank. A soul full of empty. Shattering! I sat all day in a café, drinking endless cups of coffee, wondering what to put in all that emptiness — apart from coffee, I mean."

"And what about now?" he asked diffidently. "I mean, d'you still feel like that?"

"Not completely." She smiled an oddly grateful smile at him. "In fact, that's no longer the difficulty."

Bells began to ring down in one of the Skansen exhibits. People rose, almost as if the clamour had released them, and began an orderly drift toward the exits. Katya drained the very last dregs of her chocolate. He offered her his jacket but she said the night was too warm. On the path down to the exit she slipped her arm through his and said, "You don't mind, do you?"

"On the contrary," he said, slightly breathless.

"It helps preserve the illusion."

"Illusion?"

"That we are not alone. That's what I was starting to tell you when they started ringing the bells. The difficulty now is not that I don't know who *I* am — it's that I don't know who anybody *else* is. That I *never will* know who anybody else is. You remember the masked ball I mentioned?"

"With the snow?"

"Yes." She laughed. "Anyway, when midnight came and everybody unmasked, I suddenly realized — *it didn't matter!* It made no difference. They were as unknowable without their masks as they were with them. Actually, it was something Max Lejonkrona said made me realize it. He said it would be pointless to go to a masked ball where all the guests were strangers to each other — because it would just be like everyday life."

"And then it snowed! For some reason I find that perfectly believeable now. Perhaps because it's such a beautiful image — a balmy summer's night, and snow gently falling, and you waltzing with such elegance on the terrace at Valholm! Ah, you've given me an image I'll never forget." After a little pause he said, "*Another* image I'll never forget."

She turned the handle as quietly as she could and poked her head into the apartment. "Lejonkrona?" she murmured. "Max — where a-a-a-re you!"

There was a groan from the direction of his bedroom.

She came right in and closed the door behind her.

"No!" he groaned again when he heard her footfall in the passage.

"What d'you mean *no?*" she called out. "You don't even know what I'm going to say."

"I am not responsible."

She reached out a finger and pushed wide his bedroom door. The endless summer twilight, which would now last until dawn at around four, revealed him, recumbent beneath a single sheet. *"Responsible* is the last thing anyone would ever accuse you of being," she remarked. "Can I come in?"

He groaned yet again and raised himself on one elbow. "I can't imagine any power on earth — nor in the waters beneath the earth nor in the firmament above — that would stop you. What d'you want at this hour?"

"I simply have to tell someone." She crossed the room and sat on the edge of his bed. "I'm just bursting with it. Klint is a human being, Max. A real live flesh-and-blood human being!"

He rolled over on his back and lay utterly immobile.

"Well?" she prompted.

He sighed heavily and continued to stare at the ceiling. "It's very pleasant to have one's doubts cleared up — I grant you that — no matter how trivial the topic ..." He broke off and stared at her in alarm. "You're not in love, are you?"

"No!" She laughed. "Not like that, anyway."

"Not like what?"

"Not like I love you, for instance. Oh, don't be silly, Max. Don't provoke me into saying silly things back. Why does everyone think of *love* all the time?"

"It makes the world go round?" he suggested.

"But it doesn't. That's the point. *Liking* people makes the world go round. Love is ... it's ...it's like wading through waist-deep glue. How much movement of any kind is there with Declan and me? And Magnus and me? But I've gone a thousand miles with Klint this evening. And what about you and me?"

"What about you and me?"

"We're always on the move — and we don't love each other. That's what I suddenly realized, sitting out there overlooking Skansen this evening, watching the sun set over Gamla Stan ... looking at Klint ... thinking of you and me ... liking a man is so much better than loving him. It's so much easier on the nerves. It doesn't cause arguments. It doesn't worry anyone. Nobody takes you aside and warns you against it. It's not veiled in mysteries. Why *should* I be in love, eh? Riddle me that! Where's the law that says every female heart must be going pittapat with love all the time or it's in danger of shrivelling up?"

He cleared his throat. "Are you trying to tell me you're no longer in love with anyone?"

"For example!"

"Not Declan? Nor ..."

"I don't think I ever was really and truly in love with him. It was just infatuation. My parents were right, you see. What did it ever bring me but misery?"

"It brought you to Sweden."

"Don't quibble! All right, it brought me to Sweden, but precious little else."

"It has enabled you to understand that what you thought was love is, in fact, mere infatuation. Indeed, there's only one thing it *hasn't* done for you."

"What's that?"

"It hasn't enabled you to recognize the *real* thing when it finally comes along. You're going to be as ignorant about that — and as vulnerable — as you were about this earlier feeling you *now* call infatuation. How many steps are there, Katya, on this climb toward enlightenment? Is each of them going to seem like the summit plateau — only to be revealed, when you reach it, as just another stage in the endless ascent?"

"What's the alternative? Should I just deceive myself into thinking that whatever plateau I'm on is the summit? Never raise my eyes upward again?"

"That's what most people do, you know. What makes you think you're any different?"

She slumped on the edge of his bed, spreading her thighs and pressing her fists into the hammock of her skirt. "Damn you, Lejonkrona," she said at last. "You make me wish I could be in love with you."

"Why?"

"Because I don't know anyone else who could say what you've just said and make it sound interesting. I mean you paint this picture of me endlessly climbing up and up and never being sure when I've finally arrived — and you make it sound more interesting than all the other possibilities."

"But you don't know any other possibilities," he pointed out.

"Yes I do!"

"Name one."

She cast about desperately, not even sure what they were talking about any longer. "You say I shan't know real love when I see it. Well, I shall. So there!"

"How?"

"Because it will rise up out of some mad ... impossible ... absurd act. It won't be anything I can predict. And it will be too impossible to argue with. It won't grow out of the past — d'you know what I mean? I shan't be able to see it coming — which one always can with things that come sweeping forward out of one's past. It'll just be *there*, suddenly — bang! In front of me. It'll be all future and no past. Have you got any brandy?"

"I'll get some." He threw aside the sheet and slipped from the bed. To her amazement she saw he was naked.

He grinned back at her from the door, over his shoulder, and said with a wink, "Don't worry, Princess. As you say, yourself — it's all past and no future."

He was in his dressing gown when he returned. She took her glass with a trembling hand and said, *"Skaal!"*

He toasted her in solemn silence.

She surveyed him, head on one side, as if she were only just beginning to notice one or two things about him. "There's something ... different about you tonight, Max," she said.

"Froeken Rydqvist has gone," he replied. His voice was neutral.

"Marianne!" She almost dropped her glass.

He raised a languid eyebrow. "Was that her Christian name?"

"Gone?"

"Gone."

"But ... I mean ... where? How can she just go?"

"I was rather hoping you'd know, Princess. I think you were the last to see her?" He fixed her with a sharp eye.

She squared her shoulders. "Why shouldn't I have gone there? Why did you give me the directions, otherwise?"

"Did my tone imply criticism? I'm sorry. I'm delighted you went, in fact. She may have told you things she'd rather I didn't know."

Her heart bled for Max, who was obviously (to anyone who knew him, that is) more distressed than his flippant manner would suggest; but she felt she had certain loyalties to Marianne, too.

Or did she? Had Marianne, by walking out like that, cancelled them all?

"Did she take anything?" Katya asked.

"Nothing of mine — except ..." He laid his hand mockingly on his breast and bowed his head for a brief silence.

"And she didn't leave a note?"

"Only a poem — a single verse." A sheet of paper protruded between two books on his bedside table. He fished it out and handed it to her.

She read:

> *Love, not as my loves of old,*
> *would swoop upon my servant heart,*
> *would catch my cries in webs of gold,*
> *and cherish me in faithless arms,*
> *soars eagle-like —*
> *a vulture.*

"D'you think she really means that comma after *old* in the first line?" he asked. "That hurts me, I must say — after all I did for her."

She passed it back to him. All joy had suddenly gone out of the evening. "And that was all?" she asked. "Not the slightest clue as to her whereabouts?"

"Not in the *house*," he said with a certain odd emphasis.

"In the garden, you mean?"

"No — I thought she might have left it in your head, Princess. It's the sort of thing she enjoyed doing."

"Oh, Max!"

"If she did, she meant you to tell me — perhaps even to taunt me with it. You may be sure of that."

She sat on the empty half of his bed then, pulling her legs and skirt in under her. "God forgive me if I do wrong!" she murmured.

"She did tell you something, then!"

"She didn't exactly tell me, but I *learned*, let us say. So much more than you're going to believe, I'm afraid."

In a thin voice that she hardly recognized as his he said, "Was — or is — Leif von Kieler her lover?"

She put a hand to her brow and massaged it hard. "I didn't even ask you how he is! I was so full of my silly ... self!"

"No change," he said. "Which is good news, at least. So ... was he?"

She drew a deep breath and said, "He was her half-brother, Max. I mean he *is* her half-brother."

"Impossible!" he said at once.

"Well, that's what they claimed. I'm sure they're not lovers. There was no ... spark between them of that kind. In fact, I'm almost certain I know who her lover is."

"Who?"

"Ursus. I don't know his real name."

"Bjoern, of course. Bjoern Lindgren."

Of course! she thought, for *bjoern* is the Swedish for bear.

"Did she tell you?" he asked.

"Not in so many words. She spoke of a married man — a ne'er-do-well whom she was trying to forget — a man of magnetic personality. Then Leif turned up — that's where we met, of course, not on the bridge to Kungsholm. She said he was her half-brother — they certainly behaved more like brother and sister than lovers. When I left he followed me out into Fleminggatan and pestered me, and *pestered* me, until I agreed to go and see Ursus with him. And then the first thing Ursus asked was, 'How's your sister?' But then, once he became aware I was there, too, he wouldn't talk about her — even when I mentioned her by name to him, which I did, to test him."

"What does that prove?" he asked morosely.

"That he was trying to smarm himself into my good books. No man bent on that sort of purpose is going to mention his present amour, is he!"

"By God!" Max slapped his thigh. "Doesn't instinct beat logic every time! You're right, of course. Ursus is the lover and Leif von Kieler — somehow, God alone knows how — is her half-brother. But old Pappa von Kieler is the very last man one would ever suspect of that sort of thing. I wonder if it was Mamma von Kieler! Now there's a thought!"

"Leif is the elder of the two," she pointed out.

Unusually for him he did not at once see the connection.

She added, "A woman may hide a little by-blow contracted *before* her marriage."

"I see what you mean." After a moment's thought he added, "I wouldn't have thought there's all that much age difference between them, actually."

She grinned and replied, "I wouldn't be at all surprised to find that Leif is almost exactly nine months older."

He closed his eyes and bent his head. "My God, Princess, you do keep piling them on! Any more while you're in the mood?"

She licked her upper lip cautiously and said, "Just one, perhaps."

He heaved a sigh. "Let's have it, then." He looked up at her and, placing a finger between his eyes, right on the bridge of his nose, said, "Just here — hard as you like!"

"I don't think *you* should worry about the placing of that comma, Max. I think it's a problem for Ursus to ponder."

She leaned over and kissed the spot where he had invited her verbal fist to fall. "Shall I stay with you tonight?" she asked.

He kissed her tenderly on the cheek, too moved to say more than a few words: "Not tonight, Princess — thanks all the same."

ormally Katya would walk up Sibyllegatan on the same side as the hôtel. But on the morning after her meeting with Peter in Skansen, she crossed the street and strolled up the opposite side, where she could see the whole of the place — *his* place. His home. Indeed, you could call it his creation, for he was the one who had shaped the hôtel and made it what it was. Dear Herr Svensson was a charming man — and certainly a better ambassador among the guests than Peter — but Peter was the power behind it all. His was the vision that had inspired the staff and shaped the Sibylla into the superb establishment it was.

She stared up at the façade. What a different place it seemed now that he was her friend! She counted along the top-storey windows to find his — the seventh.

And there he was, staring down at her rather solemnly!

But that was odd. He was usually busy downstairs long before this hour. And why didn't he wave? No one could see him, except her. She blew him a kiss, but it produced no effect.

Perhaps he was telling her, *"Pas devant les domestiques!"* They were to be their old, formal selves during working hours. Well, if that was the way he wanted it ...

She walked gaily into the foyer and said to Albert — as she would have said on any other day, "Something seems to have bitten old Klint this morning!"

He spun round and stared at her aghast. "How can you talk like that?" he snapped.

"Like what?" She took a pace or two back in surprise.

He saw the consternation growing in her and softened. "You haven't heard what's happened, then?"

A dreadful foreboding filled her; she felt her blood take chill. She tried to say, "No," but managed only to shake her head.

He came out from behind his desk and put out a hand to steady her. "Herr Klint died during the night, Froeken Silver."

She sat down abruptly, but the faintness that overcame her made her stand up again just as swiftly. She was not going to faint. She was not going to faint. "He can't have." The voice was hers though she barely recognized it.

"I'm afraid so." He stared deep into her eyes, full of anxiety for her. "I'm sorry I snapped at you. I thought ..." He left the rest unsaid.

"But he can't be ..." she repeated, pointing at the ceiling. "I just saw him — standing at his window."

Albert shook his head. "That must have been Herr Svensson — or the doctor. They're both up there now with the ... with Herr Klint."

Sophie, the chambermaid, came into the foyer at that moment. "Oh, Froeken Silver," she exclaimed, tears on her cheeks. "Isn't it awful about Herr Klint!"

"But I've just seen him at his window!" she insisted.

"Must have been Herr Svensson," Albert explained to Sophie over Katya's shoulder.

She realized his attitude was that of one mature, responsible adult addressing another in the presence of someone who was mentally deranged. "I tell you I did!" she insisted, knowing it only made her sound worse. "I'm going up to see. It must be some mistake."

They called after her to dissuade her but she barely heard. She took the stairs two at a time. On the third floor Arthur Dalyrimple came out of his room, wearing a ridiculous brocade dressing gown and a fez. "Ah, Miss Silver!" He spoke as if every word were a painful duty. "I distinctly recall your promising me ..."

She did not pause in her ascent and he got no further with his protest. "You crapulous old toad," she shouted back at him — the words she had longed to speak for weeks. "Go and boil your head."

He just stood there, eyes aglow, blowing bubbles that would not come. She did not even look round. Before she reached the final landing she had entirely forgotten the incident.

She entered Peter's room without knocking. The moment she was inside she knew that Albert and Sophie had been right. Death was the only true presence in that room. The doctor, Herr Svensson, and herself — they were mere transient shadows. She went straight to the window where she had seen Peter. It had not been either of the other two men — she was absolutely certain of it. Svensson, as she already knew, was too portly, and the doctor, as one glance revealed, was shorter and fatter still.

No, it had been Peter himself, waiting to see her one last time, waiting for his release.

"Who is this young person?" she heard the doctor ask.

"A very close friend." Herr Svensson's reply was little more than a whisper, imploring respect for a grief that might lead to trespass.

It took her several seconds for the reply to sink in. Friend? Very close? Had Peter ever discussed her in those terms with Herr Svensson? It could not be.

She forced herself to approach the bed, where a white sheet covered his body. Her every sense was alert for a twitch, a groan, some sign of breathing. "I saw him at the window," she said, amazed at the evenness of her voice. For some reason she was not even out of breath, after running up all those flights of stairs. Her heart, however, was galloping.

The two men exchanged glances.

"How did it ..." she began but could not finish.

"I don't know, Froeken ...?"

"Oberg," she said, thinking more of Peter than of him. Incongruously she held out her hand.

"Loenneborg, Froeken Oberg," he said, shaking hands with her. He raised an eyebrow at Svensson for he had seen the man start when she gave her true name. Svensson merely shrugged. He turned back to her. "On the face of it, it looks like a sudden heart attack. There are no marks on the ... about him — no sign of a struggle. And no ..." He waved vaguely around the room rather than say straight out that there was no bottle of poison and no suicide note.

She shook her head. "I don't understand."

"He did not wish it known," Svensson told her, "but he had been suffering from abnormally high blood pressure. It started in January. And palpitations, too."

"He thought if he ignored the signs, they'd go away," Dr Loenneborg said. There was a smugness in the pronouncement, as if Peter had issued an arrogant snub to medical science, and to Dr Loenneborg in particular, and had now reaped the just reward for his folly.

She wasn't going to allow that. "I killed him," she said calmly.

They stared at her open-mouthed.

"I met him walking around Skansen last night. We had chocolate˙ and Viennas at Idunshallen ... and talked and talked. Then we were late for my ferry to Gamla Stan. We ran all the way down Allmaenna-graend to the jetty. That must be what killed him. I had no idea he had trouble with his heart."

"But *he* knew it, Froeken Oberg," Dr Loenneborg reminded her. "Think of that."

She would have said more but she realized that this conversation was turning into a contest as to which of them was more responsible for Peter's death. Instead she turned to Svensson and said, "He was so ... different last night, somehow. I felt I was meeting him for the very first time."

The manager smiled wanly. "He was not an easy man to get near. A bit of a lone wolf, as they say."

He did not know why the words had such a profound effect on Katya ... why her lips trembled suddenly, why she turned from him and almost staggered toward the door. He followed her anxiously, pausing only to say to Dr Loenneborg, "I suppose I'd better send a telegram to the wife."

"And I'll see to the rest here," the doctor replied, but by then Katya was out in the corridor again.

"Take the rest of the day off, my dear," Svensson murmured, laying a gentle hand on her shoulder.

She stiffened at once and said, "No!" She spun round and faced him. "*He* would have hated that sort of weakness. We must do what *he* would have liked. We must carry on precisely as if ... as if he were just on holiday."

He dipped his head dubiously. "As you wish," he said.

She corrected him. "As Peter would wish."

*T*rue to her word, Katya put in a day of ferocious effort — far longer than the four hours for which she was contracted. She tried to hoodwink herself that she was doing it for Peter's sake ... keeping his hôtel together ... and so on. There was also the comforting feeling that he had not gone too far away as yet, that he was there, cherishing their newfound friendship ... watching over her ... approving.

But the end of that same day brought her the most graphic proof that Peter was, indeed, no longer there — neither watching over her nor approving. Herr Svensson called her into his office, handed her an envelope containing sixty-four crowns, and dismissed her for being offensive to one of the guests.

She had so completely forgotten the incident on the stairs with the absurd Dalyrimple that at first she denied it. Then, when some faint memory of it began to return to her, she pleaded the distress of the occasion in her defence.

"No amount of distress can excuse what you said to one of our guests, Froeken Silver," the manager responded primly. "Mister Dalyrimple claims you called him a crapulous old toad. He says you told him to go and boil his head."

It sounded much worse in Swedish and Katya, in her tiredness, was hard put not to chuckle.

"It's no laughing matter," Svensson snapped.

She pulled herself together and promised to apologize to the man. But Svensson said his decision was final.

Katya was too exhausted to plead. In any case, it was just beginning to dawn on her how oppressive it would be to go on working in this place now that Peter was no longer there. A week earlier and she'd have laughed at anyone who had dared predict such a thing. She turned to leave.

"Mind you," Svensson said, as if he now felt he had possibly been a little too harsh, "if you were willing to be re-engaged at, say, ten crowns a *day* ...?"

"But that's little more than what I earn in an hour."

"Not quite, Froeken Silver — or is it Oberg?"

"Oberg. What d'you mean, 'not quite'?"

"You said it's what you *earn*. I'd say it's what you've been *getting*. But it must be crystal clear, even to you, that you haven't actually been earning it."

She stared at him in amazement. "Then why on earth have you been paying me, may I ask?"

He smirked. "You may ask, by all means, Froeken Oberg, but you'll hardly expect me to answer."

"I don't see why not. You're hinting I haven't been worth my wages — so of course I want to know why you've been paying them." She sat down pointedly, implying she'd not leave until he answered her.

"Very well, since you insist. You were given eight crowns an hour because Herr Klint decreed it so — and he was an extremely valuable man to us. We regarded it as a small price to pay in order to keep him ... how shall I say?" He leered. "Contented? And, of course, we did not inquire too closely as to *why* he insisted on paying you so outrageously." He smirked.

The colour drained from her face. "How dare you!" she exclaimed.

"Come, Froeken Oberg — we are men and women of the world in this business. A young fellow like Herr Klint, in the prime of life — living apart from his wife — meets a pretty young girl ..."

"What did you say?" Katya asked.

"A pretty young girl — like yourself."

"No — about Herr Klint. Was he married?"

Genuine sympathy showed in Svensson's face for a moment. He nodded. "I'm sorry. Did he not mention it?" He consulted his watch. "She'll be here in half an hour, in fact. She had to come up by train from Gothenburg."

"And you think ... you thought ... all this time you've been thinking ..."

"Please!" His hands parcelled up a large helping of worldly generosity and pushed it at her. "We are not, I repeat, men and women of the cloisters. We know what we know. Let's leave it at that, eh?"

She walked out of his office, out of the hôtel, without another word. He ran after her, advising her to think over his more realistic offer because she wouldn't get a better.

She did not even turn round.

She drifted in a daze down theshaded side of Sibyllegatan and across the quay to Grefbron. There she took the ferry that sailed under Skeppsholm bridge to her usual landing stage on Gamla Stan; it was a ferry she had never taken before — which was precisely why she took it now; it held no associations for her, neither sad nor happy. And, if the printed timetable told the truth, it actually cut three minutes off her best previous time, so she wondered why she had never even tried it.

All the other things she had never tried, too …

They were all around her, just like the ferry. Waiting to take her on to the next stage of her life.

What *was* she going to do now? She was just beginning to realize that she was out of work — and what it would mean to her. Saturday would come around and no one would put an envelope containing two hundred and twenty-odd crowns into her hand. Mealtimes would come around and no commis-waiter would place a menu before her.

What was she going to do?

Poverty stared her in the face. She thought of Ursus and that dreadful hovel in Getgraend. A day's wages for her would probably pay a year's rent on a place like that. How was she going to pay the hospital bill for little Olof — yet what an easy promise it had seemed at the time!

The safety valve opened on the boiler and steam filled the ferry cabin. She looked up and saw they had arrived — indeed, that they must have arrived some time ago, for she was the only passenger left aboard; she had gained three minutes and squandered them. The helmsman was smiling at her consternation.

"I'm sorry," she murmured to him as she passed.

"We've all been in love, darling," he replied.

Fru Torbjoernsson came to her door the moment she heard Katya letting herself in. "Froeken Silver was moving around late last night," she snapped.

"I've neglected my diary shamelessly lately," Katya replied pleasantly. "Perhaps — if I bring it down — Fru Torbjoernsson could very kindly fill in the blanks?" She started to mount the stairs.

"Froeken Silver no doubt thinks she's very witty. But these late-night *goings-on* make the dog bark."

"We had a dog like that, once." Katya slowed her pace to get in all she wanted to say. "But we cured him of it. We ate him. I stewed him, in fact, but it wasn't a success. He was very stringy."

Behind her she heard Fru Torbjoernsson's door slam shut before she finished speaking.

"It was a waste of marjoram, really," Katya added to herself.

Max stood on the landing, grinning with approval. Katya's heart leaped up at the sight of him. At first she thought he was keeping quiet in case Fru Torbjoernsson was still listening, but when she drew near him he made several brief stabs with his finger in the direction of her door. "Your Tante Anna," he whispered. "She's in there with Rosie. Rosie asked me to warn you."

She grinned and kissed him briefly on the lips.

"I say!" he murmured as they broke contact. "Do you have any *closer* relatives coming to visit — or is that too much to hope for?"

"You had your chance last night," she sneered playfully. "And fluffed it! Is it only my Tante Anna? Not Onkel Kurt?"

"Only Tante Anna."

"I can't say it's entirely unexpected," she told him. "Listen, I'll get rid of her and then I want to get drunk. Would you like to get drunk with me?"

"For example," he said, eyeing her suspiciously.

"If I explain now, I'll cry. Promise you'll wait?"

He nodded. "I'll take a bath while I'm at it."

"Tante Anna!" Katya sailed into her apartment like a clipper under full canvas. "How wonderful to see you — and how clever of you to run me down!" They kissed on both cheeks. "But you needn't have bothered, you know. I was going to call on you this week — now that there's no need for secrecy any more. I see the Grand Duchess has been looking after you. Is there a cup left in that pot?"

Her aunt, a little taken aback by this display of confidence, kissed her in a bewildered fashion and said what a surprise it was.

"Yes, isn't it," her niece responded. "How is Onkel Kurt? Not with you today?"

"Cheeky boy!" came the cry from down the passage.

Rosie stood up, murmuring, "I'll leave you to your reunion, then."

They made conventional demurrals, which she, equally conventionally, declined.

When they were alone, her aunt leaned forward and whispered, "Is she really a Grand Duchess?"

Katya reeled off several other imposing titles Rosie had gained down the marriages.

Her aunt continued shaking her head. "It's going to place your uncle in some difficulty." Then she smiled and added, "I still can't believe it's you, dear."

"Perhaps it's not me," Katya said bleakly as she poured herself a cup. "I've had an absolutely beastly day — the worst day of my life, I think. D'you want to hear?"

"If you want to tell me, dear."

Katya did, indeed want to tell her. Even in her distraction she knew perfectly well why her aunt was here. She was *scouting the ground* — one of her father's favourite phrases. Her father must have wormed her directions out of Declan. So here she was, scouting the ground for Onkel Kurt, who would, in turn, be scouting the ground for his brother. Life was becoming depressingly predictable again.

Her tale was soon done, for she confined herself to its essentials, right up to today's ejection from the Sibylla. Her aunt cried when her niece spoke of Peter Klint's death and was rather surprised she did not join in — indeed, that she remained quite calm and unmoved throughout the entire recital.

"Well!" the older woman fanned her face as the tale was concluded. "I must say, Katarina — it's all very ... it's not at all the sort of thing I expected to hear."

Katya smiled wanly. "It's not exactly what I'd have expected to *happen*, either, Tante Anna!"

"I don't know *what* your uncle's going to say!"

"To my father? Or to me?"

"To both, I suppose."

"Is my father coming to Stockholm?"

Tante Anna looked away uneasily. "I don't know, dear. They don't tell me these things." Then she realized what she ought to have said. "But how silly of me!" She laughed awkwardly. "Of course he's coming. In September. How could I forget! He always comes in September — as you know."

Katya did not pursue the point. She hardly cared now whether her father came or not.

"What will you do next?" her aunt asked.

Katya shrugged. "I'm not even going to think about it until tomorrow. I have several hundred crowns saved up in the bank, so it's not as if I have to take the first thing that's offered. The Exhibition opens this week. There'll be plenty of call for interpreters. Perhaps Bolinders will employ me!" She laughed but with no humour in it.

Tante Anna merely gaped.

"What now?" Katya asked.

"The change in you! I can't get over it. How old are you? Twenty?"

"In thirty days I come of age."

Tante Anna shook her head again. "And to think I came here today to try and talk you into returning home voluntarily before you ... before you were ... before you discovered ... oh dear! You know what I mean."

Katya said gently, "Don't worry, Tante Anna. I *do* know what you mean."

The woman's face was still troubled. "It's your Onkel Kurt, I'm afraid. You know how ... how ..."

"Peppery?" Katya suggested. "Despotic? Autocratic ...?"

"Adamant," her aunt put in. "You know how adamant he is. I'm afraid it is his intention to come here — with police, if necessary — and take you into custody. Our custody, of course, not the police's. But, to be frank, he intends to more or less imprison you in our house until your father can come and collect you. That's putting it as bluntly as I possibly can."

"Today?" Katya asked — and then sank her head in her hands. "Why ask! Of course it's today. One, two, three — these things always come in threes, don't they. That can only mean Pappa's on his way already. Otherwise just think of the expense of a long incarceration for poor Onkel Kurt!"

Tante Anna tried desperately not to laugh. "Oh, my dear!" she said, yielding at last. "You are going to surprise us all."

Katya frowned. A new thought had just struck her. "Does Onkel Kurt *know* you're here?" she asked.

Her aunt shook her head. "It was quite a little victory for me, I may tell you — though he insisted he'd be the one to put my little plan to you. He doesn't trust me. So I thought I'd just slip in and explain it to you and slip quietly away — if you could pretend it comes as a complete surprise when *he* puts it to you in his own way?"

"Of course." Katya smiled. "And what is your plan?"

"Well, you see," her aunt went on, "I thought if I could persuade you to live with us *voluntarily*, your Onkel Kurt could put it about that you'd come to Stockholm on an ordinary visit — starting today. There'd be no gossip among the servants, which is so important. Also, nothing would get back to Bolinders. That's the *one* thing they're afraid of. Your father is *most* insistent that not a breath of this ... this *escapade* of yours, as he calls it, must get back to them." She smiled engagingly. "Would it be so utterly dreadful, dear? To come and live with us in Goetgatan?"

Katya sighed. Not five minutes since she would have let herself be seized and taken back to Dublin without fuss; indeed, she would have gone voluntarily — so low were her spirits just then. But the mere mention of her uncle's plans to descend with a column of police and take her into custody — "by force if necessary" — had restored all her fighting spirit.

"Of course it wouldn't be dreadful," she said. But the smile vanished from her aunt's face when she went on. "Nonetheless, I'll decline the invitation, thank you very much all the same. I'll come and visit you now and then, of course." Offhandedly she asked, "When exactly *is* my father due, by the way?"

Tante Anna almost fell into the trap, but she recovered just in time. "September, dear — I told you," she said — though she hardly bothered to make it sound convincing.

The bell rang down in the kitchen, making both women jump.

"Oh dear! That sounds horribly like your Onkel Kurt!" Tante Anna stood up in an extreme of agitation, sat down, stood up again, smoothed bits of her dress ...

"It's all right, Tante Anna," Katya said. "There's absolutely nothing to worry about. You've just given me the answer, in fact. I'll go downstairs and let him in."

Still the woman dithered. The bell clanged again; it sounded as if it was almost dancing off its spring. "Please, Tante Anna!" Katya assured her yet again. "I promise there won't be any more violence than is absolutely necessary."

Out on the landing she hammered urgently at Lejonkrona's door. She needed his help now as never before.

Franz answered.

"Tell Herr Lejonkrona to come and save my life," she said, already edging away toward the stairs. The bell was now ringing continuously in her kitchen.

"He is taking a bath, I fear, mam'selle," the man replied.

She turned round at the stairhead. "Tell him this is *even* more important than his bath. Tell him he's to acquire a large shareholding in Bolinders — in the next five minutes!"

"Large?" Franz asked. "Any particular size?"

"Large enough to threaten someone with."

Franz was impressed. She only hoped he would manage to convey the urgency of the situation to Max.

Uncle Kurt looked like a plethoric rodent. His face was scarlet, his eyes small and fierce, his moustache bristling. He was wearing a heavy Irish tweed, waistcoat and all — far too warm for a summer's day. And if he were pumping out a sinking ship, he could not have moved his arm more vigorously.

"It doesn't come off, Uncle," Katya told him. "Everybody's tried."

It wrong-footed him. He had been prepared for brazen defiance, or weary submission, or tears — almost anything except frivolity. "Eh!" he barked, staring at the bell-pull.

"Do come in," she said. "I'm one floor up. Tante Anna has explained how matters stand."

"Tante Anna?"

"Yes, she's upstairs with me now."

"Ah!" He blinked rapidly and peered about him until his eyes grew accustomed to the gloom of the hallway. This encounter was not going as he had anticipated. "Well ... I must say that's ... ah ..."

He was struggling to get events back onto the course he had planned for them.

As they started up the stairs he recovered somewhat. "You must have been out of your mind," he barked. "Of course, I blame my brother. He never raised a hand to you when you were young. Too squeamish. But a good thrashing on the bare posteriors never did a girl any harm — you ask your cousins." He paused at the half-landing, quite out of breath, and whacked the side of his leg with his cane walking stick.

"Why did you put on your Donegal tweed?" she asked. "It's much to hot for the day that's in it."

He frowned. "What d'you mean — 'the day that's in it'? In *what*?"

"That's what we say in Ireland," she told him. "Can't you say that in Swedish?"

He mopped his brow and shook his head in exasperation. "You're talking gibberish, girl."

They took the remaining flight at the rate of one step to every three sentences. "I shall tell your father when he comes to collect you — a dozen good cuts with a fresh cane. It'll work wonders on you. I've seen it happen. You're not too old. You haven't come of age yet. I'll do it myself if he won't." He slashed the air with his stick a couple of times to prove it.

She remembered being afraid of him once. A lifetime ago.

The luxury all around him began to register. He frowned at her again, "How can you afford a place like this?" he asked.

She shook her head and sighed. "It hasn't been easy, Onkel Kurt."

He gripped her arm. "I don't like your tone, my girl. And that's hardly an adequate answer to my question."

She shook his hand away with a gesture that bordered on contempt. He, expecting no resistance from her, was shaken. "Now see here..." he began.

"This is my apartment, Onkel." She opened the door and stood back to let him in. "Please keep your voice down. The Grand Duchess is taking her nap."

Angrily he pulled the door shut again, leaving them both out in the corridor. "I'll enter when I'm ready, my girl. And I'll shout as loud as I ... what Grand Duchess?"

"Roseanne, the Dowager Grand Duchess Straczjinskaya. I am engaged as her companion."

He gaped. "Your aunt told me nothing of this," was all he could think of to say.

"That's hardly surprising," Katya told him. "She has only just learned of it, herself."

He gazed about him again, this time with relief. "So this is *her* apartment. You said it was yours."

"It is mine. Shall I ask Tante Anna to bring your coffee out here?"

He almost grabbed her by the wrist again but, thinking better of it, wagged a stiff finger underneath her nose. "You're not too old, Katarina! I've warned you once and I shan't do so again." Once more he thwacked his cane against the side of his leg.

She gazed calmly into his eyes, wondering why she had ever felt afraid of him. Slightly to her surprise — and greatly to his — he looked away first. "Come!" he snapped. "Let's get it over with."

She heard Max making noises in his apartment. Relieved, she opened her door again and this time he went in.

His first words to his wife were, "I thought we agreed *I* should be the one to tell her?"

She smiled serenely and handed him a cup of coffee. She had had ample time to think what to say. "I ran into Katarina in the square below, dear," she said. "I could hardly just sail on by."

He grunted. He didn't believe her but there was nothing he could do about it. "I suppose you've told her everything, too," he went on.

"To save a lot of wasted breath, Onkel Kurt ..." Katya began.

He ignored her. "This coffee's cold." Looking around the apartment he said, "How can you possibly afford a place like this?" He turned to his wife. "We didn't have a place like this until we'd been married ten years at least. How can she afford this?"

What was delaying Max?

"To save a lot of time," Katya insisted, "I should say at once that I'm very happy here and, kind though you are to think of taking me to lodge with you ..."

"D'you hear her?" Onkel Kurt spluttered. "Kind though we are!" He turned to his niece. "Are you under the illusion, Miss, that you have some sort of choice?"

Katya sipped her coffee. "It is cold," she said. Then, staring directly at her uncle once more, she said, "It is no illusion."

Where *was* Max?

He rounded on his wife. "It's you! You've told her something. You've ruined it."

"We didn't know about the Grand Duchess, dear, when we decided what was best to do with Katarina."

Katya was about to tell them that nobody had the power to *do* anything about her when Max called from her door: "May I?"

"Herr Lejonkrona!" she called out, rising and going to greet him. "How nice of you to drop by! Do come in."

"What's this about Bolinders?" he whispered as he closed her front door behind him.

"You own a lot of it," she replied. "Just mention ..."

"I know that."

"You mean you really *do* own a lot of it?"

"Of course. That's why I couldn't understand what Franz was ..."

"Wonderful! No time to explain. Just bring it up naturally." Raising her voice she went on, "Do come and meet my aunt and uncle."

There were introductions all round. Then Max said, "And where is the Grand Duchess?"

"Taking a nap," Katya told him.

"Oh no she is not!" Rosie stood in the doorway "in full armour," as she liked to call it — dressed more or less as she had dressed for the Valholm ball, apart from the mask. She stood in the doorway, looking like nothing so much as a three-tier wedding cake, and surveyed them with a gaze that could have scythed down a hundred acres of ripe mustard.

All rose — and remained standing until she had taken her seat. "Iced coffee," she said to Katya when the introductions were done.

Katya, wondering how on earth she was going to manufacture ice out of nothing, went down to the kitchen and banged about a bit, as if she were having trouble with some complicated ice-manufacturing engine. She was on her way back with a plain cup of cold coffee when she heard Max saying it. She paused and listened.

"I seem to recall your niece telling me that you, sir, work at Bolinders? Or am I thinking of someone else?"

She could just imagine how her uncle started up at that!

"Someone else, sir," he replied hastily. "I am an insurance broker, here in the old city."

"Ah! Pity!" Max said — as if Onkel Kurt had just turned down the hottest tip since the Baggboele Scandal.

"Er ... why ... may I ask?" her uncle came back hesitantly.

"Oh, nothing, really," Max said offhandedly. "It's just that I have family connections with the firm."

"Ah. You mean you ... work there, yourself?"

"No-o-o!" Max dribbled out the word in a long, tolerant chuckle. "I own a modest share of the stock, that's all." After a lethal little pause he added, "Twenty per cent, I believe. I'm not quite sure, to tell the truth."

Katya sailed back into the room. "That wretched ice-making contraption has decided to go on strike again, Your Highness," she said. "So I just made the coffee with cold water. I hope that'll do?"

Rosie glared at her.

A fairly happy marriage, that, I'd say," Max commented when Tante Anna and Onkel Kurt had departed. Then he added, "As marriages go, that is." Rosie, complaining that she'd die if she stayed in her armour a minute longer, went off to change. Katya retired to the kitchen, where she threw away the cold coffee. Max followed her there. "You are getting very good at dealing with people," he said.

"Do you really own twenty percent of Bolinders?" she asked.

He sniffed. "It may be two percent, actually. When I heard myself say it, I thought twenty sounded a bit high. But I'm awfully bad with decimal places." After a pause he asked, "Are we going to get drunk here or in my place?"

"I've gone cool on that idea." She opened the door of her little larder and slumped. "And when she got there, the cupboard was bare!" she said in English.

He capped her: "And so the poor dog had none."

She looked at him in surprise. "D'you even know English nursery rhymes? Frida Carlsson said they're the things you never learn unless you grow up in a country."

"I had an English nanny," he explained. "I think the dinner Franz has prepared will stretch to three."

Franz served his dinner in Katya's apartment, out on the little balcony, overlooking the square. It was so narrow that they had to open both french windows wide, to allow Rosie to sit in the bedroom.

Katya told them about Peter Klint's death and then added, almost as an aside, that she had lost her place at the Sibylla, too.

"Good!" Rosie exclaimed — with such heartfelt (and seemingly heartless) fervour that the others stopped eating and stared at her.

"It was an unnatural thing for a young girl to be doing," the old woman explained. "It was no true preparation for life. It was a game." She smiled at Katya. "I'm glad you played it, my dear, but I'm even more glad it's behind you now and you can settle down to the serious business of life. For a mature young woman, I mean."

Katya and Max exchanged glances. "And what is that, Highness?" he asked.

Her look was withering. "You know very well. Don't try to provoke me. Look at her! She has beauty — well, that will fade. But she has charm. She has wit. She is intelligent. She can sing like an angel — you heard her yourself. And yet you can sit there and ask me what her proper business in life might be? She could have the whole of Stockholm at her feet — the whole of Europe, given the right impresario. And a bit of luck, of course. We all need that."

"One knows so many *chanteuses*," he murmured. "All of them so *happy*, too."

"If they're not, it's their own fault," she snapped. "They fall in love and then they're ruined." She turned to Katya and explained earnestly: "When God created woman he had six long days of practice behind him. He'd made all his mistakes — and learned from them — the camel, the dinosaur ..."

"Adam?" Lejonkrona suggested.

"Of course. Adam was his most ambitious failure of all. So by the time he created woman he *really* knew his trade and he was determined to get it right at last. Unfortunately, when he stepped back to admire his handiwork — as all artists do — he saw at once that by making woman perfect he'd committed the most fearful blunder of all! It was like looking at a Raphael Madonna in a daub by ..."

"Winterhalter?" Max suggested.

She ignored him. "... by whatsizname — that muddy French painter. Courbet! So either he had to start all over again and remake the rest of Creation up to the standard of woman, or he had to deliberately mar us in some way. And alas, as we know all too well, he chose to mar us."

"By ...?" Katya asked.

"By giving us this ridiculous capacity for love, of course. Oh, Katya! Imagine what we could achieve if we could just stop falling in love! If a dashing uniform simply made us laugh! If a man with hypnotic eyes found every one of us a Medusa, ready to turn him to stone! If our pulse never quickened when a tenor sang! If our innards never melted! If our flesh could not tingle! Why, God himself would hang his head and say, 'What have I done? What have I done?' But I'll tell you what he would have done — he'd have made this world a paradise — which, as we know well, is not what it's meant to be."

"And what *is* it meant to be?" Katya looked at Max to see if she were asking the question on his behalf as well.

Rosie misinterpreted her gesture. "It's no use asking *him!* He's the chief beneficiary of that deliberate flaw in woman's nature. This world is meant to be a battleground, darling, not a place of ease. It is *the* battleground in the eternal struggle between Good and Evil."

"And we women?" she prompted.

"We're supposed to be camp followers, of course — nurses, cooks, and so on. But some of us have a bit more intelligence than that." She grinned happily.

Katya frowned. "I still don't understand."

"You do," Rosie assured her. "You just don't realize it yet. Listen! When any particular battle is over, who is the winner? I'm talking about an actual war now. Napoleon versus Wellington, say. Who was the *real* winner at Waterloo?"

The obvious answer was too obvious for her to risk. "You mean who wins no matter which general may claim the victory?" she asked, playing for time. And then, of course, the answer was clear. "The man who's sitting at home, snug by his fireside, counting his profits. He *always* wins."

Rosie laughed. "You see — you did know it all along, you clever thing! And I'm sure I hardly need add that the great difference between military war (which is for grown-up children in fancy dress to fight) and moral war (which is for the rest of us) is that the one who sits all snug and warm by the home hearth is more likely to be counting *her* profits."

Katya was so excited by this analysis she felt a tingle run up and down her spine — until she recalled that tingling was bad for you.

"And tell us, Highness," Max said, "how have you applied this wisdom in your own life?"

She looked him up and down contemptuously. "If I had, would I be here to tell you of it?" she asked

After their dinner the Grand Duchess settled to read a novel and eat her daily allowance of chocolate. Katya and Max, finding their apartments rather airless, went out for a stroll. They wandered in a deliberately aimless fashion, turning this way or that at random whenever they came to a corner. The narrow streets, flanked by tall houses, amplified the little breezes that played between the two reaches of water, fresh and salt, on each side of the island.

"Rosie was eloquent tonight," Katya commented.

"She's been saving that for some time," he said. "Waiting, I think, for your work at the Sibylla to end."

"I must go back tomorrow and clear out my cupboard. I was too shattered today." She raised her eyes and stared at the narrow strip of powder-blue sky overhead. "Funny! I don't feel in the least bit shattered now. Rosie's right, you see — feelings *do* get in the way. If I'd had a knife this afternoon, I'd have stuck it in Svensson as soon as look at him. But now I wouldn't walk to the end of my finger to tell him what I think of him. Feelings — *eeurgh!* I shall be the Queen of the Frost from now on, Max."

After a thoughtful silence he said, "I should have some crushing riposte ready for Mister Dalyrimple, if I were you."

She darted her head forward and peered into his face, sure he was joking. "I doubt I'll ever see him again."

"You will," he assured her. "Now he knows you're penniless and your landlord is about to throw you out, he'll be round you like a wasp round honey — making you an offer he'll imagine you'll be in no position to refuse."

She laughed. "I can't deny there's some savage part of me would love to scourge that man. But the fact that he'd actually be enjoying it ..." She sighed at the strangeness of it all. "My more civilized parts would rebel."

"Civilized? Are you sure they're not actually the most savage parts of all, Princess?"

"I'm not sure of anything, Max."

"Except that you'll be Queen Frost from now on."

"Of course." She took his arm and hugged it. "Have you found a new mistress yet?"

"I've decided to redecorate the house in Kronoberget," he told her. "I think that's where I went wrong. You saw it, did you?"

"Yes. I thought it was very nice."

"There you are! It was. It was like any *haut-bourgeois* home in the country. That brass bed! And the charming rustic wallpaper! It gave the girls the wrong ideas. I'm going to redecorate it so that it'll be dripping with gilt and plaster and silks and bows and frills and mirrors and ormulu and voluptuous paintings and tasselled cushions. I shall design special divans. No girl will be able to enter that house without knowing precisely what she's there for. It will shout at her from every wall. I don't know why people speak of the idle rich. I shall be very busy this summer, I can tell you."

"I'm very good at hanging wallpaper," she put in, "if you need a hand. I don't seem to have anything else to do this summer."

He grinned at her. "You'd love that, wouldn't you — being my judas goat!" He became serious then. "In fact, I'll sell the house — like a reformed drunkard locking his cellar and throwing away the key. It's time I reformed. I'll spend the summer at Ekeroe. Modernize all the farms."

"And then?"

"Drown myself, I should think." He shrugged. "I don't know what I'm going to do, Katya."

"So that makes two of us."

By chance they arrived at the little restaurant in front of the bourse. The waiter recognized them and was quite content for them to sit and take no more than coffee and a sorbet.

The buildings on the eastern side of the square were ablaze with colour, for the sun's rays struck them almost at right angles and its reddened fire was reflected out of every window. The two of them sat and stared into the shadows that fell across the columns of the bourse, which were made to seem fantastic by the interplay between the sunlight and its reflections.

Two tables away from them a solitary middle-aged man was slowly downing schnapps after schnapps, doggedly drinking himself into oblivion.

After a long silence Katya said, "For the first time since coming here I feel more Swedish than Irish."

"For example?" he asked.

"That conversation we had on the way here ... I can't think of anyone in Ireland I could have spoken with like that." She let her eye travel toward the solitary drinker, so that Max saw it, and saw what she meant. "We're half-Russian, aren't we," she added. "In our blood. We try to be German — or English — and we'd *love* to be Italian. But we've got one foot nailed to the floorboards all the time."

He winced.

"It's true, though, isn't it," she insisted.

He agreed with a sigh.

"Shall we go and drown ourselves now?" She laughed gaily in a deliberate attempt to change their mood.

"Not until I know whether I own two percent of Bolinders or twenty," he replied.

"Why is that important — if we're going to die anyway?"

"It isn't — which is why I have to clear it up first. I know it would worry me as I sank beneath the waves for the third and last time. And it would make me so angry if my last thoughts proved so trivial. It would show that death changes nothing — for I've been nothing but trivial all my life."

"Good." She settled herself comfortably now that a decision had been arrived at. "I'm rather glad, actually, because I've just thought of one or two things to say to the Grand Old Man of English Letters."

*T*he following morning Katya went down to Raentmaestare Stairs and took the ferry she had discovered yesterday. The helmsman noticed how much more cheerful she was. "Amazing what a good night's sleep will do, eh?" he remarked as she stepped ashore at Grefbron.

"I keep meaning to try it," she told him.

Herr Svensson was not at all pleased to see her, though he could hardly object to her collecting her things. They were still there, in the cupboard up on the first landing — the spot where she had taken the tray from Sophie and carried it straight back to Dalyrimple's room. Standing between her galoshes, however, was a slim volume which she was sure had not been there before. She carried it to the light and saw it was a calf-bound edition of *The Doll's House* by Henrik Ibsen. Inside was a label bearing the emblem of a gymnasium school in Gothenburg and the rubric: *Peter Klint — First Prize for Studies in the Mother-tongue, 1888.* There was also a dedication, written partly over the label: *For Froeken Katarina Oberg, with respect and affection — however incredible it may seem — P.K.*

He must have put it there immediately after returning to the hôtel two nights ago — had it been only two nights? Once again tears pricked at the backs of her eyelids, but now her sorrow was complemented by the happiness that she had something of his to hold and to keep for ever.

A moment later, however, tears were the last thing on her mind for she turned to discover Dalyrimple, waddling downstairs from his room, tweaking his gloves on, finger by finger — Magnus's gesture when she first set eyes on him. "Miss Silver!" he said affably, "I was so sorry to hear of your dismissal. It was the last thing I desired."

The sheer megalomania of the sentiment left her speechless — but not for long. "God love you, sir, not a bit of it!" she responded merrily, putting on the brogue a little. Her father always said that an insult delivered with an Irish lilt and an Irish smile was ten times more lethal than any other.

"Oh!" He eyed her warily.

"Sure it left me with but one desire ungranted — for many's the hour I wished I'd told you my opinion of you and your works."

"Ah ..." He fingered his cravat nervously.

"And now the Stockholm University Literary and Philosophical Society has saved me the effort. Did you not read the report of their meeting in today's papers? They discussed you up hill and down dale last night. I wasn't there myself, but it was a grand meeting by all accounts. Every man there had to have his say. Your ears were surely burning?"

"Really?" He touched an ear gingerly. "How ... how very ..."

"Of course, there was the usual captious element, too. No meeting's complete without them — critics who can't write one original word themselves — and detest those who can."

Colour suffused his cheek. "Indeed, Miss Silver, but you're right there. I've suffered in my time. Yes — even I!"

"Last night would have been familiar ground to you, so. But wasn't it Ibsen himself who said that the writer who dare not face his critics sets himself lower than the lowest of them?"

"Was it? Ibsen, eh? I don't seem to ... er ..." He frowned, being less interested in Ibsen than in his own fate at the hands of these critics. "And what, pray, did they, ah ..."

"I want to tell you, Mister Dalyrimple, they left little enough of you to wake, and that's a fact. But sure isn't that the way of them?"

"Indeed. Indeed. But, um, in particular?"

"Well, as I recall, they compared you to Byron and Gibbon and Doctor Johnson and suchlike."

"Oh?" He bucked up. "Well, I wouldn't call that too ... terrible, you know."

"One said you were Gibbon without the grammar. Another that you were a Johnson-jejune. And a third that you had all the qualities of Byron save his overwhelming modesty and restraint. A fourth was of the opinion that you had borrowed more than the *qualities* of all three, for you'd borrowed many of their *words*, as well. And a fifth added that it did you no good, for your borrowings lay 'like lumps of marl upon a barren moor — encumb'ring what they could not fertilize'." She smiled sweetly.

His eyes narrowed. "That's from Sheridan, isn't it? That last bit."

She had not expected him to be so astute; it was, indeed, from *The Critic,* which the Dram. Soc. had read in Dublin just before Christmas. She decided it was time to go; over her shoulder she said, "But isn't that the way of them, sir? They can't take a leaf out of *your* book and be *original* in their borrowings!"

Her stress on those two words and her seemingly complimentary tone prevented him from realizing what she had actually said until she was back downstairs in the foyer. And then it was too late.

Out in the street she set off toward Grefbron once more. At the domestics' entrance to the hôtel she found Sophie waiting to speak to her. "Remember that Irish family you took to Drottningholm Palace last week?" she asked.

"It was more than a week ago," Katya said. "Anyway, what about them? I thought they'd gone touring in Dalecarlia somewhere."

"Well, they're back — and very disappointed to learn you're not here any longer. They wanted you to take them round Skansen. I said I'd see if you'd do it privately, like. What shall I tell them?"

"That's very kind of you, Sophie."

The maid shrugged. "I owe you a favour, ever since you put that Dimple-Dample man in his place for me."

They shared a giggle at the memory then Katya said, "Tell them I'm very sorry but I have other things planned for today. Perhaps tomorrow — I'll see. I'll telephone them."

Sophie pulled a face. "They didn't tell me what to say if you couldn't. If I ask them to come out here, will you tell them yourself?"

"Of course. Only say I'm a bit late already."

"Just hang on there," Sophie called back over her shoulder.

She left the door open. Katya turned her back to it and stood there, swinging the holdall that contained her belongings and trying not to show her impatience. She hummed a little tune, admired the window boxes in the apartments opposite, watched some removals men wrestling with a huge carved bedframe ... until a gentle tap on the shoulder made her spin round in alarm — for she had heard no one come up behind her.

And when she saw who it was she fell back against the wall and screamed his name out loud: "Declan!"

*H*e grabbed her by the waist and pulled her into the entranceway, where he started to kiss her with some passion. At first she was too dazed to respond; then, by the time a small fire had begun to light up inside her, he became aware of her coolness — as it seemed — and let go of her again. They stared at each other, a little out of breath, smiling with embarrassment. A fluttering of suppressed giggles somewhere down the dark passageway did nothing to help.

"I'll kill that Sophie when I catch her," she said. "You gave me the start of my life."

"You almost gave me the end of mine," he replied.

It was not his usual style of speech at all; she stared at him in bewilderment and asked, "When? Just now?"

"No!" he exclaimed sulkily. "When you left Dublin."

"Oh, really? Talking of which — where were you that day?"

"What d'you mean — where was I? Wasn't I in Dublin. Isn't that what I'm after saying."

"Well of course I know *that!* I mean exactly where? Doyle's? Grogan's? Mooneys?"

"Oh I see what you're after!" he sneered. "Was I drowning my sorrows — is that it? Well, this is a nice welcome and no mistake!"

"You certainly didn't show up to see was I drowning *myself,*" she pointed out. "And what sort of welcome did you expect? A letter would not have gone amiss. A postcard would have helped. We even have telegrams in these latitudes now."

He turned his back to her and faced the street. "And I thought you'd jump over the moon for joy," he complained.

The stubborn cut of him made her smile and softened her feelings a little. She reached out and gently touched the back of his arm. "I'm sorry, love, but you could have warned me. This isn't the North Pole. You let me languish the best part of two months without a heartening word from you — then you fall from out the sky and fill my mouth with lips and teeth. What d'you expect?"

"D'you want me to go?" he asked.

"Of course not, Declan."

"What do you want, then?"

She took the Ibsen from the holdall and slipped it into her handbag. Then she called down the corridor, "Sophie? Are you still there?"

There was an embarrassed admission from out of the gloom. Katya dropped the holdall and called out, "See one of the pageboys takes this back to my apartment in Jaerntorget, will you? There's a dear. And I'll talk to you about *this* later!" She jabbed a finger at Declan's stubborn figure.

Sophie began sidling reluctantly up the passage; before she arrived, Katya slipped her arm through Declan's and started walking him down Sibyllegatan toward the water.

"What d'you want?" he repeated.

She held out her other hand. "Twenty-five crowns, please — my fee as personal guide-interpreter — twenty-five crowns per half-day. And you also buy me luncheon." She moved her hand nearer him.

He stared at it and laughed, not in the greatest humour; but when she continued to hold it out he said, "You don't mean it seriously?"

"I am quite serious, Declan. This is a working day for me. I can't afford to be out of pocket."

"But you've been given the order of the boot."

"That's a very pessimistic way of looking at it, my lad. I prefer to think that the Sibylla has released me in order to move on to better things. Are you going to pay up?"

The minute she said it she wished she hadn't; now she had made it a matter of wills. As if to prove it he said, "Damned if I shall!" and stuffed his hands tight into his pockets.

"Very well," she said lightly — withdrawing her arm from his — "I have to go to Skansen anyway. There's something I have to do there. You may follow or not, as you wish."

They were within hailing distance of the steps at Grefbron. The ferry helmsman called out to her, "You see, young lady — the darkest hour comes just before the dawn."

She laughed and told him she'd remember that in future. Then she turned back to Declan and asked, "How did you know to find me at the Sibylla?"

"You told me in your letter, didn't you?" he replied.

"I did not. I wrote that letter even before I went for the interview."

"Then I must have heard it from that sea-captain's wife."

"Did you meet her? She never said."

"Is this a catechism or what?" he objected.

"There's something you're not telling me, Declan. I don't give a fig how you knew to find me at the Sibylla — but I care very much that you won't tell me."

He raised his eyes to the sky above. "Dear God! Would you just listen to that for logic!"

"Did Count Magnus Hamilton tell you?"

"Who?"

"Your man at the Lifeguards of Horse — you know."

"Oh yes!" He laughed with relief. "Yes, he told me. That's the fellow sure enough."

Had she ever considered Declan a *good* liar? she wondered; she couldn't remember thinking of him as a liar of any kind — so had he changed or had she?

"You were lucky to get a room at such short notice," she went on. "Stockholm is jam-packed for the Exhibition."

"I believe you there!" He was glad to move on to a point of agreement. "In fact, they only let me in because somebody died. Grisly, what?"

She managed not to falter in her stride. It did not make matters any easier that they were approaching the old bridge to Djurgaarden, where, only two days earlier, she had followed Peter onto the island. Fortunately it was now closed to all but Exhibition traffic — the new bridge having been opened that very morning.

Crossing it they met a family from the Sibylla, coming toward them. They had just been to the Nordiska Museum, the paterfamilias told her ... had a wonderful time ... seen all the things she had recommended ... would be ever grateful to her. She thanked them in return and said it was probably the last time they'd meet — just because she'd told Mr Dalyrimple to go and boil his head! They laughed at that and the husband said he'd been longing to do the same ever since they'd met the man. They wished her luck, smiled at Declan, and parted.

A little farther up the road they met a counter assistant from Augusta Lundin's. She stopped for a brief chat, too, and mentioned that they had some beautiful silk blouses just in from France.

And no sooner had she gone than an errand boy, riding his bicycle no-hands, blew her a cheeky kiss and shouted, "Monkey-monkey!"

She levelled a warning finger at him. "I'll give you monkey! I'll box your ears, you little devil!"

She had never seen the lad in her life but he must have watched her in the ape house, two days earlier. To Declan, however, it must have seemed that they exchanged mock insults daily. He had gone rather quiet by now.

And at the Skansen ticket office, of course, old Loefgren told her all the museum's domestic gossip and said that Simeon was his old mischievous self again and proving a great success with the children.

Inside, Declan — who had had the grace at least to pay for the tickets — said, "You'd think you'd lived in Stockholm for years."

"Some days are like that," she told him.

"You seem more at home here than you are in Dublin."

There was resentment in his tone — and something else. Relief? Regret? She could not be sure. "Did you bring the remounts for the cavalry?" she asked.

"I did, of course."

"Are they pleased? God, man, do I have to drag every bit of the crack out of you?"

He shook his head in an irritable, slightly bewildered fashion. "This is not what I expected, I must say."

They arrived at a sort of pedestrian circus half way up the slope. From it several paths radiated. He asked her what each of the fingerboards said and she translated them all except the one that read, "Wolves and wolverines."

But he noticed the omission and asked about that one, too.

"It's the perimeter path," she replied.

"Does it go to the restaurant?" He felt she was being reluctant and wanted to pick away until she said something to reveal why.

"It does if you follow it far enough. But this is the shortest way." She took a few steps up another path and looked back at him. "Come on! Aren't you hungry?"

They went straight up the hill to the Idunshallen restaurant; it was a little early for lunch but, she explained, they'd be able to eat it in peace, ahead of the main crowd. They took a chance on the showers and sat out on the terrace, where practically the whole of Stockholm made a panorama around them.

"Is *this* what you expected, then?" she asked when the girl-waiter had taken their order. She made a grand sweep of her arm across the view. "Or isn't that what you meant?"

"You know very well that isn't what I meant." He knitted his brow and stared at her. "I feel I hardly know you any more."

"I'm bound to have changed. Mind you — I don't think it's all that much. I think I was always like this — only there was no way for me to show it." She made another, smaller gesture at the view. "Opportunity," she said vaguely. "That's all I needed."

"And who gave it you?" he asked.

"Gave me what?"

"Opportunity — you said."

"No one *gave* it me! I had to make it for myself." She could see he didn't believe her.

"People helped," she admitted. "The Grand Duchess — I told you about her. And my landlord ..."

"This Lejonkrona lad who owns half of Bolinders!" he exclaimed.

If he hadn't immediately looked so guilty for his outburst she might never have twigged; she was so eager to show him how resourceful she had been that she only half listened to his interruptions. "How d'you know that?" she said.

He looked away awkwardly. "The service here isn't up to much."

"Declan!"

"What now?"

She reached across and grabbed his arm. "You know what: Where did you learn that Lejonkrona owns half of Bolinders? It's actually no more than a fifth, but never mind that."

When he drew breath to reply she could tell from his expression it was going to be a lie. She cut in: "And don't tell me Count Marcus Hamilton let it slip — because I know both gentlemen very well and they never discuss business affairs. Money for gambling or pleasure — yes. Money for business — never!"

He did not pick her up on her deliberate misnaming of Magnus, she noticed. But in any case her warning wrong-footed him. He closed his mouth ... opened it again ... closed it once more.

She turned from him and stared across the Salt Sea to Gamla Stan. "My Onkel Kurt told you, didn't he," she said. It had to be. Who else knew of it?

The girl-waiter brought their luncheon — two smoergaasar, some Baltic herring in dill, and Ramloesa water.

"It *was* my Onkel Kurt, wasn't it," she insisted when they were alone again.

Poor Declan sank his head in his hands. "God, he'll kill me!" he said unhappily.

"Onkel Kurt?" she asked in disbelief — and then the full truth hit her. "My *father*, of course! Onkel Kurt didn't tell *you*, he told my father! And you were there."

He twitched. "He'll only kill me! He'll never believe you worked it out without a word from me."

"My father!" she said again, with a kind of wild relish. "He'll be staying at his club, I'm sure." But other possibilities began to dawn on her. "Unless my mother is here, too? Is she?"

He shook his head miserably.

"And you travelled all the way with him, didn't you!"

Another nod; he stared at her with hunted eyes.

"Why?" she asked in a puzzled tone. "Are you in his good books now? Why would he suddenly change like that?" A smile spread slowly on her features as this and that began to fall into place. "You're the bait, of course! He wants me back in Dublin — and you're the bait to get me there." She laughed. "I've been wondering why you haven't put a fist between my eyes before this! Poor man — haven't I provoked you enough!"

"Sorely!" He began to regain some of his spirit — and suddenly she remembered the thing she liked about him most: the fact that you could never keep him down for long. He'd taken some terrible insults from her father in his time — and he'd suffered fierce reversals of fortune in his business, too. But he'd always give that characteistic little grin, dust himself down, pick himself up, and rebound like a boxing kangaroo.

"I'm not going back, Declan," she warned him. "You may tell him so from me. And you'd better make up your own mind which foot you'll be kicking with from here on. You can't hope to straddle both sides. We're too far apart."

He closed his eyes and uttered a brief prayer: "God send I'm doing the right thing!" He opened them again and looked at her. "He has a grand little scheme for us, Katy — all worked out."

She laughed harshly. "When has he not!"

"Wait till I tell you!"

"I'm not interested, Declan. You'd be wasting your breath — just as you'd be wasting your time to believe a word of it."

"Oh but he means it — that I'll swear to."

"And so will he. And he'll mean it, too — honestly and sincerely. But the minute we got back to Dublin it would be 'circumstances alter cases' all over again. He'd rewrite every pledge he ever gave us. Listen! Did I ever tell you of the famous incident in our family — of the shaving mug?"

He shook his head. "It sounds like a Sherlock Holmes yarn."

"Well, it would take a Sherlock Holmes to fathom that man. Listen to this now. He broke a shaving mug once — a penny piece of delph off a barrow down by the Liberties. Unfortunately for him he'd just ticked off one of our housemaids for breaking some valuable dinner plate or other — she said 'twas an accident and he told her there was no such thing as an *accident* with porcelain. Typical of the man! Can't you just hear him saying it! Anyway — no word of a lie — he spent *two days* gluing that mug together again and painting over the cracks with patent enamel. I'd swear Sherlock Holmes himself couldn't have found a trace that it was ever broken. Pappa could have gone and bought the perfect replica for another penny. But no! He had to put *that* mug together again — and then deny it ever happened." The savage curl of her lip made him shiver. "And *that's* why he wants me back in Dublin — so he can deny the crack in our lives ever really happened! And the question you've got to ask yourself now, Declan, is do you believe for one moment that the man who behaves like that is ever going to admit to his Dublin cronies that he was wrong about you? Because that's what he'd be doing if he dared fulfil even the smallest promise he made to you."

He closed his eyes again and shook his head. "It's your own father you're talking about, Katy."

"And who should know him better! Even so, I'm amazed at *you* — falling for his promises like that. What *did* he promise you, as a matter of interest?"

"He said he'd arrange for me to get capital enough to start an auction ring of my own," he admitted.

She thought it over and realized she had forgotten precisely how clever her father was. Honesty made her say, "By God, he might even do that! Not to honour a pledge, of course — perish the thought! But because he could see you making a fortune at it — with a nice fat dividend for himself, to be sure. But as for marrying *me* — you may forget all that!"

His attempt at disappointment was laughable. And it put the last bit of the puzzle in place. "That was the promise *you'd* have gone back on, isn't it!" she taunted. "Lord, but don't the pair of ye deserve each other!"

He gave an expressive shrug of his shoulders and stared vaguely over her head.

She laughed and took up his hand between hers. "And now comes the best bit of all," she said.

He groaned.

"No, listen! It's nothing like that. All that's behind us now, love. It's all spent and exploded. Shure there's no harrm in it, yer honour," she added in a Dublinese whine. "The best bit of all, Declan, is that we can now be *friends*. Plain and simple — just good friends."

"How can you say that?" He struggled to get his hand back, but not very strongly.

"I don't blame you — not one little bit. You never pretended to love me. You were flattered by my infatuation, which is only natural — but you never took the advantage of it that people always warned me against ..."

He was staring at her open-mouthed by now.

"Of course they warned me," she assured him. "And of course I was too headstrong to listen. You could have left me belly-out on half a dozen ..."

"Katy!" he exclaimed in horror.

"Hold your whisht, man! You know you could have — and you didn't. I have a higher opinion of you than my father has, I may say." She grinned accusingly and added, "... though I suspect my mother has the highest opinion of all!"

He adjusted his tie. "I don't know what you may mean by that!"

"I've seen a bit of the world and its ways since Saint Patrick's, my dear. I think I know what my mother's *indisposition* was that night — and the *cure* you devised for it!"

"Be all the holy ... colleen!" He had wounded innocence all over his face.

"Fair dues to you, Declan," she continued remorselessly. "Mamma was quieter and more contented that night than I'd seen her in years. But to get back to the point — which is that we may be good friends now because, for the first time since we've known each other, we satisfy the basic condition for friendship. D'you know what that is?"

He lifted an eyebrow and waited.

"We seek no selfish advantage from our connection with each other. Isn't that the truth?"

He breathed in deeply and then breathed all the way out again before assenting with a solemn nod. Or rather, he began solemnly enough but soon a smile spread across his face until it threatened to divide it from ear to ear. "Dear God, Katy!" he exclaimed. "I have a month's mind to start all over again from the beginning with you."

She released his hand at last, thrusting it from her. "Save your powder!" she advised.

"Is there someone else, then?" he asked.

"A fair few," she assured him. "None to take seriously. And you?"

He nodded ruefully. "As usual."

They laughed, the first genuine, unqualified laugh between them since they had met.

"Did you say you had business up here?" he asked.

Her smile faded. "Sombre business, I'm afraid," she warned him. "I have to tell ... someone ... that a mutual friend of ours is dead."

"Oh." He stared away down the hill, wondering whether to offer to wait or to leave her at once. There were so many things he ought to tell her father without delay — to prevent him from making a fool of himself now.

"You may come with me," she said. It was more of a command than an invitation. "It won't take long."

The wolf was waiting at the corner, just where he had been waiting the evening before last. He stared up at her incuriously, as he must stare at hundreds of other visitors every day, and then returned his gaze to the bend in the path where Peter had always appeared. Her heart went out to him. She wanted to pat him, to tell him she knew just how it felt to lose a friend like that.

She pulled off her glove, squatted, and reached a hand toward him through the bars.

"What in the name of God are you at, colleen?" Declan asked, staring at her in horror.

She remained silent.

The wolf, alerted by his cry, glanced at her — then snarled and backed away from the inner railing, his mane bristling.

"For heaven's sake!" Declan exclaimed.

She reached into her handbag and took out the book Peter had given her. She held it out toward him, as if she wanted him to accept it. Then the realization that he might, indeed, do so made her grip it more securely.

The wolf was now trapped between wanting to snarl a fresh warning and the promptings of simple curiosity. Then he must have caught a remnant whiff of Peter on the book for his whole manner toward her changed.

He returned to the inner railing with his ears down, his tail down, whimpering. He made the same frantic efforts to squeeze his head between the bars as she had seen him make with Peter. Her shoulder being slimmer than his, she managed to get her hand close enough for him to touch.

Declan watched aghast, afraid she'd have her fingers bitten off — yet also afraid to pull her away in case a sudden movement should trigger just such a calamity.

But biting was the last thing on the wolf's mind — not even to fight her for possession of the book, which even a playful nip would have forced her to drop. He licked it all over and then licked her fingers, too. The rasp of his tongue startled her for it was much rougher than a dog's.

When he had finished he stared at her a long while. She had an eerie feeling that he was somehow reading her thoughts. Then, without so much as a glance toward the bend in the path, he turned his back on them and vanished into the forest.

"His eyes!" she murmured, standing up and shaking her right leg gingerly, for it had developed pins-and-needles. "So deep, so pale ... and yet, somehow, so vulnerable — don't you think?"

He gave her an odd sort of smile. "Haven't you seen them before?"

She shook her head. "Only once. Last Sunday."

"No!" he exclaimed scornfully. And when she continued to stare at him in bewilderment, he added, "They're *your* eyes, Katy — that's what I mean." He turned away and made to leave that area. "Anyway," he added, "that was a she-wolf, not a he. Let's go and see this friend of yours."

Her gaze lingered on the bend in the path, where *he* would never appear again. "Oh, Peter!" she whispered. "Will I ever, ever, ever understand *anything* before it's too late?"

*K*atya returned alone to Jaerntorget and bumped into Max just as he was setting off to the Skeppsbrokaellare restaurant. Athough Franz had the evening off, she was suspicious of that "bumping into"; she felt sure Max had been waiting to engineer it. Not that she minded. In fact, she felt more in need of his counsel tonight than ever before.

He wanted to hear all about Dalyrimple, of course, something she had almost forgotten by then. She had a quick bath (for her) and, within an hour, he set off once more for the restaurant, this time with Katya on one arm and Rosie on the other.

"The eve of the Exhibition," Katya remarked. "The town will be packed tonight. We'll be lucky to get in."

She might as well have saved her breath. The restaurant was, indeed, crowded, but the *hovmaestare* bowed them to the best table, overlooking the Salt Sea. The island naval base of Skeppsholm stood between there and the Exhibition grounds on Djuurgaarden, but over it they could see the tops of the tallest buildings, including Liljeholm's gigantic replica of a candle, which, when it was turned on at midnight, would consume prodigious quantities of electricity and send a beam over the entire city.

Katya told them of her final encounter with the GOM of English Letters but for some reason Max did not find it as amusing as she had hoped he would.

"Laugh!" She nudged his arm. "I spent hours last night working it all out."

"Mmm." He nodded. "A mistake, I think."

"Well, I like that! Who was it told me to have something crushing ready for him?"

"Oh, the mistake was mine, Princess — I'm not seeking to dodge it. You always think better — and *do* better — when the crisis is presented to you, *fait accompli!*"

Slightly mollified by this compliment she went on to tell them of her much more significant meeting with Declan.

"*Voilà!*" Max exclaimed — and she saw that her story did, indeed, confirm his point. But beyond that he gave her none of the cheer and encouragement she had counted on. Instead he grew thoughtful. He asked her how far she thought her father might go to get his own way. She replied that hundreds had asked themselves that question before him and no one had yet found the answer.

More sombre still, he begged their leave and went to make a telephone call. He returned in much happier mood, saying, "The carriage will be here in half an hour, so we may dawdle deliciously over the coffee."

"Where are we going?" they both wanted to know.

But he would only grin and tell them it would spoil the surprise if he said any more.

"Am I invited, too?" Rosie asked.

"Highness!" he cried reproachfully. "It was only by mentioning your name that I was able to arrange anything at all. Do you imagine the *hovmaestare* gave *me* this table?"

She didn't believe him, of course, but that didn't prevent a blush of pleasure on her cheek. "I must look a fright," she said and went off to preen herself.

Max's eyes followed her affectionately. "Isn't it extraordinary?" he murmured. "If she lives to be a hundred — which, all things considered, she probably will ... even then, one little touch of gallantry will make her a schoolgirl again."

"But it's all for your benefit," Katya grumbled. She had no objection to a touch of sentimentality in Max — but he ought to pick its object with greater care, she thought. "It's like my 'hôtel smile' at the Sibylla. Behind it, all the little brain cogs are whirring away still."

He patted her hand. "God help us all when they stop, Princess — especially in your case — and most especially tonight, eh?"

"D'you think so?"

"I do."

The carriage was something of an extravagance for it took them no farther than the landing stage at Raentmaestare Stairs. And there a steam launch called *Vulkan* awaited them. Katya caught sight of the pennant at her stern and exclaimed, "This is a Bolinders launch!"

"Isn't she a beauty!" Max said. "The best in the land."

She touched things as she climbed aboard — the decorative deadeyes and brass bulwark rails — as if being *Bolinders* invested them with some special quality.

"I discovered I was right about the decimal place after all," Max told her. "It's most dreadfully embarrassing to discover one can be truthful by neglect."

"Are we going to tour the Exhibition?" she asked excitedly. "Have you arranged a special Private View — just for us? Oh, Max, you are so clever!"

"For example," he said.

Katya was used to the great, wallowing ferryboats, with their medium-speed steam engines and crudely balanced crankshafts. But *Vulkan*, the pearl of Swedish engineering, had a high-speed turbine one could neither hear nor feel. The moment they cast off — with as much pipe-blowing and gaff-gymnastics as if the king himself were aboard — the master opened the steam valve, the whole vessel rose several inches higher in the water, and her twin screws sent out enough backwash to soak another half dozen steps on the landing. They skimmed over the wavelets to Djurgaarden, leaving a slick calm behind them as broad as any ocean liner might lay. Their coming to rest was as dazzling as their getting under way had been; the master throttled back and she settled into the water like a swan in the evening.

When they tied up Katya continued to sit there with her eyes closed, still entranced with the thrills of that brief crossing. Max touched her shoulder. "Not bad, eh?" he commented.

She rose and followed him up onto the landing stage, where Rosie — too aristocratic to show vulgar delight in expensive toys — was waiting patiently. "That was the most thrilling voyage ever," Katya enthused. "Can we go back in it?"

"I thought we'd stroll home through the festive throng," he replied as he handed her ashore. "We can borrow this old tub again one day next week, if you like. Steam up Maelaren to Ekeroe — or even Valholm?" He turned to Rosie and added, "I'll get the carriage to take you home, of course, Highness. I know how nervous you aristocrats feel about mobs — and rightly so, when you look back over history."

Laughing, they made their way up a broad gravel path between the Hall of Machines and the Hall of Industry. Katya's gaiety fell away as she gazed about them. "Is it all going to be terribly *worthy?*" she asked.

Max swept his hand vaguely before them and said, "Beyond this *worthy* area you may find the Trolls' Grotto, a Biblical Waxworks, a restaurant where we could have eaten for forty oere each, a ride in a gas balloon, a Roentgen machine — you stand on it and watch the bones of your feet wriggling inside your shoes — and also, in case you hadn't noticed it, the world's largest artificial candle."

He glanced at Katya sternly. "Are you taking this all in, Froeken? This could be your job next week. Other wonders include a cascade or fountain, out in the water, lighted from *underneath* by over a hundred coloured lights of staggering candlepower ... what else? Oh yes — a biograph, where you can watch moving pictures of Bolinders' band marching forward through the park and then backward, retracing their steps precisely. Also a pugilist giving the Man-in-the-Moon a black eye."

Rosie interrupted him with the only item of interest to her: "I'm informed that there's an Italian sculptor who will carve my bust while I wait." To Katya she added, "And for only fifteen crowns!"

"Immortality on the cheap, eh!" Max lifted her hand and kissed it. "It's just round the corner. So!" He quizzed the pair of them. "Which is it to be?"

"All of them!" Katya said at once.

"So be it!" He raised his stick and flourished it like a sword. "On with the motley! But first" — he held up a finger — "a matter of courtesy. We *must* drop in on Bolinders and say our thank-yous."

He ushered them toward the imposing entrance to the massive Hall of Industry. "About that Roentgen machine," he said. "There's an amusing bit of scandal doing the rounds."

The two women turned to him, eyes agog — which had been his intention. "Apparently," he went on, "they've had to put special rails round it because boisterous young men and women were lying down upon it — revealing to each other and to the world at large everything that trousers and corsets were intended to conceal."

As their laughter died Katya began to look around her for the first time. They were now in the heart of the hall, which was packed with impressive machinery; but, since none of it was working, the overall effect was rather dead. Worried men in dark suits were walking around checking the labels and making lists of last-minute things to be done before tomorrow's official opening.

Max leaned toward her and murmured, "D'you remember what we were talking about earlier, Princess? How you always manage life's little crises better if you don't have too much time to think about them in advance?"

"Yes?" she replied suspiciously.

He took her arm as if to steady her. "Well, cast your eyes to our left here — just beyond the machine with the big brass dome ..."

She did as she was bid — and then breathed in sharply; he felt her whole body stiffen. It was an especially thrilling moment for him, for he literally had not the faintest notion what she would do next.

Turn and strike him? Faint? Run away and hide? Go all to pieces?

In fact, she did the one thing he would never have predicted for her. She cast decorum to the wind, picked up her skirts, and flew the twenty-odd paces that separated them.

"Pappa!" she cried, turning all the heads in earshot.

*K*atya flung herself into her father's embrace and swung him dangerously off-balance as she spun him round. "Pappa! Pappa! Oh, Pappa!" she kept repeating. People looked at one another in bewilderment but they could not help smiling, so infectious was her joy.

Rosie looked at Max and raised a puzzled eyebrow.

"Nor me!" he assured her.

When his daughter had calmed down a little, Larry O'Barry of Dublin — Lars Oberg of Stockholm — presented her to all the Bolinders nabobs. He held her by the arm, tight at his side, she noticed, and would not even let go of her if a colleague took him aside while she was still in conversation with someone else. She just had to smile her apology and let herself be carried away in his wake.

Her joyous greeting had been quite instinctive, even if those instincts had been more in her head than in her heart. But it must now be clear to everyone, she realized, that she and her father had not seen each other for some time. And, since they must also know that he had arrived in Stockholm within the last day or so, the question of her whereabouts in the meanwhile must now be forming in at least some of their minds. Why had she not called on any of them? Why had he sent no letters of introduction? She waited to see what sort of answers her father might offer.

He offered none.

It did not really surprise her. "Never mend a wheel while it's rolling," he liked to say. "If *they* don't ask, *you* don't tell them."

One man, however, did ask — an old opponent of her father's named Gran. He was to be the senior man in day-to-day charge of the Bolinders stand at the Exhibition. "Am I right in thinking you've been in Stockholm some time already, Froeken Oberg?" he asked.

"What makes you suppose that, Herr Gran?" she responded.

"I believe I saw you taking Mister MacKenzie and his family around Skansen the week before last?"

"The Canadian gentleman," Katya said, thinking quickly. "Very nice people."

"And one of Bolinders' largest customers in North America," he added. "Of course, I didn't realize whose daughter you were then." He turned to her father. "I suppose *you* arranged it, though, Oberg?"

Katya cut across her father: "You amaze me, Herr Gran. I had no idea Mister MacKenzie had any connection with Bolinders."

Her father shot her a swift, baleful glance and she knew she had been right to get in before he could lay claim to the arrangement. Gran became aware of the tension between the two and pretended to be embarrassed. "I'm sorry ... I don't quite follow?"

It came to Katya in a flash — what she must do. She squeezed her father's arm, hoping he'd understand it as her reassurance she was not about to let the side down, and said, "The truth is, Herr Gran, this dear man and I had one of those ... er, *interesting* discussions that daughters and fathers so often have these days. Independence and that sort of thing. Perhaps you have daughters of your own?"

He rolled his eyes, which was answer enough.

"So," she continued, "when he decided we were to come to Stockholm for the Exhibition, I challenged him to a wager. I bet him that if he let me come six weeks or so in advance, I could earn my own independent living for at least that period."

Gran looked rather askance at his colleague.

Lars Oberg saw a chance and took it. "What my daughter means by *independence*, Gran, is not at all what you and I would have in mind. My brother lives in Soeder and Katarina has other relations all over the city. Still" — he rubbed his hands energetically — "for a girl of her age that is heady independence, indeed!"

Gran was disappointed with his meagre trawl.

Katya was determined her father's word should not be the last. She smiled engagingly and said, "What I have not yet had a chance to tell my father, Herr Gran — and why I was so excited to see him just now and break this wonderful news to him — is that I have managed the whole thing without troubling a single one of my many relations in Sweden. I was determined to make it a *true* test of independence, d'you see." She spoke these last words as much to her father as to Herr Gran.

"But how admirable, Froeken Oberg!" Gran said. Katya's qualification of her father's assuring speech had heartened him greatly; he did not in the least object to being used as a sounding board in this urbane sparring match between father and daughter. "Do tell us how you managed it?"

Lars Oberg gave his daughter's arm a little tug. "I really think we should leave these post-mortems until ..."

Once again Katya spoke across him to Herr Gran. "Why, I did what you saw me doing with the MacKenzies. I worked at the Sibylla — partly as a professor, teaching the staff the sort of English and French they might meet day by day, and partly guiding guests to Skansen, Drottningholm Palace ... and so on. It was wonderful. And so very easy! It's little wonder you men make such a mystery of the world of work!"

Her father, tight-lipped at her side, saw another opening. "Naturally we provided her with *plenty* of money," he said.

She had felt that one coming and was ready to cap it at once: "And I didn't need to touch a *penny* of it! In fact, I managed to save most of what I earned." She smiled warmly at her father. "I am, after all, this clever man's daughter. I was paid eight crowns an hour and I only worked ..." Her voice trailed off when she saw the information had produced the desired effect.

Both men just stood there gaping at her.

Her father's arm went so slack that he actually let go of her at last. She moved slightly away from him, placing herself at an equal distance between the pair of them.

"You mean eight crowns a day, surely?" her father said.

"No. Eight crowns an hour, but I only worked four hours a day. So I didn't earn as much as you might think. Even so, I've managed to save over four hundred crowns this month." She smiled playfully at her father and concluded: "So I'm afraid that's five pounds you owe me, Pappa dear!"

"What?" he asked.

"Our wager," she reminded him. "I think any fair-minded person would agree that I've won. Don't you think so, Herr Gran?" She held out her hand to her father. "That's ninety Swedish crowns, please?"

Gran, not quite understanding what sort of battle had been waged before him, but understanding very well that his ancient rival had somehow been trounced, began to laugh. "Ah, Oberg, my dear fellow! Blood will out, eh! There's no doubting whose daughter she is! She's her father by daylight, all right!"

Katya could almost feel sorry for her father. Which way was the poor man to jump now? Part of him must be "bucking wild," as Declan's horsey fraternity would say, at what she had done; but surely the rest of him could not help feeling a little glow of pride — when even an old opponent like Gran could say that her success was no more than one would expect of an Oberg?

However, if she thought she might count on that pride to help her turn her independence into something more permanent, her father's next words shattered it.

Thinking she might prevail upon Gran to offer her a place on the Bolinders stand at the Exhibition, she said, "However, I've left the Sibylla now. In fact, I was wondering ..."

Her father pounced before she could say it. "Yes! We've great plans for her now — back in Ireland." To her he said, "You remember? We only discussed it vaguely but it's now quite firmly decided. I'm to put up the capital Declan Butler needs for his new auction house — and you're to manage his office." He smiled knowingly at Gran before he turned back to her. "And you'll look after the Oberg family interests, of course — now you've *earned* your independence."

His emphasis implied that she had previously wanted it handed to her on a silver tray. This was obviously the scheme he had duped Declan into believing. Her problem now was that she did not know whether Declan had managed to speak to her father since she had disabused him of the idea at Skansen.

She, too, smiled at Gran. "Well," she said airily, "the man who made time made enough of it to let me sleep on that. When I spoke to Declan this afternoon, he seemed to have gone very cool on that whole idea."

From the sudden pallor in her father's cheek she knew he had not seen Declan at all that evening. Now it was she who rubbed her hands vigorously. "However, Pappa dear, we don't need to vex ourselves with these trivialities, I'm sure. But there is one thing I'd like to ask Herr Gran before we let the poor man go ..."

Gran encouraged her with a lift of his brow. Her father, still desperately working out the implications of her last remark, was too late to stop her saying: "I've been thinking I might look for a place as an interpreter, here at the Exhibition. There can't be very many people in Stockholm with fluent French, fluent *idiomatic* English — and, of course, native Swedish." She smiled at Gran. "Or have you been inundated with people like that? Perhaps you have."

"Ah ... no." He fingered his tie nervously — wondering how far he dared provoke Lars Oberg, who, disliked though he was, still wielded considerable power in the firm.

Katya pressed her point relentlessly. "Perhaps you're not looking for them though?" she suggested. "Perhaps you can ... you know — muddle through somehow?"

She knew that in any list of words calculated to run against the Bolinders grain and raise the hackles of any true company man, *muddle through* would be right at the head.

"As a matter of fact ..." Gran eyed his old adversary, longing to serve him out, but desperate not to trespass too far.

Lars Oberg's face was expressionless, except that the muscles of his jaw and temple were rippling.

Katya saw that Gran's nerve was about to fail him. "Never mind," she said swiftly. "Pappa and I haven't had a chance to discuss it yet. So perhaps Herr Gran will just think it over, eh?" She slipped her arm through her father's and said, "Come on, darling, I want you to meet some of *my* friends, now."

Gran, seeing his chance slip away for ever — as he thought — called after her in an anxious tone, "It's just that figure of eight crowns an hour, Froeken Oberg."

"Oh" — she waved a hand vaguely around the great hall — "I'm sure to be offered it *somewhere*, Herr Gran. I can assure you, interpreters — especially good ones — are like gold in Stockholm this summer. Good night — so nice to have met you at last. My father has spoken of you so often."

After several paces her father stopped and turned — not to her but to seek out Gran, who was no longer where they had left him. "You've won," he murmured. "Look at him! Off to find Gyllenhammar to get permission to offer you eight crowns an hour."

"Damn, I should have said *ten*!" she responded bitterly.

His head jerked toward her in astonishment. She smiled regretfully.

"But that's always been our problem — us Obergs — hasn't it, Pappa. We cannot tell a lie!"

"Are you telling me you *didn't* ... ah, stretch the truth a little when you said eight?"

She nodded. "Eight Swedish crowns it was — not an oere more, not an oere less."

"They'll verify it with the Sibylla, you realize?"

"Then *they* will also know I'm telling the truth." She smiled cajolingly up at him. "Did I let you down? Be honest with me now — and with yourself — isn't poor old Gran back there going home tonight to complain to Fru Gran that, once again, the Obergs have left him standing?"

He closed his eyes and shook his head. "Katy!" he murmured in English. "What has become of you, at all?"

"Did I let you down?" she insisted in English, to show him that a change of language did not imply a change of subject.

"No ..." he allowed reluctantly. Then, in rather a pained tone: "Do you really intend working for Bolinders?"

"Of course not," she replied at once.

He stopped dead and stared at her.

"I wouldn't *dream* of it," she assured him. "I just said that so that they'd know Lars Oberg's daughter would never work for mere pin money — just to buy hair ribbons."

She was so emphatic in her denial that a suspicious glint crept into his eyes. "Come on! What's the real reason?"

"My real reason?"

He nodded.

"All right. I shan't work for Bolinders because if ever I did, you'd never trust me again."

He laughed and put an affectionate arm around her. "Dear God!" he said. "When 'poor old Gran back there' said you were *my* daughter, he was *wrong!*"

"I resent that," she told him.

"What he should have said is that I am *your* father!"

That was the moment when she ought to have distrusted him the most — she really ought.

*L*ars Oberg did not wait until the iron was hot; he struck while it was still warming up — the very next day, in fact. He had not intended moving against his daughter so swiftly. He wanted to leave it as near to sailing time as possible, which was on the day after the Exhibition opened. But when, on the opening day itself, his daughter came aboard the *Suecia*, all unsuspecting, hoping to talk things over with Frida Carlsson ... it was too tempting to resist. He had already persuaded Captain Carlsson that a father could not be guilty of abducting a daughter under the age of twenty-one — and, he pointed out, Katya would not reach her majority for a few more weeks, by which time they would be safely over the seas, back home in Dublin.

"And then?" Carlsson asked.

Oberg, confident of his persuasive skills over a two-week voyage, simply waved away any objections. Besides, when Katarina realized he meant to honour his pledge to Declan, she'd soon see which side her bread was buttered on.

"My wife will kill me," was the man's next objection.

"Show her who wears the trousers, then!"

And poor Captain Carlsson could not admit to a man like Larry O'Barry — a man who respected him — that he was not the thorough master of his own family, much less his own vessel.

So when Katya reached the head of the gangway, calling out, "Yoo-hoo! Frida!" her father said to the captain, "This is our chance!" and went out, all smiles, to greet her.

She was not particularly surprised to see him there, of course. One glance at the plimsoll line had told her the *Suecia* was laden and ready to sail — though she did not, as yet, fly the blue peter, nor were her hatches battened.

She kissed him warmly and asked where Frida was.

"Come on," he said, as if he'd lead her to a meeting with the captain's wife.

Katya was so eager to see her friend again that she dashed into the stateroom and on into the cabin. She did not hear her father turn the key in the lock. "Frida?" she called out uncertainly. "Agneta?"

Oh no — she suddenly remembered — the children were with their grandparents in Scotland.

"Frida?"

It was obvious by now that both rooms were empty. This was her father's idea of a joke, of course!

And sure enough, there he was, grinning at her through the open porthole. "Say goodbye to Stockholm, Katy," he called.

A little squirt of fear stirred her bowels as the thought dawned on her that this was something more than a joke. "Don't be absurd, Pappa," she warned him.

"You'll see how absurd I mean to be, young lady!"

"Who d'you think owns ..." She faltered. Frida had said she never boasted about owning this vessel — for the sake of her husband's pride. If her father knew nothing of it, she might use that to persuade Captain Carlsson to release her behind her father's back. In any case, she should say nothing that might be useful to him if this ridiculous threat proved serious.

"Owns what?" her father asked.

"Me!" she shouted back. "D'you think *you* own me?"

"Until the twentieth of next month, yes. And I don't suppose anyone will be offering you ten bob an hour in Dublin! There's only one office I know of where they need *Swedish* translators!"

"D'you think that's going to stop me?" Tears stung behind her eyelids; she fought to retain control of her fears. Above all she was determined not to give him the satisfaction of seeing her weep or plead with him.

"And what else can you do?" he sneered. "You can't sew, you can't knit, you can't cook, you can't paint, you can't sing, and you can't play the piano — not well enough to earn a living at any of them. So what'll you do, eh?"

It was a mistake to make so long a speech, for it gave her time to realize that silence was her most potent weapon now. She seated herself gracefully in a chair and folded her hands in her lap.

"What now?" he asked warily. "What are you doing?"

"Submitting," she replied.

"D'you expect me to believe that?"

"I submit to your will, Pappa."

"You're playing some trick."

"I submit to your will, Pappa."

"Oh! No doubt you think you're being *very* clever!"

"I submit to your will, Pappa."

"Wriggle and squirm all you like, Miss! You won't ever get the chance to disobey me again."

"I submit to your will, Pappa."

"Stop parroting that ridiculous phrase!"

"I submit to your will, Pappa."

"I'll come in and leather you — don't imagine you're too old."

Silence; she stared into space.

"Well?" he asked peevishly.

She continued staring ahead of her.

"Hah! Nothing more to say, eh!"

"You told me to be silent, Pappa. I am — dare I say it — submitting to your will."

He turned on his heel and stalked away in search of Captain Carlsson. She sprang to her feet and crossed swiftly to the porthole — but saw at once that escape by that means was quite impossible; even Agneta would have had difficulty squeezing through it. She went to the drawer where Frida had always kept a spare set of cabin keys — on the same ring as she hung her "landlubber's keys," as she called them. It was not there.

She went back to the porthole and, after some effort, succeeded in attracting the attention of one of the crew.

"D'you remember me?" she asked as he came toward her. If only she could recall his name!

"Froeken Oberg," he replied. "You came with us on our last voyage to Stockholm — back at the end of March."

"Where is Mrs-Captain Carlsson?"

"Gone back to Scotland, Froeken."

She stared at him in disbelief.

"We're due a refit in Glasgow after we clear this present cargo through Dublin."

"But I saw her only last week. She said nothing about it then."

"We blew a pipe leaving Stadsgaarden, Froeken. She's patched up now but the skipper says it's an omen. We're in for a refit — there's no two ways about it."

Katya believed him then, especially when, about five minutes later — having established that none of Frida's things were in her wardrobe or in the sea chest by the bed — she found a discarded draft of a note in the wastepaper basket. It began: "Dear K. — Our meeting will have to wait until next time, I'm afraid ..."

So the one person who would have put a stop to this nonsense and sent her father off with a flea in his ear was now either on her way by train and ferry to Scotland or had already arrived there. That left her husband, an altogether less certain quantity in the equation she now had to balance. Her father would realize she was up to some trick or other. She would not get two chances to summon help.

She might not even get one.

She wasted two hours in calling seamen to the porthole and asking them to fetch Captain Carlsson to speak with her; each of them came back to say that the captain was too busy. Eventually he must have realized she was not going to give up, for, when the eighth seaman came with the identical request, he rose wearily from his bunk, filled his pipe, and set off to put a stop to it, once and for all.

"Can't you come inside?" she asked when she saw him standing beyond the porthole.

"Your father has the only key, Froeken Oberg."

"Well get it from him!"

"He's gone ashore, I'm afraid."

That, of course, was what she hoped to learn. "Then break open the door and let me go," she said.

He laughed. "I can't do that, Froeken. I assure you — it's more than my life is worth."

"My father is a very clever man, Captain Carlsson. How d'you think he got where he is today? It wasn't by adding up columns of figures, I can tell you! He's always had this uncanny ability to persuade decent, reasonable men to perform acts of utter insanity on his behalf."

Captain Carlsson licked his lips nervously.

She continued, "Of course he's never around when they do it. Like now — he's ashore! What you should have said is he's *safely* ashore and — bless me — you're all alone here, doing his dirty work for him. I don't know how he manages it, but you've got to admire the fellow. Many's the laugh we've enjoyed around the dinner table when he's described how the profit flowed in one direction while the blame, quite against all justice, has flowed in the other." She laughed dryly. "Of course, the joke's on the other foot now — or whatever the saying is — now that *I'm* the victim. There's justice in *that*, I suppose!" Then she smiled sweetly and added, "I wonder if you'll be able to laugh quite so heartily when the axe falls on you?"

He looked up and down the deck and then, approaching her more closely, asked what he might be doing wrong. She was, after all, a minor still — if only just …

She let him get no further for the last thing she wanted was to get bogged down in technicalities like that. "But minors have *rights* in Sweden, Captain Carlsson — far beyond those they enjoy in *our* medieval islands." She was guessing, of course, but he' wasn't to know that. "My friends know I came here today." That was another lie, too, but, again, he would have to take her word for it. "Any minute now …" No! She need not set so fine a time limit. "Any minute now they'll realize I haven't returned. Granted, they may suppose I am dining here freely with my father and you. Their suspicions may not be roused until after we sail tomorrow. But this is not Gothenberg, Captain. We do not simply head out into open ocean from here. We hug the Swedish coast for two long, nerve-racking days and nights! We could be hailed down anywhere between here and the Kattegat. How long are your fingernails?"

"All right!" He put up his hands to ward off anything more she might say. "Enough! You've said enough, Froeken." He tipped back his hat and scratched his brow. "But if you think I can simply smash down the door and set you free — think again. Your father has a certain hold over me, too. I won't go into details …"

"I can imagine," she said sympathetically.

"So if I am to help you, I must be able to cover my tracks. He must not be able to trace it back to me. No incriminating note … no plain message that could be bribed out of the messenger's mouth."

"Nothing easier," she assured him — having had all afternoon to think it out. "Send word to a certain Herr Max Lejonkrona, saying he was right and I was wrong." She gave him Max's directions.

"And that's all?"

"He'll understand. He warned me something like this might happen and I laughed at him."

After that she felt a lot happier. In fact, she was singing when her father returned later that evening.

"Message for you!" he said, tossing her a piece of paper with a gesture of contempt. "From your friend Lejonkrona."

It read: *I warned you, Princess — I am the world's greatest physical coward. I dare not lift a finger to help you. Sorry! Max.*

There was little enough singing after that.

C ount Magnus Hamilton walked through the horse lines of *Lifgardet till haest*, seeking the two biggest, burliest, plug-ugliest troopers in the regiment. He was spoilt for choice but he found them in the end. "You and you!" was all he said, and they followed him without a word.

Ten minutes later they rode out of barracks — a pair of immaculately turned-out Life Guard troopers in ceremonial blues, led by an officer. It was, on the face of it, a strange little squad; but then, what with the Exhibition and all the dignitaries coming and going, there was a lot of it about.

Magnus had considered taking a more regular-looking squad — a dozen troopers with a corporal-of-horse and a colour sergeant — but eventually decided against it. As far as he was concerned this whole sortie was a precisely calculated provocation on his part against the military mind and military tradition; he only hoped his superiors would calculate with the same precision. His purpose was to be "invited to resign" not to be court-martialled. Actually, if he had taken a whole troop, they might have skipped even the court-martial and committed him straight to an asylum. When you tread the borders of lunacy, millimetres count.

Besides, two men was all he needed for this particular foray.

To the people of Stockholm even a brace of troopers and an officer made a scene to stir the blood — the magnificently disciplined horses and the iron-jawed men, parading down the street with the early morning sun gleaming on their silver helmets, their spurs and harness jingling, and the officer with his white-gloved hand on the hilt of his sabre. No wonder that street cleaners rested on their brooms, tram drivers reined in their horses, errand boys pulled their bicycles to the side of the road, elegant carriages drew to a halt, office workers and shop assistants came briefly to their windows — all to watch a tiny fragment of living history go past in all its glittering pride, the full length of Sturegatan.

"They must be going to the Exhibition," they told one another with many a knowing nod.

But that theory had to yield when the detachment reached Stureplan and turned westward into Kungsgatan. Then there were murmurs of "Central Station" — they were to welcome the King of Albania, to be sure. Then, when they passed beyond the Central Station, it was "Drottningholm Palace" — the royal family were moving there early this summer. The destination that was on no one's lips, of course, was "Bolinders' wharf on Kungsholm."

But fifteen minutes later that is where Magnus's arrival delayed Able-Seaman MacAlister as he was about to untie the ropes at the foot of the *Suecia's* gangway. The Count's ringing cry of "Detatchment ... halt!" brought the entire deck watch of the *Suecia* — and her captain — to the rail, abandoning for the moment their preparations for casting off.

In all its chequered history that grimy industrial wharf had never witnessed the like of it. Magnus posted one of his troopers at each end of the vessel, where the shore parties stood ready to unbend the breast ropes and stem lines.

"The first man who makes a move to cast off will answer to this trooper," he said to each shore party.

As organized shore parties, they dissolved at once; as a rag-bag of spectators, they regrouped a hundred paces clear of their respective stations. Captain Carlsson might as well have been letting fly his curses at the moon.

They died in his throat, anyway, when he saw this lunatic of an officer face his horse — a splendid white Lippizaner gelding — directly toward the gangway and give it the merest touch of his heel. A rare silence fell on that busy industrial wharf as, without a demur, the haughty creature set one hoof, then two, then all four, upon the wooden incline — and then strode up as if it had never walked on any other surface.

The crew fell back. Captain Carlsson, aware that there was suddenly more light and air in his immediate vicinity, glanced nervously about him. By then the charger had gained the deck, where he stood impassively, champing at the bit.

"To what do we owe ..." Carlsson began.

"Captain Carlsson?" Magnus barked.

"How dare you, young man?" he replied. "This is the grossest outrage. I command you to leave my ship."

Magnus, calm as a summer's day, dismounted. "Where is she?" he asked — though it was obvious the captain had no intention of telling him.

He heard a frantic knocking, as of knuckles on glass, from a little way down the deck. He threw his horse's reins to the skipper — who was too startled *not* to grab them — and strode off in that direction.

He was just in time to catch a glimpse of Katy as her father pulled her away from the porthole. At least he knew which cabin she was being held in.

The door was locked.

"Now see here, young fellow ..." The captain had given the horse into the charge of a deckhand and was now bearing down on him again. "I don't care who you are, or who sent you, or by what authority, but this is ..."

Magnus, having found a fire axe, splintered the door from its lock at the first blow.

"... an outrage," the captain concluded feebly.

Magnus drew his sword, levelled it at the man's chest, and said quietly, "You stay out of this. You're in trouble enough without adding to it."

Captain Carlsson, pale as a sheet by now, merely nodded.

Magnus, sword still drawn, went inside.

"You're mad!" A frightened Lars Oberg stood with his back to the wall, desperately trying to lift up one of the chairs, to use it as a shield. "Absolutely stark, staring mad!"

Katya stood in the doorway between stateroom and cabin, tears of joy in her eyes, and her heart overflowing with love.

Magnus sheathed his sabre and said to her, "Go on! Go out and hold my horse."

She drifted outdoors as if in a dream.

Her father, watching her go without a murmur, now felt absolutely sure he was in some kind of dream. "How in the name of God did you do that?" he asked.

Magnus took the chair from him and set it down. "Your servant, sir," he barked, holding out his hand. "May I present myself? Lieutenant Count Magnus Hamilton, King's Squadron." He cleared his throat and murmured, "Just."

The other straightened up and shook the proffered hand. "Lars Oberg," he said.

Magnus dropped his hand and bowed again. "May I have the honour to ask for the hand of Herr Oberg's daughter in marriage?"

It was all too much for the poor man. Before he altogether lost his grip on sanity, his mind scrabbled desperately for the last moment of reality it could comprehend — when he was in a tramp steamer on a grimy wharf in industrial Stockholm in the year 1897 taking his unruly daughter back home. "Now see here, young man — whoever you are ..."

Magnus lifted his sabre a few inches out of its scabbard and resettled it menacingly. "I asked Herr Oberg a question," he said.

"You can't just ... invade this ship, break your way in here, and ... and abduct my daughter."

"I asked for her hand in marriage. I said nothing about abduction."

"You ask *me?* That only proves to me that you cannot possibly know *her!*"

"Herr Oberg takes the words from my mouth. I not only know his daughter, I love her with all my heart and all my soul. Who takes her liberty takes mine. Who harms one hair of her head will answer to me and this sword. Does Herr Oberg know the Hamilton motto? *Through!* He would be wise not to put it to the test."

Lars Oberg stared deep into his eyes. "By God you *are* mad!" he said. "That's the only other explanation. You are determined to marry Katarina?"

"If she will have me."

"I will!" Katya stood in the doorway. "I will!" She ran to him and threw her arms around his neck. "Oh Magnus — you dear, dear man! I knew you'd come. When Lejonkrona sent that note I knew he'd told you — and that you would do something *magnificent* like this — darling, darling Magnus!"

Behind her she heard her father sitting down heavily and yielding up a sigh. "What's the matter, Pappa?" she asked in a much colder tone. "Are you sure you're feeling quite well? You're not usually so slow to join the winning side."

Magnus held her away from him then, gripping her shoulders sternly. "A daughter should speak more respectfully to her father," he said angrily. When he was in danger of smiling he added, "To his face, anyway."

It broke the miniature battle of wills between them. Katya hung her head and turned pentiently to her father. "Forgive me," she asked — adding, "as I have already forgiven you — for without you I should never have known what a marvellous son-in-law you're going to have!"

He rose again and approached them. "You are both certain you know what you're doing?" he asked.

"Yes," Magnus said.

"I was never more certain of anything in my life," she told him.

He did not take his eyes off Magnus. "Did you hear that, young man? Ten words to your one! It's an omen if ever I heard one. Are you *still* set on it?"

Magnus grinned. "I can always go one better, sir: I, *too*, was never more certain of anything in my life."

Lars Oberg laughed at last. "By God, you deserve each other!" he said. "Go on — away with you."

When they reached the door Katya turned and ran back to him, tears welling in her eyes again. "Oh, Pappa!" She flung her arms about his neck and kissed him. "You old rogue!"

"What now?" He eyed her with nervous suspicion.

"I wouldn't put it past you to have done the whole thing deliberately — just to see if anyone here cared for me enough to do ... what Magnus has done."

Back on deck, Magnus helped her into the saddle. It lacked the side-saddle's knee post but she gripped the pommel as best she could; he threw the right stirrup across to the left and shortened it for her. Then he took the horse's head and led her back to the safety of the quayside. That first twenty paces down the gangway was the journey's worst; after that she felt she could have climbed an alpine pass on this superbly steady — and sturdy — creature. Magnus flourished his sabre and the two troopers fell in behind them.

"Good luck!" her father called from the deck where they had left him; Captain Carlsson stood morosely at his side.

"Did he really shanghai you deliberately?" Magnus asked. "As a sort of test of me or ... anybody?"

"I don't think so for a minute," she said. "But a year from now he'll swear it was so. This is starting to be very uncomfortable, Magnus."

"I'm sorry. If it's any consolation, you make a splendid picture."

"I'll stick it out a bit longer, then," she told him. "But I don't know if I could go all the way to your lines."

"Well, actually, Lejonkrona's waiting for us in my carriage in Kungsgatan. I couldn't take you into barracks — things will be hot enough there as it is."

"Will you be cashiered for this?"

He smiled up at her concerned face. "I hope so!"

When they reached the bridge he said, "You don't have to marry me — just because of what happened back there." He jerked his helmet downstream toward the *Suecia* — the plumes danced in the bright sun.

"Getting cold feet already, are you?"

He smiled at her again, an endearingly shy smile, and shook his head, rather solemnly.

She said, "I told Max — I said to him — or, rather, he said to me that I wouldn't know real love when I saw it. And I said I should. And he asked me how. And I said it would rise up out of some mad ... impossible ... absurd act. I said it wouldn't be anything I could predict. And it would be too impossible to argue with. I said it won't grow out of the past — by which I meant I shouldn't be able to see it coming — because you can always see things that come bubbling up out of your past, can't you. I knew it'd just be *there*, suddenly — boomps! In front of me. And the past would be obliterated and there'd be nothing there but the future. And wasn't I right?"

He laughed. "I'm sure you're always right, Katya — on things that matter, anyway. Do you really love me enough to marry me? I'm asking you seriously now."

A faraway look came into her eyes. "I've just thought of something," she said.

"Never mind that — answer my question."

"*Jawohl!* I am answering it, actually. I've just realized that if I marry you, I'll be a Hamilton."

"And a countess."

"Well, that's nice, too. But the main thing is I'll become a Hamilton, won't I?"

"Yes."

"And will you love me when I'm a Hamilton?"

"Of course."

"And I'll love you. So then we'll love each other *Through!* and *Through!* — won't we!"